The **Devolution** of **Adam** and **Eve**

By Mit Sandru

Disclaimer:

This is a fictional story. All names, persons, organizations, businesses, occurrences, and some places are fictitious and spring from the imagination of the author. Any resemblances to actual people or events are completely coincidental.

Table of Contents

A Trinity Investigation Organization Case

Chapter 1. For Sale: Biochemical Nerve Agent

On a peaceful morning in Southern California, Prescott, Claire, and Travis, dressed in dark gray buttoned-up suits and wearing wraparound shades, stood and observed the well-manicured grounds of the Queen of Heaven Cemetery. They had been asked by Maximus to meet at a particular gravesite. The bronze memorial plaque on the ground read:

RIP

Derek Dodd

2017 - 2062

"Who's he?" Prescott, the shorter of the two men, wondered aloud.

"Either a saint or a villain," said Travis. "I put my money on the villain."

"We'll find out soon," said Claire, as she initiated the holo-conference with Maximus.

The holo-conference was held in each of their Personal Audio-Visual (PAV) virtual visors, a device that resembled dark wraparound glasses when activated.

"Thank you for being here." Maximus appeared in the hologram as a bald Caucasian man with dark glasses, but in fact, Maximus was an Artificial Intelligence (AI) entity and the head of Trinity Investigation Organization (TIO.) "We have a new investigation requested of us. Fresh intelligence has surfaced of a new biochemical weapon available on the black market. This weapon seems to affect the nervous system, specifically the brain, but without killing or physically incapacitating the victim."

"What mad scientist could have ever developed such a biochemical weapon?" Dr. Stark, another virtual participant, appeared in their PAVs. He was the chief scientist at TIO, a skinny, weathered man who resembled a pale mummy.

"It is unclear what this weapon is, or who developed it, or where," Maximus said.

"Has this biochemical agent been analyzed? Are there any countermeasures against it?" Claire asked.

"Negative," replied Maximus. "Only the aftereffects have been discovered recently, prior to it being offered for sale."

"So it has been used against people already?" Prescott asked.

"Yes. The intelligence community heard a rumor that this biochemical weapon was recently sold to warlords in the Middle East."

"Why are we involved?" Travis asked. "Chemical or biological weapons are not our specialty."

"For one reason," said Maximus. "The arms dealer who allegedly sold this agent is dead, and there is no information on to whom he sold it. The buyer may have killed him after the transaction was complete."

"That's why you asked the three of us to gather here at his gravesite," said Travis, looking down at the memorial plaque.

"Derek Dodd was that dealer, now dead and buried," said Maximus.

"And what are Prescott, Claire, and Travis supposed to do—exhume him?" Dr. Stark asked. "A dead man tells no tales."

"We have ways to make the dead talk," said Travis, raising one eyebrow at the doctor's hologram.

"Oh yes, your hocus-pocus," Dr. Stark smirked. "Why am I here, then?"

"Your expertise is required to identify the biochemical agent," said Maximus. "When it's found."

"What are you three going to do, sink into the grave to have a chat with the deceased?" Dr. Stark wisecracked.

"Surprise, surprise—Dr. Stark has a sense of humor." Claire chuckled. "No, this does not involve getting our hands dirty."

"In that case, get to work," said Dr. Stark. "Don't keep the dead waiting."

"Stand by, it won't take more than a second." Claire, Prescott, and Travis joined hands and closed their eyes.

Chapter 2. The Interrogation Room

Derek Dodd looked around the gray cinderblock-wall room with disgust and trepidation. The dreary room seemed to be made worse by the random flickering of one of a group of neon tubes on the ceiling, enclosed in a heavy-duty grill. As he attempted to move his right hand, he discovered that he was handcuffed to the arm of a gray metal chair. The table in front of him was gray metal as well, and across, on the opposite wall, he could see himself, in his gray suit, in a large mirror. His red tie—the only colorful item in the whole room—was askew, and he instinctively adjusted it with his free hand.

He didn't remember how he got there or why he was handcuffed to the chair. He turned his head and assessed the rest of the room. Other than the mirror in front of him, the walls were gray and bare, with no windows. Was he in a police interrogation room? Perspiration formed on his brow. What the heck was going on? Where was he?

"Hello!" he called out to no one in particular. "Hello? Anyone behind that mirror?" No one answered. He swallowed hard and tried to remember how or why he was in this gray room. "I demand to know who is holding me in here and for what reason!" His voice echoed in the room.

Only the dead silence of a crypt surrounded him.

Derek inhaled deeply, trying to calm himself. Whatever this situation was, it would unravel eventually. Whoever was holding him in here wanted to soften him first through silence, and then the interrogation would start. He propped his cheek in his left hand, but then, at second thought, he sat up straight. With his free hand, he checked his pockets. They were empty, not surprisingly.

He pounded on the table with his fist. "Let me out of here! I know my rights."

"I'm glad to hear that, Mr. Dodd," said a voice from behind him.

He turned quickly and saw a man in a dark gray suit, his eyes masked by dark wraparound glasses. Where did he come from? Derek never heard a sound, but he saw a gray metal door behind him that he hadn't noticed before.

"Who are you?" Derek asked the man.

"We are the Capuchin Trinity Team," a voice said from the direction of the mirror.

Derek turned back and saw a woman and another man standing in front of the table. They were dressed in dark gray suits as well and wearing the same dark glasses. All three of them wore a white collar, as if they were ordained priests. There was a triangular insignia on the front of the collar, with a cross inside it.

He looked back at the taller man behind him.

"Are you a religious group?" Derek asked, turning his head around frequently to keep an eye on these strangers. "Is this a joke? Who put you up to this?" He tried to smile, hoping that this was just a charade.

"You and only you got yourself into this situation," replied the man standing next to the woman.

"What situation? What's going on?" Derek felt his blood pressure rising. "Where am I?"

"What does this place look like to you?" asked the taller man.

"Am I at the police station, in an interrogation room? What are the charges? Who are you people?"

"My name is Travis St. John," said the taller man, who now moved to the front of the table, closer to the other two. He pointed to the woman first. "This is Claire German, and he is Prescott Alighieri. As Claire said, we are the Capuchin Trinity Team."

"So you're not cops."

"No, we're not cops."

"Have I been kidnapped? I can pay ransom."

"You have not been kidnapped, but you are being detained," said Prescott. "We are investigators."

"If I am being detained, I have the right to a phone call with my attorney." Derek attempted to fold his arms.

"Certainly." Claire pointed to the side of the table on Derek's left, where there was a black, old-fashioned dial phone.

Derek's eyes opened wide. The desk had been empty seconds before—where did it come from? Or maybe he hadn't seen it.

"A rotary dial phone? These haven't been used since the late 20th century." He couldn't hold back his dismay and burst out in laughter, shaking his head at the absurdity of it all.

"But it is a phone and you can make your call," said Claire, pointing to the phone.

"Yeah?" He picked up the phone by the cradle and noticed that there was no cord attached to it. That was not a problem, since wired phones were rare nowadays, but an antique like this should have had a cord. "Joke's on me." He picked up the receiver and heard a dial tone.

"Who are you going to call?" asked Prescott.

"My lawyer," Derek barked. "And when he answers, I'll find out who's behind this poor attempt to scare me." He dialed the number, one dial turn at a time. It felt as if it took forever to finish dialing the ten-digit number.

The phone rang twice before someone answered:" Stanley, McCormick, and Davidson law office. How may I help you?"

"Get me Jim, please."

"You mean Mr. James McCormick?"

"Yeah, yeah, and make it snappy, boy."

"Right away, sir."

A voice came on at the other end: "This is James McCormick."

"Jim, thank God. This is a good joke, getting me drunk and then setting up an arrest—ha, ha, ha—"

"Who is this?"

"Dodd, Derek Dodd, your client." He ran his fingers nervously through his hair, wondering if maybe this wasn't a joke. "If this is not a hoax, maybe I'm really in jail, and I need to get out."

"Now, listen, buddy, I don't know who you are, and you have some nerve—"

"Jim, it's Derek Dodd. Hey, I'm in jail and need your help." Derek rolled his eyes, guessing that his lawyer and buddies would put him through this for all it was worth.

"You're Derek Dodd, huh? Yes, I give you that—you sound like him, but it can't be him. So, knock it off. It's in poor taste."

"Jim, it's me. I need you to get me out of jail. What's going on?"

"OK, now listen carefully before I hang up and call the police. You cannot be Derek Dodd, because Derek Dodd has been dead and buried for over a week now."

Chapter 3. Dead?

Derek's call was disconnected. He sat with the receiver at his ear, stunned and confused. It took a few moments until the rage exploded inside him. He stood up and hurled the phone to the floor, pieces of it shattering in all directions.

"Enough of this bullshit! Who are you and what do you want?"

"Did your lawyer tell you that you're dead?" asked Claire, with a trace of a wry smile.

"Who are you and what do you want?" asked Derek through clenched teeth.

"First, you have to be at peace with the fact that you are dead," said Claire.

"How can I be dead? I'm sitting here, talking to you, with all my functions intact. You are real, I am real." He pounded his chest. "Dead people don't feel as if they're alive!"

"How do you know how dead people are supposed to feel?" Prescott asked.

"Mr. Dodd has a point," said Travis. "Considering how many lethal weapons he sold around the world, he should know a thing or two about the dead. Isn't that true, Derek?"

"Ahh! You are with some government agency investigating my business transactions."

"No, we're not," said Travis.

"Then what is this all about?" Derek huffed. "You must be the government. My competition and enemies would have beaten the shit out of me and then popped me, not arrested me and pretended to interrogate me."

"Unfortunately for you, your last client did *pop* you. That's how you died," said Travis.

Derek touched first his chest, as if checking for bullet holes, but soon stopped, realizing he hasn't been shot. "And yet, I feel alive."

"You were shot in the back of the head and died instantly. You have no recollection of seeing yourself with a hole in your head," said Claire.

"Really. And if I'm dead, you must be dead. I'm talking to dead people." Derek raised his arms and realized that he was not cuffed anymore. There were no cuffs on the chair's arm, either. They must have removed his cuffs when he was distracted on the phone. He pointed to his right wrist.

"What's the matter?" Travis asked.

"My cuffs. You removed them."

"No, we haven't. We did not put them on you and did not take them off."

"Then who did?"

"You did."

"Me?"

Travis nodded and waved his arms at the room. "Just as you placed yourself in this interrogation room."

"I did that? Well, let's see how omnipotent I am." He grabbed the chair and hurled it into the mirror across the room. The chair smashed the mirror into a thousand shards that clinked onto the concrete floor. Only the mirror's frame remained, but there was no room behind the broken mirror, only a gray cinderblock wall. One last piece of the mirror broke loose and fell to the floor, startling him.

"What the fuck is going on?"

"You tell us," said Prescott, with his fingers steepled.

"I, I don't understand why I am in this fake interrogation room."

"Maybe your guilt for what you did in your life placed you here on your way to Hell," said Claire.

"What guilt? I don't feel guilty at all for selling weapons to people who wanted a better life or to defend themselves."

"And yet you ended up where you thought you'd belong," said Claire.

Derek stared at her. He rubbed the back of his neck and asked, "When will I be released?"

"Which part of the word 'dead' don't you understand?" Travis asked.

Derek looked fearfully at Travis. "But someone is holding me here."

"No one is holding you," said Prescott.

"Really." Derek strode to the gray metal door. "Then I'm out of here!" He opened it wide and froze in horror.

Outside, he saw a blackened landscape with blown-up buildings, fires burning all around, emitting black smoke, and thousands of dead or dying people littering the ground. Dodging combatants were firing automatic weapons, while explosions blew up bodies every so often. Assailants with flamethrowers chased other retreating fighters and incinerated them. The screams of pain and horror were louder than the gunfire and the explosions.

The Devolution of Adam and Eve

Mit Sandru

Chapter 4. Mossad

Claire, Travis, and Prescott opened their eyes. They were back on the grassy field of the cemetery.

"Well?" inquired Maximus.

"We found him," said Travis, who could see everyone else as talking heads in his PAV.

"But you were gone just a split second," commented Dr. Stark.

"Time is different in the other realm," said Travis.

"As a scientist, it is hard for me to believe what you claim you did," Dr. Stark bristled. "Anyway, other than in his grave, where else did you find Derek Dodd?"

"In a purgatory of his own making," said Prescott. "His soul and his mind are still united, and subconsciously, he has major misgivings about what he did while he was alive. While alive, subconsciously, he thought he was going to Hell to roast, and so he created a temporary purgatory that resembles an interrogation room to delay his departure."

"And he believed he was alive, until he opened the door and saw Hell outside," added Claire.

"I can imagine his lawyer's face when he got a call from a dead and buried man," snickered Prescott.

"What?" Dr. Stark asked. "He talked to his lawyer?"

"Sure, he made a phone call on an imaginary phone to his lawyer, James McCormick, to spring him out of jail," said Claire. "In a way, Derek Dodd called from the dead to find out he was dead. Or, better said, his mind and soul connected to the lawyer's phone."

"This mind and soul stuff sounds so unscientific," said Dr. Stark.

"It seems perfectly real to me," said Maximus.

"Of course. You're not alive, Maximus. You are only an AI, and you don't fear death or what happens when you're turned off," Dr. Stark said.

"True, nonexistence is not a concern for me," agreed Maximus. "But the whole of humanity may plunge into nonexistence, I was told, if we don't get to the bottom of who Derek Dodd did business with."

"So, did this dead man give you any information?" Dr. Stark was skeptical.

"Not yet," said Prescott. "But he will."

"Hopefully, he will cooperate, although from the beyond," said Maximus. "The intelligence agency that is most interested in Derek Dodd's dealings is Mossad, the Israeli Mossad."

"They cannot solve their own cases?" Travis asked.

"I'm sure they can, but time is against all of us, and they cannot do what you do," said Maximus. "We are working with an agent, code name 'Daniela Rock.' She is an officer with Mossad, and she'll be your contact until this case is solved. I invited her to join us."

A hologram of a cute brunette with hazel eyes came to life in their PAVs.

"Agent Daniela Rock, I am Maximus, the head of Trinity Investigation Organization, TIO for short. I have with me Prescott Alighieri, Travis St. John, and Claire German of the Capuchin Trinity Team, or CTT. They are an investigating unit specializing in paranormal and supernatural crimes that science and law enforcement cannot solve. Also with us is Dr. Stark, our doubting scientist assigned to assist CTT."

Dr. Stark did not even blink.

Agent Daniela Rock nodded and said, "Nice to meet you. Please call me Daniela."

"Certainly, you can call us by our first names as well," said Travis.

"Maximus assured me that you people can do incredible things," said Daniela. "Including talking to the dead. You must be some psychics."

"We are not," said Claire with a smirk. "That's the usual reaction when people are told about our capabilities."

"We are not clairvoyant," said Prescott.

"And we cannot make objects float in the air, either," Travis said.

"Then what do you do?"

"We located Derek Dodd," said Travis, making a face as if to say, *how about that?*

"We know where Derek Dodd is buried," said Daniela, frowning.

"So do we. As a matter of fact, we're standing on top of his grave, six feet above his decaying body," said Travis. "His dead body is irrelevant, although it helps to locate his soul and mind quicker. We spoke to him briefly."

"I'll give you the benefit of the doubt and believe you for now," said Daniela with a straight face. "Did he give you any information?"

"No, at first he didn't even know that he was dead," said Travis.

"Our first priority is to find out to whom he sold the biochemical agent," said Daniela. "Derek Dodd sold a terrible weapon to some bad people who intend to use it on a selective basis or on a global scale, but for sure against Israel."

"If this agent is airborne, I fail to see how it could be an effective weapon," said Prescott. "And if it needs to be ingested, it would be of limited impact in infecting a large population."

"We don't know how this agent is administered, but we know its effects," said Daniela. "The victims don't die, but they become demented."

"That's stupid. A weapon's task is to kill, not debilitate," said Travis.

"Sure, but this one does not kill," said Daniela. "Imagine an army of 100,000 soldiers who are turned into idiots."

"Armed idiots," added Prescott.

"Exactly, but that's not the worst part, even if the idiots know how to use their weapons," said Daniela. "What do you do with 100,000 nut cases? If they were dead, you'd bury or burn their bodies. But they are alive and don't even know how to open a bottle of water. They still know how to kill to eat, but they would starve next to an unopened can of corned beef."

"How do you know this?" Claire asked.

"We have knowledge of three incidents in which groups of people became demented, with little faculty to think or reason. The first one was in 2061, in Afghanistan, in a remote area near the border with Pakistan. Three hundred people in a small village lost their minds, behaving like apes. They were not discovered until after the snow melted, in late spring. The population was down to less than a few dozen people. The others died of starvation or injuries, or were eaten by the survivors. There were untouched cans of food stored in the village, but just as dogs cannot open cans, neither could the survivors. They weren't able to speak, other than to make guttural sounds. Their former brain capacity was reduced to that of animals. They hunted their own sheep, instead of herding them as they did before. And whatever clothes they had on them were rags. Many were completely naked. Not surprisingly, they copulated, and a couple of the women became pregnant."

"Were there any traces of this biochemical agent?" Dr. Stark asked.

"The dead and the living were tested, and their bodies contained an elevated level of cyanide," said Daniela. "No other toxin traces were found in the immediate environment of the village, not even in the surviving sheep or dogs. We don't know how the biochemical agent was introduced into the valley, but it affected only the people, not the animals or plants. It seems that this was a field trial experiment performed by an unknown group."

"The cyanide could be explained in other ways. But please continue," said Dr. Stark.

"Yes, but wait until you hear the rest of the gruesome facts," said Daniela. "The second occurrence was in Brazil, in a remote upriver village in Alto Rio Negro.

Same symptoms as in Afghanistan, except that less than ten percent of that village's population survived by hiding in the jungle. Cyanide was found in the living and dead there as well. There are no gold mining activities anywhere upstream of the river to explain the cyanide. The toxin was not found in the waters, vegetation, soil, or animals, only in the people.

"The third occurrence was found in a remote village in the Congo—the situation identical to that of the other two sites. Although some of the survivors stayed in the village, many others were found in the jungle in small groups. The jungle groups often raided the village for food. There may be a fourth site like this in China, but the Chinese government has quarantined that area and has not allowed the World Health Organization access to it, nor have the Chinese shared any information about it.

"The people from all three sites were quarantined and studied by an elite group of scientists from the WHO. The investigation is being kept highly confidential. They don't want to spread panic in the world. Although, over time, the cyanide level has dropped in the survivors, their minds have not returned to normal, and they continue to behave like apes. The three sites are all located in remote, unregistered areas of the planet, as if selected to give the perpetrators time to study the effects of the biochemical agent and not have the outside world interfere with them."

"It looks as if the experiment was tried on four different races, if China is included," said Dr. Stark.

"Anything like this in Europe?" Travis asked.

"No, I guess the Afghanistan experiment represented the Caucasian race."

"Could China had developed this biochemical agent and experimented on their own people?" Prescott wondered.

"Anything is possible."

"What makes you suspect, besides this happening in three remote areas, that this is a biochemical agent and not some natural toxin?" Claire asked.

"Originally, this was considered an outbreak of some unknown pathogen, although it was highly suspicious, considering it occurred in several unconnected areas," Daniela explained. "But then we heard rumors about a new biochemical agent available for sale to the highest bidder, and hints were made that it had been proven through field tests."

"Who could have developed such a weapon?" Dr. Stark asked.

"If a country developed such an agent, it would not try to sell it," said Daniela. "It would be a well-kept secret in the arsenal of a nation. It must be a rogue organization. Derek Dodd was the broker peddling this deadly agent. All the leads start and end with Derek Dodd, so far," said Daniela. "And we're afraid that some of our Muslim enemies would love to release it on Israel."

"In that case, we will resume our investigation in Purgatory," said Travis.

Mit Sandru

Chapter 5. Derek Dodd

Derek Dodd slammed the metal door shut to hide the inferno raging outside. He touched the door, but it was cool. He placed his ear to the door, but it was deadly quiet outside. The three strangers, those cappuccino weirdos, were gone, leaving him alone in the room.

"What the hell," he said to himself and opened the door again. The fighting, shooting, blasting, and burning had not abated outside. In front of the door, the blackened face of a man missing his legs crawled toward him, begging for water. Nausea overcame Dodd, and he slammed the door shut, leaning his forehead on it, trying to dismiss what he had just seen.

Dumbstruck, he retreated and leaned on the desk, staring at the gray metal door, behind which a real inferno was raging. "Someone's fucking with my mind," he said out loud. "I bet I'm alive, drugged or hypnotized, and someone's trying to extract information from me."

The shards of mirror glass on the floor attracted his attention. One simple way to find out if all this was real or a dream was to slash his wrists with one of the glass pieces. He walked determinedly to the pile and picked up a medium-sized triangular piece.

"I'm going to slash my wrists if you don't let me out of here," he demanded aloud. But no one responded. "Hell!" he shouted, and with one stroke, he ran the sharp edge of the glass across his left wrist.

Blood spurted out of his cut wrist, followed by a sharp pain. "Shit, shit, shit!" he screamed. He pulled his tie from around his neck and wrapped it around his slashed wrist to stop the bleeding. He used his teeth and his good hand to make a knot on the tie wrapped around his wrist. For good measure, he clamped his hand over the makeshift bandage to prevent more blood loss. Luckily, the tie was red, hiding the blood's color.

"So, this is not a dream," he mumbled. "I am being held somewhere near a battlefield. But by whom?" He collapsed in the chair, waiting for the pain and the blood flow to subside while he stared at the ceiling.

He was in a concrete box, maybe a bunker, to protect him from the battle outside. Then why was everything so quiet in here, while outside the explosions were deafening? What if there was no real battle outside, just a Hollywood hologram of a battle? Cheap trick, he thought. When he opened the door, the hologram would be turned on, and when he closed it, it would be turned off.

Time to test his latest suspicion: He walked to the door and opened it just a crack, peeking outside. The battle was on. He closed the door and opened it as fast as he could to be able to see the hologram going on and off, but he couldn't discern any difference. He again opened the door wide and stared outside. The heat from the fires outside was horrendous, forcing him to retreat behind the door.

"Damn it!" he shouted.

They must have used a furnace blaster to simulate the heat. He ran his left hand through his hair and stopped midway, pulling back his hand. The wrist did not hurt anymore. He pulled the knot loose, the tie came off, and he stared dumbly at his unscratched wrist. There was no cut anywhere. There was no blood, either.

Confused and depressed, he collapsed onto the chair. It was obvious. He was drugged, and external stimuli were being transmitted to his brain to give him the impression that this was real. Probably someone burned his wrist to give the impression of the glass cutting his flesh. His mind added the details, making him a prisoner of his own drug-affected brain.

Nothing was real; it was all just an illusion to make him divulge information about . . . He thought hard but couldn't remember much. Suddenly he realized that trying to remember might be exactly what his captors wanted. His thoughts would become words, and he'd give away what those bastards wanted from him. A blank mind was the best thing for now.

Without any timepiece, Derek did not know how long he had been in here. Would his captors nourish him intravenously? He didn't feel hungry or thirsty. He didn't feel euphoric, as if he were drugged either. Aside from the pain he suffered when he allegedly slashed his wrist, and the searing heat from the fires outside, he didn't feel any discomfort. For sure he was drugged, lying on a bed, with tubes and probes coming in and going out of him.

Screw this. He was not going to allow the SOBs to torment him anymore. Without hesitation, he walked to the door and stepped outside.

"Oh, for the love of God!" he shouted, looking at what he just stepped on. His right foot had landed on a pressure-triggered land mine. The latching pin flew into the air, forecasting what was about to happen if he moved his foot. The heat from the fires around him singed his hair. A bomb detonated above his head, and he felt the shrapnel penetrating his skull like nails and cutting his face like razor blades. His hands were blistering from the heat. The pain was beyond his tolerance, and he had to retreat to the safety of the room, but the moment he lifted his foot, the mine would blow up. His left foot was still on the threshold, and he couldn't move his other foot planted on the mine, while at the same time he was being roasted and shredded alive.

"Help!" he shouted, feeling the hot air searing his lungs as he inhaled.

A hand grabbed him by the scruff of his neck. Another hand gripped him from the back of his jacket and pulled him in, but not fast enough to prevent the mine from detonating. The explosion propelled Derek Dodd inside the room, and he slid across the floor and under the table, stopping when his head hit the block wall. His vision was blurred, but he noticed the door being slammed shut, ending the scorching heat and noise. He lay on his back, panting and recovering from the burning pains he experienced outside, when an excruciating pain came from his right leg. He lifted it and saw with horror that his leg was missing its foot and that below the knee his leg was mangled, bloodied, and scorched.

He blacked out.

Chapter 6. Purgatory

"Are you OK?" Claire bent over him, gently slapping his face.

"Wha-, what happened?" he asked, opening his eyes just a little.

"You walked out into Hell. Luckily you kept a foot on the threshold for Travis and Prescott to pull you inside. Otherwise, we would have found only pieces of you."

Derek Dodd sighed. The pain in his leg was subsiding. He opened his eyes and saw the other two standing over him.

"I suppose you want me to thank you," he said. "Not a chance in hell." Then he remembered his leg and began to cry. "I need a doctor for my leg."

"I'm a doctor. Which leg?" Claire asked.

"Are you blind?" Derek mastered the courage to lift his right leg, dreading what he was about to see.

But his leg and foot were intact. He bent it but felt no pain. Slowly, just in case he was injured and holding his leg bent, he scooted himself to a seated position, leaning his back against the block wall. He then remembered that he must have been sitting on a pile of broken glass. But the floor underneath him was clean.

Of course, they must have cleaned up the broken glass, but what about his leg? This was not reality. It was a drug-induced hallucination. Just as he never cut his wrist, he never stepped on the mine and mangled his leg. Who was holding him captive, and what did they want?

"Let's stop playing games," Derek said calmly. "Tell me what you want and let me out of here."

"You're the voice of reason," said Travis. "Who was the buyer?"

Derek blinked rapidly, trying to understand the question. "Buyer of what?"

"Derek Dodd, we know you're an arms dealer," said Claire. "To whom did you sell biochemical weapons?"

He recalled his memories. They called him a merchant of death, and he sold any weapon under the sun to kill, maim, or conquer. It was a lucrative business, once you knew what you were doing and developed a clientele, which—with twenty billion people on the planet, and constant fighting—was never lacking. The fractured world they lived in was hungry for arms, and he prospered by finding the weapons, the sellers, and the buyers.

"What agency did you say you represent?" he asked.

"The Capuchin Trinity Team," said Claire.

Derek Dodd laughed bitterly. "So you're here to get my confession? Sorry, I don't believe in God."

"You'd better change your mind about God," said Travis. "You could use his help now, more than ever."

Derek Dodd looked at him sideways with contempt.

"We would like to hear your confession, though," said Claire.

"In return for what?" Derek Dodd asked.

"Maybe we'll show you a way to get out of Hell," said Claire.

"Sure, pull the tubes out of me and let me wake up," Dodd scoffed.

"You still don't believe Hell is behind that door," said Prescott, walking to the door and touching it. "It's getting hot."

"It was cold before." Dodd stood up, leaning gingerly on his previously injured leg that now felt fine. He walked to the door to feel it for himself, but he didn't have to touch it to feel the radiating heat. "Of course, now it feels hot. You're playing with my mind to make me think that the door is hot."

"When you stepped outside, you touched Hell, and it's coming for your soul now," said Travis.

"Really, and what is this?" Dodd gestured at the gray room. "Purgatory?"

"That's exactly what it is," said Claire.

"If I don't divulge who my customer was, you'll crank up the heat." Dodd chuckled nervously at his own joke.

"You don't believe you're dead. But you are dead, and you are in Purgatory, and Hell is there for you." Prescott pointed to the door.

"If you want to save yourself, you'd better confess who your customer was," said Claire.

"Or you get what's outside." Prescott pointed to the door again.

"Ha, ha, ha. Good cop, bad cop," said Dodd. "What are you going to do, Prescott Alighieri? You and your pal here will throw me into Hell?"

"Claire is the bad cop. She will throw you out," said Travis, motioning with his head toward the door to reassure Dodd of the inevitable outcome.

"Go to hell," Dodd said defiantly. He leaned on the wall but quickly jumped away when he felt how hot it had become.

"Feeling the heat?" Prescott asked, raising his eyebrows.

"You know, this Hell is not the only hell you'll encounter," said Travis. "The ultimate Hell will be based on what you sold last. Do you remember that?"

Dodd didn't remember selling biochemical weapons to anyone. Maybe the drugs they were giving him had affected his memory. "Frankly, I don't remember. But if you bring me back from this nightmare and let the drugs clear my brain, my memory will come back and I'll tell you what you want to know."

"You think you are in some drug-induced hallucination, Mr. Dodd?" Prescott asked.

"Isn't that obvious?" said Derek. "I don't believe in God or hell or heaven, for that matter."

"It is not what you believe, Mr. Dodd. It is what it is," said Claire.

"Yeah, sure. Burn me to make me talk," said Derek. "And if I were to tell you what you want to hear, you would show me a way out of here?"

"We will show you paths away from the most excruciating pains you are about to encounter," said Claire. "To prevent you from living them over and over again."

"But not out of Hell?" The walls around him became unbearably hot. The steel door turned red from the heat outside. "This is not real, this is not real," Derek repeated, with his eyes closed and holding his temples.

With a thunderous boom, the ceiling blew away and the walls collapsed outward into heaps of broken cinderblocks. They were left standing on the cement slab of the former interrogation room, as thick, black, acrid-smelling smoke drifted around them.

Mit Sandru

Chapter 7. Hell

Derek Dodd began coughing his lungs out from the toxic black smoke. Claire, Prescott, and Travis stood by, seemingly unaffected. Luckily for Derek Dodd, the wind shifted and cleared the air—temporarily.

"Congratulations, Mr. Dodd. You are out of Purgatory," said Claire, gesturing at the surroundings.

"Welcome to Hell," said Travis. "I hope it will meet your expectations."

Derek Dodd looked around with horrified, bloodshot eyes. "This is not—" he coughed, "—real."

On the ground a line of dust puffs created by a fusillade from a machine gun approached in rapid succession. It barely missed them, but Derek Dodd wasn't taking any chances. He dropped down onto his belly, covering his head with his arms.

"Real enough for you?" Prescott asked, standing above him.

"I, I don't understand. Why aren't you affected by these explosions and this poisonous smoke?" Derek asked.

"This is your Hell, not ours," said Claire. "We are not affected by the punishment you're meted."

Derek Dodd jumped to his feet and dusted off his suit. "Fuck, fuck, fuck!" he shouted. "I'm alive and drugged, and all this is fake."

From the blackened ruins of a nearby apartment building, a single shot was fired. It hit Derek Dodd in the stomach. The hole into his stomach was insignificant, but his guts exploded out of the exit hole. He clenched his stomach, wobbled, and then collapsed onto the cement floor. His body convulsed as dark red blood spilled onto the gray floor around him.

Claire, a trained doctor, couldn't help him even if she wanted to. "We'll have to wait until he dies and wakes up again," she said calmly.

Derek Dodd opened his eyes. He was lying in a fetal position, holding his stomach. His teeth were still chattering from the pain he had just experienced.

"It's over." Claire bent down to speak to him. "You'll remember this pain, just as you'll remember many more pains to come. And then you'll have seconds, and thirds, and so on, forever."

"Was I shot?" Derek asked.

"Yes, by a sniper, who is still out there and will shoot you again if we don't find shelter," said Claire. "Get up and follow us."

Derek Dodd didn't wait for a second invitation—he got up and ran after the CTT people, who were walking briskly upright, without fear of the bullets flying around them. He ran, hunched over, somehow hoping that the bullets whizzing by wouldn't hit him again. They managed to get underneath the partially collapsed concrete upper floor of a building.

"How come you didn't get shot?" he asked them.

"We told you, this is your Hell, and only you are subject to the painful experiences," said Prescott. "We don't exist here and cannot be harmed."

Derek Dodd leaned against a wall. "Who the hell are you? Why is this happening to me?"

"Stop denying your situation," Claire said.

"OK, let's start from the beginning," said Prescott. "You are dead and in Hell. What you are experiencing now is what the victims of the weapons you sold in the past experienced as they died or were maimed by them. And you will continue going through this Hell forever. Understand?"

Derek Dodd nodded dumbly.

"You were an arms dealer and were in the process of selling a new biochemical weapon. The buyer, or his agent, shot you in the back of the head after you completed the transaction. Remember that?"

Derek Dodd stared, wide-eyed, at the three of them. "If, if, if I'm dead, why are you here with me? Are you dead, too?"

"You are the dead man!" Travis shouted. "We're alive, and in real life, the three of us are standing on top of your grave. Your body, six feet under, is being eaten by worms as we speak."

"Yeah? Prove it to me."

The Capuchin Trinity Team flashed the picture of the memorial plaque on Derek Dodd's grave.

"Shit, shit, shit! Is it true? It's true! How could it be?" He covered his face with his palms.

"The sooner you face the truth, the better," said Claire.

"Why are you here with me?"

"We want information about your last deal," said Claire impatiently. "The biochemical weapon you sold will obliterate a lot of people, and you'll experience Hell for that, too. Prevent more pain for yourself by telling us the buyer's identity."

Derek Dodd looked at them, bewildered. "Am I really in Hell?"

A loud explosion detonated nearby. "What more proof do you need, man?" Travis shouted at him. "Your leg was blown away by a land mine, you got shot by a sniper. You will die many times, over and over again, and feel the pain of death as your victims suffered from all the weapons you sold."

"All the weapons?" Derek Dodd began hyperventilating. "That means the nuclear bomb, too?"

A blinding flash lit the sky behind the building. The wind began blowing in that direction for an instant, and then it reversed away from the explosion, roaring toward them. Derek Dodd held his ears, but it was too late. He went deaf. The destroyed building sheltered them, but Derek felt the searing heat engulf everything. The few broken trees nearby exploded into flames. Bodies and charred body parts, cars, rocks, sand, and any imaginable debris flew by at hundreds of miles per hour.

Above the wrecked building, a mushroom cloud formed.

Chapter 8. Who Was the Buyer?

"You miserable creature!" Prescott shouted a few minutes later, after it was quiet again. "You were the one who sold the nuclear bomb to the Kurds?"

Without looking at him, Derek Dodd said, "They deserve to have their own country."

"Sure, and half a million Kurds were gassed by the Turks in retaliation," said Prescott. "Did you sell the poisonous gas to the Turks?"

"I was an intermediary between the Turks and . . . " His voice trailed away. "I guess I'll die by poisonous gas as well." He laughed bitterly.

"And if you don't like it, you'll die repeatedly while gasping for air, until you repent," said Travis.

"How can I be in Hell?" Derek stared in disbelief. "I'm an atheist. I don't believe in those myths."

"Just because you don't believe in those *myths* doesn't preclude Satan from believing in you," said Travis, narrowing his eyes. "Snap out of it."

Derek Dodd turned pale, as if realizing for the first time that Satan and Hell were real. "What am I going to do?"

"Tell us about your last transaction," said Prescott.

"I sold a shipload of shoulder-held rocket launchers to the Janyah Liberation Front, the Chinese Muslims rebels, two months ago. The cargo went up the Yangtze River."

"Your very last deal, man," Travis said. "To whom were you selling the biochemical agent?"

"I was negotiating the price for personal laser guns, just after that, with a Catalonian liberation group."

"Are you dense?" said Travis, losing his temper. "Your last deal, man! The name of the buyer!"

Derek seemed to think hard and then shook his head. "I don't remember." He froze, as several bloodied and smoke-blackened fighters came by in a small truck. They jumped out and, with guns drawn, assailed him. "Help me!" screamed Derek Dodd at the CTT.

The fighters didn't seem to notice the CTT, but they sure saw Derek. They grabbed him, strip-searched him, and dragged him to the truck by his feet.

"What are you doing?" screamed Derek Dodd at them. "I'm a civilian. I'm not your foe."

"I don't give a shit what or who you are," growled one of the assailants. "We haven't eaten in days, and I bet you'll roast well on a spit." They dumped him in the back of the truck, climbed in, and drove away, while Derek Dodd continued to yell for help.

"We'd better not lose him," said Travis. "It'll be hell to find him again in this Hell."

They followed the tire tracks through the war-scarred land to a nearby mud-brick outpost, where they found the truck parked along a wall. There was the stench of burned meat, and although they suspected what they would find, they were not prepared to see Derek Dodd on a spit, roasting like a pig. Some of the fighters were already eating his organs, which they had cooked in skillets over the fire.

"That's unexpected," said Prescott.

Claire covered her mouth and nose.

"Kind of spoils your appetite for roasted pig," Travis said.

"I feel like throwing up." Claire turned around to avoid seeing the red and brown roasted body of Derek Dodd.

"Let's take a break," said Prescott.

They reemerged from Hell while still standing on Derek Dodd's grave.

"Sorry, guys," said Claire. "I'd seen corpses in medical school, but none on a spit, awaiting to be eaten."

"And this might be just the beginning of what he may go through," said Prescott.

"I hope his Hell experiences will jog his memory," said Travis. "At first, he didn't believe he was dead and in Hell. Now he does. Why doesn't he remember his last deal and the buyer?"

"What if he was curious and sniffed the stuff he was selling?" Prescott speculated.

Travis and Claire's eyes widened.

"Like sample it?" wondered Claire. "He wouldn't be that stupid."

"Maybe it was an accident. He might have become demented before the buyer killed him," said Prescott.

Mit Sandru

Chapter 9. Who Was the Seller?

Travis rubbed his chin. "Then we should ask him about the seller, not the buyer."

The CTT members joined hands and descended into Derek Dodd's Hell.

He was not where they had last left him, on a spit, but they sensed his soul hiding in a nearby bombed-out neighborhood. The turmoil of war around him hadn't ceased for a minute. A squadron of hovercopters flew overhead and began strafing part of the ruined town with heavy caliber machine guns. A ground-to-air missile fired from the ruins blew up one of the hovercopters. The remaining hovercopters didn't retaliate but fled.

"This Hell is not for Derek Dodd alone," Travis commented.

"For him and everyone like him," said Prescott.

A few minutes later, they entered the bombed-out neighborhood, skirting the barricade of burning tires and climbing over piles of rubble to reach a once-large boulevard, now narrowed by demolished concrete buildings on both sides.

"Derek Dodd!" shouted Travis.

From a dark alcove in one of the bombed-out buildings, someone began firing at them in short bursts.

"That must be him," Travis said, as he approached the shooter's hiding place.

Prescott ran quickly along an alley to block Derek's escape, while Claire climbed up on some ramps made of fallen walls to get a higher vantage point.

"Don't come any closer!" shouted Derek Dodd from the shadows. "I'll shoot you."

Travis approached, unperturbed, and Derek fired at him, but his gun stopped after two shots; he was out of ammo. Travis found Derek crammed into a crevice made by the collapsed walls and ceiling.

"Is this how you greet a friend?" said Travis. "You look like a trapped rat."

"It's better than being a sitting duck in the open," Derek replied, recognizing Travis. "Besides, I have allies here. That hovercopter was shot with missiles I sold to—"

"Good for you, but how many times have you been killed since we saw each other last?"

"Lost count." Derek lowered his head and trembled. "The pain seems to get more intense with each death, and I'm terrified of what will follow. The worst is when I'm not killed outright, and I'm left to die slowly, drowning in my own blood, my eyes pecked out by crows or my guts torn out by rats and feral dogs."

Claire approached. "Maybe praying to God would help."

"I don't know how to pray."

"Do you know how to ask for forgiveness?" Claire asked.

Derek lifted his eyes and then nodded slowly.

"OK, Derek, we're back to find out who your last customer was," said Travis.

"I've thought about it, and I cannot remember a thing," said Derek. He looked sincere.

"Too bad. If what you sold is released into the real world, you're about to experience hell in Hell," said Travis.

"Shhh," Prescott said, entering the collapsed room. "There are several patrols coming this way."

They waited in silence until they saw them pass down the narrowed boulevard.

"Do you remember who the seller of the biochemical agent was?" Claire asked.

Derek thought for a long moment, visibly trying to recall. "I don't remember dealing in biochemical weapons. For some reason, it is hard to recall anything just before I awoke in the gray room."

"I suggest you go back to the point you do remember and talk your way forward, as far as you can remember," said Claire.

Derek Dodd closed his eyes and began. "Well, I remember being in Mexico, in Cabo. I was a wanted man in most registered zones in the USA and some other parts of the world. I had become infamous, and it was getting hot for me. I was on my way to New Zealand, where I owned a ranch." He chuckled. "My neighbors were the megarich from Silicon Valley, and the new Big Agro and Big Pharma tycoons, you know—those do-gooders who helped create the mess and the population explosion we see today. I didn't care if I was going to live among hypocrites who had enriched themselves with cheap labor from destitute countries, preaching peace and brotherhood, and whose social technology fueled the anarchy, death, and destruction that had engulfed the world since the Apocalypse.

"While there, I received a message from someone I didn't know, and he asked me if I wanted to do a big deal. His name was, was—I remember! It was Alexei Perchenko, and he was Russian."

Chapter 10. The Miracle Medicine

"How did you know this Alexei Perchenko was Russian?" Claire asked.

"I checked him out. He was an old Russian oligarch, a megabillionaire who had survived the Apocalypse in '29 and kept his wealth."

"Isn't it unusual for an oligarch to get involved with the black market in weapons?" Claire asked.

"Hell, no. I bought weapons from rich capitalists, communists, and fascists, and sold them to nationalists, religious fanatics, and the political crazies. Where there was a need, I had the connections to procure and sell the weapons."

"Tell us what happened," said Claire.

"As I said, I was waiting for a turbojet hydrofoil yacht that was going to take me from Cabo to Auckland. I couldn't fly from registered zones, because I could have been arrested, and I didn't trust the banana-airlines flying from nonregistered zones. Anyway, I called Perchenko back, just out of curiosity. He needed someone like me to sell medical drugs to warring zones. Medicine, for crying out loud!"

Travis, Prescott, and Claire exchanged meaningful glances. As far as Derek Dodd knew, he was selling medicine, not biochemical weapons.

"I thought it was a joke," he continued. "Taking me for some doctor without borders, or a dilettante with a death wish, but he knew exactly who I was and what I did. I had the right connections for his medicine. It didn't take me long to realize that profit was what matters, not what I was selling. Heck, if all those people didn't die, they would continue to fight another day, and I could sell more weapons. And more medicine. Win-win."

"And you wonder why you're in Hell," said Travis.

"I didn't think that far ahead," said Derek Dodd, pulling an innocent face. "What the heck, money is money—the people killed didn't have to die from what I sold. It would be good for a change to be on the side of the white-hat crowd. But then again, if this guy were peddling some bad medicine, my buyers would come after me, so I declined. Besides, why sell medicine on the black market if the medicine is good and could be sold officially? I asked him if it was stolen. To my surprise, Perchenko told me that the medicine was not stolen, but it was not approved yet. Anywhere. And he didn't expect it would be approved because it would ruin Big Pharma. His medication would destroy trillions of dollars of their wealth. The politicians would not allow this medicine to come to market. So what was this miracle medicine? A serum that cures body wounds when inhaled. According to him, it was an incredibly fast-acting medication that could cure the open wounds caused in war-afflicted areas. With time, it could even grow limbs. That was extraordinary, if it was true.

"He told me that they were very concerned about the wars raging throughout most of the Muslim world and Africa. Billion of innocent people died in or were mutilated by the continuous fighting, and he wanted to help the ones who survived, and perhaps those people would come to their senses and stop the wars. I couldn't care less if the world population kept growing from twenty billion today to a hundred billion because of their new miracle medicine. I had found my piece of heaven in New Zealand, among the rich, and it was far away from the hordes that had invaded North America and Europe.

"The more he talked, the more it made sense for me to broker this deal. He was like a grandmother of the past, who grew pot in her garden and then didn't know where or to whom to sell it. He sent me the price for the medicine, and it was lucrative—very lucrative. Although I was already well-off, I could always use more money. Who knows what politicians, judges, police, or warlords I would have to buy off once I was retired? After the transaction details were worked out, we needed to agree on how to execute the transaction. He didn't want to meet face to face to seal the deal, which was fine by me. I didn't want to go to Russia to acquire the goods, and he told me that he could send the stuff to the US. That was a nonstarter for me. Then he proposed Mexico, somewhere south of the US border. We shook virtual hands and promised to get the deal rolling."

Several explosions broke the silence in their quasi shelter, causing Derek Dodd to wince.

"Tell us the rest," said Claire.

"I asked for proof, and he showed me a holovideo of a mouse having its hind legs severed, after which the wounds healed in minutes and, a few hours later, the mouse was growing new legs. They told me that they would provide additional proof once we were on the verge of making a deal. The medicine came in liquid form,

54

colorless and odorless. It could pass for water, and they would sell me 1,000 cc, a liter of the stuff, in one hundred 10cc tubes. I haggled with him on the price, as I usually do, and he gave me another ten percent off. I told him I'd get back to him."

Chapter 11. No Honor Among Thieves

"I think I contacted my largest intermediary in Riyadh, Mohammad Abadi al Medina, but I remember this only vaguely. I had done many big deals with him in the past, and he had many contacts among the Sunni and Shiite Arab warlords. He didn't take sides, just like me. I could make one transaction through him and be done. His biggest objection was proof, so I forwarded him the holovideo. Mohammad Abadi al Medina agreed to my price, and he placed his money in the dark cloud escrow. To satisfy him, I was going to wear an *eye* so he could see and hear the upcoming transaction in Mexico. I placed my money in another cloud escrow to pay Perchenko and to be transferred to a Bermuda bank upon the delivery of the goods.

"A week later, I flew to an unregistered airport near Mexicali and received a message from Perchenko about where to pick up the medicine. I rented an all-terrain SUV and drove south to a ranch designated in the message. I brought with me a drone to follow me in the air and keep an eye out for any trouble. Even with repeat vendors and customers, you can never be too careful or protected. Although the money transaction would happen electronically, the delivery of the medicine was physical, and I was the mule. My concern was more about the anti-smuggling Federales than the local bandidos. The drone didn't signal any dangers, so I drove south on Mexico's highway 5 and then west on 20. The GPS guided me to a dirt road that led to a ranch, whose location I had verified previously from the satellite maps.

"The so-called ranch was a dilapidated hacienda in the middle of nowhere, ideal for smuggling drugs or weapons or even slaves. Inside, Perchenko greeted me on a hologram display, as he had promised in the message. Unbeknownst to Perchenko, Mohammad was seeing and hearing everything I was, thanks to my hidden eye. The only one at risk at the time was me, but everything played out without any hint of danger. Besides, I had a laser gun on me and several self-propelled dart-grenades in case of trouble.

"On a table, I found a small box and inside there was a tiny vial labeled 'proof.' Perchenko told me that the best proof was to try it on myself. I was to be the guinea pig. He instructed me to open the vial and sniff the contents, after which I was to make a small cut on my arm with the knife in the box. I opened the vial and sniffed it first. There was no malodor, only an almond scent. I made a cut on the back of my left forearm. I clamped my other hand over the wound, scowling and swearing, but then the bleeding stopped rather quickly. I looked at my forearm and, although there was blood around the wound, I could see only pink flesh where the cut was, free of blood. I began arguing with Perchenko about what all that meant and by the end of the argument, my wound had closed up, leaving a white line over the cut. It was a miracle medicine, for sure.

"Upon hearing in my ear the approval from al Medina, I asked Perchenko for the delivery of the medicine, and he guided me to a wood credenza in the room. Inside, I found an aluminum case with 100 sealed vials of clear fluid, cushioned in foam packing. Perchenko clarified that the medicine worked as an inoculation against wounds, and it would work for the life of the individual. Because of its short shelf life, the medicine had to be administered to as many people as possible. One 10cc vial was good for hundreds of thousands of people. Since the medicine's effects were airborne, all that was needed was to open a vial and spread it around in a populated area. It would evaporate and cover a very large area. We ended the first part of the transaction. Next was for me to deliver the product to my buyer."

"Do you usually deliver the merchandise in person?" Travis asked.

"No, not usually. Except this time, it was a small case and so I took it."

"Then what?" Travis asked.

Derek Dodd shook his head. "After that, it's all foggy. I don't remember anything else. The next thing I remember was the gray cinderblock room where you found me. I thought that I had been arrested and was about to be interrogated." He took a moment. "Where was my body found?"

"In a ditch along highway 20," said Travis. "You had been shot in the back of the head, as we said. There was no trace of the so-called medicine."

Derek Dodd chuckled bitterly. "There is no honor among thieves."

"What would you have done under normal circumstances?" Prescott asked.

"I would have taken the case back to Cabo, from where I would have waited for instructions from Mohammad Abadi al Medina for a pickup."

"Why did you go to Mohammad Abadi al Medina for this sale? Why not to your other sources?" Claire asked.

"I made the biggest deals with him," said Derek Dodd. "He was a broker."

"I thought you were the broker," said Claire.

"I was a seller's broker, and in most cases, I dealt with buyers' brokers. It was clean and safe. I didn't know the ultimate buyers, and my suppliers didn't know to whom the weapons were sold. Everyone got their money and was shielded from too much knowledge."

"In this case, you didn't know who Mohammad Abadi al Medina's buyers were," said Claire.

"In this case and in most cases," said Derek Dodd. "And I didn't care, as long as I got paid. In due time, I may have heard that a certain warring group used specific weapons that I had sold, but I was not curious to find out more details."

"Did you ever meet Mohammad Abadi al Medina face to face?" Travis asked.

"No, never met the guy in person. There was no need. He transferred the money into cloud escrow. I had the merchandise delivered as instructed."

"Can you describe Mohammad Abadi al Medina?" Claire asked.

"Typical towelhead—big beard, bushy eyebrows, dark shades, and a mark on his forehead."

"Could you identify him in a lineup or a picture?" Prescott asked.

"Not a chance," said Derek. "I don't know who the real man is."

"Could he be a AI hologram?" Prescott asked.

"He could." Derek Dodd laughed bitterly and shook his head. "Why didn't I think of that and conduct my business that way?"

"And Perchenko?" Claire asked.

"Typical Russian—wide face, salt-and-pepper hair, beard and mustache, and blue eyes. I only saw his head in the hologram."

"How did you contact Mohammad Abadi al Medina?" Prescott asked.

"On the dark net. He or I posted on a bulletin board a cryptic message, and that's when we arranged the time and net-address where we would be e-meeting. Not being caught was paramount, and we never used the same cryptic message twice."

"How could we contact him?" Travis asked. "What message would you use?"

"How would you impersonate me? Don't you think he knows I'm dead? He probably ordered my execution. Did you find his payment for the medicine, 100 billion goldbits in my account?" Derek Dodd asked.

"We haven't checked yet," said Travis.

"Probably not. That son of a bitch stiffed me," whispered Derek Dodd. "My Bermuda account number is the dark net address, and the next cryptic message is the phase of the moon on the second day of Ramadan."

"Thanks," said Travis.

"But good luck finding him. Even if you could find him, he probably used the same methods to contact his buyers. In the warring world, the people who pull the strings are *respectable* citizens. Unmasking them would be catastrophic for them. They surround themselves with layers and layers of intermediaries to avoid identification."

"We'll find him," said Travis.

"May I ask you a question?" said Derek Dodd.

Travis nodded.

"What was that liquid, a medicine or a poison?"

"You said you sniffed the liquid," said Claire.

"Yes, and it healed my cut."

"The moment you did that, you were contaminated and began losing your mind."

Derek Dodd looked stunned—more stunned than when he realized he was in Hell.

"Any more questions?" Claire asked.

"But I'm not mad, I'm me," Dodd said in a trembling voice.

"This is my evaluation of what happened," said Claire. "Whatever you tested may heal wounds, but it also began a process in your brain similar to Alzheimer's. That's why you don't remember much afterward. A genetic process began in your body to reduce you to an ape-like intelligent biped."

Derek pointed to Travis. "He said that it will get worse for me here in Hell. Why?"

"Because there could come a time when you'll meet the men-apes you helped create, as this biochemical agent spreads throughout the real world."

Derek Dodd rolled his head as if to overcome a stiff neck. "Use the account numbers from the Luxembourg bank to access the other dark net contacts and history of transactions. You will find everything I did recorded in there."

"Finally, you just did the right thing," said Prescott.

"Can you tell me now how do I get out of Hell?" Derek asked.

"Yes," said Claire. "But you're the only one who can find the way out."

"How?"

"You'll meet Satan or the other devils helping him."

"Satan?"

"Oh, yeah," said Claire. "If you can convince him that he does not exist, your soul and mind will depart from Hell."

"How do I do that?"

"You, and only you, have the answer. Repent and prayer helps, too."

Mit Sandru

Chapter 12. Derek Dodd's Demise

Prescott, Claire, and Travis opened their eyes and rejoined the holo-conference with Maximus, Dr. Stark, and Daniela Rock.

"What's the good news?" Maximus asked. The CTT proceeded to inform the others of all Derek Dodd had told them.

"Therefore, we have two names: the seller is Alexei Perchenko, a Russian oligarch, and the buyer is Mohammad Abadi al Medina, a weapons broker in Riyadh," Travis said.

"We know of a few al Medinas," said Daniela.

"Alexei Perchenko, the Russian oligarch, died five days ago." Maximus displayed a picture of the late Perchenko, who resembled the description given by Derek Dodd.

"They are covering their tracks," said Prescott.

"And there are 67 Mohammad Abadi al Medinas in our terrorist databanks," said Daniela.

"And all have beards," said Travis.

"No, not all, only 43 of them," replied Daniela.

"How about a zebiba, the prayers mark on the forehead?" Claire asked.

"Twelve," said Daniela and she displayed the pictures of the twelve.

"Even Derek Dodd wouldn't know who the right Mohammed is," said Claire. "He was wearing dark glasses when Dodd contacted him."

"We'll start an investigation on the twelve immediately," Daniela said.

"It seems to me that you in the CTT have another appointment with the dead," said Dr. Stark, raising his eyebrows. "Alexei Perchenko."

"Unfortunately, Perchenko died in a plane crash over the White Sea, and the wreckage has not been recovered yet," said Maximus. "Without the body, CTT cannot talk to him."

"Did any of the al Medinas die within past ten days?" Prescott asked.

"No," replied Daniela. "But one died three months ago."

"Maximus, can you identify if our Mohammad Abadi al Medina might be an AI?" Travis asked. "They used a dark net, and Derek Dodd's Luxembourg account may give us access to it."

"Investigating," said Maximus.

"Did the money from al Medina ever get into Derek Dodd's account?" Travis asked.

"There is no evidence of such a large transfer into any of Derek Dodd's legal or illegal accounts," said Maximus. "But there was a debit of 10 million goldbits sent to an account in Luxembourg."

"What if al Medina did not take possession of the one liter of the biochemical agent?" Travis began. "What if he was double-crossed?"

"What makes you say that?" Claire asked.

"Al Medina did not pay Derek Dodd for a reason," said Travis. "This business relies on some amount of trust. Al Medina and Dodd had gotten to know each other over many deals, and al Medina would have deposited the money in Dodd's account if he took possession of the agent."

The others expressed various levels of agreement or doubt.

"Derek Dodd and Mohammad Abadi al Medina believed they were transacting a deal for medicine," said Travis. "Someone else knew that the medicine was instead a biochemical agent, but he didn't have the money to buy it and stole it instead from Derek Dodd."

"More suspects?" wondered Claire. "But wait—Dodd had a drone that monitored him. I wonder where that drone is and if it recorded what it saw? Maximus, Dodd was communicating with the drone before he died. It had to be via a satellite link. Do you think there could be any recordings stored somewhere?"

"I'm checking drone transmissions south of Mexicali during that time," said Maximus, and after a few seconds he continued, "Something was recorded. Watch the images."

A video showed an SUV traveling on a highway and then stopping behind a stranded motorist on the side of the road. The car's hood was up and steam was coming out of the hydroengine. Someone got out of the SUV, presumably Derek Dodd, and approached the person who had flagged him down. They seemed to have a short conversation, and then a second individual got out of the stranded car and joined them to look under the hood.

The hood obscured Dodd and the other two, but suddenly Dodd fell down onto the road. The assailants grabbed him by the arms and legs and threw him into the ditch by the side of the road. One of the culprits stepped inside Dodd's SUV, while the other closed the hood of the supposedly disabled car. Then he looked up and ran to the trunk of the car. He looked up again, and the image went blank.

"Repeat, magnify, and refine resolution," said Maximus.

The same images appeared again, but this time it was obvious that the two individuals were most likely women wearing dark shades and baseball caps. Derek Dodd was shot while looking under the hood. The woman who opened the trunk had pulled out a laser gun and blasted the drone out of the sky.

Chapter 13. The Plague

"And that's why we've got recorded images," said Maximus. "The last two minutes of its transmission were saved because the drone failed to end the communication per protocol."

"Now we have two new suspects possessing a deadly agent," said Daniela. "Can you magnify more to see the two women better?"

"Unfortunately, that's all we can see," said Maximus. "But I'm checking if there are satellite images from that time over that location." A second later, Maximus continued, "Yes, here they are."

The video showed Derek Dodd's SUV and the car on the side of the road. The image resolution was about the same, but from a different angle, which revealed who the assassins were. One was a blonde woman and the other a brunette. Unfortunately, their dark shades made them all but impossible to identify. Once they ditched Dodd, the two cars sped down the highway, and then they turned off onto a dirt road. After a few miles, the two cars drove under a shed on the side of a house, and that was it.

"And the following are the real-time images of that location," said Maximus.

The house, the shed, and the burned–out carcasses of a car and a SUV were all that was left.

"It's likely that the two women stayed there until dark, set the vehicles on fire, and fled without a trace," commented Travis.

"These two seemed to be professionals," said Claire, smirking. "And deadly."

"Unless we discover who those two women are, all paths to find the culprits are cold," said Maximus. "And I'm finding out that al Medina was an AI after all, and the link to it is dead as well."

"We need to set up a worldwide alert about this biochemical agent," said Dr. Stark.

"Someone beat you to the punch, Dr. Stark," said Maximus. "A worldwide alert has been initiated by WHO, the World Health Organization. A possible plague has been reported in West Africa. Travel bans have been imposed into and out of the areas."

In their PAVs, Claire, Prescott, and Travis saw the map of Africa and a red semicircle, spreading out from Senegal to Kenya.

"I'm sorry, people, but I'm being called away from this conference," said Daniela. "This alert seems to be very serious. Nice meeting you." Daniela disconnected.

"I don't think I can be useful any more here, but I need to get involved with WHO and this plague." Dr. Stark disconnected.

"Maximus, what's this plague all about?" Claire asked.

"The communications with many countries in the danger zone have dropped off," said Maximus. "Preliminary information indicates that people have begun rioting and killing each other, as if they have lost their minds."

"What are the chances that it may be caused by the biochemical nerve agent?" Claire asked.

"There's not enough information to determine the cause," said Maximus.

"They would not even know how to determine that," said Claire. "Daniela said nothing was found in the three affected areas, other than cyanide."

"That is correct," said Maximus. "The French authorities raised the alert and identified the breakout as a plague of unknown origin. There is a bulletin from WHO asking to identify and isolate any person who has traveled from the area in the past week."

"I don't think we can do anything else about this," said Prescott.

"Affirmative," said Maximus. "It is a global matter for the health organizations to contain. And if the biochemical agent is causing this, then the law enforcement organizations must find the culprits. In the meantime, stand by, and if you can think of any paranormal ideas, let me know. Maximus out."

Prescott, Travis, and Claire stood over Derek Dodd's grave, wondering what to do. Derek Dodd had told them all he knew. Even if he were to remember the women who killed him, they would be as mysterious as al Medina.

"Any ideas?" Prescott asked.

Travis folded his arms and sighed, shaking his head.

"Let's go to my place and see if we can come up with something while watching how this plague unfolds," said Claire.

Mit Sandru

Chapter 14. A New Apocalypse in Africa

They decided to go back to Claire's condo on the Santa Monica Bay to observe the developments in Africa and brainstorm alternative ways of finding the culprits who had unleashed such a catastrophic believed-to-be-plague on humanity. Travis summoned a robotaxi to pick them up at the Queen of Heaven Cemetery.

The robotaxi departed north on Fullerton Road, and soon it took the ramp to the gravimag tracks running at 1,000 meters above the old 60 freeway. The robotaxi's speed increased to 300 km/h, and it joined the gravitational-magneto paths high over the Interstate 10 freeway, skirting downtown Los Angeles, and on its way passing over registered ritzy complexes and communities, and over the unregistered parts of Los Angeles, where crime and squalor varied in degrees, from very little to horrible.

The world's socioeconomic and political structure had collapsed in 2029, in an event known as the Apocalypse or the Armageddon, but it had recovered, and the world population exploded by the year 2062 to 20 billion souls. The United States alone had three billion people. The world population increase was caused by the technology progress in energy (using hydro engines,) robots that could work 24/7, genetic-medical advancements, and Manna, the Biblical food that could feed populations all over the world with little cost or labor.

Of the USA's legal or illegal able-to-work population, some 70% of the labor pool was "Idle," or not working.

Formerly, they had been called the unemployed, but they did not have to work or live in poverty because every man, woman, and child received an income allowance that kept everyone above the poverty level. The other 30% of the able-to-work population did work, if they so chose, and they were called "Active."

The world was also divided into two zones: the registered and the unregistered. With the use of Chemical Composition Scanners, CCS, every individual could be identified by his or her GeneID. All the people in the registered zones were identified by their GeneIDs and tracked anywhere they moved within the registered zones. Civil liberties were surrendered in exchange for very little crime, no terrorism, and a clean and safe environment for the population. Most Active people were registered and lived in registered communities, but the property taxes there were higher. Many Idle people lived in unregistered zones, although their GeneIDs were recorded and recognized if they entered the registered zones. In the United States, half the population was registered by consent and lived in registered zones, mostly in the cities.

Although the old Interstate 10 freeway ended at the Pacific Ocean, the magneto-tracks continued above the water to the circular floating islands in Santa Monica Bay. These islands, which were registered zones, supported tall tower condos. The expansion of habitats over the bay was a necessity, as just the greater LA population consisted of 75 million people.

The robotaxi descended to the rooftop of one of the condo towers, where CTT disembarked. On their way to Claire's condo, they had watched on their PAVs the developments coming out of Africa. It was getting worse with every new report, as the plague expanded. Officially, the media could only speculate about the cause of this pandemic, as very few medical facts had emerged from the affected areas.

"If this spreads beyond Africa, humanity may become extinct," Claire commented as they descended in the elevator to her place.

"We know from Derek Dodd that the agent can be dispersed aerially, but how could it cover such a large area?" wondered Prescott.

"If that's the case, the agent must have been released from many planes, as in crop dusting," speculated Travis. "But why Africa?"

"If that agent is the cause," said Claire.

They entered Claire's condo and made themselves comfortable, popping beers while watching several hologram screens reporting from different sources about the African pandemic. There were many reports of journalists who had gone to those areas and reported briefly on the situation on the ground, the riots, and the carnage. After which, they and their camera crews, if they had any, had gone berserk. Some of the cameras left on tripods or on robodrones continued to record and transmit the progress of the infection. The reporters became agitated at first, speaking through grunts and wild

74

gesticulations. Then they would assault each other or defend themselves from the deranged locals. In most cases, the fights resulted in quick retreats or flights. Occasionally a few ended in macabre deaths. After the initial burst of madness, the people turned into zombies, walking around aimlessly or hiding in fear, displaying ape-like behavior.

"Look at that one," said Claire, pointing to a woman who was crouched in a corner. "A few minutes ago, she was all scratched and bloody, and now her wounds have healed, and she's up and roaming around as if nothing happened." Just as Claire said that, the woman and another heavier woman began pulling on a bag, trying to claim ownership.

"If they're not killed, their injuries heal, just like Dodd's." Prescott shook his head in disbelief.

Urgent calls for help came from the infected areas, as did warnings to stay away, but all lessened or ended as time passed and the infection took its course. Satellite and drone pictures showing the mayhem on the ground were the only ways to obtain information on the disaster that was unfurling. The drones were not retrieved for fear of infecting the operators at their bases, and so they were left to fly indefinitely in circular patterns, for as long as they could retrieve water vapor for fuel or until they crashed due to malfunctions.

The pictures transmitted were gruesome. People lay dead in the streets. Cars and buses ended up in accidents or off the roads in ditches or smashing into trees or houses. Fires and thick plumes of smoke erupted in different parts of the cities, although the causes of the fires were unknown.

"This is the new Apocalypse," Claire commented.

It was in the afternoon when Maximus came to life on each of their PAVs. "We have new reports from Africa. It seems that the plague started 24 hours ago in Senegal and continues to spread east and south over the continent, although not as fast and with only spotty infections in Chad, South Sudan, eastern Kenya, Tanzania, Zambia and Angola. For some reason, it has stopped south of the Sahara. Recently, new hot spots of the plague have appeared as far east as Somalia and south in Mozambique." A map of Africa with swaths and blotches of red showed the contaminated areas.

"Do we know for sure if the biochemical nerve agent is the cause?" Claire asked.

"No, there is no proof of anything causing it," said Maximus. "There is no indication that WHO knows about the biochemical agent that Derek Dodd attempted to sell. As far as they know, this is a pathogenic contamination."

"Do they have samples of the pathogen?"

"WHO is in the process of equipping several drones with auto-labs to land and analyze the infected people and the environment," said Maximus.

"Why aren't you telling WHO about the biochemical agent we investigated?" Claire asked.

There was a short pause before Maximus replied. "That is classified information at this time. Besides, there is no cure for it, and WHO has data from the three sites in the world where this infection occurred previously. Although no pathogen or any other chemical, besides the cyanide, was found at those sites, either."

"I don't think anyone knows yet what the cause is," Travis said to Claire.

"In my opinion, the more info the better," said Claire.

"Point taken. I'll relay to WHO the similarities in Afghanistan, Brazil, and Congo," said Maximus. "If they haven't yet realized it."

"Could this be an offshoot of the Congo contamination?" Claire asked.

"I made a note about that as well," Maximus said. "New information has just been released. Based on the analysis of images collected from the capitals and other cities in the affected countries, the following timetable on the spread of the contamination was compiled: The intense infection began in Dakar, Senegal, at 17:25, and it continued to spread east and south for 24 hours, until it reached Niamey in Niger, and Abuja and Port Harcourt in Nigeria. It is still spreading slowly."

"How could it have spread so fast?" Prescott checked a few geographical facts in his PAV. "Some 2,000 km separate Senegal and Nigeria. That's 84 km per hour. What carried it?"

"It looks like it could be a deliberate biochemical gas attack from low-flying planes," said Travis.

"Negative. No signs of such spraying have been spotted from ground stations or satellites," said Maximus.

"Maximus, what do you mean by 'the intense infection'?" Claire asked.

"Intense infection is from the time people start acting erratically until they settle into a complete zombie state, which takes one hour."

"Maybe they used drones." Travis attempted another guess.

"Negative," said Maximus. "No such vast numbers of drones were detected by ground radar in those countries. However, let me share with you the rest of the report. Past the 2,000 km radius and the first 24 hours, the infection fans out slowly as a medium infection, reaching Chad, South Sudan, Tanzania, Zambia, and Angola. 'Medium infection' is described as the process from erratic to zombie, taking from two to four hours. This medium infection is spotty, as I mentioned. It may have lost its potency."

"It's slowing down, but did it stop?" Claire asked.

"It's undetermined if it has stopped completely. It may be slowing down as it's dispersing."

"Maximus, repeat the time stamps of this so-called intense infection," asked Prescott.

"The intense infection began in Dakar, Senegal, at 17:25. An hour later infection reports came from Conakry, Guinea. Two hours later Monrovia in Liberia and Bamako in Mali were affected. Three hours after it began it reached Abidjan in Cote d'Ivoire and Kumasi in Chad. By the fourth hour the intense infection showed up in Niamey in Niger, and Lagos in Nigeria. After 24 hours it reached all the way to Abuja and Port Harcourt in Nigeria," repeated Maximus. "After that it appeared in certain spots in the surrounding countries, as I mentioned earlier."

"Why so rapidly at first?"

"Unknown at this time. The infection expanded southeast, covering in 24 hours a distance of 2,500 km as an intense infection," said Maximus.

On the holo-screens the images of masses of people clogging the roads, trying to escape the oncoming infection, were shown from different parts of African countries. Panic and flight from the outlier countries in the plague zone had made a bad situation even worse. The airports were crowded with people trying to fly away from the inevitable disease and death. More people might have died during the mass exodus than from the pandemic itself in those specific areas.

"My God, that continent can't get a break," sighed Claire.

"We've been alerted that Namibia, Botswana, Zimbabwe, and Mozambique have mobilized their militaries and are closing their borders," said Maximus. "Most airports in the world have refused arrivals from any African countries. Also, all those who had arrived within the past 48 hours have been quarantined."

"The symptoms from this infection are similar to the three sites but not what Derek Dodd experienced," said Prescott. "He didn't go berserk."

"We don't know that. Remember his confusion about what happened before he was killed?" said Claire. "Or he could have been exposed to something milder."

"We're speculating," said Travis. "It may be the biochemical agent, or it's something unrelated."

"The official position at WHO is that this is a pathogen," said Maximus. "They're scratching their heads about the speed at which the disease initially propagated. The wind wouldn't carry an agent or virus that fast and that far."

"Then the source of the infection was in Dakar, Senegal," said Prescott. "But was that the epicenter or where it began? What if the distribution began in Dakar?" Prescott checked a few more facts in his PAV. "What do you know? The 2,500 km bulge from Dakar to Abuja and Port Harcourt is only 2,000 km from Monrovia in Liberia."

"Good point," said Maximus. "The time when the intense infection began in Monrovia, Liberia, was 19:30. This is based on images we have from different locations on the ground. The distance between Dakar and Monrovia is approximately 1,200 miles."

"Dodd said to spread the agent in the air," said Travis. "Do you think it was dispersed between Dakar and Monrovia? By truck? No, too far, too slow. By airplane then."

"Geometrically, what are you proposing is correct," said Maximus. "In the first 24 hours it spread at a 2,000 km radius from a path between Dakar and Monrovia."

"A jet flying between the start and the end locations," said Travis. "But why did it spread so evenly from that path over Africa?"

"It propagated like a wave," proposed Prescott.

"At an average speed of 83 km/h," Travis said.

Prescott shrugged. He didn't know, either, what caused the contamination to expand over such a large area.

"Let me inquire," said Maximus. "I'm forwarding your question to other agencies that are investigating the source of the pandemic." A second later, Maximus continued, "Now this is interesting. I initiated a search of all the aircraft flying during that time on that path, just in case a plane dispersed the pathogen. There is a flight that coincides with the suspected time stamps. The transponder of the plane, tail number N560AE, ceased to transmit near Monrovia in Liberia. The time of last contact is 19:26—about the same time the intense infection began in Monrovia."

Chapter 15. The Plane Crash

"Where did the flight originate?" Prescott asked.

"Oakland, California. It left the US mainland via Miami and approached Africa's coast near Dakar, Senegal. And the time it reached Senegal was 17:19 local time. From there, it flew along the eastern African coast, where the transponder quit over Monrovia at 19:26. Another thing—the flight path is 1,220 km."

"The flight path and times corroborate our theory," said Prescott, "as if the plane flew along the coast from Senegal and discharged the nerve agent up to Liberia, where it quit. Afterward, the epidemic started spreading east, all the way to Tanzania."

"Where is the plane now, Maximus?" Travis asked.

"I'm searching about the plane. There has been no warning issued about this plane being missing, but it is not accounted for in the air or on the ground."

"Are there other planes that are unaccounted for, Maximus?" Prescott asked.

"Yes, and the transponders show the crash sites all over Africa, mostly in the hot zone."

The news about the many plane crashes shocked them.

"The infection impacted planes in the air?" Claire asked.

"Maybe they got infected before taking off," said Travis.

"But what if they were infected while in flight?" Prescott proposed.

"Now you're complicating the matter," said Travis. "An infection that affects airplanes at high altitudes?"

"What if it does, Travis?" said Prescott. "The suspect plane could still be flying on autopilot with a dead transponder. Or the pilots may have landed in an unregistered zone." Prescott shook his head, disbelieving what he had just said. "Or the transponder is dead because the plane crashed near Monrovia."

"The black box would have signaled the crash," said Travis. "Monrovia's area flight control would have identified it."

"Unless the flight control personnel were zombies by then," said Prescott.

"Sometimes black boxes are destroyed in crashes," said Maximus.

"Wouldn't the satellites pick up the crash?" said Claire.

"No, it was already dark and overcast," said Maximus. "I'm checking the infrared. Nothing definitive there."

"Back to infecting the airplanes in the air," said Prescott. "This is not the behavior of a pathogen or gas, right, Claire?"

"Not unless it flies through a cloud of it. But the pathogen would take time to incubate."

"This other information is curious." Maximus paused and then said, "I just found images from WHO about the infection on the ground from different places where cameras are active. This is from the cameras inside the James Spriggs Payne airport terminal, in Monrovia. Just watch this."

Claire, Prescott, and Travis saw on their PAVs the interior of the airport's small terminal, where people were seated or milling around. Typical terminal behavior, until something atypical happened. Suddenly the people stopped doing what they had been doing. Even the seated and sleeping ones tensed up and then began walking around aimlessly, as if disoriented, for about five minutes, followed by their making erratic movements. Later, the first sign of trouble came when a big man pulled a woman down to the floor and pulled her skirt up, intending to rape her. The woman resisted and pounded with her fists on the man's chest. He hit her back, ripped her and his clothes off, and proceeded to rape her. Some of the people watched, others ignored it, as if nothing out of the ordinary were happening. Similar violations began in other areas in the terminal, although not as successful as the first one. Fights broke out, but it wasn't clear if they were to protect the women or to be the first ones to rape them.

"Oh my God," said Claire. "Basic instinct—sex."

"Look at what's happening near the fast-food outlets," said Prescott.

People began looting the food shops, getting whatever food they could get their hands on and eating it on the spot. Some snatched food from others' hands, and more fights ensued. They didn't fight as humans fight, but as animals—pushing, pulling, scratching, biting, clawing, and stomping on the ones who fell down. The ones who didn't fight were jumping up and down like apes, excited, or to scare away potential attackers.

A faucet with running water attracted many people, who pushed and shoved to drink from the flowing water. They ignored the many bottles of water or other drinks, seeming to not know what was in the bottles or how to open them.

84

Two bigger men took possession of the spigot as if claiming ownership, but soon they were overtaken by the thirsty mob.

"They are acting on the basic physiological needs," said Travis. "Food, water, sex."

"Yes. I'll magnify a particular area. Watch again from the beginning, over the crowd, through the windows, and on the tarmac," said Maximus.

Outside, through the glass windows, a flash occurred, followed by a brief fire and lots of smoke. The emergency fire trucks arrived immediately at the crash site, and firefighters sprayed the burning area of the crash briefly with foam. But then, for no apparent reason, before all the flames were put out, the firefighters stopped and then wondered off in different directions, as if disoriented.

"A plane crashed," said Claire. "Do you think it is the same plane, Maximus?"

"I found new visuals," said Maximus. "The following images were recorded from Monrovia's Key Hole Community, according to the video feed."

The video was taken from a balcony of sorts, showing a black plume of smoke rising in the dusky sky. The intent clearly was to record the plane crash, which had happened shortly before, and the camera was focused on the spot where the crash occurred. The background noise changed from people talking about the crash to silence and then growls, snorts, and screams. The camera pointed down in the street at the panicked people losing their minds. Masses of people were running back and forth with no specific aim. A truck rumbled on, running over some people and eventually crashing into a wooden electrical pole that broke and fell onto the street, strewing its wires, which electrocuted many innocent people who stepped on them. More screams came from within the house where the camera was located, but the camera videoing the street below continued, as if it had been forgotten on the tripod and kept downloading the live feed onto the WorldVideo.

"It is as if the people went mad, just like in the terminal," said Claire. "When were those images recorded, and by whom?"

"The images were posted on the WorldVideo, clock time 19:28, by code name Black Mamba Kid," said Maximus. "There were efforts made to contact this individual, but there was no response. Most likely, the individual went mad as well and left the camera running. There has been no response at all from anyone in Monrovia since the incidents you've just seen. This is similar to all the other areas infected."

"And the fire and smoke in the distance came from the plane crash?" Travis asked.

"That is James Spriggs Payne Airfield, and it is a plane crash," said Maximus. "The Kid videoed the aftermath of a crash. I'll connect images taken from the satellite during daylight, when the weather was clear."

The images in their PAVs changed to a city with some smoldering structures. There were no people in the streets. The image redirected to the airfield and zoomed in on the wreckage of a jet plane that crashed on the runway in its attempt to land.

"I am able to identify the plane's tail number, N560AE, the same American registered hydrojet originating from Oakland Airport in California," said Maximus. "It says it was carrying rat poison."

"The mystery of the dead transponder is solved," said Travis.

"From the looks of it this plane didn't crash on landing, it just crashed," said Prescott.

"I'm checking the flight paths for the James Spriggs Payne Airfield," said Maximus. "The normal landing is east to west. That jet came down the opposite way."

"Meaning?" Claire asked.

"Something might have happened inside the cockpit of that jet, and they were trying to emergency land."

"Are you thinking the biochemical agent, if it was onboard, leaked into the cabin, and the pilots went mad?" Prescott wondered.

"We don't know if this plane was transporting the biochemical agent," said Claire. "The flight originated in Oakland, and the agent's heist happened south of the border, in Mexico."

"I don't know," said Prescott. "I have a funny feeling about this."

Claire replayed the airplane crash as seen from the terminal. "It exploded on impact. Then it burned briefly, emitting black smoke. If the biochemical substance were inside, it would have been incinerated in the explosion."

"Or the explosion blew the biochemical gas sky high, and it drifted in the winds over Africa," said Travis. "Let's see. A plane from California, transporting rat poison, flew to Africa, then flew south along the African coast line, and then it crashed after the pilots nibbled on the poisoned grains intended for rats. Was it a coincidence that the timing and flight path were on the west boundaries of the pandemic, from where the wind blows?" Travis paused for effect. "I think not."

"Even if it was the plane that carried the biochemical substance, there isn't proof yet," said Claire.

"There could be proof," said Maximus. "Preliminary scanning of the ground around the crash shows an abnormal level of cyanide."

Prescott, Travis, and Claire stopped, their mouths opened in surprise.

"Mossad detected the chemicals and alerted me," said Maximus. "Travis may be right about there being no coincidence. The records show that this jet also flew south of the border, to the Mexicali airport, at the time of Derek Dodd's demise."

"It's getting warmer," said Travis.

"Well, to paraphrase Dr. Stark," said Maximus. "We have dead pilots, and only you can talk to the dearly departed to find out what happened."

Mit Sandru

Chapter 16. The Mission

"Go there?" said Travis, pointing with his hand, although he was seeing a virtual holo-image.

"If we go, we need HAZMAT suits," said Claire.

"They'd better have cooling capabilities," said Prescott. "The temperature must be 40°C on the ground."

"And 95% humidity," added Travis.

"I sent a note to Dr. Stark to find the right gear for you," said Maximus. "I've just placed you with the WHO agency, specifically with their Pandemic Alert and Response, EPR, as investigators, and requested transportation for you to go there," said Maximus.

Dr. Stark joined them on their PAVs. "The best protection I suggest for your new mission is to wear light astronaut suits. They will be available at Vandenberg."

"Are we going suborbital to Monrovia?" Prescott asked.

"The US Air Force has dispatched a suborbital jet for you at Vandenberg Air Force Base," said Maximus. "The US is taking this very seriously."

"Any contacts on the ground in Monrovia?" Travis asked.

"Unfortunately, you'll be the first to land there representing WHO," said Maximus. "Everyone's afraid to go there, even with proper protection."

"Will we land in Monrovia?" Prescott asked.

"Negative," said Maximus. "You'll be dropped over Monrovia. They don't want to have any more people exposed to the pathogen than necessary."

"Lucky us," said Claire, displeased by the news.

"Claire, as a medical doctor, you'll be the team lead," said Maximus. "In case you're wondering, you're going there as a medical and scientific investigating team, not as paranormal investigators."

"Then we must conduct a medical assessment and gather pathological evidence on the ground," said Claire.

"Correct," said Maximus. "Drs. Nellie Henderson and Fred Warner, both with WHO-EPR, want to speak to you in a few minutes. WHO doesn't know about your interest in the plane crash, and you'll just stumble over it while you're down there."

"Why don't they know about the crash?" Prescott asked.

"Officially, Africa has been infected by an unknown pathogen. No one at WHO suspects that this is a man-made agent."

"But haven't they learned yet about the other three sites where similar infections occurred?" Claire asked.

"I informed them, but the pandemic is officially attributed to a naturally occurring pathogen, although they have no proof of what pathogen that is."

"In that case, we'll be doing field evaluation for them and assessing the possibility that this was the same agent Derek Dodd tried to sell," said Claire.

"That is correct, Claire," said Maximus.

"I know you're a doctor, Claire, but how are you going to bluff your way by these experts at WHO?" Travis asked.

"Watch me," said Claire with a smile.

"We have connection with Drs. Henderson and Warner," said Maximus. "And Dr. Stark, feel free to pitch in, if needed."

Dr. Stark mumbled his agreement.

"Hello," said a gray-haired woman with a raspy voice.

"Hello, Dr. Nellie Henderson and Dr. Fred Warner." Maximus made the introductions.

"Dr. German, I'm told that you are the team lead," said Dr. Nellie Henderson. "Have you ever done work in an infectious area?"

"No," answered Claire. "But I'm sure I'll be able to manage both gathering the pathogen and performing autopsies on the deceased. I hope I can administer medical help to the survivors."

"And what is the expertise of your associates, Prescott Alighieri and Travis St. John?"

"Prescott Alighieri is our technical specialist," intervened Maximus. "And Travis St. John will serve as security."

"Hmm, is that normal for your organization—let's see, the Trinity Investigation Organization—to assemble such a team? And who exactly are you, what is your responsibility?"

"As explained to you," began Maximus, "we are an organization called upon when extraordinary events occur in the world, such as this pandemic of unknown origin. And yes, a team is composed of such members as described."

"Interesting. At this time, I cannot be too choosy, given that we have no other volunteers." She sighed. "Dr. Warner, would you take it from here?"

Dr. Warner was a bald man with a small moustache. "Hello. I want to thank you for volunteering for this mission to Monrovia. I sent from L.A. complete medical and scientific kits to use on the ground, to collect the pathogens, and if possible, to conduct biopsies on victims. Self-help information explaining what we are interested in achieving is included in the kits, and we will standing by for assistance."

"Rest assured, we know what we're doing," said Claire.

"Yes, we will maintain audio and visual connection, if we can, and we will assist and direct you as needed," said Dr. Henderson.

"Good luck to you, and we'll reconnect when you're on the ground," said Dr. Warner.

The conference ended.

"Boy, they must be desperate to get anyone there to assess what happened," said Prescott.

"And they found three fools," quipped Travis.

"You knew your job requirements when you took it," smirked Dr. Stark.

"Mingling with the dead and the devil, yes—not becoming one of them," said Travis. "If we die, we're going to come back from the dead and haunt you, Dr. Stark, and you, too, Maximus."

"Good luck haunting me," said Maximus, the AI entity living in the cloud.

"We'll come back as a virus."

"I'm immunized against viruses. Travis, you are a well-trained former CIA agent, and a TIO agent. I'm confident you'll do a good job."

"I'm looking forward to your visitations," said Dr. Stark dryly. "Besides, when Travis is joking, he's ready for the mission."

Travis looked surprised.

"I hope we can find out what happened with that plane and the pilots," said Prescott.

"Remember, I'll be in touch as well," said Dr. Stark. "Whatever you do, protect yourselves, and guard your suits from punctures or rips."

"I presume we have duct tape in our emergency kits," said Travis.

"I think you do," said Dr. Stark. "Yes, you do."

"Any more questions before the hovercraft picks you up for Vandenberg?" Maximus asked.

"Are we still working for Mossad?" Travis asked.

"Yes, and you also work for WHO, for now, but I'll be your liaison as usual," said Maximus. "Anything else?"

"Yeah, how are we going to come back if we're dropped in Monrovia?" Prescott asked.

"That detail hasn't been finalized yet," said Maximus.

"Oh, dear!" exclaimed Dr. Stark.

"What?" Travis jumped up. "What if the powers that be determine that all these regions must be sterilized by nuking them? Us included."

"No such plan has been made," said Maximus. "But, in truth, you'll be on your own on the ground."

"How long can we survive in the suits?" Travis asked.

"Forty-eight hours," replied Maximus.

"Two days before we can bail out to safety," pondered Travis unhappily.

The Devolution of Adam and Eve

Chapter 17. Free Drop

The hovercraft picked them up from the roof of the tower and departed northwest to Vandenberg Air Force Base, where they arrived after a half-hour. The base contained several gravimag sky-jump towers of different sizes to accommodate craft that were catapulted either into suborbit or full orbit. Their flight was a suborbital jump, and the craft would be catapulted by gravimags to an altitude of 50 kilometers, after which the hydrorocket engine would ignite, propelling the rocket-plane to an altitude of 200 kilometers. Traveling at hypersonic speed at such an altitude, the flight would be smooth and frictionless. Any point on Earth could be reached by rocket-plane suborbital flights in 60 minutes or less. The flight to Monrovia would take 40 minutes, just 20 minutes longer than their atmospheric flight from Santa Monica to the Vandenberg base.

Ten minutes after they arrived, they were in the suit-up area to get ready for their flight. After shedding their gray suits and bagging them to be taken along, they took the necessary physiological steps required to wear space suits, after which they dressed in the environmental jumpsuits that fitted snugly to their bodies and finally inserted themselves into the astronaut light suits. The suits were called "light" because they were not radiation hardened; they were designed to be used in more sheltered places in spacecraft or in the lunar underground complexes. After they made adjustments and were comfortable in their suits, packs with scanners and their personal suits were inserted

97

into their arm and leg pockets, and then backpacks with jets and parachutes were latched onto their backs, completing their resemblance to three fat white bugs. A shuttle-elevator took them deep underground to the sky-jump launcher's base. The sky-jump was a vertical shaft, beginning one kilometer underground and continuing for another kilometer above the surface. The suborbital rocket-plane resembled a combination of blunt-nose rocket and airplane, with wings tightly folded back to minimize its profile in the launching shaft and the friction in the lower atmosphere. The wings would deploy later to assist upon landing. At this time, the gray rocket-plane with its white US Air Force insignia was positioned horizontally on its gravimag track. This military craft's body was slim, accommodating only eight seats, two per row, behind the pilot in the cockpit. They entered the craft and specialists strapped them into the seats, giving them safety instructions about what to do in case of an emergency. Their suits were connected to the craft's environmental support but would disconnect automatically when the drop would happen.

"How are you civilians doing back there?" asked the pilot over the comm.

"Peachy," said Travis. "What's your name?"

"No name needed, just Pilot."

Claire and Travis exchanged knowing looks. He was not a mere US Air Force pilot, probably a CIA or DIA pilot.

"How are we going to be dropped?" Prescott asked.

"I will descend to 50 km and you will be ejected through the ceiling hatch," the pilot said, probably holding back a chuckle. "Don't worry. They fitted your suits with parachutes, jet assistance, and guiding systems. Everything will operate automatically and land you on a dime at your destination. During the free fall, you'll experience weightlessness, just as in suborbit. If you handle the suborbit weightlessness, you'll have no problem during the drop. You were provided with the VIP parachute package. That means a gentle jerking when they deploy and jet assistance in landing. Any other questions?"

"Anybody ever get flattened from these drops?" Travis asked.

"Not lately. They've been perfected, even for civilians," said the pilot. "I'll let you know, about five minutes before the drop, when to place your mouth guards in to protect your teeth and then to lock your helmets' visors. After that point, you'll be breathing air supplied from your suit. Any other questions?"

Travis wanted to ask him if being a wiseass was a prerequisite for his job, but considering his life was in the pilot's hands, he refrained.

Prescott and Claire, all cocooned in their suits, had no questions either. Everything would be on automatic from that point on. At least, that was the promise.

"Good luck, then."

"We must be insane to do this," whispered Claire.

"C'mon, Claire. You've been on suborbital flights before," said Prescott.

"Yes, but not ejected through the ceiling to land," she replied.

"What about you, Travis?" Prescott asked.

"I'm cool," said Travis, blinking frequently. "Thank God, there is a hereafter."

The rocket-plane moved on its tracks until it reached the vertical launch position. Over the comm they could hear the pilot communicating with the flight control. In the cabin, there were red numerical displays counting down to launch, and other green displays showed the altitude—below sea level at the moment—and the interior cabin pressure, temperature, and other parameters.

The count reached zero and the gravimags engaged, propelling the craft at 2g acceleration toward the sky and pushing them back into their seats. They exited from the two-kilometer tube after 32 seconds and continued to accelerate for another 50 km, achieving the final speed of 5,000 km/h, or 1.4 km/sec. From that altitude and speed, the hydroengine fired and stayed on until they reached the speed of 8 km/sec at 200 km altitude, according to the displays, achieving low orbit. The engine went silent as they traveled ballistically, imparting weightless. Through the small portholes, they could see the curvature of the magic blue Earth covered by white curly clouds.

"Well, lady and gentlemen, we are approaching our destination and descending to 50 km alt," said the pilot 35 minutes later. "About five minutes to drop. Place your mouth guards on and seal your helmets' visors. The environmental supply will disconnect, and you'll rely on your suits' environmental systems. The cabin will depressurize shortly. Remember, you don't have to do anything. You'll descend on automatic maneuvering mode. I suggest you grab onto each ring on your waist belt to keep your arms from flailing when you hit the first blast of air 20 km above the ground."

They did as told and braced themselves for the wild ride about to begin.

"Wait a second," said Prescott. "We'll reach ground during darkness."

"Don't worry, you have night vision in your helmets."

"I'm worried about the landing."

"You can direct your landing choice verbally," said the pilot.

Prescott didn't seem happy to be free falling to the ground in the dark, but at that moment, Earth would not alter its rotation to suit him.

"Lady and gentlemen, get ready for the eject in one minute," said the pilot. The display inside their helmets began the countdown. "Keep you hands tight on those rings on your belts, and you'll do fine. Thank you for flying with your friendly US Air Force, compliments of the US taxpayers, however few they are, and good luck."

When the countdown reached zero, the ceiling hatch retreated, the seat belts snapped open, and they were unceremoniously ejected. For a second or so they rose over the aircraft, and they would have achieved a slightly higher suborbital trajectory, if the jets on their suits did not fire. But they fired and slowed them down to begin the descent back to mother Earth.

Free falling is not an enjoyable experience if you're not a parachutist or daredevil. And free falling in the dark is downright spooky. Claire, Travis, and Prescott took a few seconds to calm their panicked nerves and remind themselves that it was safe, as safe as it could be to fall at hypersonic speed through the stratosphere. At 50 km above the ground, the air was thin, and they felt no wind gusts at first. The parachute-assist units mounted on their backs had jet stabilizers that kept them on the vertical as they fell toward the ground. Inside their helmets, the displays showed their speed, which was diminishing as the air resistance slowed them down. The altitude to touchdown was decreasing fast. It was not until they passed the 20 km mark, and entered the troposphere when they began to feel the jerking of the heavier air and high wind speeds. Their stabilizer jets fired more often to keep them true to the landing spot.

They punctured through dark-gray clouds and kept on dropping, although at subsonic speed by then. After exiting the cloud layer, city lights became visible down below. As they approached the ground, at the 7 km mark, yellow lights began pulsating in their helmets, alerting them to the imminent parachute deployment at 5 km above ground. The yellow lights turned to green when the parachutes deployed its first stage. They felt the jerk from the parachutes, and their speed began diminishing fast. At

3 km, the parachutes' second stage opened, followed by another jerk, and the speed decreased even faster.

"I see the airport and the plane wreckage," said Prescott, watching through the night vision deployed inside the helmet.

"The lights in the city are still on. That's good," said Travis.

"The generators are still running," said Prescott.

"There are no more fires anywhere in the city," said Claire.

"We're going to land 50 meters upwind from the plane wreckage," said Prescott. "Ten seconds until we kiss the ground."

"If I didn't have this helmet on, I'd kiss it for sure after I touch down," said Travis.

Their backpack jets began firing, slowing them down and guiding them to the drop site. The displays in their helmets showed the distance to the ground in meters. At the one-meter mark, the jets intensified and their feet touched the ground softly. At that moment, the jetpacks and parachutes unlatched and floated away. They stood on the ground, safe and unharmed after the 50 km-high drop. Their pulse rates were as high as the altitude they had come down from.

Staying unharmed from now on would be another story.

The Devolution of Adam and Eve

Chapter 18. On the Ground

"Everyone OK?" Claire asked.

"In one piece," said Travis.

"It was kind of exhilarating," said Prescott.

"Claire, hold him while I slap him silly," Travis grunted.

"I'm glad we didn't wear the regular space suits."

"Oh come on, the astrosuits aren't that bad," said Prescott. "It's just like wearing heavy clothes."

"And we are being kept alive inside them," said Claire.

Travis grunted again.

They stood on the tarmac of the James Spriggs Payne Airfield, an old-fashioned airport without any signs of modern airport magneto-tower launchers or magneto-grab lander infrastructures. The lights were on around the airport, even the ground guidance lights, as if they were waiting for airplanes to land. A few airplanes and two military hovercrafts were parked near the airport hangars.

Their exterior microphones picked up no troublesome noises, other than occasional animal sounds or the banging of a sign stirred by the wind somewhere. The jet wreck, no more than a pile of debris by now, was not far away. No one had touched the broken parts nor searched for bodies. The crash site was undisturbed, as it was after the fire was partially put out.

"Command center, we're safe on the ground," communicated Claire. "Local time 01:25, and all seems to be quiet."

"Good to hear that, CTT," said Dr. Stark.

"Excellent news," said Dr. Nellie Henderson. "The preliminary air sample readings from your suit sensors show no bio-danger. That's good news."

"Except there are traces of cyanide, hydrogen cyanide, HCN," said Dr. Warner. "But nothing dangerous in the amounts detected so far."

Prescott, Travis, and Claire exchanged apprehensive glances when they heard about the HCN.

Claire read the findings inside her helmet display. "Nothing dangerous in large amounts of anything."

"The readings may change when you encounter humans," said Dr. Warner. "Will you be able to do much work in the dark?"

"We have night vision capability. The sky is overcast, but there is sufficient light, and we can assess the situation on the ground without difficulty," said Claire.

"We're seeing a crashed jetcraft on the tarmac not far away from where we are," announced Prescott. "We're approaching it as I speak."

"Are you saying a plane crashed nearby?" Dr. Fred Warner asked.

"That's correct," said Prescott.

"When did it crash?" Dr. Warner asked.

"A while back, I suppose. It's not burning or smoking anymore," said Prescott. "Tail number is N560AE."

"This is Maximus. This plane stopped communicating two days ago at 19:26."

"Any significance to our case, Dr. Warner?" Dr. Henderson asked.

"I don't know. Depends on when the plane crashed, before or after the pandemic started."

"We can examine the remains of the pilots and find out," volunteered Claire.

"Please do so, Dr. German," said Dr. Warner.

"We'll report back when we have additional information," said Claire.

"And we're on private comm," said Prescott, reminding the others that they could communicate privately among themselves. "And they accepted the plane crash as part of our investigation. Good job, Claire."

"Don't mention it."

Travis made sure his gun was ready for any eventuality. "First thing first—let's see what remains of the plane and crew." He walked toward the wreckage, followed by the others, to where parts of the cabin and cockpit survived in larger pieces. Since it was a hydrojet that used water as fuel, the fire after the impact did not do much damage.

The fire-extinguishing foam had been washed away by recent rain, and the wreckage was in a pile of twisted metal parts inside a shallow crater filled with water. Many more broken parts littered the area around the wreck. They walked carefully among the shattered airplane pieces, making sure not to cut or tear their suits.

"Should we turn on our helmet lights?" Claire wondered.

"No, let's inspect with our night goggles first," said Travis. "Who knows who's watching out there."

They used the Chemical Composition Scanners (CCS) on their suits, bouncing the examination rays among the suits for the chemical analysis of their surroundings. Carefully they made their way to the center of the wreck. If there were any bodily remains, it would be hard to identify them. The fire-extinguishing foam that covered the biological parts prevented vermin or maggots from consuming the remains for the time being. The flight records mentioned by Maximus showed that only the pilot and copilot were onboard.

"Not much here," said Prescott.

Travis pointed to a portion of the aircraft's cockpit that resembled a broken eggshell, and he and Claire entered cautiously.

Claire bent down and lifted a charred forearm from inside and scanned it. "A relatively large piece of remains." She took initial bio readings and opened the comm with WHO–ERP. "Doctors, we found a forearm. How are the bio readings?"

"This is Dr. Warner. The readings show nonthreatening biohazards. Please perform an autopsy to get internal bio readings."

"This arm belongs to Captain Tom Bradwell, according to the GeneID," said Dr. Stark, who was on the comm as well.

Claire motioned to Travis to help her, while Prescott ventured deeper into the crater filled with mangled parts. Travis held the captain's arm for Claire to work on, and she inserted a probe into the unburned part of the flesh, observing the readings inside her helmet.

"Hold it tight, Travis. I need to cut across the arm and reach the marrow in the bone." Claire retrieved a scalpel and cut the flesh longitudinally all the way to the shattered ulna. She dissected the flesh around the cracked bone and inserted the probe inside.

"Dr. German," said Dr. Warner. "We're receiving lots of data, which is excellent. It would be helpful if you could find a head, even a partial one. Please scan the brain."

"Acknowledged," said Claire. "Prescott, can you detect any head pieces down there?"

"No, but I can see brain matter scattered all over the inside of a remaining windshield."

Claire and Travis walked down to reach Prescott.

"Here," Prescott pointed. "This section of windshield was not contaminated by the fire or the fire-extinguishing foam."

Considering the violent crash, a relatively large section of the windshield, crisscrossed with spidery cracks, had survived, and it was coated with a reddish-brown substance on the inside surface. Claire pointed the probe at it, taking readings while Travis stood on the other side for the CCS scans.

"The readings are good," said Claire.

"It's the captain's brains, Tom Bradwell's," said Dr. Stark. "Can you find the copilot's remains?"

"I'm reading different GeneID outside the cockpit," said Prescott, who was performing CCS scans as well.

"That's the copilot, Chuck List," said Dr. Stark.

"I found portions of a head," said Prescott.

Claire went to the spot to where Prescott was pointing and took readings from the partial remains of the head and brains of the copilot, Chuck List. She then lifted the head and placed it in a portable imaging scanner they had with them in the kit. The device performed a complete interior scanning of the remaining brain. They continued performing more scans of the few human remains as dawn approached.

"That's all the scans we can provide you with for now," said Claire.

"Thank you, Dr. German, we much appreciate your work down at the site," said Dr. Warner. "This will give us some insights into the premortem physiology of the pilots. Could you do the same type of work on the people in the terminal?"

"Yes, we will. But first, we must rest. Dr. German out."

"Still all quiet here," said Travis, turning in place and surveying the landscape around them. "The locals must be asleep."

"Good, we satisfied the scientists from WHO. Now let's see what story the pilots can tell us," said Claire.

"What is that?" Prescott pointed to a distorted aluminum case among the debris.

Chapter 19. The Vial

Prescott lifted a few smashed pieces covering the metal case and dislodged the badly banged-up aluminum case. "Guys, this is the case described by Dodd. What are the chances that this was holding the biochemical agent?"

Claire turned her exterior helmet lights on. "I think there is an intact vial inside."

Inside the deformed case, cushioned by its foam crate, one vial had survived the crash. With a great deal of care, Claire and Prescott pried open the case and retrieved the intact vial, which was in the shape of a test tube with a rubber seal. There were more broken vials inside, shattered by the impact.

"Is the tube intact?" Travis asked, watching Claire examine it by the light of her helmet.

"Pristine," said Claire. She opened comm with TIO. "Dr. Stark, do you see what I see?"

"I do, and I'm looking at the readings," he said. "This is unbelievable."

"What's in the vial?" Claire asked.

"Water and cyanide," said Dr. Stark.

"Water? Are you sure?" Travis asked.

"Positive."

"What's so unbelievable about that?" Travis asked.

"It's plain water, not what I expected."

"What did you expect?"

"Anything else but water."

"How about the cyanide, Dr. Stark? What type?" Claire asked.

"HCN, hydrogen cyanide. Not a great amount. But more than enough to kill one human if the contents of the vial were to be swallowed."

"This makes a poor nerve gas," said Claire.

"I have to agree." Dr. Stark sighed. "Actually, not even a nerve gas, since it's in a liquid solution."

Prescott scanned the case's interior. "What are the readings from inside the case?"

"Nothing, except for traces of cyanide."

"Then the agent has evaporated from the broken vials," reasoned Prescott. "It rained here recently, and there is plenty of water to dilute the agent."

"Just as with the other three sites Daniela Rock mentioned," said Claire.

"You're in the right place then," said Dr. Stark.

"Lucky us," said Prescott. "But what or where is the biochemical agent?"

"That's the puzzling problem. There are no detectable traces to cause any harm to anyone," said Dr. Stark.

"Are you saying the contamination has ended?" Prescott asked.

"Remember that WHO suspects a pathogen, not a nerve agent," said Claire.

"And there are no signs of any pathogen, either," said Dr. Stark. "The only way to analyze the vial's content is to open it up in a lab environment."

"Which we don't have," said Claire. "We'll need to return with it."

"There is more work to be done, and you must continue your work on the ground," Maximus said.

"But we're finding nothing," said Prescott.

"Maybe we're not looking for the right thing or in the right place," said Maximus. "We're going on the premise that the agent was a nerve gas substance. WHO suspects a bio agent. But the spread of the contamination in the first 24 hours does not match any known vector carrier."

"We're not out of the woods yet," Claire sighed.

"That's correct," said Maximus. "We need more detailed test results from the pilot scans to determine what the cause of this contamination is."

"How about the intact vial?" Claire asked.

"Hold it safe, don't break it," said Maximus. "Something has caused this widespread contamination, which we cannot detect. Opening that vial may kill anyone that's unprotected, along with the scientists analyzing it."

"Are you saying that the agent is unknown to us and that we may be surrounded by it, or that the agent is safe only inside the vial?" Claire asked.

"Those are two possibilities, among many more," agreed Maximus.

"Maybe it is a good thing we're inside our suits," said Travis from other section of the wreck, as he continued searching among the debris.

Claire ripped foam from the case, rolled the vial in it, placed it in a plastic bag, and then in a breast pocket. "I'll be the keeper of the vial for now."

"Can you locate the black box?" said Dr. Stark. "It should be at the craft's tail end."

"Travis, have you seen an orange box, which is the so-called black box?" Prescott asked.

"No, but guess what I just found." Travis lifted a mangled system of tubing attached to a portion of the aircraft's skin. "A dispersing system. I can see small shards of glass and pieces of rubber in the injection section."

Chapter 20. The Dispersing System

Claire and Prescott joined Travis to inspect the equipment purported to be the spray system used to distribute the nerve gas. It was the size of a large suitcase, now badly battered. It had tubing manifolds inside, a few broken digital displays, and a feeder for the vials. There was a mechanism that punctured the vials with a needle to extract the fluid and then ejected the spent vials into a sealed orange container that was no longer sealed. A ribbed hose attached the system to the exit nozzle on the outside of the plane's skin.

"This is definitely dispersing equipment of some kind," said Prescott, examining it thoroughly. "Except they were not crop dusting."

"This is Maximus. It seems that you found the smoking gun."

"Indeed," said Travis. "This plane was spraying Africa with the agent. We'll find out more from the dead pilots when we visit them in the afterlife."

"Is the vial dispenser chamber sealed?" Dr. Stark asked.

"It was originally, but it is broken and open now," said Prescott. "You think that the dispenser leaked the gas in the cockpit and doomed the pilots and the plane?"

"Something malfunctioned. I hope you find out soon what happened onboard."

"Judging by what I see here, this system is not a military-grade nerve gas spraying system but an industrial-grade system made for spraying hazardous substances," said Prescott. "It should not have leaked into the cabin."

"Don't forget to look for the black box," said Maximus. "It will tell us a lot about the moments before the crash."

"I'm walking toward the tail section now," said Travis, making his way around small pieces of aluminum brackets. "It broke and catapulted toward the front section of the plane down the tarmac."

Prescott went over to join him, while Claire remained behind to scan and video-record in detail the dispersing equipment.

"The box is orange-red, a cylinder attached to a shoebox-sized container," Prescott said as he joined Travis.

They searched the debris, but other than a few hydraulic cylinders and screw-drive mechanisms for the rudder, they couldn't find any such orange device.

"I'm scanning on the wave band Maximus gave us, but I'm not receiving any signals from the box," said Prescott.

"It is definitely dead," said Travis, looking around. "Say, Prescott, how come the tail is in front of the cockpit?"

Prescott looked over the wreckage. "The jet came down at steep angle, exploded, and the tail was blown forward. Funny things happen in a crash."

"There are parts littered behind the plane as well," said Travis. "Claire, can you check the debris behind the plane?"

"Sure. I'm done with the scanning." Claire walked toward the rear, inspecting the broken parts. "Sorry, nothing here is that large."

"What happens if the black box ends up underwater?" Travis asked.

"It transmits from underwater as well," said Maximus.

"Do you think the box fell in the ocean?"

"No, it is too far away," said Travis.

"Wait, Travis has a point," said Prescott. "We can't hear the underwater locator beacon because we're on land. And the land beacon, unless it is broken, will not be heard if it is underwater. We need to check the ditches or waterholes on the side of the runway."

"Time for dirty work." Travis walked to the edge of the runway, inspecting the ditches and water holes.

Prescott did the same on the other side, and Claire also at the opposite end.

"I found something!" Prescott lifted a box from a small pond. "I'm getting the signal now."

"Great job," said Maximus. "At the box end, there is a wireless connection over short distances. Position it near your suit's chest system. I'll extract the information from the CVR and FDR."

Prescott did as instructed and all three walked back to the plane's cockpit.

"Just another minute, and we'll have all the preliminary data," said Maximus. "Excellent work. Hang on to the box—there's more detailed information to be extracted from it."

Travis unfurled a sturdy white plastic sack, and Prescott placed the box inside it.

"Well, girl and boys, it is time to do what you do best—talk to the dead," said Dr. Stark, joining them online.

"And then we can come home," said Travis.

"No, we can't," said Prescott. "Our WHO work is not done here and . . . "

Claire and Travis looked at him, confused.

Prescott raised his gloved hands. "We cannot make skin contact with each other."

"A small detail we completely overlooked." Claire sighed. "Dr. Stark, as long as we're in the astrosuits, we cannot hold hands to make skin contact and talk to the dead pilots."

"It will have to wait then," said Dr. Stark.

"We have company," Prescott announced. "Lights off."

Along the tarmac, alerted by the helmet lights, a group of people approached cautiously.

Chapter 21. Shelter

From the south, a bestial howl split the air. The approaching group stopped, looked to where the sound had come from, and ran away in the opposite direction.

"What was that, a lion?" Claire asked.

"There are no more lions in Africa, and that was no lion, or anything I've ever heard before," said Travis. "Get your guns ready."

"If that is a feral animal, we don't want it to come here and contaminate this area," said Claire.

"Then we'd better meet the creature head on," said Travis, who began scanning the neighborhood from where the howl came. "I see movement. It's another group of humans. I'm relaying the images to Maximus."

"They are coming at us without hesitation," said Prescott. "This group doesn't seem to be afraid, like the other one."

Among the approaching group, a woman stopped, opened her mouth wide to the sky, and howled the same feral sound. The large men around her began making guttural sounds and bouncing around, as if they were apes.

"Is she encouraging them?" Prescott wondered.

"They are carrying sticks and stones," said Claire, looking through her zoom night vision.

"Maximus, do you see what we see?" Travis asked on the comm.

"Considering that we don't know the complete danger of the infection, I suggest avoidance," said Maximus.

A stone bounced off the pavement in front of them.

"They know how to use stones as weapons," commented Prescott.

"We could shoot them, or we could blind them with our helmet pinpointing lasers," said Travis.

The three of them opted for the lasers and turned them on in the direction of the group, just as another stone flew by them. The lasers temporarily blinded some, which was better than deadly bullets. The people stopped, screaming in distress and rubbing their eyes. No understandable language came from any of them. The lasers did the job, and the stone throwing stopped, leaving the group in temporary disarray.

"Let's move toward the terminal building," said Prescott.

"We may find shelter behind metal doors there," said Travis.

Their light astronaut suits were not cumbersome, but they were not exactly safari garb. The good aspect of the suits was that they maintained a stable temperature inside as they walked at a brisk pace toward the dark terminal.

"Do you remember the mayhem we saw in the terminal from two days ago? It may not be safe," said Claire.

"The air traffic control tower, then," Travis proposed.

The control tower looked as if it had been a water tower at one time, probably repurposed as the air traffic control center. Access to the control room at the top was up a coiling set of stairs on the outside of the tower's shaft. They climbed to the top only to find the door locked. A numerical keypad was near the handle.

"Hold on a second." Prescott squatted in front of the numerical pad to disable it.

"Hurry up. I see movement across the tarmac, coming toward us," said Claire.

Prescott smashed the keypad box, exposing the wires inside and then short-circuiting the device. The door unlatched and they rushed inside.

"With all your electronic know-how, that's the best you can do?" Travis quipped.

"We're inside, aren't we?" said Prescott.

"There is no one in here. Good." Claire went to the window, inspecting the surroundings. "They lost track of us."

Travis busied himself barricading the door with a sofa, and Prescott inspected the archaic equipment inside.

"Four hours till sunrise, and we are self-imprisoned," said Travis, clicking his tongue.

"The characters outside are humans, but they don't behave like humans," said Claire, watching from the window.

"They're bipeds," said Travis. "But behave like apes."

"I'm glad we're sheltered here, otherwise we would have to kill a lot of them out there in the open," said Prescott.

"In the meanwhile, I'll see if Dr. Stark can make any sense of the bio data our detectors collected." Claire slid down against the wall into a sitting position. "Dr. Stark, any new information?"

"WHO and our computers are hard at work, but so far nothing out of the ordinary could be determined from what you scanned and inspected," said Dr. Stark. "There are no unusual bio hazards of the magnitude we thought would be present. There are chemical contaminants, but that's to be expected after an airplane crash. There is no indication of any micro- or nanotechnology, either."

"And yet the people outside are behaving like apes," said Claire.

"Yes, as observed at previous sites," said Dr. Stark. "You should venture out during the day, in the heat."

"Agreed," said Claire.

"More data from the affected people, dead or alive, are necessary," added Dr. Stark.

"Will do, when it's safe," said Claire.

Chapter 22. Monrovia

The sun rose, shedding light on the partially devastated city that at the moment seemed void of humans. The only life visible through the tower's windows was some birds, a few stray dogs, and an occasional goat or cow.

"Do you think the dogs ate from the dead people?" Prescott wondered.

"It's possible," agreed Claire. "We'll need to take readings from the dogs or any other animal we may find."

"In that case shall we venture outside?" Prescott asked.

"The sooner the better," Travis said. "I'm starting to itch in this suit." He pulled away the sofa and cracked the door open, inspecting the outside. "No one outside." He opened it wider and exited, holding his gun at the ready.

Prescott ventured behind him with his gun drawn. Claire was last, carrying the lab kits. They descended to the ground, where everything was quiet. Travis pointed to the terminal building, and they walked quickly over without a word. Inside they found a few bodies scattered here and there on the floor and under the seats, with maggots and flies swarming over the corpses.

"God, even inside the suit I can smell the stench," said Prescott.

"That's because you're smelling with your brain, not your nose," said Claire. "Let's walk across the terminal and do a drive-by scanning. Turn your cameras on. Command center, are we connected?"

"Yes, we are, Dr. German," said Dr. Warner.

They holstered their guns in order to free their hands to use the medical probes and obtain readings from the bodies lying around.

"Dr. Henderson, are you seeing the images?" Claire asked.

"Yes, I am. Horrible."

"Dr. German, this is Dr. Warner. It seems that all the dead have suffered some form of trauma."

"That is correct. As far as I can tell, everyone here was bitten or battered to death."

Travis signaled to go private comm. "There are far fewer people in here than we saw in the videos from the time of the airplane crash," said Travis.

"I'm sure many must have escaped from the terminal, injured or otherwise," said Prescott. "Remember what Dodd told us—this agent acts as a wound healer."

"Not if they were killed," said Claire, moving and turning over bodies as she inspected them. "None of these show any signs of healing."

"Dr. German, are you there?"

"Yes, we're here, Dr. Warner," Claire said after switching the comm back to conference mode.

"Please perform brain scans on as many bodies as you can."

Claire motioned to Prescott to help her place the victims' heads in the scanner. Travis had his gun drawn again and walked around the terminal, making sure there was no risk of an ambush. But nothing stirred, except for the maggots.

"We scanned seven heads. Do you need more scans, Dr. Warner?"

"That will do for now. But we will need to scan one of the survivor's brain."

"As soon as we catch one," said Claire. "We'll go in town and see if we can capture anyone alive." As they walked toward the door, she and Prescott removed maggots off their legs, arms, and even the visors.

They pushed the doors open to get out of the terminal's hall, and swarms of more flies flew in. Outside, a large black dog began approaching them, growling as if it were ready to attack. Without hesitation, Travis shot him.

"We cannot take any chances, with our suits as our only protection," said Travis apologetically.

Claire scanned the dead dog's body and head for a brain analysis. "Dr. Warner, did you receive the data from the dog?"

"Thank you, we did."

"Anything unusual we should be aware of? Are animals affected as well?"

"From the satellite surveillance, it doesn't seem so. The animals are behaving normally. We'll let you know if there are any kind of pathogens affecting this dog."

"Maybe it was just one mad dog," speculated Prescott.

"You need to analyze a few survivors," said Dr. Henderson.

"Trying to find some volunteers, but they're all hiding." Claire addressed her teammates, "Where do you think survivors would be?"

"They must be hiding in some of the buildings, or houses, in the shade," said Travis, looking at the sun getting up in the sky.

"The concrete buildings would be my preference," said Prescott, pointing to the buildings nearby. "It is cooler inside those."

They were at the gates of the airport, and the streets around them were deserted. No other dog challenged them. Cars were strewn around the main road, most left with their doors open, abandoned in a hurry by their drivers.

"Let's commandeer that SUV," said Prescott, pointing to a nearby vehicle. "We'll cover more terrain, and it is safer."

"I'm sure the owner won't mind," said Travis, getting into the driver's seat.

They drove slowly, assessing if there were any signs of living people out in the streets, but there were none. Sheets strung across the roads, raised to catch Manna, were left neglected and sagged under their load. Many had collapsed under the load. In corners, alcoves, or any other dead ends, the Manna had accumulated like dirty snow. Black bacteria had begun feasting on the putrid lichen-algae.

"No one is harvesting the Manna," commented Prescott. "They must have forgotten that it is food."

"There, a cow!" said Claire, pointing. Although it was in the middle of the city, the cow has found its way in the streets, eating grass from the green belt. "A good candidate for scanning."

Luckily, the cow was accustomed to people and didn't run when Prescott and Travis approached it. The cow kept eating the grass, unconcerned.

"Her head is too big for the scan," said Prescott.

"Stay on the other side and I'll do a CCS walk scan," said Claire.

Travis stood in front of the cow and petted her head. The cow appreciated the rub and stood still while Claire worked the CCS.

"Watch the horns," said Claire, while scanning. "And . . . I'm done."

"It is docile," said Travis.

They continued driving into the uninhabited town, searching for signs of living humans. No one waved or peeked out from the buildings' windows at the moving SUV.

"More dogs, but most are sleeping," said Travis. Some of them raised their heads but ignored the SUV and quickly went back to sleep.

They saw a few more bodies in the ditches, covered in flies and maggots.

"Where did the others all go? We have to check inside the buildings," said Claire.

"There is a supermarket." Prescott pointed ahead to a store on the ground floor of a multistory building. "Survivors will hang around food."

Travis pulled the SUV in front of it, and they exited to inspect the supermarket. The automatic doors were still operational and opened when they came near them. At least the survivors were not trapped inside, not knowing how to open the doors. The store was in disarray, as if a pack of wild pigs had just ransacked it. The aisles were strewn with ripped bags and broken boxes. The only intact items were the nonedibles or the foodstuff in cans or jars. A few jars lay broken on the floor, and bloodstains were visible near some of the shattered glass jars.

"I think those jars broke when they fell off the shelves and crashed onto the floor. They don't seem to be smart enough to break the glass jars to get to the food," said Claire. "Anything that was edible and easy to access, they ate. They haven't figured out how to unscrew the caps on the plastic water gallons."

They continued to walk around the aisles, inspecting the piles of torn packages of food. The produce aisle and meat displays were empty, but beer and alcohol containers remained intact.

"No one here," said Prescott. "This is surprising, since there is food remaining in this place. But it's unattainable, given their level of reduced intelligence."

"Let's inspect the upper floors in this building," said Travis.

All three drew their guns and followed Travis out of the store and into the lobby of the building. There were no dead bodies in the atrium. After locating the stairs, they climbed cautiously to the floor above. This was an office building, and most suites had been abandoned or ransacked. Two floors up, it was the same: no one was in any of the offices.

"It was evening when the contamination began. Not many people were working late hours," said Travis. "Or if they did, they must have run home. If they could remember where home was."

Prescott stared out a window. "That must be the Mesurado River. Maybe they went there for water. They should know at least that much."

"That river is a sewer stream," said Claire.

After they were satisfied that there were no people in the offices, they exited and continued driving in the SUV along the empty streets. Food stands were overturned, pillaged as the people raided them, just like the supermarket. Occasionally, an audio commercial blared advertising specials for one store or another, interrupting the silence. Most buildings and houses did not caught on fire and remained intact; some windows and doors were left open, while others were shuttered to protect from the sun's heat, but there was no sign of curious eyes peering from behind cracked shutters. Three brown and white goats sprinted away as they passed near them. A dog barked and gave the SUV brief chase.

"Turn back, Travis. We have to scan the goats," said Claire.

"Sure," said Travis, turning the SUV around.

"I'll shoot one with the tranquilizer gun." Prescott pulled a gun from their kit and loaded a dart. "Just drive slowly by their side." Prescott rolled down the window and shot the nearest goat.

The other goats ran away. The shot goat dropped on its knees about a dozen yards away and then rolled over. The other two stopped shortly, as if waiting for the tranquilized one to catch up with them. Claire and Prescott got out of the vehicle and scanned the goat, while Travis stayed at the wheel, constantly checking the surroundings. After the job was completed, Claire injected the goat with an antidote. It rose on wobbly legs and joined the others that were eating grass nearby. The team resumed their search.

"There!" Travis shouted, pointing to an alley. "I saw someone there." He pulled the SUV to an abrupt stop at the entrance of the narrow alley.

They came out holding their guns at the ready. Several cats scattered away when they saw them. In the alley were three Africans, a woman and two boys, lying on the ground.

Chapter 23. Brain Dead

"My scanner indicates they're alive," Claire said, approaching cautiously.

"What's wrong with them?" Travis asked.

"Dehydration," said Claire, getting closer to one of the boys.

The woman moved an arm, opened her eyes, and made a feeble effort to push away. She was dry as a prune. Fresh wounds on the woman showed signs of complete healing. Claire pointed at the healed wounds for Prescott and Travis to notice, which they did.

"Can you hear me?" Claire asked the woman through her external speaker.

The woman opened her mouth and made low, throaty noises.

"Doctors," Prescott called the command center. "We've found some people alive, but in bad shape. They need help."

"We hear you, but until we assess the contamination level, we cannot send rescuers into the area," said Dr. Henderson. "Dr. German, please scan the people you've found."

Claire kneeled down and probed the two boys. "They are almost dead from dehydration."

"There must be water somewhere here," said Prescott.

"I'll go into the next building and look for water." Travis exited the alley. He returned soon with a plastic water bottle. "I found it at the abandoned information desk." He unscrewed the cap and gave the bottle to Claire, who poured it into the woman's mouth. At the taste of the water, she gulped the whole bottle down.

"I don't get it—the water was just around the corner," said Travis.

"What good does it do if she doesn't know how to unscrew the cap?" said Prescott.

The woman opened her eyes and scooted away from them, wailing.

"Analyze her before she gets away!" Dr. Henderson, observing the scene from their helmet cameras, shouted.

Prescott walked around and blocked her escape. She looked fearfully at him and Travis.

"I suggest holding her by the arms and legs." Claire had the head scanner ready.

"Careful, Prescott. Don't let her tear your suit with her nails. Grab her above the wrists." Travis, in turn, immobilized her above the knees.

The woman squirmed and thrashed, snarling at them. Claire did not hesitate and placed her head in the scanner. Once that was completed, she did additional scans on the woman's furiously thrashing body.

"Release her," Claire told them.

The freed woman turned and scrambled away on all fours for a distance, then she stood up and looked at them with wild eyes. She was breathing heavily, and then she collapsed due to exhaustion.

"What should we do for the boys?" Prescott wondered.

"They are unconscious," said Claire. "Can you get more water, Travis?"

Travis ran back into the building and returned with another bottle of water. "That's all I could find.

Claire opened the younger boy's mouth, and Travis poured water into it. The boy did not respond. She opened the other boy's mouth, and Travis tilted the bottle into his mouth. He drank for a while and then faded away. Claire scanned both boys and their heads.

"Have you received the readings, Dr. Henderson?" Claire asked after completing the scanning.

"Thank you, very good. Good readings."

"Would you share some of your findings?" Claire asked.

"The brain scans are alarming."

"Please explain," said Claire.

"So far, the scans you sent us from the pilots and some of the dead in the terminal show most of the neurons' dendrites shrunken or missing completely," said Dr. Warner.

Claire addressed her teammates: "Learning and memory are affected if dendrites die."

Travis gave a long whistle. "You mean like brain death?"

"No, but the brain capacity is seriously reduced," said Claire. "No wonder these people don't know the simplest of modern survival skills."

"It's as if they've suddenly become primitive," said Prescott. "That explains the violence. They were reduced to primitive instincts."

"Did the animal scans show the same brain degradation, Dr. Warner?" Claire asked.

"No. The animals seem to be normal."

"What is worse, we haven't found any chemical or bio agent residues, or anything that could have caused this phenomenon," said Dr. Henderson. "There are no bio agents in the animals, either."

"Are the animals immune?" Claire wondered.

"Possibly," said Dr. Warner.

"I think we're done here," said Claire to her teammates. "We did everything we could. Dr. Henderson, we request evac and emergency teams to treat the victims."

"Sorry, Dr. German, until we assess the level of contamination, we cannot send for your evacuation."

"Are you serious?" Travis asked. "We were told that you found nothing bio contagious."

"That is correct, Mr. St. John," said Dr. Warner.

"Because you cannot identify an agent, you suspect that we're contaminated anyway?" Claire questioned.

"Our inability to identify an agent does not dismiss the possibility that it exists," said Dr. Henderson. "It could probably be on the exterior of your suits. Until we are sure that you're not carrying the agent, or until we can cleanse you properly, you must be quarantined in situ."

"Did you just give us a death sentence, Dr. Henderson?" Travis asked.

There was a long pause. "We're sorry about the situation, and we're working frantically to identify what's caused this brain deterioration among the human victims. And if it is still contagious."

"The danger is that, if we bring you back, you may contaminate everyone on your arrival," added Dr. Warner.

"You realize that we have only 36 hours of air in our suits?" Travis shouted.

"Mr. St. John, we understand, and we'll do our best to find a solution," said Dr. Henderson in a businesslike tone. "But our hands are tied."

The communication ended.

Chapter 24. Stranded

"Wonderful, just wonderful!" Travis was furious, walking around to dissipate his frustration.

"We're stranded," said Prescott.

"And you thought I was being ridiculous when I said we could be nuked," Travis said.

"Too much real estate to nuke," Prescott rebutted.

"What if the suits kill us?" Travis wondered. "Or if they aspirate air from the outside to contaminate us?"

"What if this agent is gone? Disappeared. It's done its job, and it is no longer to be found?" Prescott countered.

"It could be. The agent might had mutated into harmless bugs," said Claire. "But they need proof that the agent is extinguished. And they still need us to keep searching."

"What if this agent is not a physical agent?" Prescott proposed.

"What do you mean? It is a fluid. Claire has a vial of it," said Travis.

"Yes, it's a fluid when contained, but when it evaporates, it may emanate an energy wave," said Prescott. "A form of radiation."

"Is there anything like that existing today?" Travis asked.

"No, except for radiation itself, and this is not radiation," said Claire. "You cannot provoke a disease this quickly with energy waves." She thought for a moment and scanned the vial in her pocket. "Just as I thought—there is no radiation of any kind coming from it."

"Maybe this is paranormal? Is Satan at work here?" Travis countered. "Destroy the brain, keep the body and soul, and leave no trace of the cause."

"We haven't sensed any evil," Prescott said. "Satan or not, this is the ultimate mass murder weapon. Look how far and fast it spread from the crash site all the way to Nigeria. There is no substance that can last for that long and not diffuse itself."

"Let's talk to our headquarters." Travis switched on the comm. "Maximus, have you heard about our situation?"

"Yes, I have, and I called for Dr. Stark. We underestimated the severity of this agent."

"What do we do now? In 36 hours, we'll die, asphyxiated, or we can open our visors and become idiots."

"Uh, that's not a good solution," said Maximus.

"What did I hear, you're stranded?" Dr. Stark joined the conference.

"Yes, this is our chance to have medical buildings named after us," said a sarcastic Travis.

"No, no, we'll get you out of there before your good air expires," said Dr. Stark.

"I realize we're quarantined, but animals, and birds especially, are free to move around," said Claire.

"And they may spread the contamination," Dr. Stark concluded her thought. "But I don't think so. The contamination spread east, carried by the winds, not birds. Or none of those, considering the speed."

"Dr. Stark, Prescott floated the idea that this agent is not an agent but a paranormal energy field that affects the brain," said Claire.

"If it is, it is highly selective," said Dr. Stark. "I'm reviewing the results from the dog, goat, and cow's brain scans, and they were not affected at all."

"Sure, how much lower can you reduce an animal's intelligence?" said Travis.

"Dendrites are dendrites," said Dr. Stark. "The animal have less gray matter and are not as intelligent as we are. But their dendrites did not deteriorate."

"Isn't the shrinkage of dendrites reducing the human's gray matter?" Prescott asked.

"You are correct," agreed Dr. Stark. "It destroys the dendrites and axons."

"Were the brains of the people in the three previous infected sites scanned?" Claire asked.

"I'll search," said Maximus.

"It is obvious the agent is designed to affect only humans, not animals," said Claire, observing several birds doing what birds do. So far they saw no dead birds, either, only people.

"Anyway, Dr. Stark, if Prescott is right about this being a nonphysical agent, what can be done to identify it?" Travis asked.

"As I'm talking to you, I'm scratching my head, looking for an answer," said Dr. Stark. "Now, you still have a vial with that agent."

"Yes, I do," said Claire. "Do you want to retrieve it?"

"Sure, but we have the same dilemma. We cannot extract anything from where you are." Dr. Stark paused. "I can't believe I'm saying this, but if that vial contains paranormal elements, you three should analyze it."

Travis, Prescott, and Claire looked at each other with a great revelation.

"Satan. Paranormal," said Prescott.

"This is right down our alley," said Travis.

"Maybe we could analyze it," said Claire. "Whatever is in the test tube is inert matter, not a living thing—"

"Claire, Prescott—we've got to get out of here!" said Travis.

"Of course, that's what we're discussing with Dr. Stark," Prescott retorted.

"I mean get out of this spot." Travis pointed across the street, where several people, mostly men, were coming out of the lobby of a building. They were dressed in shirts or T-shirts, but with no pants or underwear. Some were carrying sticks and brandishing them menacingly.

A woman among them stopped and howled the bestial cry they had heard at the airport the night before.

"The same gang that threw rocks at us," said Travis.

Travis, Claire, and Prescott ran to the SUV and got inside, rolled up the windows, and locked the doors just before the mob reached the vehicle. They encircled the SUV and began jumping and hollering at them. They looked mad, with bloodshot eyes and flaring nostrils. They were foaming at the mouth, and constantly bellowing and shouting. The more daring ones pounded on the windows.

Two climbed onto the SUV and reached through the opened moon-roof, grasping at them.

"Floor it!" Prescott shouted, as Travis did just that.

They accelerated down the street as the mob ran after them. They lost one who was on the roof, but the other one held on to the opening's edge. Claire hit the man's knuckles and he flew off, bouncing on the pavement.

Out of nowhere, another man walked in front of the SUV, and they ran over him.

"Watch out!" Claire screamed.

"I never saw him coming." Travis concentrated and reduced the SUV's speed. "It is as if he was never aware of the danger of walking in front of our vehicle."

"Are you alright?" Maximus inquired.

"We were attacked by a mob of people, but we managed to get away," Prescott said. "It might be the same mob that attacked us at the airport. We're in a car, speeding around."

"This group seemed to have adapted as a gang," said Claire. "They communicate with each other somehow."

"Fascinating," said Dr. Stark.

"Chances are that your SUV motion will attract others' attention," said Maximus.

"True, but they can't catch us," said Travis. They drove near a large intersection, where Travis stopped under a bus stop overhang. They looked around, but the streets were quiet again, except for the usual dog here and there. The sun was beating down on Monrovia, heat shimmering from the pavement.

"Dr. Stark, any other ideas on how to get out of Monrovia?" Claire asked.

"I'm working on it," he said. "But it would help if you could do your hocus-pocus stuff and find out what that agent is."

"We can't do our 'hocus-pocus' for the same reason we couldn't find out what the pilots experienced before they crashed," said Travis.

"Why is that?"

"We're in suits and have gloves on our hands. We need to make skin contact."

"Why?"

"That's how we join our life energies and are able to do what we do."

"I didn't know that."

"For the deep beyond, that's what's needed," said Travis.

"Uh-huh, I see. For what it's worth, is that life energy of yours electromagnetic energy?"

"I don't know," said Travis.

"Wait, Dr. Stark has a point," said Prescott. "If we can channel our life energy via conductors, we may be able to make contact with the dead pilots."

"I'm glad to be of help," said Dr. Stark.

"Good, then figure out what we need to do," said Travis.

"I guess I'll do that."

"Dr. Stark, one more thing," said Travis. "Did you tell WHO that we retrieved an intact vial of the agent?"

"Of course not. They are not looking for a manmade agent dispersed from an airplane."

"Why aren't they?" Travis asked.

"Because it is inconceivable that such an agent exists. They believe this is a pathological agent born in Africa. Besides, if this were a manmade agent, the US military would be involved in the investigation."

"Why aren't they involved?"

"They are," said Maximus. "Why do you think the US Air Force provided you transportation? They are watching right now to see what conclusions WHO is coming to."

"Are you providing them information?" Travis asked.

"Of course. If Mossad knows about this, the US military and the appropriate intelligence agencies must know as well."

"Why didn't you tell us?"

"It is very simple, Travis. No one in the government wants to admit that they rely on a paranormal team such as yours to resolve cases. Officially, they're letting WHO handle it, but I'm feeding them information through the right channels, so they keep clear of any misinterpretation."

"Then they could rescue us," said Claire.

"That's what I'm working on," said Maximus. "Why did you ask Dr. Stark if he had divulged information to WHO about your findings?

"I have a funny feeling about our doctors at WHO."

"What's your suspicion, Travis?" asked Maximus.

"The brain scans of the victims," said Travis. "The pilots especially."

The Devolution of Adam and Eve

Chapter 25. The Flight Data

"You think that they already knew about the biochemical agent's effect?" Maximus asked.

"Well, yes. But the pilots died in the crash and were not infected. Why did Warner and Henderson ask us to check their brains? They had to have known what the plane was transporting."

"Your logic is correct," said Maximus.

"I'm not suspicious of WHO, but of some of their scientists. Scientists in an advanced lab developed this biochemical agent. And they know of each other."

"That's a stretch, to accuse scientists of being involved with such a disastrous killer agent," said Claire. "That happens in holo-movies, not in real life."

"I didn't mean to say WHO developed it," said Travis. "Whoever developed it or knew about the agent may have contacts at WHO."

"And you think they're keeping this under wraps?" Claire wondered.

"Just as they're keeping us here," said Travis. "They are distrustful of us, my suspicious mind whispers to me."

"I'll keep that in mind," said Maximus. "A quick update for you that may not cheer you—an absolute quarantine has been imposed from the sub-Saharan countries down to Angola, Zimbabwe, and Mozambique."

"Is this contamination contained, or is it still spreading?" Claire asked.

"This is Dr. Stark. New update—the contamination has spread to all major urban centers in sub-Saharan countries, all the way to South Africa. Now the whole of Africa south of the Sahara is quarantined."

"Are there any areas that are uninfected?" Prescott asked.

"Yes, most areas outside the initial 24-hour zone are partly safe," said Dr. Stark. "The new hot zones are around airports. That means the pandemic was spread by air traffic."

"What are the people outside the infection zone doing?" Claire asked.

"Most people are behind barricades to protect themselves from the wild ones."

"They're fighting zombies," said Travis. "Just as we did a short time ago."

"Dr. Stark, do you think that the original airborne agent has done its damage and the afflicted people are carrying the infection now?" Prescott asked.

"That would be a good supposition. It was voiced by several health agencies, but there are no data to support it yet."

Silence fell on the conversation. Much speculation could be made, but without data and scientific analysis, nothing was for sure.

"Maximus, what info do you have from the airplane's black box?" Prescott asked after a while.

"The jet came down at a 45-degree angle and the auto pilot was off, but no malfunction of any kind was reported," said Maximus. "The cockpit voice recorder for the prior three hours shows nothing abnormal, other than the copilot mentioning it was time to 'feed the vials in the hopper.' Then, six minutes before the crash, the copilot started screaming, and soon after the pilot did the same. They began to fight in the cockpit and continued until they hit the ground."

"It fits the characteristics of the infection," said Claire.

"Very much so," agreed Dr. Stark. "Somehow, the dispersing system leaked, and the pilots went berserk."

"The flight manifest filed in Oakland said that they were to fly from Oakland straight to Riyadh," continued Maximus. "However, the flight recorder shows that when they reached the coast of Senegal, near Dakar, they slowed down to 600 km/h, dropped altitude from 12,000 meters to 3,000 meters, and flew south, following the African coast, until they crashed in Monrovia."

"I wonder if they tried to land, if they had enough mental capacity to know they had a problem," said Travis.

"Further detailed analysis of the voice recorder may shed more light on the matter," said Maximus.

"By the way, are Henderson and Warner aware of the black box content?"

"I don't know, but I'll direct them to the pilots' conversation and see what they say."

"Do they know about the spraying system?"

"No, only we know about that. Let's see if they question the copilot's statement, 'feed the vials in the hopper'."

"Speaking about the vials—considering the spray system and unused vials we found at the crash site, they might have intended to contaminate the whole of Africa," said Travis.

"We have to talk to the pilots," said Prescott. "We'll find out what they were doing and who hired them."

"The conspiracy theorist in me thinks that the pilots were on a one-way mission," said Travis. "The leak was planned after the last vial was dispensed. Maybe the system malfunctioned."

"Or something else," said Prescott. "If this agent spreads as an energy wave, it may have caught up with the plane and the pilots."

"The plane was flying way too fast," said Maximus. "The expansion speed of the infection was just 83 km/h. Fast, but slower than the plane."

"Anything else on Perchenko?" Claire asked.

"The Russian authorities are investigating his background, connections, financial ties," said Maximus. "I'm scanning through some of the information gathered so far, but nothing catches my attention."

"Are we sure that he died?" Claire asked.

"Last GeneID of him was at Oakland Airport—"

"Oakland seems to be a hotbed of happenings," said Travis quickly. "Where was he flying to from Oakland?"

"To Moscow. He was flying on his private jet, and flight control from Finland lost contact with the plane over the White Sea," reported Maximus. "They found debris in the water, and satellite imaging recorded an explosion in the area where the plane was lost."

"If his hydrojet plane exploded, it was likely a bomb," said Travis.

"Deadly endings are associated with this biochemical agent," commented Claire.

"By the way, preliminary CCS scans at the crash site in the White Sea show traces of Perchenko's GeneID," said Maximus. "This is not definite, but we can presume he has been killed."

"Or blown to pieces. Any investigations conducted in Oakland?" Travis asked.

"We're compiling all the data and we'll submit it to the FBI for investigation," said Maximus.

"Any news from Mossad?" Prescott asked.

"No, but I see electronic traces of them snooping in Russia. I wouldn't be surprised to detect them in Oakland as well."

"What's so important in Oakland?" Prescott wondered.

"A hotbed of malcontents?" Travis speculated.

They returned to the tower and sneaked quickly up the stairs into the control room. No one had visited that place since they left, and after barricading the door with the sofa, they lay down on the floor to get some sleep.

Someone pounded at the door.

The Devolution of Adam and Eve

Chapter 26. Confidence

They looked at each other, more with surprise than fear.

"Did somebody order a pizza?" Travis approached the door and turned on his suit's external speaker. "Who's out there?"

"Please, sir, let me in. I'm afraid," a female voice responded.

Travis pulled his gun and Prescott moved the sofa barricading the door. Travis cracked the door open and poked his gun through the narrow opening. He saw an African girl, a teenager, in a restaurant uniform, looking at him with wide eyes. Travis reached out, grabbed her by the arm, and pulled her inside. He shut the door, and Prescott pushed the sofa against it.

"Who are you?" Claire asked, scanning her.

"Confidence Azango," said the trembling girl.

"I'm Claire. What happened, Confidence?"

"I don't know, I don't know." She began crying. "Everyone is dead or mad."

"Where are you coming from?" Travis asked.

The girl, who didn't look older than sixteen, wiped her tears with her hands. "From the terminal."

"Tell us what happened," Claire gently led her to sit on the sofa backing the door.

The girl seemed to be disoriented. "I don't know."

Travis and Prescott looked at each other and opened their personal intercom.

"Maybe she was mildly affected by the agent, not like the others," said Travis.

"I think she's just in shock," Prescott said. "How did she survive when everyone else went berserk?"

"Confidence, are you hungry or thirsty?" Claire asked.

She shook her head.

"I need to check you out." Claire pulled a small light-probe and scanner from her pocket and examined Confidence's eyes. Claire read the diagnostic in her helmet display and said, "You are healthy and normal. You said you came from the terminal—where in the terminal?"

"The walk-in cooler."

"What?"

"I work in the cafeteria and I went into the walk-in cooler two days ago, I think. I got locked in. I pounded on the door, but no one came to open it."

"Oh, you poor thing," whispered Claire.

"How did you get out?" Prescott asked.

"The cooler stopped working and the door unlatched yesterday. I went out and I was horrified at what I saw." Confidence began crying. Claire took her in her arms. "I ran home from the terminal, but everyone was dead—in the streets and at home. My mom, my brothers, and my sisters." She began crying again.

Over the suit's intercom, Prescott said, "Do you think the cooler was sealed well enough that she was not affected by the agent?"

"Either that, or she's immune to it," said Travis.

"You're safe with us, Confidence," Claire said through the external speaker.

The girl quieted down. "Are you rescuers?"

"Yes—no, we're scientists," said Claire.

"How did you manage to stay alive in the cooler?" Travis asked.

"There were food and drinks in there. I raised the temperature on the thermostat above freezing and used the burlap sacks that held onions and potatoes to keep warm."

"Where did you go when you left the terminal?" Prescott asked.

"I tried to stay in my home, and then I went to the church nearby to see if there was anyone who could help me. Mad people inside wanted to hurt me. I ran, and they chased me all the way back to the terminal. They didn't follow me inside. Maybe the dead people scared them. I hid back in the cooler where I felt safe."

"Did you see us in the terminal?" Claire asked.

She nodded. "But I was scared. Why do you wear those suits?"

"Confidence, a terrible thing has happened. There was a plague, and we came to inspect the situation," said Claire. "These suits protect us."

She looked into the distance for a while. "Will I be affected by the plague?"

"Chances are that you are safe for now, but I have to scan you more thoroughly to determine if you're healthy," said Claire. "Can I scan you?"

The girl nodded. Claire told her to lie down and she scanned Confidence's head first and then her entire body. The information was transmitted back to headquarters.

Monrovia was an unregistered zone, but Confidence's GeneID was recorded because she worked at the airport. She was who she said she was.

While Claire was performing additional tests with CCS probes, Prescott and Travis moved closer to the windows to discuss this latest development. The dusk settled, and fewer lights turned on around the airport. The generators were shutting down.

"What do you think—are there more survivors like her?" Travis asked.

"If they happened to be in a sealed room, as she was," said Prescott. "Also, it depends on how long it took for the agent to expire."

"Then the agent is definitely airborne, and it survived until it reached Lagos in Nigeria," assessed Travis.

Prescott thought for a moment. "The walk-in cooler must have metal walls."

"Meaning?"

"It acted like a Faraday cage," said Prescott. "It blocks electromagnetic waves."

"Then all the people in reinforced concrete buildings should have survived," said Travis. "But that wasn't what we discovered in the city."

"Maybe this agent acts both ways, as an airborne contaminant and as an energy pathogen."

"Energy pathogen?" Travis pondered. "Is that even a term?"

They were interrupted by the comm.

"This is Dr. Henderson." Her voice startled them. "We just received data about a survivor. That is good news."

"What are the results of the girl's brain scan?" Claire asked.

"Prelim, normal. No sign of neuron damage. Where was she?"

"In a walk-in cooler," said Claire.

"If she survived in the cooler and she is healthy being out for a day, I would say we're safe to come out of our suits," said Travis.

"I don't advise you to do that, Mr. St. John. We need absolute proof that it is safe to do so."

"Well, we've got only 29 hours of air left," said Travis.

The Devolution of Adam and Eve

Chapter 27. The Red, Orange, and Yellow Zones

The communication ended without any promises of help. Travis mouthed a few well-chosen swear words.

Confidence couldn't hear what they were saying inside their helmets and looked inquisitively at them. "Are we going to be rescued from those mad people?"

"Soon." Claire coaxed Confidence to lie down on the sofa and go to sleep.

Claire switched to the intercom and pulled the vial of the agent from her pocket. "How can water mixed with small amounts of cyanide become such a mind-destroying agent?"

"Whatever is in there is definitely voodoo," said Travis. "Keep it safe, don't break it."

"We need to analyze it with our mind." Prescott opened the comm to the TIO headquarters. "Maximus, any news from Dr. Stark about channeling by conductive material?"

"This is Dr. Stark. I have bad news for you. There is not enough metal inside your suits that you can touch with your bare skin. Sorry."

Claire looked at the vial again. "How could such a small amount of this agent have contaminated such a large area and then disappeared without a trace?"

"It is mostly water," said Travis.

"Water is the key," said Prescott.

"Homeopathic dilution?" Claire wondered.

"Something like that," Prescott said. "The agent is just the starter. It combines with water molecules in the air, diluting itself and spreading out."

"If that's the case, the whole world would be covered by this homeopathic poison by now. But it petered out," said Travis. "Maximus, shouldn't the crashed plane's flight path to Riyadh have been more over the Saharan countries?"

"Yes."

"They didn't start spraying in Morocco but in Senegal," said Travis thoughtfully. "The air would be too dry over the Sahara. Moisture was needed for the agent to spread, and so they flew over the wet part of Africa."

"That sounds like a good theory," said Dr. Stark.

"Since we're talking about water, Dr. Stark, please analyze the water composition in the victims we scanned in the city, and in Confidence," said Claire.

"I'm initiating analysis," said Dr. Stark.

"Why?" Travis asked.

"Not all waters are the same," replied Claire. "Maybe the water in Confidence's body prevented the agent from metastasizing."

"The results show no significant differences," said Dr. Stark. "The concentration of deuterium oxide in the bodily fluids is the same."

"Then the agent indeed petered out," said Travis with a smile.

"How do you explain the infections beyond Nigeria?" Claire asked.

"It's losing its potency," said Travis. "I can't wait to get out of this suit."

"Not so fast," said Maximus. "Just received reports from Shanghai showing the same symptoms as in Africa."

"Jesus, from Africa to Shanghai," said Prescott.

"Air travelers," said Maximus. "There is a new assessment posted by Interpol, correlating the flights originating from Africa and the infected areas within and outside of Africa. There is an advisory, just issued, to shut down all flights in the world."

"Incredible," said Travis. "How would we get out of here?"

"Working on it," said Maximus.

"Dr. Stark, are the cyanide levels diminishing the farther the contamination spread out in Africa?" Claire asked.

"I'm checking the readings from drones," said Dr. Stark. "I'll have to get back to you after I contact WHO to analyze what you proposed. Dr. Stark out."

"What are you suggesting?" Prescott asked Claire.

"The original agent, as it combines and replicates homeopathically, will not replicate the cyanide molecules, although it will leave an impression of the cyanide in the homeopathic solution. People are made of mostly water. The infected people are carriers of the agent, but with less and less cyanide molecules to leave a trace."

"I'll relay this information to Dr. Stark as well," said Maximus.

"I need to get some sleep," said Claire all of a sudden. "It's night here, and we've slept little in the past 36 hours."

"How can you sleep under these circumstances?" Travis commented.

"We have to do the same thing," said Prescott. "We can think better after we've rested."

"Anything else we need to know, Maximus?" Travis asked.

"Nothing new. Claire and Prescott are right," said Maximus. "Get some sleep. We'll wake you up if something happens."

At five in the morning they were awakened by Maximus and Drs. Stark, Henderson, and Warner.

"Good morning, people," Dr. Henderson said. "I congratulate you for the observation you made regarding the cyanide levels. Based on the data we obtained from different spots in Africa and from Shanghai, we can determine that the primary zone was hit by a direct infection of the pathogen, airborne perhaps, and the secondary infection was spread by people, without any cyanide residues."

"Look at the attached map of the infection spread," said Maximus. In their helmets, a map of Africa showed a red swath from Senegal to Nigeria. "The red arc is where the intense infection zone occurred within 24 hours and where the cyanide level is the highest." An orange band covered Africa farther east, past Cameroon and Gabon to the Central African Republic. "The orange swath indicates the medium-intense infection zone, which took place 24 hours after the infection started. It has a radius of 3,000 km. Only small traces of cyanide levels can be found in this

160

zone. The yellow areas reaching out to China indicate the low infection zone, which spreads out only as transmitted by infected people. The yellow area has no traces of cyanide."

"Are the people in the yellow zone quarantined?" Claire asked.

"Yes, each country as it detects infected people quarantines them," said Maximus. "But all travel had been shut down, even among countries that are in the green."

"Maximus, in reading the map, it seems that the red zone is the contamination, and the yellow zone is the infection. Am I correct?" Travis asked.

"Correct."

"What happened in the orange zone?"

"That's contamination as well, although it propagated at a slower pace."

"Besides us, are there any other scientists in the red or orange zones?" Claire asked.

"You are the only ones alive—I mean, coherent—in these zones," said Dr. Warner. "And, of course, Confidence Azango, who miraculously escaped contamination."

"If the pathogen had subsided by the time she exited the cooler, she was not infected by the people she came into contact with later on," said Claire.

"Did she touch or was she touched by any infected people?" Dr. Henderson asked.

Claire woke Confidence up and after a few moments asked her, "Did you touch any of the dead people?"

"Yes, my mother and brothers, but they were dead," she said. "And I probably brushed against some of the dead in the terminal."

"How about the living?" Claire asked her.

Confidence shook her head. "They chased me, but no one touched me."

"From what she says, the contamination is not spread by the dead," commented Dr. Henderson. "However, it is undetermined if the survivors can transmit the infection by touch."

"I'll request that information from the personnel observing the infected people in the yellow zone," said Dr. Warner.

"Do you have personnel on the ground in the yellow zones in Africa?" Claire asked.

"Yes, in Luanda, Angola, in Kinshasa, the DR of Congo, in Addis Ababa, Ethiopia, and Nairobi in Kenya," said Dr. Warner. "WHO teams were already on the ground there. And, of course, in China we have Chinese doctors monitoring the infection."

"Dr. German, in light of what we're learning, we will need to scan more of the living people," said Dr. Henderson. "You have tranquilizer guns in your scientific kit. Feel free to use them as needed."

Chapter 28. New Scans

"We're familiar with them—we already used one on a goat," said Claire. "We'll start again at daylight."

"Why wait? We're already awake," said Travis.

"It's dark, but we can see better than the people out there," agreed Prescott.

"What do we do with Confidence?" Claire turned toward her. "Can you wait here for us, honey? We have a task to do."

"Wait here while you're out?" she asked fearfully.

"Yes, you're safe here," said Claire.

"I'm afraid to be alone. Can I come with you?"

"That might be dangerous. We're looking for live people to examine."

"I can show you where they are," Confidence said.

Prescott felt like scratching his head, but his helmet was in the way. "Shall we take her with us? She may follow us anyway, unless we tie her down."

"Where are these people, Confidence?" Travis asked.

"Near my house, in the church."

"How many are there? Men, women?" Travis asked.

"I think three men and two women chased me," said Confidence. "Maybe a few kids, and I think the old pastor was there, too. He looked crazy."

"What do you think?" Travis asked his teammates. "We can find them quickly and not have to search the whole town."

"Confidence," said Claire. "Tell us what happened when you went inside the church."

Confidence thought for a few seconds. "The church was empty, or it looked empty, but I saw the pastor behind the altar. I was so relieved when I saw him, I ran to him, but he jumped on the altar when he saw me and screamed, pointing at me. From somewhere, two mad women came out, with a few kids around them, and pointed at me as well, shrieking. I backed away, but three men came out from behind the altar and ran toward me. I ran out and they followed me, but they stopped outside for a moment. I think the midday sun blinded them for a time. They chased me until I reached the terminal and ran inside. They didn't follow me inside."

Claire pointed to her glass-beaded necklace. "Were you wearing that necklace?"

"Yes, it was my mom's. I took it from her to remember her."

"Let me see it, please."

Confidence gave her the necklace, and Claire scanned it.

"There are no cyanide traces on the necklace," Claire said to Prescott and Travis. "But these shiny beads may have caught the mad women's eyes. Confidence, honey, you'll have to leave the necklace here if you want to come with us."

"If a shiny trinket caught their eyes, what do you think they'll do when they see our LED lights on our suits and inside our helmets?" Travis asked.

"We can turn them off," said Prescott. "Just tell your suit to go to energy-saving mode."

"OK," said Travis. "But Confidence, you will have to wait in the car when we enter the church."

She nodded.

Not long after they left the terminal, Confidence pointed down a dark, side street toward a yellow church with a steeple. "That's the church." The white wood doors stood open, and it was dark all around.

They exited the SUV and, as agreed, Confidence stayed behind. It was still dark outside, and CTT hoped to find the infected people asleep. All three checked their tranquilizer air guns. The gun would shoot only one dart at a time, after which a new dart would have to be reloaded.

"If there are three men, we shoot them first," said Travis. "Drag them out and protect Claire while she's scanning them."

"Sounds like a plan, if the men show up," said Prescott.

"We'll shoot whoever comes at us," said Travis. "We have three shots each, and we can shoot a new dart every two seconds."

"What's plan B?" Prescott asked.

"Protect yourself with a real gun." Travis opened his arms and attempted to raise his shoulders as if to say, that's a given.

"Very well. You two go first," said Claire. "Remember, I'm the scientist and your leader. Protect me."

"Yes, ma'am," Travis and Prescott chorused.

Each of them held their tranquilizer guns with two hands for better accuracy as they entered the church. The night vision in their helmets gave them a fair picture of what lay ahead. There were no people in sight, but they could have been asleep, hidden under the pews.

"Shall we make a noise to wake them up?" Prescott asked.

"They may scramble and run out," replied Travis.

"Let's get deeper inside until we spot them," suggested Claire. "Try not to shoot the kids. The darts are for adults."

They walked down the center aisle, fanning their surroundings with their guns, until they reached the altar. The pastor jumped onto the altar into a squatting position, and began hollering at them.

Claire, who was in the middle although behind, fired a dart, and it hit the pastor in the chest. It was quick; the man swayed and fell forward, head first, to the carpeted floor. He rolled down the few stairs and rested at the bottom in a lump. After placing another dart in her gun, Claire approached the unconscious man, while Travis and Prescott stayed vigilant. No one appeared.

Claire used the scanner and determined that the pastor was sedated but alive. She pulled the dart out of his chest, then placed his head in the scanner and recorded his brain structure, after which she scanned him head to toe.

A scream came from outside.

Chapter 29. Bad News

"Confidence!" shouted Claire, and all of them ran out.

Two big men outside the SUV were pulling Confidence by the hair through the half-opened car window. Prescott and Travis shot a dart on the run at each man, but the distance was beyond the guns' accuracy, and they missed both of them. Claire took time for a better aim, but when she was about to squeeze the trigger, someone jumped on her back. She bent forward and flipped over a woman, who screeched with anger. Another man attacked her next, but she had time to pull the trigger, and a dart struck him in the neck. The man grabbed his throat and collapsed shortly.

Before Travis or Prescott could pull out their real guns, the two men let go of Confidence and assailed them. Travis kicked the man attacking him in the chest and knocked him down. But from the side, a woman jumped him, her fingers latched onto his suit. He hit her with his left elbow, but she wouldn't let go. He turned and knocked her down with the back of his right fist. She scarpered away, followed by the other man Travis had kicked.

Prescott was caught half-turned, trying to pull his gun, but the big mad man toppled him and landed on top of him. The man was foaming at the mouth, trying to gnaw at his face, but Prescott's visor held and protected him from the bites. He was pinned down and had no other option, but pull his gun and shoot the man in the side of his torso. The man rolled over and ran away, half-bent, holding a hand over his wound.

Travis and Claire remained with their guns drawn, expecting another round of attacks. Prescott jumped to his feet, breathing heavily, and turned in place to spot if anyone else was coming at him. Confidence was on the ground, screaming.

Claire ran to her side. "Are you hurt, Confidence?"

The girl was wailing. Her forearms were bloody and scratched, and she had a bite on her forehead.

"Prescott, scan that man's head." Claire opened the door of the SUV and pushed the crying girl inside.

Quickly, Prescott performed the scan. "Done."

"Let's get out of here!" shouted Claire.

Travis and Prescott got in and Travis accelerated toward the airport.

"How bad is she hurt?" Prescott asked Claire over his shoulder.

"I don't know. I'm cleaning the wounds right now. God, she has a bite on her forehead. The nail scratches on her forearms are bleeding badly too." Claire pulled additional gauzes from her emergency kit and wrapped the wounds in them. "Sit still, Confidence. Let me check your head."

The bite had ripped the skin, and teeth marks were clearly visible. Claire applied antiseptic ointment and sealed it with an adhesive bandage, as the girl sobbed quietly.

"How are you guys doing?" Claire asked them.

"Not bad," said Travis.

"I had no choice but to shoot my assailant," said Prescott. "I hope I didn't crack a rib when he fell on top of me."

"This didn't go exactly as planned," said Travis. "We thought we were dealing with deranged people. This was more like dealing with wild animals."

"They're not human anymore," said Claire.

They pulled up to the bottom of the tower at the crack of dawn. Claire helped Confidence climb the stairs, followed by Prescott and Travis climbing backward with their guns drawn. No one was stalking them as they entered their shelter and barricaded the door with the sofa.

Claire initiated transmission of the data immediately and opened comm with headquarters. "Maximus, we're back but we were attacked."

"Are you all right?" he asked immediately.

"Confidence was scratched and bitten. I applied first aid, and she's suffering from mild shock—"

"That's not good," said Maximus. "You'll need to scan her. What else happened?"

"Prescott got knocked down and had to shoot his assailant. Travis had to fight off a man and a woman, and I fought with a woman and shot a dart into the throat of another man."

Claire lay Confidence down on the sofa and began scanning her.

Travis looked intently at Prescott.

"What's the matter?" Prescott inquired, seeing his concerned look.

"Turn your helmet to the left, would you?"

Prescott did as told and Travis approached, turning his helmet lights on.

"What's the matter?" Prescott asked again.

"Your visor is cracked on the right side," said Travis.

"What?" Prescott turned his head inside his helmet to the far right and saw the crack. "Shit." He applied pressure over the crack with his gloved right hand.

"Check the interior pressure of your suit," said Travis.

"Shit," repeated Prescott. "It must have cracked when I fell down—hit it on a sharp rock or something. It's leaking, but slowly. Bad news, nonetheless."

Chapter 30. More Bad News

Travis opened a small tool kit and found inside a roll of one of the most useful items in a handyman's toolbox—duct tape. He pulled out a strip and taped over the crack. Then he added several more strips for good measure and patted it down.

"Did it seal?" he asked Prescott.

"It did." Prescott exhaled. "But if I'm infected, just shoot me."

"Of course not," said Travis indignantly. "We need you for experiments."

"What are you talking about?" Claire asked from where she was just completing Confidence's scan.

"My visor has a crack in it," said Prescott.

"Did you say your visor is cracked?" Maximus asked. "How badly?"

"I've lost ten percent of my air, but Travis duct taped it. The leak stopped."

"Claire, you have to scan Prescott and his suit's interior air," said Maximus.

Without another word, Claire walked over and scanned him. Through his visor, she read the air composition. "I'm transmitting the data," she told Maximus.

"Maybe it only leaked out and not in." Travis tried to encourage Prescott.

"I doubt it. I didn't sit still. I moved around. It's bound to have pulled external air in while I was in close contact with the infected man." Prescott sighed. "Besides, it won't make much of a difference. I've lost ten percent of my reserves, and I have only nine hours of breathable air left."

"I'm sorry, Prescott," said Claire.

"Don't worry. I don't feel that I'll die here."

Travis slouched on a chair. "Maximus, any update yet on an extraction mission?"

"I'm sorry, but the entire world is in quarantine. As a last resort, they'll parachute down a biohazard habitat for you. NATO is patrolling around the entire African continent by air to prevent anyone from flying out."

"Any news on the man's and the pastor's data, Maximus?" Claire asked.

"Not yet. Keep an eye on Confidence—you may want to sedate her. If she was bitten, she might be infected. Word from China is that infected Africans returning from Kinshasa bit all the people who went mad in Shanghai. However, their cyanide levels are negligible."

"Poor girl," lamented Claire, looking at Confidence. "She survived the agent, only to be infected by one of her mad compatriots."

"Other reports from WHO teams on the ground in Africa confirm that the infection is transmitted to others through bites, and the cyanide level is undetectable," said Maximus. "And I have new data. Bad news and good news, sort of. The man's and pastor's scans show a maintained level of cyanide, comparable to the scans you collected from the other infected people on the ground there."

"What's the good news?" Claire asked.

"That was the good news. The bad news is that Confidence's cyanide level is very low."

"What exactly are you saying?" Prescott asked.

"Intense infection victims who came into contact with the nerve agent maintained their cyanide levels, while victims infected through bites did not."

"That's actually good news," said Prescott. "I haven't been bitten, and if the agent is gone, I may not be infected."

"It seems that way," agreed Maximus. "The problem is that WHO hasn't been able to identify yet the pathogen that infected the secondary victims, just as we don't know for sure if Confidence is infected."

"But if she is, she'll show symptoms," said Prescott. "How soon?"

"Unknown," said Maximus.

"Besides Shanghai, are there any other places with secondary infections beyond the known yellow zones?"

"Unknown at this moment. However, there are many planes that crashed over Africa or disappeared over the water on flights from Africa. The infected people may have gone mad while in flight."

"Even Satan couldn't come up with a more apocalyptic plan," said Prescott. "Are there any estimates on casualties?"

"Estimates are from 500 million to one billion people."

Prescott, Claire, and Travis were stunned that this agent had affected so many people. And it was far from over yet.

"Considering that we may become some of the casualties, one way or another, we will have to talk to the dead pilots before we expire," said Travis. "They may be able to tell us who did this."

"I agree," said Claire.

"Me, too," said Prescott.

"But what do we do with Confidence when she goes mad?" Travis wondered. "Maximus, are there tertiary wave infections beyond the yellow zones?"

"Unknown at this time. But the only victims who were isolated and are under study are the Chinese. Only by infecting another healthy human can it be determined if the infection keeps spreading."

"I wouldn't put it past the Chinese government to test that with condemned men from their prisons," said Travis.

"The world would censure such an act," said Maximus.

"Sure, sure." Travis walked to where Confidence lay sleeping. "Just as we have to make a decision here. Let Confidence go mad and turn into an animal, or euthanize her."

"What?" Claire shouted.

"If she goes mad, do we throw her out and let those outside kill her?" Travis asked.

"Fuck," said Claire. "Why do we have to be like the gods and decide if she'll live or die?"

"Just as humanity, WHO in our case, decides our fate," said Travis. "Or all of Africa's fate." Travis bent down to examine Confidence.

"Travis, don't move," said Claire. She walked over to him and reached under his left arm. "Your suit is breached."

Mit Sandru

Chapter 31. In Plain Air

"You don't say." Travis chuckled bitterly. "I thought I felt a draft under my arm, and now I know why. The woman I knocked down must have used her nails effectively."

Prescott came closer to examine the rip. "I'll need to seal it with duct tape."

"Yeah, sure, but it's too late. I've been exposed for over an hour to the outside air. Screw it." With one swift move, he opened his visor.

"That's not wise, Travis!" cried Claire.

Travis looked under his left arm. "This opening is so large that the suit's delta pressure monitor couldn't detect any difference. Whatever's happened, happened."

"I have to scan you," said Claire.

"Please do, but I need to get out of this outfit and put on my TIO suit." Travis ripped the seals covering the suit's zippers.

"Do you think that's smart?"

Travis unzipped the suit and pulled it off. "First, I need to go to the restroom." He took with him his bag.

Claire turned to talk to Prescott and saw him with his visor opened. He shrugged.

"I think you're both contaminated and mad," she said.

"I don't think so. I'm more worried about Confidence and if she's infected." Prescott began taking his astrosuit off and soon followed Travis to the restroom.

Claire examined Confidence, who was still asleep. If she were indeed infected, she would be a danger to Travis and

Prescott. In the emergency medical pack, Claire found a tranquilizer syringe, which she used to inject Confidence. The girl did not even wake up.

Without hesitation, Claire opened her visor and breathed in. The air, even in the flight control tower, seemed to be fresher than that inside the suit. Unlike Prescott and Travis, she pulled the zipper seals off carefully. After she took her astrosuit off, she placed Confidence in it. She closed the visor and opened the suit's air valve to the outside air. In case she became violent, she would not be able to harm them while she was in the astrosuit with the visor closed.

Travis, Prescott, and Claire were dressed in their dark gray TIO suits, feeling a lot more comfortable. From this point on, they had protection against bullets, but not against the biochemical agent, or its mutated variant. Claire scanned the men and then Prescott scanned her.

"Maximus, we are out of our astrosuits, and I just sent over our scans. Please advise," said Claire.

"Are you all right?"

"It's been a half-hour for me, and longer for Travis and Prescott, and we don't feel any symptoms," said Claire. "Confidence is in my astrosuit. I turned the auto scan on, and the data will show the metastasis in progress."

"I'm calling a conference with the WHO doctors, considering that you are exposed now."

"Very well," said Claire. "After the conference, we'll go to the crash site and attempt to interview the dead pilots."

"This is Dr. Stark. What have you done? You're naked!" he exclaimed, referring to their being out of their astrosuits.

"Yes, Dr. Stark, and both Travis and Prescott look great *naked*," said Claire, winking at the men. Prescott and Travis mimicked man-posing while trying not to laugh. It was good to release the tension.

"Looking at your scans, everything looks normal," said Dr. Stark. "But the data streaming from Confidence are mind-boggling. How long will she be out?"

"For a normal person, a couple of hours, but in her case, I don't know," said Claire. "Let's make this conference short. We need to find out what the pilots know."

"Sure thing," Dr. Stark said. "We now have a connection with WHO."

"Hello, CTT, this is Dr. Henderson."

"And I'm online as well," said Dr. Warner.

"As I'm talking to you, I'm scanning the data, and you are healthy," said Dr. Henderson.

"What made you take your suits off?" Dr. Warner asked worriedly.

"Prescott's and Travis's suits were compromised, and they were exposed to the outside air," said Claire. "Maximus and Dr. Stark can fill you in on the details. What else can we help you with, other than watching Confidence go mad?"

"Containing her in your suit was a brilliant idea, Dr. German," said Dr. Henderson. "Yes, please record her external actions."

The conversation continued for a few more minutes, and they signed off.

Claire turned to her teammates. "Let's find out what happened in that aircraft."

A few minutes later, they had gathered in the shallow crater of the crash to transition into another realm.

"It's hot," said Travis. "Maybe we should have stayed in our air-conditioned astrosuits."

"I thought you didn't like them," said Claire, shaking her head. "Let's find out what our pilot boys remember."

They joined hands and transcended into—to human eyes—a world of confusion. Upon death, the soul and the mind leave the body behind in what we call "the real world." Depending on each individual's circumstances, the soul and the mind linger around the dead body, not aware it is dead. In this case, there were two pilots, and if they knew each other well, their souls and minds may still be together. The pilots' souls and minds appeared as two nebulae of light within the cosmos of chaos they experienced.

The melded minds of Travis, Claire, and Prescott joined the nebulae.

Chapter 32. The Pilots

They found the two pilots in white short-sleeve shirts, blue pants, caps, and aviator glasses, strolling in an airplane graveyard. It seemed that for these two pilots, an airplane graveyard was like candy land, with vintage and modern planes littering the dry field. They seemed to be content, walking around, touching, and discussing the quality of each "bird."

"Good day, Captain Tom Bradwell and Pilot Chuck List. I'm agent Claire German, and these are my teammates Travis St. John and Prescott Alighieri with the US Secret Service. We have some questions for you."

The two pilots had not noticed them until Claire spoke. They stopped talking, slightly surprised, and stared at the three strangers in dark gray suits and dark shades, and at their badges. All three showed the pilots their TIO IDs, which displayed convincing Secret Service badges at that moment.

After they shook hands, Tom Bradwell said, "The Secret Service?"

"Do not be alarmed, Captain Bradwell," said Travis. "We require information regarding your last flight, tail number N560AE."

"Yes, and what does the Secret Service have to do with our flight? It is all documented in the flight plan."

"It certainly is," said Travis, smiling. "However, your testimony is required since your mission was changed from the flight plan."

The two pilots exchanged unsure glances.

"It was changed, wasn't it?" Travis asked.

"That's correct," said Captain Bradwell after some hesitation. "Why, was that a problem?"

"Not a problem. But your flight was a matter of national security."

List and Bradwell looked surprised.

"We want to hear your account of what happened during your last flight. But first, some preliminary information to make sure we're talking to the right people. Who owns the plane, Captain?"

"O&C Private Jet Co."

"Are you employed by that company?"

"Yes, both of us."

"Who chartered the flight?"

"OTTM Chemical Corporation, I think."

"For what purpose?"

"To transport rat poison to Riyadh."

Rat poison transported by jet seemed bizarre but not illegal, Travis thought.

"Was that your final destination?"

"After we left the continental United States, we received a message that our mission had changed. We were to fly along the western coast of Africa and discharge a new mosquito insecticide that was given to us in an aluminum case. There was not rat poison in the case, but insecticide."

"Didn't you find it curious that the mission had changed, and that you had become crop dusters instead of rat exterminators?"

"When the owner of the company gives the order, you don't question the job."

"Which owner?"

"Don O'Halloran, the president."

"Tell us what happened."

"Mr. O'Halloran told us that our mission had changed and requested we view an instructional video of our revised mission," said Captain Bradwell "We were surprised to find out that the ground crew had installed onboard a special spraying machine, which was connected to one of the exit ports."

"Please tell us the details of this spraying system."

"It was the size of a large suitcase. It had some tubing manifolds and digital displays, and it was connected by a hose to the exit port. It had a receiver for the insecticide vials, and Chuck was to insert the vials into the feeder."

"Ten at a time," added Chuck List.

"Where were those vials stored?"

"In an aluminum case the size of a briefcase. They gave it to us just before the flight."

"You thought it contained rat poison?"

"That's correct."

"When did the spraying begin?

"When we reached Senegal, and it continued until all the vials were exhausted."

"Did you complete your mission?"

"Yes, we landed in Cape Town."

Prescott, Claire, and Travis exchanged knowing glances, visible only to them inside their PAVs.

"Did you see the spraying system being installed on the airplane?" Travis asked.

"No, as I said, the ground crew did that without our knowledge. It was already onboard when we arrived."

"How about the aluminum case with the vials?"

"Just before departure, a ground crew member came over and gave us what we were supposed to take to Riyadh. Actually, she gave it to Chuck after we were onboard."

"Mr. List, did you recognized the woman who gave you the case?"

"No, never saw her before."

"Can you describe her to us?"

"She wore the ground crew uniform and a cap. She had a blonde ponytail sticking out through the back of the cap. I couldn't see her eyes, she had sunglasses on."

"What other details do you remember?"

Chuck List thought for a moment and then shook his head. "Nothing else. She was young, judging by her skin."

"Was she pretty?" Travis asked.

"Yeah." List shrugged.

"You were above her and she was on the ground, right?"

"Yes, she handed me the aluminum case. I was onboard."

"Did you see her face from above?"

"No, the cap's bill covered her face. She didn't look up at me."

"Nice breasts?"

"Nice, medium, firm," said List, blushing.

"Tattoos?"

"No. But she had a golden necklace around her neck and it had a pendant monogrammed with two letters, A&E."

"Was the pendant gold?"

"No, it was wood or plastic. A reddish color."

"Do you know what A&E means?"

"No. Somebody's initials?" said Chuck List.

"You've never seen it before? How about you, Captain?"

They shook their heads.

"Who gave you the instructions on how to load the vials?" Travis asked.

"It was another video, showing some hands loading the vials with a narrator describing the tasks."

"Were the hands of a man or a woman?"

"Woman, definitely a woman," said Chuck List.

"How about the narrator?"

"A man."

"Have you ever done a job like this before?" Travis asked.

They shook their heads.

"Did you wonder what was in the vials?" Travis asked.

"Insecticide, we thought," answered Chuck List.

"What if I tell you that you dispersed a nerve agent?"

"A nerve agent?" they said in unison.

"We weren't required to use gas masks," said Captain Bradwell.

Travis shook his head slowly. "Please continue describing your revised mission."

"When we reached Senegal's coast, the autopilot descended to a 3,000-meter ceiling, and Chuck loaded the first ten vials in the feeder."

"And then I pushed a button to begin spraying," added Chuck List. "That was it."

"Were the vials labeled?"

"No, just 10-cc glass test tubes with rubber plugs. I suppose a syringe penetrated the rubber plug to extract the insecticide."

"When did you run out of vials?"

"Hmm. I don't remember."

"How about you, Captain Bradwell? Do you remember what happened after the spraying began?"

"No, not much. What do you mean by a nerve agent? I was in the Air Force, and no way such an agent could be distributed by us and from that altitude."

Travis nodded. "Tell us more about the flight."

"The craft flew at an altitude of 3,000 meters along the continental coast."

"How did your flight end?"

"We landed in Cape Town."

"Have you landed there before?"

"Yes, many times," said the captain.

"Are you sure?"

"Of course." Captain Bradwell chuckled.

"Where are we now, Captain Bradwell?" Travis looked around.

"In Lancaster, California. I promised Chuck that I would take him to see some vintage planes after we returned, and here we are."

"What about you, Mr. List? Do you remember the same thing?"

"Yes, we were talking during the flight about what we'd do in Cape Town."

"Any malfunctions of the dispersing unit?" Travis asked.

"No, not that I remember," said List, shaking his head.

Prescott pulled Travis and Claire aside. "Just like Derek Dodd, they don't remember a thing after being infected. Not even when they switched from auto pilot to manual control."

"Yes, they were just two expendable pawns," said Travis.

"Should we tell them that they crashed in Liberia?" Prescott asked.

"How long do you think they'll linger in this yard?" Travis wondered.

Prescott shrugged. "By telling them, we'll help their souls and minds to move on."

"They just did a job. Little did they know that they were spreading nerve gas to exterminate millions," said Claire. "I'll tell them that they passed away."

"Be gentle," said Prescott.

Claire approached the two pilots with a solemn face. "Gentlemen, thank you for your cooperation."

"Sure," said Captain Bradwell. "I hope everything is OK."

"I'm sorry, but I have bad news for you," Claire said.

Bradwell and List listened, horrified, with their mouths open.

Mit Sandru

Chapter 33. A&E

Claire, Travis, and Prescott opened their eyes, emerging from wherever the pilots' souls and minds were. They had only been gone for an instant, but they surveyed the airport just in case there was trouble they hadn't noticed before. Then they contacted TIO headquarters and informed Maximus of what they had found out.

"We have new suspects," concluded Travis. "The owner and the president of the O&C Private Jet Co. and the OTTM Chemical Corporation, and the blonde ground crew woman with the A&E pendant."

"The NTSB has interrogated the company's employees regarding the crash," said Maximus. "There is no mention of a spraying system installed onboard. And the cargo is identified as a small briefcase, aluminum, containing rat poison, which did not raise any eyebrows among the employees. The FBI needs to be involved now."

"Who on Earth charters a flight to carry rat poison?" Prescott wondered.

"Some unnamed Saudi Arabian prince," said Travis.

"At least we found a thread," said Prescott.

"Yes, that's a good start. Now, this A&E pendant," said Maximus. "An A&E monogram was found in Alexei Perchenko's house and on other virtual documents he possessed. The Russian investigators have found out that it stands for the Adam and Eve Historical Society," said Maximus.

Travis, Claire, and Prescott didn't understand what Maximus was alluding to.

"Meaning?" Claire asked.

"A secret society, I presume. The Russians haven't found any leads about this secret society or its members. There are many other A&E organizations, and we'll investigate in the meantime, but there is no connection whatsoever with Alexei Perchenko, except for this one. Nor is there any connection between Perchenko's private jet and O&C Private Jet Co. Also, there is no OTTM Chemical Corporation," said Maximus. "Don O'Halloran was found dead, according to the NTSB inquiry. The cause was suicide."

"They're covering their tracks well," Travis remarked. "A thought just came to mind—could you ask Daniela Rock if Mossad knows anything about this A&E Historical Society?"

"I will."

"Damn it!" said Travis in frustration. "We came all the way here and found nothing."

"I wouldn't say that," said Maximus. "The blonde is part of the A&E society. We can follow that lead."

"If they haven't killed her by now," said Travis. "Maximus, I wouldn't tell the FBI or anyone else about the blonde, yet."

"Understood."

"Maximus, since we are not infected, when can we be retrieved from here?" Prescott asked.

"We're working on several possibilities," said Maximus.

"Put some pressure on whomever," said Travis.

"I am, but I'm dealing with people, not machines," said Maximus.

"The only thing left for us to do here is to observe Confidence," said Claire. "And determine what to do about her."

"And in the meantime, we will inspect some of those hovercraft around the airport," said Travis, motioning with his head to the planes around the airport.

"You cannot fly out of Africa. You'll be shot down," said Maximus. "I have a suspicion that WHO is tracking you and knows where you are."

"You mean our astrosuits?" Travis asked.

"Not only your astrosuits but your bodies. The inner jumpsuit you wore under the astronaut suit coated you with nanobots, which by now are under your skin."

"Sons of bitches. No wonder I was itching," said Travis. "We probably glow under the right light spectrum."

Prescott started scratching involuntarily. "Are the nanobots sophisticated enough to transmit our conversations?"

"No, but that does not mean they didn't bug your astrosuits," said Maximus.

"When did you learn about this?" Prescott asked.

"As I was talking to you, I read an internal text from a US intelligence source to WHO that said that if you went missing they'd track you through the nanobots. Sorry, I didn't know about this safety scheme."

"Safety scheme?" Prescott shouted. "More like, if we were to go AWOL, they would find us."

"I smell a rat," said Travis. "So they know everything about us, what we said, where we are. Including about the vial of the biochemical agent."

"The extent of their eavesdropping seems to be patchy," said Maximus.

"We tried to help WHO," said Prescott.

"In all honesty, we had an ulterior motive, too," said Claire.

"WHO is not alone. Someone in the government has set us up," said Travis.

"I'm inquiring. And the tracking is standard procedure. It may not have been intentional."

"But opportune," said Travis.

"I checked on methods of getting rid of the nanobots," said Maximus.

"We're all ears," said Travis.

"They can be extracted by magnetism. The nanobots will migrate from the north polarity to the south polarity of a magnet, but only to another living host. Simply put, you place a magnet on your forehead, south polarity toward your feet. You place another magnet on the host's forehead, north polarity toward the host's feet, and touch your bare feet to the host's bare feet. The nanobots will migrate like ants to the new host."

"And how do we know when we've cleansed ourselves of the nanobots?" asked Claire.

"You could use a magnetic compass. If you placed a compass on your body now, it would gyrate, unable to settle on the North Pole. When you're clean, it will point north."

"We have a compass capability in our suits," said Travis.

"You'll need a magnetic compass, not the GPS type," said Maximus.

Travis and Prescott smiled from ear to ear.

"Let's find some magnets," said Travis.

"But first, we need to see how Confidence is doing," said Claire.

"And magnets," said Travis.

"And a functional hovercraft," said Prescott.

"It's a plan," said Travis.

Mit Sandru

Chapter 34. Cleansed

They returned to the control tower and found Confidence still asleep, which was good. Claire reviewed the suit's scanners, and Confidence's vitals showed disturbing deviations from the norm. Her rate of metabolism had increased, along with her heart rate and pulse.

Travis and Prescott used duct tape to cover the external microphones on her astrosuit and retreated to the other end of the room to plot their next moves. Claire opened communication with WHO.

"This is Dr. Warner."

"Hello, Dr. Warner. I'm calling to find out the final results on Confidence's infection."

"Not good." He sighed. "She is transforming rapidly. Please do another brain scan, Dr. German."

"Sure, but what are her brain readings from the last scan?"

"The dendrites are deteriorating, just as in the first wave victims, but slower. It's a given that she will become violent and you will have to restrain her."

"If we restrain her, she'll die."

"She's not human anymore. She's changing into an animal."

"How much did her mental capacity deteriorate?" Claire asked.

"About 60 percent. She will be completely demented in another two hours."

"Thank you, Dr. Warner. By the way, we're restraining her in an astrosuit. I'm signing off." Claire scanned Confidence's brain for the benefit of science. Unfortunately for Confidence, she had ceased to be human.

Prescott and Travis looked at Claire from across the room.

"What do you think? What should we do with her?" Claire asked them.

"Release her into the wild," said Travis, opening his arms as if to say, what other choice do we have?

Claire rested her forehead in her hands, shaking her head.

"She'll either attack us, or she'll run," added Prescott.

"She's a living entity," said Claire.

"So are we. Perfectly healthy and left here to die," said Travis. "Or they'll retrieve us later for additional studies."

"What could we do with her?" Prescott pondered. "Why don't we take her out of the astrosuit, move her to the terminal's walk-in cooler, and leave the door open so she can get out. There is plenty of food there, and maybe we can leave some bowls of water for her to drink."

Claire sighed. "Without proper care facilities, I'm resigned to admit that's the only option."

Some time later, they had moved Confidence into the walk-in cooler, and there they took her out of the astrosuit. They opened many cans of vegetables and meats, and poured bottled water into large bowls from the cafeteria's kitchen. The cooler's refrigeration system was working, and it was cold inside. They hoped that the flies would not gather to feast on the food.

"We need magnets first to cleanse ourselves," said Travis.

"We'll find them in the cars," said Prescott. "We need to visit that hangar to get tools."

They took the SUV to the large hangar. A magnetic compass in the shape of a ball was mounted on the dashboard of the SUV. It gyrated wildly in their presence, just as Maximus said it would. Prescott ripped it off the dashboard and pocketed it for later use.

Inside the hangar, they found all the tools they needed, including several vehicles from which they extracted two magnets from the electric motors.

"I think we're all set with the magnets," said Prescott, after finishing the removal work. "I wonder what's in the smaller hangar next door?"

They followed Prescott to the smaller hangar, but the entry door was locked. Prescott used a magnet to smash the digital access pad to gain access.

"What do you know?" Prescott was all excited, looking at the hovercraft parked inside.

"This must be the presidential jet-hovercraft," said Travis. "Liberia's finest."

"Why aren't they keeping the jet at the international airport?" Prescott wondered.

"Monkey business." Travis wiggled his eyebrows.

Prescott unlatched the door, which unfolded downward, providing steps to access the craft. It was plush inside, and after closer inspection, they found the bar well stocked.

"Maximus, we've found the presidential hover-jet, and we will use it to fly back," called Prescott. "Could you chart the safest flight path back to California, without being shot down?"

"I'll prepare it."

"At least we'll travel across the Atlantic in luxury," said Claire.

"Indeed." Travis was delighted by what they'd found. "But first, the nanobots."

They drove to the church, where they found the mad pastor hooting from the altar. The other men nearby seemed unsure about whether to attack these newcomers. Claire, Travis, and Prescott were not dressed in the white astrosuits, but in their dark gray outfits, and the mad people seemed confused about their identity. The women, peering from behind the men, were sheltering the kids. The maternal instinct had never died, even in their brutish condition.

"These two front men are good, and we need one of the women for Claire," said Travis, raising the tranquilizer gun and shooting one of them. Prescott shot the other man, and Claire shot one of the women. The three victims collapsed shortly, and the others, led by the pastor, fled through the back door.

"We'll do you first, Travis." Prescott dragged one of the men into the isle and positioned him on his back. "Take off your shoes and touch the bottom of your feet to his."

While Claire was keeping watch in case the survivors returned, Travis lay down on his back and touched the bottom of his feet to the other's man feet. Prescott placed one magnet on Travis's forehead and then the second magnet on the other man's forehead, the polarity aligned as Maximus had instructed.

"Is it working?" Claire asked.

"I hope so." Prescott pulled the compass out of his pocket and ran it along Travis's body. At the head, the compass detected the north pole of the magnet, but soon after it aligned itself with the real North Pole. The compass gyrated wildly when Prescott ran the compass over the other man's body. "It worked. Claire, you're next."

Prescott repeated the procedure with the sedated woman and Claire, cleansing her of the nanobots. Claire repeated the process and cleansed Prescott in turn.

"Maximus, we're clean of bugs," communicated Claire.

"As far as WHO is concerned, Maximus, we went mad and are roaming the streets of Monrovia," said Travis. "We're getting the hell out of here."

"I'll tell them I do not know what happened to you," said Maximus. "And that I'm unable to communicate with you and have no way of tracing you. I'll have to contact WHO and ask for their help in tracking you down."

"Please do," said Travis. "Perhaps Dr. Stark should call them and sound worried about our fate."

"Have faith, Travis," said Maximus. "I can put a concerned tone in my voice."

"Sure, but they won't believe you. You're not supposed to have feelings," said Travis.

"All right," said Maximus, sounding disappointed. "In the meantime, I'll reroute all your transmissions through a convoluted satellite network."

Back at the airport, Travis and Claire managed to open the gates of the smaller hangar, while Prescott disabled the craft's transponder. Once finished, Prescott took the pilot's seat and Travis, the copilot's.

"Where to, Captain?" Claire asked, while serving them cold sodas.

Prescott didn't get a chance to answer as Maximus made contact with them. "How are you doing down there?"

"We are in the jet hovercraft and about to depart Monrovia," said Prescott. "Do you have the flight plan for us?"

"Yes, but it would be prudent to wait for darkness."

"Oh, no!" Claire exclaimed.

They saw Confidence running toward the craft.

Chapter 35. Close Call

"Confidence is awake!" Claire shouted.

Travis adjusted his PAV to magnify her face, and it was not pretty. Her clothes were torn, her left breast exposed, her eyes bloodshot, and she had an expression bent on killing. "Let's get out of here, Prescott."

"This is an aircraft, not a car," replied Prescott.

"No, we can't go without checking on her," said Claire.

"Claire, she's mad," Travis said over his shoulder.

Claire didn't listen. She opened the hatch and got out to meet Confidence.

"Damn it!" Travis followed her, grabbing one of the tranquilizer guns.

Claire took a few steps from the craft and waited. Confidence sprinted toward her, ready to rip Claire apart. When she was near, she lunged at Claire, howling like a beast. Claire moved out of the way, but Confidence recovered quickly and returned to grab Claire by the neck. Claire held her arms at the wrists, away from her face, but Confidence jumped on Claire, wrapping her legs around Claire's waist while attempting to bite her. Claire bent backward to avoid Confidence's vicious bites, and she fell on her back, Confidence on top of her. She was pinned down with a foaming-at-the-mouth-Confidence snapping at her.

Travis had no choice but to shoot Confidence in the back with a tranquilizer dart. He grabbed her by the hair and pulled her off Claire. The girl's contorted face relaxed from the dart's drug, and she fell to the ground. Besides her ripped clothes, she had scratched away all her bandages, and many of her wounds were bleeding.

"Claire, you are hurt," said Travis, kneeling down to help.

"She only scratched my hands. I need to disinfect the scratches." Claire ran inside the craft, retrieved the medical emergency kit, and rubbed her hands with alcohol.

After Travis was inside he pulled the hatch up and closed it. "Screw the preparations, Prescott. Let's fly out of here." He slid into the copilot's seat and latched his belt.

"Wait!" shouted Claire from the back.

Travis and Prescott turned to look at her, worried about her.

"We'd better wait until we're sure I'm not infected," said Claire. "Besides, night will be upon us shortly. If they're watching us, it's better to leave under the cover of darkness."

"Yes, you're right." Prescott got out of his seat to check on Claire. "How are you faring?"

"I'm fine, other than some superficial scratches from her nails."

"Are you infected?" Prescott asked.

"I'm monitoring my vitals," said Claire. "Right now, my pulse is high because of the skirmish with Confidence. If I see any signs of infection, I'll let you know. Don't hesitate to throw me out."

"Claire, we can't do that." Travis had joined them at the back of the craft.

"You must, or you'll end up like Confidence. By the time it's dark and we're ready to fly away, we'll know for sure. It's my fault. Don't hesitate to get rid of me."

Prescott and Travis exchanged troubled looks.

"No rush decisions," said Prescott.

Travis opened the bar and brought back a crystal-cut bottle of scotch and two glasses. "I'd offer you a scotch, too, but . . ."

"Of course not," agreed Claire, and she opened comm with TIO headquarters. "Maximus, I have been scratched by Confidence, who is mad."

"How do you feel?"

"I'm OK for now. I'm sending the data collected on me. Please warn us if I'm deteriorating."

"What are you going to do if you're infected?"

"I told Prescott and Travis to leave me behind."

They waited for one hour. In the meantime, Travis pulled Confidence outside the hangar and closed the gates to prevent further attacks from her and the others.

Prescott scanned Claire's head several times and she reviewed the readings, which she also transmitted back to TIO headquarters.

Claire reviewed the analysis. "I'd say I'm in the clear. What do you think, Maximus?"

"Dr. Stark is reviewing the information and comparing it with Confidence's," said Maximus.

"Yes, it's negative," said Dr. Stark. "I see no evidence that you've degraded, as Confidence did."

"I notified WHO that we lost comm with you due to the possibility of infection, and that you could have gone rogue and mad. So far, no response from them," Maximus said. "I charted your course and downloaded it to your craft's computer. You'll be flying at low altitude, under a 100-meter celling, and only in the dark. Your course will be over water until you reach Mexico. There, if the Mexican Air Force detects you, you'll have to ditch the plane and make it on foot. I downloaded possible routes in Mexico and the US around the registered zones."

"And if we reach the US, then what?" Travis asked.

"You'll go to a safe house in Nevada."

"I thought we were going to Oakland to investigate the source of the nerve agent," said Prescott.

"Negative. If they discover that you've come back from Africa, you'll be quarantined for God knows how long," said Maximus. "From now on, this will be a straight police investigation. The FBI will find the culprits."

Claire, Travis, and Prescott exchanged ambivalent glances. It was better to be in the US, in a TIO safe house, than in Monrovia in the control tower.

"Daniela Rock is joining us online. She has new information about the A&E Society."

Chapter 36. The Forbidden Fruit

A second later, Daniela Rock appeared in their virtual PAVs meeting. "Hello, people. I'm so glad to see you well. From what I gather, Africa is hell."

"That's an understatement," said Claire.

"How are you doing, Claire? I heard you got injured."

"Yes, but they were superficial wounds," said Claire, looking at her hands covered with bandages. "So, what do you have on the A&E Historical Society?"

"Dr. Moshe Klein, a professor of Middle Eastern history, the Torah, anthropology, and archeology at Tel Aviv University, was contacted a few years back by two Americans, a man and a woman, claiming that they were with the A&E Historical Society. And they offered a generous donation to the Archeological Department of Tel Aviv University," said Daniela.

"Who were they?" Travis asked.

"Their names were Audrey and Sean. No last names," said Daniela. "They inquired about the latest scholarly research on Adam and Eve."

"Could Dr. Klein describe the man and the woman?" Claire asked.

"The communication was by text only," said Daniela Rock. "To get a better grasp of the discussion, or texting, that happened over several days back then, I invited Dr. Moshe Klein to join us and tell us what happened. He's not privy to our investigation or about the pandemic in Africa. And it's very important that you keep an open mind about what he's going to tell us."

"Don't tell me that he believes we come from Adam and Eve," said Dr. Stark disappointedly.

"That's not any stranger than talking to the dead," replied Daniela, raising an eyebrow.

"Let's keep an open mind," said Maximus.

"If I must believe that CTT can talk to dead men, my mind might as well be open about Adam and Eve as well," Dr. Stark quipped.

The hologram of an old, bearded professor joined their meeting.

"Thank you for taking the time to talk to us, Dr. Klein." Daniela then introduced Maximus, Claire, Travis, and Prescott by their first names only, and Dr. Stark.

"Nice to meet you," said Dr. Klein. "Daniela told me that you're interested in the A&E Historical Society and the text-discussion I had with them a few years back."

"When did it happen?" Travis asked.

"In 2057."

"We'll be certainly in your debt, Dr. Klein, if you tell us what you discussed with them," said Maximus.

"I'm not supposed to discuss our donors, but I'll do this as a favor to Daniela," said Dr. Klein.

"I appreciate what you're about to tell us." Daniela smiled at him.

"Right, then. They told me that they were a philanthropic society dedicated to the historical figures of Adam and Eve, ergo the name, A&E Historical Society. They wanted to know our wildest theories about Adam and Eve. I was obliged to share with them our latest concepts in light of their generous donation.

"Some of us, the more avant-garde scholars, believe that the events in Genesis are true and that they happened in the past. Which brings me to say that Adam and Eve were real people."

Dr. Stark rolled his eyes.

Dr. Klein might have noticed that and continued, "Everyone is born from a mother, and if we exclude the Immaculate Conception, a father is needed, too. Therefore, the modern human lineage started from a pair of prehistoric humans, Adam and Eve."

"In theory I agree with that," said Dr. Stark. "But how did Adam and Eve get to be who they were?"

"I'm not insisting that Adam and Eve were created by a supernatural force, a god, or that they were modern humans. They may have been prehistoric humans, similar to the Neanderthals or Devonians, but a mutation must have occurred before they gave birth to Cain, Abel, and Seth, followed by the other unnamed sons and daughters who became the first modern humans. As a matter of fact, Abel must have been the first completely modern human, somehow different from Cain, and for that, Cain killed him."

"The Bible doesn't say that," said Travis. "Cain killed Abel because he was jealous that God favored Abel."

"I agree about the jealousy, but not because of God's favoritism," said Dr. Klein. "Being the firstborn, Cain might have been half-Neanderthal and half-modern human, whereas Abel was a completely modern human. Afterward, Adam banished Cain, afraid that Cain might kill their other children as well."

"What was the mark God put on Cain?" Travis asked.

"The mark was Cain being born as a half-breed human," said Dr. Klein.

"That whole Adam and Eve proposition is preposterous," argued Dr. Stark. "If we all came from Adam and Eve, than we all are a product of incest, brothers and sisters of Adam and Eve's children, intermarrying and having children till this day."

"It seems so, and probably it was so," agreed Dr. Klein. "However, Adam and Eve were not the only two people on Earth. There were others like them. For sure, Adam had other wives and many other children with them. The gene pool was large enough to prevent inbreeding mutations, and later on, just as we intermixed with the Neanderthals and other early humans, the gene pool expanded. Their descendants might had been the start of the proto Indo-European race, which later migrated from the Middle East to India and Europe."

"Be that as it may, what caused the mutation?" Dr. Stark asked.

"The Forbidden Fruit," said Dr. Klein.

"An apple!" derided Dr. Stark.

"Not an apple," said Dr. Klein. "Evidence suggests that the fruit were almonds. Therefore, the forbidden fruit, the almond, was the agent of change for Adam and Eve."

"An almond caused the mutation?" Dr. Stark scoffed.

"An agent, a virus of some kind associated with that almond. A pathogen."

Chapter 37. Manna

"That would be pure speculation. We don't know of any such pathogens," said Dr. Stark.

"Dr. Stark, you know that humans have several genes, like SRGAP2, HYDIN2, and ARHGAP11b, that are unique to us," said Dr. Klein.

"And you speculate that some pathogen, a virus, mutated our genes, which changed our brains and physiques to evolve into what we are today?"

"You must know that some viruses are known to affect how the brain functions," said Dr. Klein.

"Yes, but only as parasites, not gene-altering agents."

"Let's call it a mutation agent then," Dr. Klein proposed.

"Sure," agreed Dr. Stark.

"And it may still be around," said Dr. Klein.

"What?" Claire asked, slightly surprised.

"I'm listening." Dr. Stark was unperturbed.

"The forbidden fruit almond carried that specific agent and once it was eaten, a metamorphosis occurred in Eve and Adam. The ancient people did not know of any such things, but they knew that something dramatic happened after they ate it."

Dr. Stark scoffed. "Unsubstantiated speculation."

"We've discovered many new pieces of information over the past century regarding Genesis," said Dr. Klein.

"What kind of information?" Travis asked.

"One in particular was an older clay tablet that describes Genesis in a lot more detail," said Dr. Klein. "It was found in the wall of the Temple Mount when archeologists dug at the base of the wall back in the twentieth century. The tablet dated to at least 80,000 years ago. It probably originated in the Tigris-Euphrates region thousand of years before the wall was built and was buried there."

"Hmm," exclaimed Dr. Stark, resting his chin on his knuckles. "And what did it say?"

"We were able only recently to decipher it. The tablet was inscribed in a proto-cuneiform alphabet. It described how Adam and Eve found a magic tree. They saw the Tree of Knowledge, a magic almond tree, which bore sweet almonds and bitter almonds. Eve did not pick the fruit. Instead, a branch of the tree offered a sweet almond to her."

"That was the snake?" Travis wondered.

"It seems so. Perhaps a vine on the tree gave the impression of offering the almond," said Dr. Klein. "And she picked it, and it smelled good. She removed the husk to get to the nut, and with a rock she split open the shell to get to the almond pit. And then she took a bite and ate it, and it was sweet. Eve offered it to Adam, who smelled it and ate the rest of it, and he found it sweet, too. I'm paraphrasing."

"Does it say whether they became smart instantly or over a period of time?" Dr. Stark asked.

"It said that the following day, Adam and Eve started seeing the world with new eyes. A few days later, they went back with other people in their tribe to see the miraculous tree."

"Did the other people eat of the forbidden fruit?" Dr. Stark asked.

"By then the tree was barren and dead," said Dr. Klein.

Dr. Stark swayed his head side to side, doubting. "What's the point of this latest theory?" he asked.

"Well, it is about the Tree of Knowledge," said Dr. Klein.

"All right, so it may have happened. End of story," concluded Dr. Stark.

"Ah, but the story continues in Exodus," said Dr. Klein, clearly excited by what he was about to tell them. "Aaron, Moses' brother, who did not get fair PR in the Hollywood movie *The Ten Commandments*, had a walking stick known as Aaron's Rod."

"The rod that changed into a snake and swallowed the Pharaoh's snake," said Travis.

"That's the one," said Dr. Klein. "Later on, Aaron's Rod was placed in the Ark of the Covenant by Moses, along with the Ten Commandments tablets and a jar of Manna."

"The Bible says that much," acknowledged Travis.

"Manna? Are you referring to the same *manna* that feeds billions of people today?" Dr. Stark asked.

"The same manna that appeared out of nowhere in 2030, upon the collapse of our civilization, and that prevented the deaths of billions of people."

"Is there a problem with the manna? Is it in danger of dying out?" Dr. Stark asked. "That would be an incredible tragedy, since Earth's population survives on it."

"No, manna is safe, as far as we know," said Dr. Klein. "But the appearance of modern manna indicates that the pottery jar containing the biblical Manna—and implicitly, the Ark of the Covenant—was found and opened."

Mit Sandru

The Devolution of Adam and Eve

Chapter 38. The Tree of Knowledge

"That's based on your conclusion," said Dr. Stark.

"Mine and those of a few other colleagues," said Dr. Klein. "After the sacking of Jerusalem, the Babylonians took the Ark of the Covenant away. You'd expect to find the Ark in Babylon, but somehow the Ark of the Covenant ended up in Egypt."

"How do you know that?" Dr. Stark asked.

"Based on modern manna and its reappearance location," said Dr. Klein. "Scientists conducted detailed research and found out that the origin of modern manna was in Egypt—Cairo, precisely. Someone discovered the Ark of the Covenant, the Ark was opened, and inside they must have found the Ten Commandments tablets, Aaron's Rod, and the jar of Manna. The jar was opened, and manna spores escaped, spreading throughout the world."

"Again, do you have evidence of the discovery of the Ark?" Dr. Stark asked.

"No, this is just extrapolation," said Dr. Klein. "But well-justified, as I'll continue to show. Around 2031, an ancient bronze box, claimed to be from the Ark of the Covenant, was offered for sale in the underground antique market. Manna appearing after thousands of years is a mystery, but an artifact from the Ark of the Covenant is incredible."

"Other than the location of manna's origin, I've never heard of this." Dr. Stark glanced around the virtual gathering to see if anyone else had heard that news.

"We did," said Daniela, alluding to Mossad's intelligence. "We thought it was just another fake relic in search of billionaire suckers."

"Who found the Ark?" Travis asked.

"We suspect the thieves were high-ranking generals in the Egyptian military," said Dr. Klein. "They could have been the ones who unsealed the jar of Manna in 2030. They might have been spooked by the magnitude of their discovery, closed the Ark, and left it in place. Who knows, until someone else privy to the whereabouts of the Ark reopens it again and retrieves Aaron's Rod."

"If they found the Ark of the Covenant, it would be a monumental discovery," said Travis. "Why didn't they bring it to the world to know about it?"

"And what would they get in return?" Dr. Klein asked. "The Egyptian government would have taken possession of it, and the discoverers might have ended up in jail, and definitely with no riches. I think they retrieved the bronze box to first test the market. The Ark or the tablets would be too significant to bring to the market, so they started cautiously."

"And then someone retrieved Aaron's Rod," Travis said. "To sell the rod itself is a big deal, if it's proven as such."

"I suspect there is plenty of money wishing to buy such a historic artifact," said Claire.

"Yes, but first, it would have to be proven that it is Aaron's Rod," said Dr. Stark.

"Why do you suspect it was Aaron's Rod that was brought out?" Travis asked.

"Because in 2057, shortly after my discussion with the A&E Historical Society, there were rumors on the antiques black market that the forbidden fruit was available for sale."

"Did you inquire about it?" Dr. Stark asked.

"I sure did, and I found out they were almonds," said Dr. Klein. "Just as it was written on the clay tablet."

"Did you offer to buy them?" Maximus asked. "How much did they want?"

"One billion goldbits." Dr. Klein sighed. "That's a lot of money. The university was interested, if they could overlook the price. I wanted to see them, assess what was offered for sale. Of course, just to evaluate them, you had to post a one million goldbits bond. But before the committee made up its mind, the almonds were taken off the market. Very likely sold."

"I think I'm missing something. You're talking about the forbidden fruit offered for sale, but what does it have to do with Aaron's Rod?" Prescott asked.

"The rod was famous for its miraculous powers," said Dr. Klein. "The rod would sprout if planted."

"Sprouting leaves?" Dr. Stark asked.

"Yes."

"Big deal. Many plants can do that."

Dr. Klein shook his head. "Aaron's Rod is not just a stick that sprouts. Aaron's Rod is the Tree of Knowledge."

The Devolution of Adam and Eve

Chapter 39. Bitter Almonds

"Say what?" Dr. Stark shouted.

"I got your attention, didn't I?" smirked Dr. Klein.

"Wait, wait—are you suggesting that Aaron's Rod sprouted into the Tree of Knowledge and bore fruit, almonds, which are the forbidden fruit?" Travis asked.

"That's exactly what I'm saying," said Dr. Klein.

"Do you think the A&E Historical Society bought the forbidden fruit?" Claire asked.

"Audrey and Sean of the A&E Society did not indicate that they knew about the almonds being available for sale," said Dr. Klein. "However, I told them everything I knew, just as I told you, and I told them that, according to ancient writings, the almonds came in two varieties— sweet and bitter. The sweet almonds made Adam and Eve smart, while the bitter almonds could do the opposite. They peppered me with questions about the almonds, about which I only knew from what the ancients had written."

"Did you make a connection between the Society's questions and the almonds on the black market?" Travis asked.

"Not at the time. A few historical forums discussed this subject, although it was not widespread knowledge."

"So there could have been other entities interested as well?" Dr. Stark wondered.

"Sure."

"Have you contacted the A&E Historical Society since then?" Travis asked.

"Yes, I tried to contact them yesterday, but the contact's e-addresses were nonresponsive," said Dr. Klein.

"Why did you contact them?" Travis asked.

"Underground rumor has it that a serious buyer is looking to buy more of the forbidden fruit. Big money is being offered." Dr. Klein groaned.

"Thank you, Dr. Klein, for the illuminating information." Maximus concluded the discussion.

Dr. Klein's hologram turned off soon after that.

"Well, that's an enlightening story about antiquity and the Bible. I'm sure Travis appreciated it, but what does that have to do with the A&E Historical Society?" Prescott asked.

"Agent Rock, I have a suspicion that there is more to this story. Please tell us the rest," said Maximus.

"What Dr. Klein said is true," Daniela said. "It all started in Egypt, in Cairo, at the Giza Plateau."

"Giza, where the Great Pyramids are," said Prescott.

"Exactly," said Daniela. "Only the pyramidiots claim a connection among manna, the mysteries of the pyramids, and extraterrestrial aliens. Everyone kind of shrugs it off. In 2057, when Dr. Klein alerted us about the almonds being available for sale on the black market, we paid little attention to it. The whole affair didn't seem to have anything to do with Israel's security. The information was filed away as inconsequential, although it was linked to Aaron's Rod."

"I presume we are still talking about the A&E Society, who they are, and who might had developed this apocalyptic agent," said Travis.

"Yes," said Daniela. "Maximus telling us about the A&E pendant closed the loop of our AI search. What Dr. Klein does not know is that we verified A&E electronic fingerprints on the darknet inquiring about buying more almonds. Our AI didn't think that the A&E were farmers from California interested in buying almonds, but 'A&E,' 'Adam and Eve Historical Society,' 'Aaron's Rod,' 'the Tree of Knowledge,' 'the Forbidden Fruit,' 'almonds,' 'cyanide,' and other terms caused our AI to flag a connection to the African pandemic and the biochemical agent Derek Dodd attempted to sell."

"Hmm," Travis contemplated. "A&E, almonds, and cyanide are the only things in common. It takes a stretch of imagination to associate these with Aaron's Rod and the Tree of Knowledge, which are legends. Besides, how can anyone make such a potent nerve agent from almonds? Even if they're bitter."

The Devolution of Adam and Eve

Chapter 40. The Devolution Agent

"Only according to ancient writings, for which there is no proof," said Dr. Stark. "I cannot buy into this theory. It's too far-fetched."

"There is one more thing our AI flagged," said Daniela. "The names of the generals who discovered the Ark in 2030."

"So you found them? Who are they?" Travis asked.

"General Kazaz and General Nassief, both dead of old age," said Daniela. "Now, brace yourselves for this news—each general had a son. Both sons have been confined to mental institutions since 2057. Their names are Fatta Kazaz and Ahmed Nassief."

"Daniela, you didn't give us the whole picture the first time we met," said Maximum.

"We had the pieces, but the whole picture didn't assemble itself until the past few hours," said Daniela defensively.

"Maybe the exposure to the almonds affected the mental health of the sons," said Claire.

"This changes the entire investigation," said Maximus. "Although in certain parts it is circumstantial, it seems that the A&E Historical Society is behind the nerve gas, which may have been developed from the bitter almonds of the biblical tree. The perpetrators need more almonds to make more nerve agent, and if the sons had sold them the almonds last time, the culprits are now out of luck."

"Great. We have two nutty accomplices and a mysterious organization that is responsible for millions of destroyed lives," said Dr. Stark. "We have nothing to go on."

"You forgot we have the CTT, Dr. Stark," admonished Maximus. "The FBI can track down A&E Historical Society, while CTT can get information from Fatta and Ahmed. Not all is lost."

"Then we need to go to Egypt," Claire concluded.

"Yes. I'll get you a new flight plan to Cairo," said Maximus. "Daniela, do you think Mossad can assist CTT on the ground in Cairo?"

"I'll get back to you on that." Daniela Rock disconnected.

There was a moment of silence as all of them, except Maximus, needed to gather their thoughts.

"If what we discussed is true, the bitter nuts will reverse human beings to prehistoric human intelligence," said Claire.

"Make us dumb again," commented Prescott.

"Earth becomes the Planet of the Apes," commented Travis. "Reality mimicking fiction."

"Apes can survive," said Claire. "However, billions of apes cannot. They wouldn't have enough readily available food to forage for themselves, as we just saw here in Monrovia."

"Not to mention cooperating among themselves, which made us human in the first place," said Dr. Stark. "Billions of humans are overcrowded in cities, and only by cooperating, as we do now, can we survive. They won't know how to harvest manna. Diseases and plagues will spread wildly. Not to mention what will happen when apes get guns. Fortunately, they may not know how to use them."

"There are all kinds of scenarios of how humanity will perish, but mental debilitation is new," said Maximus.

"What we're dealing with here is a *devolution* agent, not a biochemical-nerve agent," said Claire.

Naming it a *devolution agent* had a stunning effect on all of them.

"That's why no trace of it could be found," said Claire.

"You'll need to expand on your thoughts, even if you have to leave the science behind," said Dr. Stark.

"I'm thinking out loud, but this is my assessment," Claire said. "Assuming that the sweet almonds made us smart and the bitter almonds make us stupid, how did that happen? Adam and Eve ate the almonds, and a genetic transformation happened to them and successively our ancestors inherited the smart genes. Bitter almonds may do the opposite and affect our genes in reverse. Dr. Stark, was any DNA analysis performed on the current victims?"

"No, we don't have DNA samples, although we should," responded Dr. Stark. "But wait, there are DNA samples from the three previous incidents in the world."

"I've retrieved the information, specifically from the previous Congo incident," said Maximus. "I'm surprised that no one noticed this, but genes SRGAP2, HYDIN2, and ARHGAP11b show signs of damage."

"Then this is a genetic weapon," said Dr. Stark.

"This mutation agent must be either biomatter or something else we cannot detect," said Claire. "If it is

223

biomatter, it could be absorbed into the body, and whatever is left would die out. But considering the speed at which it spreads and its longevity, I don't think this agent is biomatter."

"Then what is it?" Dr. Stark asked.

"Something new we haven't seen before, and we have a vial of it," said Claire.

"You cannot open it without being infected," said Dr. Stark.

"Of course not, but Travis, Prescott, and I can do a TAP on it," said Claire.

"A what?" Dr. Stark asked.

"A Trans Axiom Paranormal examination," said Prescott.

Chapter 41. Trans Axiom Paranormal Examination

"What's a Trans Axiom Paranormal examination?"

"We have the ability to transcend into the Mind Realm," said Prescott. "The assumption Claire makes is that the devolution agent affects the mind, and we may find its essence in that realm."

"I don't even know what question to ask next," said Dr. Stark, clearly perplexed. "As a scientist and medical doctor, I understand science and biochemical facts, but what you say sounds like witchcraft."

"So it seems, Doctor," said Travis. "We're saying all living things are trinities: the body, the mind, and the soul. In the realm of reality, where the body resides, science cannot find what this agent is. But we may find it in the realm of the mind. And if we do, we may find a solution."

"Do what you have to do. I'm out of my depth here." Dr. Stark sighed.

Claire pulled the vial from its foam wrapping and placed it on the small table in the aircraft. Although they didn't have to join hands for this investigation, Prescott, Travis, and Claire did so for a more powerful amalgamation of their minds. Their three individual minds became one, and they no longer considered each self as "I" but as "we."

We are in the ether of the Mind Realm. Our human senses are limited in understanding everything that there is in this realm. Time is multidimensional, and it can even

225

stop. Space fluctuates among one, two, three, four, or even more dimensions, but we understand only three dimensions at any one time. We are limited. It is difficult to describe this realm, although calling it a hallucination would be just the beginning.

We see snowflake-like shapes of dark light. They are from the Dark Light universe, which is a surprise to us. We surround one flake and examine it. It is a symmetrical hexagon with many shoots of crystals. It has no thickness, and it stays perfectly flat, never bending. We surround another one, and it is identical to the first one. We see fuzzy yellow tendrils interconnecting the center of each flake into a twisted grid whose purpose we don't understand.

Pulses of dark colors race along the fuzzy tendrils, ending in a small burst of dark light when they arrive at the center of a snowflake. A dark aurora-like curtain floats lazily among the convoluted grid of snowflakes and fuzzy tendrils. It seems the aurora is the source of the dark colors racing along the tendrils, and it ripples every time there is contact with the tendrils.

The aurora passes through us, and we feel a surge of electricity discharging into our joined minds. Immediately, many snowflakes surround us, forming a geodesic sphere around our mind essence. We feel trapped. And then suddenly, the geodesic dome explodes outward. We see the flakes expanding fast, slowing down, and eventually coming to a stop. While this expansion is happening, those snowflakes slowly change to white-light color and then they melt into mist. We continue to pass through the dark aurora and other dark-color snowflakes, but they do not encase us again.

We must return.

"That was an experience!" exclaimed Claire.

"What happened?" Dr. Stark asked.

"This vial," Prescott lifted the vial, "contains bad mojo."

"Care to explain?" Dr. Stark asked.

"Even if you analyze the contents of this vial, you'll find nothing but water and cyanide, Dr. Stark," said Claire. "This vial contains dark-mind energy."

"Huh," said Dr. Stark, clearly baffled. "Then bitter almonds have negative energy and sweet almonds have positive energy?" he asked, stroking his chin.

"Dark and white energy," said Travis.

"Mind-boggling," said Dr. Stark. "What do you mean by 'dark energy'?"

"It is not black, if you're wondering," replied Travis. "The closest analogy would be seeing a world lit by dark light, which is visible to us when we do a TAP."

"The devolution agent is pure dark energy," said Prescott. "It is undetectable by scientific instruments."

"But what exactly did you see?" Dr. Stark asked.

"We saw snowflake shapes, which represent the water content," said Claire. "The water molecules are held in a grid by the cyanide molecules, which transmit the dark energy to each snowflake shape, and are charged by the dark aurora of the dark-light universe."

"Say it in English, please," said Dr. Stark.

Prescott and Claire exchanged thoughtful looks. Travis poured Scotch into his glass and relaxed.

Prescott raised the vial again. "This is a solution of water and the cyanide that was originally extracted from the bitter almonds," said Prescott. "It contains dark-mind energy that has the power to change DNA structure, affecting the brain. Originally, we thought that a homeopathic process took place during the propagation of the contamination, but that's not the case. Once released from the vial, the serum molecules' dark-energy vibrations replicate all water molecules in its path. The replication propagates fast initially and continues to replicate at decreased speed, until eventually it dies out. Its lifespan is 24 hours, once released into the air. The water molecules in the human body replicate as well, and the contamination takes effect."

"Based on what you said, I've just reanalyzed the contamination rate by examining visuals obtained from the field at different locations from the original dispersing path," said Maximus. "You are correct. The contamination expands in the first hour over a distance of 475 km. Over the second hour, it expands over 405 km. In the third hour, it decreases to 313 km, and so on, until by the end of the 24 hours, it crawls at 20 meters per hour until it dies down altogether. The conclusion is that the contamination started at a speed of 500 km/h and the speed decreased to zero past the 24th hour. It covered a distance of 2,000 km from the origin in those 24 hours."

"It's like an explosion," said Dr. Stark. "Question is, does the contamination remain after the initial shockwave passes?"

"No," said Claire. "The contamination happens only as the wave of dark-mind energy passes over. We could have landed a minute after the plane crash and not have been infected. That's why Prescott and Travis did not get infected when their astrosuits were compromised. That's why we are not devolving now."

"Jesus," said Dr. Stark. "Maybe I should go to church more often."

"That's right, Dr. Stark," said Travis. "It is not the substance in the serum but the energy it radiates."

"We can infer that the contamination spread radially, even to the west," said Maximus. "Luckily, half of it was over the Atlantic Ocean."

"Exactly," said Prescott. "Although people on ships were affected as well."

"How about airplanes?" Dr. Stark asked. "Submarines?"

"I'm checking to the coast of Brazil," said Maximus. "There are reported cases of ships failing to communicate. I see reports of dozens of airplanes over the east Atlantic that fell off the radar. I'm releasing a bulletin alerting WHO of the infection spreading at sea, over the Atlantic."

Prescott thought for a moment. "Although Confidence was in the blast zone, she was not affected. The walk-in cooler has a metal skin. It acted like a Faraday chamber, and since the cooler was sealed, the dark-mind energy water molecules could not get in, either, to affect the water molecules inside the cooler. In that case, submarines are

229

safe, but airplanes are not, because they have windows and composite, nonmetallic skins."

"The contamination cannot penetrate a sealed Faraday chamber," said Claire. "The chamber has to be both sealed and shrouded by metal skin or wire mesh."

"I think the perpetrators did not know how the agent spreads," said Prescott. "They thought it was spread by the wind, but it's not."

"Lucky for Africa, the plane crashed," said Claire. "If it had traveled south into the middle of the continent, it would have contaminated all the people in Africa."

"The speed of dispersion makes me wonder if the contamination caught up with the plane and the pilots," said Prescott. "But then, the plane's speed was faster."

"I've just checked the plane's travel path, and you are correct, Prescott," said Maximus. "The plane flew due south. It did not hug the coast, and it made a correctional 90-degree turn near Liberia. That's when the contamination wave caught up with the plane and the pilots were infected."

"Wow," said Prescott. "They fell on their own swords."

"And you are correct again, Prescott. The perpetrators did not know how the agent spreads," said Maximus. "Even if the plane had followed the African coast, eventually it would have made a 90 degree turn when passing Liberia into Ivory Coast, entering the Bay of Guinea. The pilots were doomed from the start."

"That solves that mystery," said Travis.

Dr. Stark scratched his forehead. "I accept your theory about how the intense infection took effect. But low infection happens only when people are bitten. Why?"

Claire raised her hands. "I can only speculate that the intensely infected people became infectious through their bodily fluids, but without further studies, we don't know what makes them infectious and for how long they will be infectious—maybe forever."

"In that case, we're back in the real world, and we can stipulate that the low infection is caused by a pathogen or a protein in the saliva," said Dr. Stark.

"I'm communicating that information as well, and hopefully the scientists will be able to isolate the pathogen-protein," said Maximus. "We still have an issue. How can we explain the dark-mind energy to WHO?"

"It is not a physical energy, they won't be able to detect it with any instruments," Claire said. She looked down at the back of her hands and paled. "Oh my God, my scratches are healed."

Chapter 42. Change of Plans

"What?" Travis and Prescott jumped out of their seats. Travis hit his head on the ceiling.

"I'm reacting just the way intense infection cases do," said Claire, pulling the rest of the adhesive bandages off her hands. "Scan me again."

Prescott and Travis grabbed the equipment and scanned Claire, including her head.

"Dr. Stark, let us know ASAP what the scans show," said Prescott.

Claire crawled into a ball in her seat. "The wounds heal only on primary infected people, not secondary."

Prescott and Travis looked at her, unsure of what she was saying.

"Confidence's wounds did not heal," continued Claire. "Dr. Stark, is there any evidence the wounds on any of the secondary infected people healed as fast as the primary ones?"

"I reviewed several pictures from China. No such healing happened," said Dr. Stark.

"I'm inquiring about healing in other WHO centers in the African capitals," said Maximus.

"Are you saying that you've been somehow exposed to the dark-mind energy?" Dr. Stark asked.

"Aside from being scratched by Confidence, Travis and Prescott weren't . . . " Claire didn't finish her thought.

"Travis, we need to scan each other," said Prescott.

Each scanned the other and sent the data to Dr. Stark.

"Where could we have come into contact with the dark-mind energy?" Travis wondered.

"In our TAP examination," answered Claire.

"What are you talking about?" Dr. Stark asked. "You didn't open the vial. Did you?"

"No, I didn't," said Claire. "But we came in contact with its energy when we performed the Trans Axiom Paranormal examination."

"For crying out loud!" said Dr. Stark. "You might be immune."

"Claire, you show no signs of deterioration," said Maximus. "I'm waiting to see the results for Prescott and Travis."

"Interesting," said Claire, looking at her healed hands. "I'm showing symptoms of being intensely infected, but I'm not devolving."

"Prescott and Travis, you're negative as well," said Maximus after a while.

"Guys, do you remember when we were enclosed in the snowflakes sphere?" Claire asked.

"Do you think we may have gained immunity from the devolution agent while in that realm?" Travis wondered.

Prescott pointed to the vial. "I would not open the vial to find out."

"Yeah, let's stay safe and not dare the devil," said Claire.

"But I can find out if I'm immune." Travis cut the back of his forearm. One drop of blood dripped out, but it coagulated right away.

"I might as well take the test, too." Prescott did the same as Travis, and his wound closed quickly, leaving behind just a few smudges of dried blood. Within minutes, the cuts appeared as pink lines.

"I've just downloaded a new flight path to reach Egypt," said Maximus. "You can take off immediately."

Prescott and Travis took their seats in the cockpit and energized the airplane's systems.

"Do you have enough water in the tanks?" Maximus asked.

"Yes, they're full," said Travis. "Why?"

"You will be flying north along the borders of Guinea and Ivory Coast, then along the borders of sub-Saharan countries east to Egypt. You'll be flying at under 100 meters over the desert through a lot of dry air."

"Got you," said Travis. "Where do we land in Egypt?"

"First, you'll stop outside the Siwa Oasis, in an industrial complex."

"Not at an airport?"

"No. The airports are intensely monitored. Besides, you're in a jet hovercraft and can land anywhere you want. Hovercrafts are allowed to fly within a country without being subject to the international air ban. Once you've landed, Nahab, your local contact—compliments of Mossad—has contracted with a company to redraw your tail number to an Egyptian hovercraft, and you'll be able to fly from there to Cairo and anywhere over Cairo, which is the only viable way to go anywhere in that city."

"Roger that," said Travis. "Are we ready, Prescott?"

"Ready," said Prescott while examining the control panel. "You'll need to go down and open the hangar gates."

Travis opened the airplane's hatch, descended, and ran to the wall where the hangar gates' open button was located. He punched the button, and the gates began to retract vertically, in sections. The aircraft systems were operating, causing significant noise and steam. As he ran back to the craft, he could see many pairs of legs under the gate's opening.

"We have spectators, Prescott," he warned. "I'll use a smoke mini-bomb and then get onboard."

Travis stood in front of the craft to give the gate a chance to open higher and then threw outside a mini-canister, the size of a lipstick tube. It skipped on the concrete floor and began spinning, emitting dense smoke while bursting into a deafening ringing. He didn't hang around to see if the people outside had run or come into the hangar. He climbed quickly inside and closed the hatch. He barely had time to take a seat and latch his belt, as Prescott moved the craft forward through the thick smoke created by the mini-bomb.

Prescott was just about to throttle the hover engines to ascend when he heard Maximus shout, "Abort!"

Chapter 43. On to Egypt

"What's going on, Maximus?" Prescott de-throttled the engines.

"You are being detected. Still."

"Do we have an implant in our clothes?" Prescott asked.

"Possibly, or even your PAVs could be giving you away," said Maximus. "There is a lot of confused chatter at WHO regarding your position on the ground."

"Do you think they deciphered our conversations?" Travis asked.

"Not recently, otherwise they wouldn't be so panicked," said Maximus. "Let me propose a new plan. Take off your clothes, including your PAVs and other electronic stuff, leave everything onboard, and exit the plane. I'll place the craft on autopilot to fly to North America to throw them off. You'll have to find another craft at the Robert International Airport to fly to Egypt on the same route I sent you. Is that a plan?"

"Butt naked and running in the jungle with these two guys?" Claire raised her eyebrows. "Eww!"

"It's OK, Claire, I won't look." Prescott pulled his jacket off.

"I will," said a not-bashful Travis.

"I hope you're not disappointed, Travis." Claire removed her clothes. "And remember—look, but don't touch."

"This is our last communication," said Maximus. "You know the protocol to reconnect. I'll give you one minute to clear the craft."

"Roger that." Travis discarded his PAV.

They ran from the plane, looking like three pale ghosts, and entered the SUV parked on the side of the hangar. The hovercraft rose and flew away in a northwesterly direction.

"I'll miss that airplane," Travis said longingly.

"I miss my clothes," said Claire from the backseat, still clutching the vial in her hand. "I remember seeing a department store near the church."

It didn't take long for Travis to drive the SUV to the department store, and they scrambled inside. First, they located flashlights under the counters of the cashiers, which helped them see in the dark.

"We need to stay together," said Prescott. "We are empty-handed."

"Follow me then, and keep watch for assailants." Claire ran up the dead escalator to the women's apparel department. "Men's clothes are on the other side." She wasn't going to be choosy—she searched for dark pants, underwear, a dark long-sleeve top, and a jacket with pockets.

Later, they met at the shoe department, where they selected socks and sneakers.

"How do I look?" Travis asked.

"Like an African," said Prescott. "I wonder if they have an electronics and sporting goods department?"

"This is a mini-mall. They have everything except guns," said Travis.

"We'll check the security room. They may have guns there," said Claire.

One hour later, they had gathered everything they thought they'd need—including two 38 revolvers, one from a dead security guard and the other from a drawer in the store's security office. They were about to exit when they saw a mob hanging around their SUV.

"Do you think this is the same gang that's been pursuing us?" Prescott wondered.

"If it is, they followed our scent," said Claire.

"We can't shoot our way out of this." Travis looked around for safety signs and spotted two red fire extinguishers on a wall. He gave one to Prescott, and together they confronted the pack.

"Pull the pin, aim, and spray from the center out," said Travis.

A few seconds later, a dozen or so black men and women were engulfed in white powder. They were so shocked at what happened that they froze in place. Only their eyelids moved. They didn't look like Africans any more, but more like voodoo creatures.

"Scram!" Travis shouted. The pack didn't need to be told twice, and they ran in whichever direction to get away from another blast of the white fog.

The team got back into the SUV with the fire extinguisher canisters, and Travis drove toward what he hoped was Robert International Airport.

"Prescott, see if the navigation system works in this SUV."

Prescott touched the menu on the navscreen and found the airport, after which he pressed the "Go" button. The navigator's female voice piped, "Make a legal U-turn at your earliest convenience."

Travis cursed and crossed over the boulevard's median, taking the right path to the airport under the gentle guidance of the navigator's voice.

"It's midnight," Claire said from the back seat. It was understood that they needed the stealth of darkness to get to Egypt, and Travis accelerated.

A half-hour later, Travis smashed through the chain-link fence of Robert International Airport and drove onto the tarmac toward the hangars.

"Go where the Liberian Air Force planes are," instructed Prescott.

Travis came to screeching halt among the air force jets. "No Learjet here."

"That's the plane we'll take." Prescott pointed to a slim gray plane with double jets.

"But that's not a hovercraft," objected Claire.

"True, but it's fast," said Prescott. "This is the brass's Learjet." He got out and tinkered with the hatch latch. He opened it, pulling down the stairway. "Let me check the cockpit." Prescott charged inside, followed by Claire, who inspected the gray leather interior with her flashlight. Travis removed the wheel blocks before going onboard.

It was not as plush as the previous craft, but it was acceptable. This was a slimmer hydrojet, with five single chairs on either side of the aisle, designed to transport ten passengers and a crew of two. There was no door separating the cockpit from the cabin.

"How are we looking in there?" Travis asked Prescott.

"This baby is ready to go," said Prescott, flipping switches. "Water tanks are full, everything else is green—let's haul ass out of here."

"We have military rations in the back, if you're hungry," Claire said. "And lots of small bottles of liquor."

Travis joined Prescott in the cockpit. "Did you bring the autopilot information?"

"No, I brought nothing," said Prescott.

"I have the vial." Claire patted a pocket on her jacket.

"I'll use the internal navigator to fly us." Prescott moved the red plastic shield covering a switch and flipped it on. "This is the benefit of flying a military aircraft—you can disengage the transponder with one flick of a switch."

"Tarmac is clear," said Travis. "We'll have to take off the old-fashioned way."

"We'll be airborne quickly. We're light." Prescott fired the engines, which spewed white-yellow flames of hydrogen reacting with oxygen, recombining into superheated steam. "After we're airborne, you'll take the controls, Travis. I need to figure out how we get to Egypt using the navigator on this craft. And keep an eye on the forward-sweeping radar image. Don't run into trees."

The hydrojet accelerated quickly, and halfway down the runway, it left the ground. Prescott leveled the jet at under the 100-meter ceiling, and Travis took over flying to the northeast.

Claire plugged into the plane's comm system and made contact with Maximus.

"Status," said Maximus.

"We're off toward Egypt, flying in a military jet," said Claire.

"Good. Be careful. The auto piloted jet from Monrovia to the US has been shot down over the Atlantic."

Chapter 44. The Smartest and the Dumbest

Claire and Prescott exchanged apprehensive looks.

"It could have been us on that plane," said Travis, concentrating on flying the jet as low as possible over the jungle canopy.

"Was it by chance that the plane was shot down, Maximus?" Claire asked.

"It's suspicious. It happened a few minutes ago over the Atlantic, with only two warnings before a missile destroyed it. Make contact with me before you enter Egyptian airspace."

Claire opened her mouth to say something but saw Prescott giving her the cut-off sign over his throat, and she disconnected the communication.

"Let's keep the communication to a minimum," said Prescott. "I charted a path below the Sahara. It's a more direct route to the Egyptian southern border, between the Nile and Libya."

"Why aren't we taking the prescribed path to get there?" Travis asked.

"That information might be known to 'WHO-mever'," Prescott smirked. He entered additional commands into the navigator. "Besides, we're flying at near the speed of sound and using a lot of water. We need to intake all the water vapor we can before flying over the desert. The auto pilot is on, Travis."

Travis released the control wheel. "Our only worry should be the satellites above."

"We need to stay strapped into our seats. At this low altitude, we'll have a bumpy ride," said Prescott.

"Anyone want coffee?" Claire asked.

Travis and Prescott nodded. Claire returned five minutes later with three mugs and strapped herself into the seat behind Travis.

Travis took a sip of his coffee, in deep thought. "That explains why the Jews are the smartest people on Earth," Travis said.

"Well, that's debatable," Claire said. "You're the historian. What's your point?"

"If the Tree of Knowledge existed and Adam and Eve were real people, then their offspring were the smartest people ever," said Travis. "The Jews claim to be descendants of Adam and Eve, and if they intermarried among themselves, without diluting their genes with those of other people who were not as pure, then the smart genes remained strongest in the Jewish race."

"But they did intermix," said Claire. "Adam and Eve were not the only people on Earth. They were part of a tribe and, as Dr. Klein said, they intermingled. So there may no longer be a pure Adam-Eve superior gene."

"Of course not," admitted Travis. "I have two percent Jewish genes. Most European descendants, like you two, may have some amount of Jewish DNA. But that's not why I mentioned the intelligence factor."

"What is on your mind?" Claire asked.

"Follow my thinking," said Travis. "Adam and Eve were the first ones to be affected by the sweet almonds from the

244

Tree of Knowledge. Their direct descendants would have been the smartest people ever. Everybody else after that inherited a percentage of the smart DNA. So how will the devolution agent affect the people on this planet? Equally or proportionately, based on how much smart DNA each one of us inherited?"

"Are you saying that the smartest people will become the dumbest when infected with the devolution agent?" Claire asked. "And the dumbest not so much?"

"We'll all become equally dumb," said Prescott.

"Not as good as being equally smart," said Travis, who took another sip of his coffee. "If this notion about the almonds and their effect on the human brain is true, it may explain how humanity transitioned from the Neolithic to the agricultural era."

"How?" Prescott asked.

"Adam and Eve and others like them were hunter-gatherers, and then, all of a sudden, man knew how to farm, domesticate animals, invent the written language and mathematics, and even name the zodiac in the sky."

"Well, humanity will survive, albeit in a Neolithic age," said Prescott.

"Very few of us," said Claire. "Back to this equally dumb devolution. The devolved people we encountered in Monrovia, displayed different intelligence. Some ganged together, wielded sticks, and threw rocks. Others were scared out of their wits."

"The smartest ones will be the survivors," said Travis. "As it had always been."

The Devolution of Adam and Eve

Chapter 45. Egypt

Prescott monitored the plane's position. They cut across from Liberia over many countries to Chad and into Sudan, and now they were flying straight toward the Egyptian border. Below was only desert. He made minor adjustments to keep the plane flying along the valley and wadis. The plane used only forward look-down radar to map the ground and prevent collisions with sand dunes. They were passively monitoring any radar signals that could track them. In that part of the world and with the current pandemic in Africa, the military was not concerned with protecting their airspace. That was not the case for US, French, British, German, and even Egyptian AWACS patrolling the south Sahara to prevent any plane from coming north.

"One hour to cross into Egypt," said Prescott.

"So far, so good. We haven't been spotted by anyone," said Travis.

"That's what the craft's monitors say. But who knows if we are being watched silently?" Travis got out of the copilot seat to get more coffee for all of them.

Claire opened comm with Maximus. "We're south of Egypt's border at 20.3362 N and 27.1962 E."

"Good. I'll beam a general broadcast every minute about any plane in your vicinity. And slow down. Contact me after you've crossed the border for a new route. Maximus out."

"I'm not confident that we can avoid the AWACS," Prescott told Claire. "Wow, look at the airborne status at the 29th parallel. It is a wall of AWACS scanning the airspace."

"How far north can we go?" Claire asked.

"I'm surprised that they haven't hailed us yet," said Prescott. "Then again, this is a military plane." Prescott looked and spotted what he was looking for. "Stealth." He flipped that switch. "This will give us additional cover."

They continued flying north and crossed into Egypt.

"Maximus, we're in Egypt," Claire called in.

"Good. Everything is set up for your arrival," said Maximus.

Just as Maximus said that, a voice came on the general comm: "Unidentified plane, position 21.6762 N and 27.0969 E, identify yourself. Turn your transponder on. This is an order."

"Let me take over the flying, and you take care of what else this plane can do," said Travis.

The voice of a man speaking with a French accent gave the order again.

"This AWACS is from Libya," said Prescott.

"Maximus confirms that two other AWACS have pinpointed us," said Claire.

"Chicken-shit stealth," mumbled Prescott. "Maximus, are we in stealth mode?"

Maximum came online. "Negative. It needed a passcode. I just downloaded the code. Activate stealth now."

Prescott pressed the switch again.

"They've lost you," said Maximus. "But they've still dispatched two Egyptian jets to intercept you. Luckily, they knew only your approximate position. Stand by for additional information." He came back onto the comm. "Head due east. Egyptian jets are coming from Mut."

"Just marvelous," said Travis.

"Here is the plan," said Maximus. "When you reach the 22nd parallel, go east toward Abu Simbel City."

"Do you want us to land at the Abu Simbel airport?" Prescott asked.

"Of course not. You're in a Liberian military jet."

"How do we get off the plane in Abu Simbel?" Travis asked. "This airplane has no parachutes onboard."

"No parachutes needed," said Maximus, "You'll land on Lake Nasser, sink the plane, and swim to shore."

"Are you serious?" Claire blurted.

The Devolution of Adam and Eve

Chapter 46. Abu Simbel

"It's the best plan," confirmed Maximus. "There is a nice cove where you can ditch the plane. I included it in the information I just downloaded to your navigator. After you splash down, prepositioned guides will escort you to meet Nahab in Aswan. 'Nahab with a B' is the code. He is a Mossad agent, compliments of Daniela Rock. You won't be able to contact me until after you get in touch with Nahab. If you don't have any more questions, we'll reconnect after you finish your trek."

Claire, Prescott, and Travis were speechless.

"What's with all this James Bond crap?" Travis wondered after a while.

"Why did he say 'trek'?" Prescott asked.

Claire mimicked a flight attendant: "In case of a landing on water, please use the seat cushions as flotation devices."

Travis shook his head. "I think Maximus has lost his chips."

"Aren't you the one who worked professionally as a spook—St. John, Travis St. John?" Prescott asked, lifting an eyebrow.

"Landing on water was not part of my CIA training, where I should have stayed in my cushy job with a pension," smirked Travis. "Do you know how to splash down gently, Prescott?"

"I never landed on water. Even in a simulator," said Prescott. "However, the auto pilot can do."

Claire and Travis began preparing for the unavoidable, while Prescott kept an eye on the autopilot and on potentially hostile aircraft.

There were many AWACS in the sky, and military jets were escorting trespassing airplanes from the south to secret airports in the Sahara. If they did not comply, they were shot down. There must have been several such quarantine airports from east to west in the Sahara Desert.

It was only the jet's stealth and low flying that kept them hidden. So far.

"Less than 20 minutes to splash down," announced Prescott. "Autopilot's on, air speed 160 km/h, altitude 50 meters."

Prescott got out of the pilot's seat and took a seat near the hatch where Travis and Claire were sitting, each holding a cushion from the seats on their laps. Claire offered him a rolled-up towelette.

"You forgot to steam it," said Prescott, unsure of why Claire had given him the towelette.

"Bite on it," Claire said. "It'll save your teeth."

"Thanks, Claire."

"We're over Lake Nasser," said Travis, looking outside through the round window.

"Three minutes," Prescott said, holding tight onto the seat cushion on his lap.

They bent down, in anticipation of the jarring ride once they were on water. CTT's fate was in the "hands" of the autopilot. The plane's engine throttled down to minimum speed before stalling at only one meter above the water.

The plane's belly, tail end first, hit the water with a big splash. The nose stayed up, keeping level and not cartwheeling. It was hard to determine how long they surfed over the water, but they knew it ended when the nose came down into the water with a slight bounce. The plane didn't stop, but the forward momentum continued moving it toward a nearby shore. Outside, the water was splashing over the windshield and on the lower part of the windows.

Prescott spit the towel out of his mouth and straightened up. "Everyone OK?"

"I'm good," said Claire.

"The plane survived." Travis looked outside. "We have a sealed bag containing our stuff for each one of us. Use the jerry-rigged straps to hold the bag against your chest. When we open the hatch, the water will rush in and it may sweep us deeper into the cabin, so you'd better hold tight onto the seats near the hatch. The whole idea is to get out before the plane sinks below the surface. Prescott, position yourself on the other side of the hatch to help me push it open. Claire, stand in front of the hatch, right here."

"Got it," said Prescott.

"As agreed—Claire, you're first, Prescott next, and I'll be last. The plane's hatch will open outward at the top first." Travis gripped the hatch handle. "Ready?"

Since no one objected, he pulled the handle to the open position and pushed the top of the hatch. Prescott pushed and the hatch cracked open, admitting in daylight at the top. They pushed harder until the water began flowing in on both sides of the opening in a continuous stream.

Claire pushed as well and when she judged the opening wide enough, she crawled out. Upon her exit, she pushed the hatch farther down, enlarging the opening. The water came in with all its force. Travis and Prescott were up to their waists in water, holding on to the edge of the doorway.

"Go!" Travis shouted and pushed Prescott out. Travis did not wait and swam out after him, barely managing to get his head out before going underwater.

They gathered closely to assess that everything was well after their disembarkation, and then they swam away from the plane, which began sinking fast. The engines in the rear, being heavier, sunk first and tilted the nose out of the water, but not for long. The rest of the plane sank beneath the surface, leaving behind bubbles of air and a greasy film of lubricants.

There was no need for talk. They swam to the nearest shore, where they arrived ten minutes later. After getting out of the water they climbed up on the coarse sandy incline.

"Do you think anyone spotted us splashing down?" Claire wondered.

They were inside a cove encircled by tall banks. A tributary to the Nile must have carved the cove when occasional rain blessed that land.

"Maximus selected it well," said Travis. "There is no sign of the plane, and there are no souls around other than us."

Prescott squeezed some of the water out of his shirt. The only sound heard was when the water hit the ground. "We were promised help here on the shore."

The sky was cloudless, signaling a hot day.

"Yeah, where are the gorgeous babes bringing us piña coladas and shrimp cocktails?" Travis wondered.

Claire walked toward the top of the bank, and the men followed, occasionally squeezing more water out of their clothes. After they reached the top, they scanned the land around them, which was a flat plateau of never-ending sand dunes.

"*Ahlan wa sahlan.* Hello, *effendis.*" They saw a boy nearby in a lower spot and four camels tied together.

"Who are you?" Claire asked him.

"Alim," said the boy proudly. "My father sent me with the camels to bring two men and one woman to Abu Simbel town, to the south fishing cove. Why are you wet?"

"We were fishing," said Travis.

"It was an accident and our . . . boat sank," said Claire.

"Who's your father?"

The boy gave them a disbelieving look. "My father is Ahmet, and he's a merchant of tourist trinkets—I mean, souvenirs—in the market. Ready to go?" Alim asked with a bright face.

"Ride the camels?" Claire couldn't wrap her mind around the low-tech turn of events.

"How much more James Bond-ish can you get than this?" Travis began laughing and shaking his head.

"You must change clothes. You look strange the way you're dressed, and you're wet." Alim opened the side bags on the camels' saddles and pulled out clothes. "I brought caftans, turbans, and headscarves. And my father said that you should put this on your faces and hands." Alim handed them a jar, which turned up to be a brown make-up paste.

Twenty minutes later, they were dressed in their new garb and their skin was darker. From a kilometer away or in the dark, they could pass for local Egyptians.

There was a reason for the camel ride, as the main highway number 75 was blocked by the Egyptian military. All traffic, although very little in that area, was stopped and the passengers questioned. No one paid attention to four camel riders crossing the desert and coming into Abu Simbel town through side streets. An hour later, they had reached a spot near the lake, where several feluccas were anchored in the small cove.

"This is the end of our trip, effendis. From here on, you'll be taken by someone else," said Alim, bowing. "*Ma'a as salama*, good-bye."

They climbed down from the camels, hoping that they didn't take any unwanted passengers along with them, as in camel fleas. They thanked Alim and sat down at the edge of the lake, wondering what would be next.

"Effendis." An older man dressed in a caftan and turban was bringing to shore a felucca, and he waved to them to get closer.

"That's our ride," Travis snickered.

The man beached the boat sideways and helped them board, after which he pushed the boat away with an oar.

Masterfully, he unrolled the rest of the triangular sail and navigated away.

The man, smiling and bowing, said, "*As salam aleykum.* My name is Ali, and I am here to take you on your special vacation trip to Aswan in my felucca. You will be delighted."

"*Wa aleykum as salam,*" replied Travis. "Ali, are we near the Abu Simbel monuments?" Travis asked.

"Sure, over there." Ali pointed to the left bank.

The two reddish-beige sandstone monuments were just a kilometer away. On the left was the Great Temple, consisting of the four colossal seated statues of Amun, Ra-Horakhty, Ptah, and Ramses. And on the right of it stood the Small Temple of Hathor and Nefertari.

Chapter 47. Aswan

They gawked at and admired the temples and the colossal carvings in sandstone, which, by some miracle, had never been covered completely by sand, demolished by the early Christians, or blown up by later generations of radical Muslims. Luckily, the monuments had been moved to prevent them being inundated by Lake Nasser.

"Travis, I'm surprised that you, the historian, have never come to see these monuments before," said Claire.

"You know—time and money constraints, and security issues." Travis couldn't take his eyes from the temples.

"Aren't you glad that you came to see the monuments on the company's dime?" Prescott said with a straight face.

Claire couldn't stop laughing on hearing that remark.

"There is so much more to see there," said Travis, ignoring Prescott while staring at the monuments. "I'll have to do some serious tourism after this is over. Or before I devolve and forget it all."

Claire looked around at they leisurely sailed along on the lake. "It's going to take us forever to reach Aswan."

And as if to prove her point, Ali rolled down the sail.

"What are you doing, Ali?" Prescott asked.

"Jets. Faster." Ali brought up from the hull storage two water jet systems, which he mounted overboard on either side of the boat. After making sure they were securely attached, he used a remote control and powered up the jets. "Move front, please."

They did as requested to keep the bow from rising too high out of the water, and the felucca/power jet boat picked up considerable speed.

"How long is it going to take to reach Aswan?" Claire shouted to be heard over the jets' noise.

"Five hours." Ali opened one hand, showing his fingers. "*Insha Allah.* God willing."

They were sailing for an hour when Travis remarked, "Maximus has gone to great lengths to segment our trip so that we are not found."

"Our local contacts are compartmentalized," said Prescott. "Now it makes sense why Maximus called this a 'trek'."

"This will be one surprising trek," said Claire. "Guys, keep your guns at the ready."

Travis looked up at the sky. "I wonder if there are drones up there keeping an eye on us?"

"Friendly or foe?" Prescott asked.

Travis shrugged.

As promised, five hours later, the rock-and-dirt Aswan Dam came into sight. Ali cut off the jets, lifted them out of the water, and stowed them away. He then raised the sail and steered toward the western shore. He maneuvered the felucca to a cove, toward no particular landing spot. Travis and Prescott searched the shore for their next contact, but there was no one there. Claire looked at Ali for any clarification, but he gave no sign of knowing about their trip's end. Then she saw over his shoulder a Lake Nasser patrol speedboat approaching them. They were trapped. Ali calmly brought down the sail and waited for the patrol boat.

"Do you think this is part of the plan?" Prescott wondered.

"Even if it's not, act as if you expected this," said Travis.

"What does Egyptian law say about guns?" Claire asked Travis and Prescott.

"Only one thing. Drop them into the lake," said Travis.

As if they were of the same mind, Travis and Prescott pulled their guns out of their pockets and discreetly dropped them overboard, so as not to be seen by the patrols or Ali.

The Lake Nasser patrol boat pulled alongside the felucca, and the captain exchanged greetings with Ali. Besides the captain, there were three other crewmembers on the boat. One of them threw a rope to Ali and pulled the two boats close together.

"Effendis." Ali bowed and smiled at the team. "You need to board their boat."

Claire, Prescott, and Travis knew they had little choice but to comply. Something must have gone wrong somewhere along the way. One by one, they boarded the patrol boat, and each was frisked for weapons. They found a switchblade on Claire, which they confiscated. They were then asked to sit down on the deck.

"*Ma'a as salama*, good-bye," said Ali, waving to them as his felucca sailed away. Only Claire waved back.

The patrol boat turned around, almost on a dime, and sped away around the bend to another cove. It approached the beach there, where a camouflage-painted, tarp-covered truck was waiting for them. On the shore were two soldiers with automatic weapons, looking none too welcoming.

A hoverjet roared above toward an unknown destination. Another larger jet was coming in low from another direction.

"Is there an airport nearby?" Claire wondered.

"Sure, Aswan International Airport," said Prescott.

The patrol boat slid onto the sandy beach. Two soldiers got out of the truck, came to the shore, and pulled them off the boat by their arms, while the two armed soldiers kept their guns pointed at them. Once on dry land, one of the soldiers with a gun motioned for them to move to the truck and then to climb into the back. They did so and sat quietly on a side bench. The soldiers climbed in after them and lowered the tarp over the tail end, obscuring their view to the outside. They took the bench opposite them, and the truck moved on toward an unknown direction.

"Hello, how are you?" Claire attempted to be polite.

The soldiers stared, unblinking, like sphinxes.

Chapter 48. To Cairo

After a while, the truck stopped and backed up against a structure. One of the soldiers opened the tail-end canvas, exposing a loading dock's corrugated roll-up door, which shortly began to creak open. Behind the door stood a tall, bearded Egyptian captain wearing dark sunglasses. He pointed to CTT and motioned for them to come in.

After they were inside, the roll-up door descended and the truck departed.

The bearded man said, "Claire, Travis, Prescott, my name is Nahab."

"Nahab with a *B*," said Travis.

"Nahab with a *B*. I'm impersonating a captain in the Egyptian Special Forces with the same name, who asked me to cover for him while he's indisposed. Time is of the essence." He spoke impeccable English.

"Is there a need to know why the real Captain Nahab is indisposed?" Travis asked.

"No, except we have 24 more hours until he's purified of his latest transgression and comes to his senses."

"Understood," said Travis. "Where are we going?"

"I'll take you by military hoverjet to Cairo." He pointed to a golf cart and motioned for them to get in, and he drove them to the restrooms. "Before we leave this warehouse, you'll need to change into the uniforms of French field officers." He handed them one large duffel bag. "Place your old clothes in the bag. They'll need to be destroyed."

They sorted out the clothes and went inside the restrooms to change. When they came out, they looked the part in their beige fatigues, the tricolor French flag emblem on their shoulders, and each with the rank of lieutenant.

"You are French military officers assigned to assist Egypt in dealing with the pandemic," said Nahab.

"I hope we don't have to speak French," Claire said.

"Insha Allah, God willing. The easiest way to travel by air in Egypt now is to be part of the military, and you don't pass as Egyptians. There are only French military in Egypt now." Nahab drove the golf cart to a gray trap door on a wall, which displayed biochemical hazard signs around it. He opened the door and dumped the duffel bag with their old clothing in it. "It will be incinerated, eliminating any traces of your previous existence. Please put your shades on." He then drove the cart to the other end of the warehouse and exited.

They were at the airport, at dusk. Jet planes landed or took off from time to time. None were tourist planes, only military or special attachments. Nahab drove the golf cart as fast as it could go to a nearby field, where many jet-hovercrafts were parked.

He pointed to one of them. "The craft is ready to go. Get in quickly and take a seat, and we'll depart for Cairo."

A guard waited at the bottom of the short stairs leading to the craft and saluted smartly. They got out of the cart and climbed in quickly. The cockpit door was closed, and they couldn't see the pilots or be seen by them. They strapped in and saw the guard outside driving away in the golf cart. The jet-hovercraft rose up vertically and flew north.

"We're safe for now." Nahab gave each of them a bottle of water. "For now, this is all military, and it is a top-secret mission. Needless to say, the military doesn't know who you are or whom you're working for."

"Can we get communicators?" Travis asked.

Nahab offered each one a pair of military-grade PAVs.

"Maximus, can you read us?" Claire asked.

"I presume you're on your way to Cairo," replied Maximus. "The world is gone mad. Although the pandemic has subsided, those who have the plague are still infectious. Hundreds of millions of people are trying to flee Africa. Air smugglers are making a fortune, but they are also shot on the spot if they're caught.

"TIO is under a lot of pressure in the US to disclose what has happened to you. WHO is behind it, and the FBI is trying to get into the TIO organization, which, as you know, has no headquarters and no employees, and exists only in the cloud. The French government and the Vatican are trying to persuade the US administration to stop investigating TIO."

"You mean the other Trinity Teams have raised the alarm?" Travis asked.

"Yes. Do you need their help?"

"Not right now," said Travis. "What's the issue with WHO? Any possible contamination from us is no longer a problem."

"The powers that be in WHO have given up on you, considering you dead or demented. They eavesdropped on our conversations and know that you discovered a non-biochemical agent as the cause of the pandemic. They don't want the secret to be divulged to the world, that a man-made agent is responsible for hundreds of million of deaths."

"What did the FBI find in Oakland?" Travis asked.

"The FBI has closed the case," said Maximus.

"Why?" Claire demanded.

"They're trying to cover up the man-made agent theory. WHO insists that it was an African pathogen of unknown origin, and they are concentrating on containing it to Africa. I think the FBI was getting too close to the culprits, and someone called back the dogs."

"In that case, there is a powerful force within WHO," said Claire. "But WHO is an international organization, and from what I can discern, it is the American section that may be suspicious."

"Yes, it is," acknowledged Maximus. "They even wanted to arrest me."

"How ridiculous! You're an AI," said Prescott.

"They think there is a real human behind me."

"What about Dr. Stark?" Claire asked.

"There is an international arrest warrant out for him," said Maximus.

"The world has gone mad," said Prescott.

"Or devious," said Travis. "What if they're trying to pin the blame of the agent manufacturing on TIO or on Dr. Stark?"

"That's a remote possibility, but unlikely," said Maximus. "With you out of the picture and me in the cloud, only Dr. Stark is left. They're hunting him. He is in comm blackout and in hiding."

"Will he be safe?" Claire was worried.

"TIO has a process to hide him, or you, in case of trouble. But TIO does not have agents to protect you. We hire contractors when needed—Nahab is an example—but that's about all we can do. We rely on law enforcement for protection, and if they turn on us, we have few alternatives."

"This has never happened before," said Prescott.

"Not to you, but we'll need to revisit and develop new procedures for the future," said Maximus.

"What else?" Travis asked.

"It is imperative that you find Aaron's Rod and destroy it," said Maximus. "There can be no more bitter almonds coming from it."

The Devolution of Adam and Eve

Chapter 49. Helwan-Cairo

Next morning, Nahab met them at the entrance to the safe house where they had stayed for the night.

"Traveling by car is more prudent at this time," said Nahab, seeing their surprise at his car.

He drove them in a large, wide sedan to the gates of the Military Production Medical Center in Helwan, south of Cairo.

Nahab continued to impersonate an Egyptian captain in the Special Forces, while CTT had changed their clothes and were now dressed in the dark gray TIO suits that showed them to be representing a medical team from WHO.

"*SabāH al-xeir,*" Nahab greeted the receptionist in the lobby.

"*SabāH al-nur,*" responded the male receptionist.

"I'm Captain Nahab, and we are here to meet with Dr. Bitar."

The receptionist scanned Nahab's holo ID and then invited each one of them to sign in by being photographed. The CTT's PAVs were capable of creating holograms to display different eyes, therefore changing their identities. Each of them were issued clip-on buttons serving as visitor badges.

Five minutes later, a fashionably dressed woman came to the lobby. "Hello, my name is Dr. Marwah Bitar." She extended her hand to Nahab.

"Hello, I'm Captain Nahab, and with me I have a specialized psychiatric WHO team that has come from America to see Fatta Kazaz and Ahmed Nassief."

The introductions were made: Claire was posing as a Dr. English, Travis was a Dr. Pope, and Prescott was a Dr. Lombardi.

Dr. Bitar took them to a small conference room in the lobby. "Welcome to our medical center. Suddenly, we have many doctors from WHO inquiring about our psychiatric patients," Dr. Bitar said.

"As you know, WHO is a huge organization, and we have different programs and ongoing research," said Claire, as Dr. English. "Do you remember their names? Maybe we've crossed paths with the other doctors."

"Dr. Henderson represented WHO, and Dr. Perkins was with the University of California at Berkemore," answered Dr. Bitar, smiling.

Claire didn't show any reaction when she heard Henderson's name. "No, I don't think I recognize the names. But they may be from different departments." Claire asked Travis and Prescott, "Doctors. Any one you know?"

"No idea, Dr. English," said Travis, as Dr. Pope.

"That's right, these doctors specialized in communicable diseases, which nowadays, with what's going on in the world, is much needed."

"Exactly, Dr. Bitar," said Claire. "Did they meet the patients?"

"No, Dr. Perkins just inquired about them and their status," said Dr. Bitar. "I'm curious about the scope of your visit and why you're interested in these two particular patients."

"Good question," said Prescott, speaking as Dr. Lombardi. "We were referred to these two psychiatric patients by Dr. Hadad. In his opinion, these two patients show the same symptoms as the contaminated patients in Africa."

"Good Allah!" exclaimed Dr. Bitar. "Are they contaminated? No wonder we were asked to isolate them at Benham Hospital!"

"I don't think there is any reason to worry," said Claire. "They've been in the psychiatric ward since 2057, right?"

"That's correct."

"And you scanned their brains recently, I suppose?"

"Yesterday," said Dr. Bitar. "Per Dr. Henderson's request."

"You found massive deterioration of the neurons' dendrites, right?"

"Exactly, very similar to Alzheimer's," said Dr. Bitar, smiling.

"And similar to the victims in Africa," said Claire.

"You've seen the scans from the victims in Africa?" Dr. Bitar asked.

"Yes, WHO has such preliminary scans."

"Time is of the essence, Dr. Bitar," interrupted Prescott, as Dr. Pope. "We would like to see the patients without delay."

"By all means. Captain Nahab, would you mind waiting here in the lobby for us?" asked Dr. Bitar.

Nahab made himself comfortable, in a way relieved that he wouldn't be seeing any screaming people.

"Follow me, please, doctors." Dr. Bitar requested a hospital van, which took them nearby to the Behman Hospital Mental Health complex.

The hospital inside did not resemble the bleak psychiatric wards of the past. It was bright and airy, thanks to the use of plastiglass walls. They walked through several partitioning hallways, all electronically locked, and reached the sector where Fatta Kazaz and Ahmed Nassief were kept.

"Here they are," said Dr. Bitar.

Both of the patients were dressed in white T-shirts and pants. They were in separate but adjacent cells that had once been painted white but were grayish now. The front wall was clear plastiglass with a pull-on drape on the outside for when the patient was to be visually isolated. As the sons of generals, they appeared well-provided for. Yet there was no rehabilitation that could ever make them well. "Each of them displays the behavior and judgment of a three-year-old, although they are adults. They are able to recognize some of the staff attending them, and they even sometimes respond by name. Their vocal communication consists of guttural sounds or shrieks. And they laugh, too, when they're happy. Keeping them dressed is difficult, as they often rip their clothes off their bodies."

"That's typical behavior," commented Claire.

"What would you like to do? Would you like to sit and observe them? We can get you some chairs." She called a couple of orderlies to assist them.

"We will need to assess each one individually, Dr. Bitar," said Claire.

"You mean, go inside with them, Dr. English?" Dr. Bitar was concerned and so were the two orderlies. "No, no—they can become violent."

"That's a risk we'll have to take," said Travis. "Just let the three of us in, and we'll take any responsibility in case of problems."

Dr. Bitar looked unsure about what these three strangers were asking her to do. Contact with demented people, who could snap at any moment and injure the personnel, was allowed only if the patients were restrained.

"We'll have to mildly tranquilize them, one at a time, and place them in restraints," she said.

Claire, Travis, and Prescott communicated with each other through their PAVs using voice-sound cancellation; they needed the patients awake, without any trace of tranquilizers. They wanted to penetrate the patients' minds to explore the memories associated with Aaron's Rod and the almonds. The whole process would be almost instantaneous to outside observers, but once in the mind of a mentally deranged patient, they could spend as much time as needed to find the information they were seeking.

"Dr. Bitar, the assessment we need to make needs to be performed while the patient is in his natural state," said Claire. "We must determine if these two patients are the earliest victims of what has infected Africa."

Dr. Bitar gasped. The two orderlies, large men, took an instinctive step back. It was one thing dealing with crazy people, but another handling crazy, infectious people.

"What exactly are you going to do, Dr. English?" Dr. Bitar asked.

Chapter 50. Fatta Kazaz

"Observe and assess them up close," said Claire.

Dr. Bitar exchanged glances with the orderlies, who shrugged. "Who do you want to see first?"

"Fatta Kazaz is right here. Let's analyze him first," said Prescott.

"Orderly, please let them in."

One of the orderlies pressed a button on a device on his upper sleeve, and the cell's transparent door slid open. Travis, Claire, and Prescott entered the cell, and the door slid closed behind them.

Fatta Kazaz was in another world and not interested in what was happening outside the glass wall or around him. He was in a squatting position, looking down at the floor. Travis, Claire, and Prescott encircled him and squatted down, while joining hands. They melded their minds, becoming "we," and transported into the mind of Fatta Kazaz . . .

We see his immediate mind as a nebula of images, sounds, and, to a lesser degree, sensory perceptions sometimes mixed together into cohesive stories, but others are just random, reflecting the current status of his impaired brain. Fatta's self-identity is illogical, reacting only to basic needs, and we don't sense a dangerous, defending self, as would be the case in a sane mind's person.

We must travel along the mind link to the mind realm, where all his past memories are stored. The path is intact and memories are free to travel between the memory realm and Fatta's mind. In an instant, we arrive in his memory realm. Stored forever, his memories begin even before he was born and continue to the present moment. There is an immense longitudinal universe of holograms depicting everything he has experienced in chronological order, and we proceed along the tunnel of memories, reviewing what's important to our case, starting in 2030.

We are attracted by the first memory relevant to our search, all seen through the eyes of a young Fatta:

A man in an Egyptian military uniform, a general, unwraps a long bronze box from a bundle of cloth. Engraved winged cherubim adorn each long side of this metal box, which is about 10cm wide by 10cm high, and over a meter long. A second uniformed man, a general as well, bends over the box holding a magnifying glass, and after a careful examination, he forces open the lid with a knife.

Inside there is a wooden rod, lying in the box at a diagonal to accommodate its length. He removes it from the box and examines it with the magnifying glass. He gives the rod to his partner, while he collapses, dejected, on a sofa. The other general taps the floor with it, shrugs, and places it on the coffee table.

The two men begin arguing and gesturing toward the bronze box and the rod. They stop, but begin arguing again, pointing fingers at each other in accusatory fashion. In the end, the man with the knife and magnifying glass grabs the bronze box and storms out of the room.

The other man sits in an armchair, unhappy with what has happened. Out of his breast pocket he pulls an old scroll. He unrolls it and examines it. Then he folds it and places it in a thick book on a bookshelf among many other leather-bound books. He picks up the rod from the coffee table and places it inside an umbrella holder that's in the shape of an elephant's foot.

We move on, advancing in time, searching for any other memories related to the rod. Occasionally, we get a glance of the elephant umbrella holder during meetings or tea parties in that room. The rod is left undisturbed among the umbrellas and walking canes. Many years pass until we see an elderly woman, helped by a grown-up Fatta, bringing into the room a potted plant and placing it on the windowsill. Fatta uses the rod as a stake to support the plant in the pot, as the woman advises him.

A few days later, we see two other women discussing the plant in the windowsill. The wood stake, the rod, has sprouted leaves, dwarfing the original potted plant, which has wilted. One of the women has a clipper and is about to cut the new sprouted plant, when Fatta holds back her hand. The new plant is left alone.

Not long after, a man in his thirties and Fatta stare at the young almond tree. The man is Ahmed Nassief. He admires the small tree, fingers the fruits, smells them, and takes pictures of the three puny almonds. They spend much time together, searching the World-Net and old thick books, talking and planning something. After a few more meetings, Ahmed removes the three almonds from the tree, which have turned dark purple by then, and places them in a self-sealing plastic bag.

On another day, a woman takes Fatta into the room to show him the almond tree, now shriveled and dead. Fatta pulls the tree out of the pot. It comes out clean, without roots, resembling the old rod that had been planted in the pot originally. He then places the rod back into the elephant-foot umbrella holder.

Fatta is discussing a transaction with Ahmed as they sit in an open-air cafe in Cairo. Ahmed is writing and rewriting figures on a piece of paper, as if trying to get Fatta to agree to a price, which in the end he does. Then Ahmed pulls one almond from the sealed plastic bag, kisses it, and gives it to Fatta. He keeps the others, and Fatta rolls his almond into a napkin and pockets it.

They part company, only to meet again in a hotel room later that same day. Ahmed places a briefcase on the bed and opens it. Inside, wrapped in plastic, are two rolls of gold coins. Ahmed opens the mini-bar and pours drinks, happy about their new fortune.

Next day, Fatta is called to a hospital, where he finds Ahmed sedated and strapped into a restraining vest. The room is full of relatives crying about Ahmed's fate. Fatta is cornered; they ask him about the gold they've found on Ahmed, but he keeps playing ignorant. Ahmed is wheeled away. Fatta returns to see Ahmed again the next day in the psychiatric ward, perhaps at Behman Hospital.

Fatta sits in the same room where the rod sprouted. He has the rod on his knees, and he's staring at it. He stands up and looks apprehensively at the bookshelf. He pulls out

278

one book at a time and shakes it, after which he discards the book onto the floor. It doesn't take long until the old scroll that the general had stashed away falls out of one book. He examines the scroll, which is a map showing three pyramids and a route through many passages, surrounded by hieroglyphs and deity symbols.

It is at night when Fatta, with a long narrow bag over his shoulder, comes down Fahmi Ali Street and climbs over the east wall, entering the grounds of the Great Pyramids. He moves stealthily to avoid attention from the guards in the nearby compound, and he climbs the hill near the pyramid workers' cemetery, heading along the funeral causeway toward Menkaure's Pyramid. At the Mortuary Temple, he takes a left and walks to the first Queen Pyramid, the eastern one. He finds the entrance to the queen's mortuary chamber, turns his headlamp on, and goes inside to the first antechamber and then into the room that holds the queen's granite sarcophagus. He runs his hand along one of the corners of the granite box, and then he pushes the box with ease to the wall. The sarcophagus's bottom and the side touching the wall open up into a stairway that leads underground.

The Devolution of Adam and Eve

Chapter 51. The Ark of the Covenant

Fatta descends the stone stairs through a passage that is tall enough to accommodate his frame. Occasionally, his headlight shows unadorned walls, just like inside the pyramids, cut smoothly into the limestone. At landings on the staircase, other passages lead elsewhere into the underground complex. At the bottom, the stairs end at the edge of a deep rectangular well. It seems to be the end, as no other passage continues from there. Fatta peers down into the well, and the headlight can barely make out the bottom. He consults the map and then walks sideways along the right-hand wall on a ledge that didn't seem to be there before. When he reaches the end, he turns into a hidden niche and finds himself inside another passage.

He walks through a tall corridor and wide enough to accommodate two people abreast. The corridor is part of a maze with many corridors branching left and right. Eventually, it dead-ends against a limestone wall. Fatta consults the map and walks right through the solid wall, as if it were a hologram. He is inside another chamber from where he goes down a flight of stairs, deeper underground. It ends in a rectangular vaulted-ceiling room, with connecting corridors at the left and right. He walks to the opposite limestone wall instead, consults the map, and places both of his palms on the wall.

It opens up, as if it were a parting curtain, into a narrow, truncated A-shaped hallway, similar to the Khufu Grand Gallery. From the landing spot, Fatta's headlamp cannot detect the bottom or the end of this gallery-corridor. A path of square stepping-stones, as if on dark water, lead toward the unseen end of the gallery. The stepping-stones are the tops of square granite columns rising from deep underground. He walks on them carefully, not to fall between them, and arrives at a chamber, containing a labyrinth path, quadratic in shape. The labyrinth's narrow paths are separated by deep chasms. The ceiling is made of a similar labyrinth, and although he looks up, the headlamp's light cannot penetrate to the top between the paths or to the bottom chasms below. In the center, where the square labyrinth ends, stands a pedestal representing a Nile boat made of red granite. Mounted on the boat is . . .

The Ark of the Covenant

We are astounded to see this religious and historical artifact. It is as described in the Bible. It is a rectangular wooden chest, one and a half meters long, and less than a meter tall and deep. The wooden chest is gilded with intricate gold designs. On the lid are two gold cherubim presiding over the chest, with their wings touching at the tips. Each cherub is about 60 cm long. A soft blue, mysterious light comes from a crystal on the ceiling above the Ark.

Fatta examines the map again, reading the instructions on it, and then walks on the labyrinth's narrow path, back and forth, nearing the Ark. After he arrives in front of the Ark, he bows and prays. Reading from the map, he then places a hand on each cherub wing and opens the lid by sliding the two halves laterally. A blue hue glows intensely

282

inside the chest. Fatta's headlamp sheds additional light into the chest, which is lined in a velvety blue cloth. Inside, he sees two black-granite inscribed tablets lying at the bottom—the Ten Commandments, facing up in all their glory.

On top of the stone tablets lies a rectangular bronze box with cherubim engraved on all sides, similar to the box that contained Aaron's Rod. There are several small sealed pottery or alabaster jars, probably containing incense, and another ceramic pot lying on its side with its lid nearby. Manna is scattered out of it, like grain.

Fatta raises his hands to his face and prays, as a Muslim would, after which he runs his hands over his face. He reaches inside and opens the lid on the bronze box. He then removes the tubular bag from his back and takes out Aaron's Rod. Inside the box lies another wooden rod. Holding it with both hands, Fatta places, with much reverence, Aaron's Rod inside the bronze box, along with the other rod. He raises his hands to his face and prays again. He scrutinizes the map one last time and then drops it into the chest. Carefully, he closes the lid on the bronze box, and then he closes the chest's lid. He steps back and looks at the Ark of the Covenant. He prays again and bows.

He takes the opposite, the return path on the labyrinth. As he walks the labyrinth path rises up, taking him higher and higher, giving him the impression that the Ark is sinking. The upper labyrinth rises as well. When he reaches the end of the rising labyrinth, the identical labyrinth above becomes a low ceiling, and a new corridor opens up, which takes him to the exit through a crack in a wall in the middle of the pyramids of the queens of the Great Pyramid of Khufu.

By the time he is back in the library room, it is dawn. He rests on the sofa, exhausted from his exploration. He then reaches into his pocket and pulls out the napkin containing the last almond. He shouts with surprise, stands up, and walks aimlessly around the room. He drops the almond into a brass ashtray, douses it with whiskey from a bottle hidden behind some books, and sets it on fire. At first, the flames shrivel the husk of the almond and then, with a pop, the almond shell cracks open and burns to ashes.

Fatta keeps staring at the smoldering ashes. The room seems to warp and rotate. Patches of color and dark shadows are the new reality of what Fatta sees. He starts screaming, as a horrible noise begins grinding inside his head.

We must return.

Chapter 52. Ahmed Nassief

Claire, Travis, and Prescott came back to reality. It took them a few seconds to accept what they had experienced. However, digesting the information would have to wait until later. The most important piece of the puzzle, the identity of the buyers of the two almonds, is locked in Ahmed Nassief's memory. Fatta Kazaz had told them all he could before he became demented.

"Amazing," whispered Claire. Fatta looked at her with sexual interest.

Travis looked over his shoulder and saw Dr. Bitar and the two orderlies staring at them. Although it took an instant for the three of them to witness Fatta's memory, the position they assumed while doing so—holding hands—must have seemed strange to them.

"Therefore, the patient's mental ability is as deficient as in those patients from Africa. Don't you concur, Drs. English and Lombardi?" Travis said in a loud voice, trying to give the impression of conducting a real psychiatric assessment.

"Screw it—let's not waste time. Let's see Ahmed Nassief," whispered Claire. Then more loudly: "Dr. Bitar, would you please let us out?"

"Sure, but has your assessment even begun, Dr. English?"

"No, not conclusively. That's why we need to see the other patient, to compare."

Dr. Bitar moved her head as if she were receiving a call in the aural device behind her ear, and she began talking.

Prescott walked to the glass wall and motioned to the orderly to let them out. The orderly pressed a button and the door slid open. They walked out, while Fatta tried to follow Claire. The orderly pushed him back in and closed the door. Prescott used his audio translator and said to the orderly, "Please open Ahmed Nassief's door."

The orderly looked at Dr. Bitar for approval, but she was deep in the telephone conversation. The orderly couldn't wait, so he nodded at Prescott and pressed the opening button. The door slid open, and Ahmed Nassief ran forward, as if to escape.

"Grab him, Travis—I mean, Dr. Pope," Prescott said.

Travis was on him. He grabbed Ahmed's wrist and pushed him back inside. Ahmed was agitated and raised his hand, trying to grab Travis's face. The orderly blew his whistle to call reinforcements and, for good measure, closed the door, entrapping CTT and Ahmed inside.

"No time to waste," whispered Travis. "Join hands."

They let go of Ahmed and held hands as they melded their minds, becoming "we" and transporting into the mind of Ahmed Nassief. It was a turbulent mind, as his actions attested. However, there was no information to be gathered in his present mind, only in his stored memories, which they soon accessed . . .

We enter the memory when Fatta is showing Ahmed the almond tree. Ahmed is puzzled over the small tree. He examines the almonds, even smells them, and takes several pictures of them. At home, Ahmed begins searching on the World-Net about almonds. He has several hologram

286

displays open with information about Adam and Eve. Some of the information is in Arabic, but much more is in English. He zooms in on *Aaron's Rod*. He contacts Fatta and discusses what he's discovered. The two get together and begin reading the old books in Fatta's library. The more they search, the more they are convinced that they have discovered a relic that has come back to life. There is money to be made from it. Both of them become very excited, and Ahmed collects the almonds and places them in a plastic bag.

We follow Ahmed's memories as he enters the shop of an antiques dealer and shows him the almonds. The merchant remembers the bronze box he sold many years before and the buyer. While waiting, the dealer contacts that buyer, who is interested in buying the almonds. It takes several days of haggling over the price, both in person with the merchant and by audio link. Ahmed agrees with Fatta at the café on the final price at which to sell the almonds to the interested buyer, but only two almonds, and he gives Fatta one almond back for safekeeping after kissing it.

Ahmed visits the dealer's shop, where he meets a blue-eyed, Eastern European-looking man, with a beard and mustache and salt-and-pepper hair. It is Alexei Perchenko, who offers a briefcase containing three rolls of gold coins. Ahmed gives him the two almonds, the antiques dealer takes one roll of coins for his commission, and Ahmed walks out with the briefcase containing the other two rolls of gold coins, which later he shares with Fatta in a hotel room. Ahmed and Fatta celebrate, drinking from the mini-bar.

Ahmed returns home and his world collapses in hallucinations and chaos.

We returned to reality.

Ahmed was agitated. Travis grabbed Ahmed by the wrists, preventing him from hitting Prescott.

"Orderly, please bring in the tranquilizer. This patient is becoming violent!" shouted Claire.

Travis and Prescott wrestled Ahmed to the floor and subdued him.

Dr. Bitar stopped talking on her comm. Her eyes were wide with unease. "Orderly, do not open the door."

The orderly, who was just about to push the open button, stared in confusion at her.

"Security, this is an alert! We have intruders in the Behman psychiatric ward!" Dr. Bitar shouted into her comm.

The orderly responsible for opening the door pushed another button. Red lights began flashing and doors slammed.

It was a lockdown.

Chapter 53. The Escape

"Dr. Bitar, what's the meaning of this?" Claire shouted. "I demand you open the door at once and tranquilize this patient!"

"All in due time, Dr. English, if that's even your real name," said Dr. Bitar, who was visibly pissed off.

Travis spoke into his PAV without being heard by anyone else but his teammates, "We've been discovered. Time to get out of here before security arrives."

Claire contacted Nahab. "We've been discovered and are locked in a psychiatric cell. Meet us at Behman's exit for an escape."

With all the commotion and alarms, Ahmed became even more agitated. Prescott flipped open a tube, which he had retrieved out of his sleeve, and had Ahmed smell its contents sedating him.

"Dr. Bitar, we are on your side. Please open the door this instant," said Travis.

Dr. Bitar folded her arms in defiance. "Tell that to the guards."

The time for reasoning had passed. Travis pulled out of his pocket a thick pen-like device, which he twisted, revealing a greasy pointer. He inscribed a generous oval onto the plastiglass wall. "I suggest you all stand back," he ordered, and he pushed a button on the resonator in his pocket, which acted as a detonator. The inscribed line on the plastiglass wall dissolved, and Travis kicked out the circumscribed oval, creating an opening in the wall. Travis threw out through the opening a small canister, the size of a lipstick, that was a smoke and noise bomb, which started smoking and ringing at 100 decibels, deafening everyone around.

The orderly and Dr. Bitar ran toward the exit and began pounding on the door for someone to let them out. The smoke diffused rapidly, filling the hallway and blinding the monitoring cameras. The central air system sucked some of the smoke out, polluting the entire facility. The outside guards couldn't see or hear Dr. Bitar, but when they saw dark smoke coming through the vents, they feared a fire, activated the fire alarm, and ran out, leaving everyone behind.

Unlike the others around them, Capuchin Trinity Team had PAVs with microwave-radar capability that gave them the ability to see through the dark smoke. They walked out of the psychiatric ward and into the hospital proper after Travis cut several openings in the partitioning plastiglass walls. Warning sirens, fire alarms, and flashing lights added to the chaos on the scene. Employees were running for the exits through the haze created by Travis's smoke bomb. Without attracting attention—no more than they had already caused—they exited through to the lobby, another area in chaos, and boarded the car Nahab was waiting in. Nahab immediately drove them away at a normal speed to avoid detection from the air.

But it was too late. A military hovercraft was flying above them and, over loudspeakers, ordered them to stop. Nahab did not stop; he accelerated once they were on Omar Ibn Abd Aziz Boulevard, cutting across the three-way roundabout over the grassy area, and plunged into the

Nile. The car floated at first, and inside the cabin, tube-bags expanded from the floor, and began filling with water, decreasing the buoyancy of the submerging car, which sank to the bottom of the Nile. It was quick, and they felt a small bump when they hit the Nile's muddy bottom. The water was murky green, allowing little visibility.

"I thought a submersible vehicle might come in handy," said Nahab. He adjusted the buoyancy of the vehicle and navigated it as a submarine, following an orange beacon on the dashboard.

"Now I see why this sedan was so wide. It's a submersible," Prescott chuckled.

"Where to?" Travis asked.

"Near here, at Paradise Hall of Military Production. They have a secret underwater outlet to the Nile and we will get back on dry land from there."

As promised, Nahab drove the craft through an underwater tunnel and emerged into a large garage that housed amphibious military vehicles. He touched some icons on the dashboard and changed the craft's exterior color to drab green, and then, using other icons on the dashboard, he applied an Egyptian Army General insignia to the outside doors. They drove out of the complex with a full military salute at the central gate, while water was still dripping from under the car. Police hovercraft were circling furiously over the spot where their vehicle had sunk into the Nile, searching for them.

"Nahab, you devil, you're full of tricks," said Claire, impressed by his actions.

"Part of the travel package," said Nahab, smiling at her. "Have you obtained what you were looking for?"

"Yes," said Prescott. "We know who we're dealing with now. We must return to the US."

Chapter 54. To Alexandria

Nahab drove into a multistory public lot, changed the outer color of the vehicle to brown, and parked in a far away corner.

"That's your vehicle." Nahab pointed to a beige car parked nearby. "It's been nice doing business with you." They shook hands, exited Nahab's vehicle, and got into their new getaway car.

Travis sat in the driver's seat and Prescott rode shotgun, guarding against trouble. Claire, in the back seat, opened comm with Maximus.

Maximus appeared in their PAVs. "Everyone's safe, I see."

"Only after a smoky escape from Behman Hospital," said Claire.

"Fortunately, you were not identified by GeneID at the Military Medical Center, or at the Behman Hospital of Mental Health," said Maximus. "Only your pictures were taken, and your PAVs reimaged your eyes. For right now, your identity is a mystery, unless they use GeneID sniffers to recognize you."

"I selected the smoke bomb to release trace amounts of phosphorus pentachloride to contaminate the premises and to destroy our biological traces in Behman," said Travis.

"Excellent," Maximus said. "I need to get you out of Egypt ASAP. Don't use the self-driver or navigator in your car. Follow the navigator in your PAVs and drive manually. You'll need to go to Alexandria."

"What's going on?" Claire asked.

"The whole world is in quarantine now, and I had to devise a torturous path to smuggle you into the US," said Maximus. "At Alexandria Port, you must go to the cargo area. In the glove compartment, you'll find a pass card to let you into the Port. Go and park the car in shipping container area G, container number RUSU 342981 0. In case they follow the car, it will end up in Sevastopol. For your info, that's why there are documents in the glove compartment with your pictures taken in the lobby of Military Medical Center. When the car is discovered, it will confuse your pursuers.

"After you park the car in the container, leave the port through the east gate and there will be two tuk-tuks waiting for you. They'll take you to Al Mina'ash Sharqiyah port, Alexandria East Port, across the peninsula to the Egyptian Yacht Club. Your names are Adam, Eva, and Seth—you men decide who's who. You'll embark on *Yolanda*, a private turbojet hydrofoil yacht, which will take you to Malta. Depending on the evolving situation, I'll let you know what your next travel plan will be."

"Can't you fly us out of here?" Prescott asked.

"Airports and air traffic are closely monitored."

"Did you hear from Dr. Stark?" Claire asked.

"Unfortunately, he was arrested by the FBI." That news stunned them. "I lost track of his whereabouts when they transferred him to Lawrence Livermore National Laboratories."

"What the hell!" Prescott exclaimed. "Livermore is part government and part University of California . . . "

"Berkemore," added Claire. "Maximus, you'll see the connection when we bring you up to date."

"Then you don't know where Dr. Stark is?" Travis asked.

"He's off the GeneID radar," said Maximus. "He might be at Livermore or elsewhere."

"What was he apprehended for?" Travis asked.

"Danger to national security," said Maximus. "He's not allowed a lawyer or to communicate externally."

"A danger to national security," repeated Travis. "He was involved in this mess only by remote communication. He was not a participant. What did we do for him to be taken into custody?"

"It is what you figured out about the devolution agent. Luckily, you are considered AWOL or dead. He and I are the only ones who know the causes of the pandemic. They cannot get me, but they've got Dr. Stark."

"He is going to blow their minds when he tells them what we've discovered," Travis chuckled.

"Or that knowledge may keep him from talking," said Maximus. "They likely suspect he has more information. Or they may even keep him safe."

"Keep him safe from whom?" Travis asked.

"From who developed the devolution agent. My speculation," said Maximus.

"Then the US government is involved," Prescott said. The three exchanged concerned glances in their PAVs.

"It's unknown at this time to what extent," said Maximus. "Or why. But they provided you with quick transportation to Monrovia, although the motive might have been the pandemic."

"Why would the government try to sell the devolution agent to Derek Dodd?" Travis wondered. "And who stole it back from him?"

"And who in the government authorized exterminating half of Africa?" Claire asked.

"Good questions, and you'll find the answers. I'm confident of that."

"Then what about us? Are we in danger?" Claire asked.

"Yes, immediately from the Egyptian authorities. Overall, considering what the situation is currently, it's yes again, although your names are specified as missing or dead, not wanted. I'm trying to keep it that way."

"This is bullshit!" exploded Claire. "Maximus, we are a paranormal investigative team, not field operatives. The six-month training we received when we formed this team is hardly enough to protect us from the dangers ahead." Claire was fuming.

"I apologize," said Maximus. "The magnitude of this pandemic, now knowing that it is man-made, was unforeseen. I will do my best to keep you safe until this is over and to return you safely to the US from Egypt."

"Thanks, Maximus," said Prescott. "We need to look on the bright side—we're alive and well. And soon, we'll be out of Africa. Unofficially, of course."

"Well, Claire, for what it's worth, this is not that bad," said Travis.

"Not bad! Weren't you the one having palpitations about parachuting from the jet?"

"I might have overreacted," said Travis. "But let me clarify. I was a field operative with the CIA and received one year's training with military Special Forces. On every mission I was assigned as an agent, the danger was imminent. I could have been blown up in many situations. Now, however, I don't feel the same level of apprehension I felt when I was a 'secret-agent man.' Maybe it's because I'm with you two in our Capuchin Trinity Team, or maybe because we have gadgets that help us get out of danger. Look how easily we got out of Behman without blowing up the building or shooting anyone."

"I agree with Travis," said Prescott. "Exploring other realms is exhilarating, but I don't feel in peril during our missions, although this is the worst one."

Claire calmed down. "Thanks, guys."

The Devolution of Adam and Eve

Chapter 55. The Suspects

"Were you successful with Fatta's and Ahmed's mind investigations?" Maximus asked after a few moments.

"Incredible what we found out," said Prescott. "We have definite suspects, like Dr. Henderson, who I wouldn't be surprised is the Nellie Henderson with WHO, and Dr. Perkins, with the University of California at Berkemore. Proximity to the Oakland connection comes into the picture again."

"I'm checking," said Maximus. "I'm finding a Dr. Matt Perkins, professor of sociology and human studies at UC Berkemore. Dr. Nellie Henderson is also a professor of molecular biology at UC Berkemore, besides her post with WHO. Now that we're dealing with the University of California at Berkemore, further inquiries show a Dr. Audrey Sontor as a dean of biological sciences at UC Berkemore, and a Dr. Sean Cohen, professor of political science and department chair at UC Berkemore. These two could be the Audrey and Sean with the A&E Historical Society."

"Scholars from Berkemore and the devolution agent?" Claire wondered.

"But we don't know if Henderson and Perkins are with the A&E Society," said Prescott.

"That's correct," agreed Maximus. "Here are the pictures of the four esteemed professors, if that would help." The pictures of two women and two men appeared in their PAVs. "You've seen Henderson, so she's not a surprise."

"Perkins!" shouted Prescott.

"That's right, Perkins," agreed Claire.

"What's the matter?" Maximus asked.

"Bring up the picture of Alexei Perchenko," said Claire.

A picture of a mature Eastern European man with blue eyes, salt-and-pepper hair, and a beard, and a picture of a younger man with brown hair, blue eyes, and a beard, appeared side by side.

"Analysis shows a 70% resemblance between the two," said Maximus.

"Are these two related?" Prescott wondered.

"Yes, they are," said Maximus with AI research speediness. "I found information that Alexei Perchenko is the biological father of Matt Perkins."

"Where was Perkins born?" Claire asked.

"He was born in 2022 in the city of Berkemore, California. His mother is Dr. Cecilia Perkins, professor of chemistry at UC Berkemore. Marital status of mother: unspecified."

"Maximus, find out if Alexei Perchenko owned a bronze box, 10 by 10 centimeters, and over a meter long, with cherubim engravings on both sides of the box," said Travis, who was driving the car on Route 75 to Alexandria, doing his best to avoid collisions with other cars that had no respect for the demarcation lanes. Even self-driven cars seemed to ignore traffic laws in Egypt.

"I'm scanning the police file on Perchenko's death investigation," said Maximus. "There isn't any such specific item listed, although . . . I detected a similar box resting on a shelf from a picture taken in a room of his house. Here is the magnification of it." A grainy, zoomed image of a long bronze box appeared in their PAVs.

"That's the box," said Prescott.

"Yes, it is," agreed Claire. "This box contained Aaron's Rod. General Nassief sold the box on the black market as the only object of value worth selling. At the time, the generals didn't know that the wooden stick was Aaron's Rod."

"Add Alexei Perchenko as another suspect, although he's presumably dead," said Prescott. "I wish we could find his body."

The Devolution of Adam and Eve

Chapter 56. The Rod's Fate

"Bring me up to speed on what you found out from Fatta Kazaz and Ahmed Nassief," Maximus said.

"Here is the short story," said Claire. "The generals Nassief and Kazaz found an ancient map that guided them through a maze under the Great Pyramids to the Ark of the Covenant. That was in 2030. When they found it, they opened the lid and inside they saw the Ten Commandments tablets, several ceramic pots, and two bronze boxes like the one on Perchenko's shelf. Based on the position of a larger pot left inside the Ark of the Covenant, we believe the generals opened it, thinking it contained gold. But instead they found inside manna seeds, which resembled worthless, desiccated grains, and they left the pot in the Ark. We think that's how manna spread throughout the world, after they carried out the spores on their clothes.

"The only thing they took out was one of the bronze boxes. Over at the Kazaz house, General Nassief opened the bronze box just to find a wooden stick inside. They didn't know what that stick was, and General Nassief sold the box to an antiques dealer, who sold it to Perchenko, we presume. General Kazaz placed the rod in an umbrella holder and hid the map to the Ark in one of the books in his library.

"Years later, Fatta used Aaron's Rod as a stick to support a plant. The plant died, but the stick sprouted. It was Aaron's Rod, after all. The new tree bore three almonds, the bitter ones. Fatta called Ahmed to show him the new tree, and the two of them figured out that they were in possession of Aaron's Rod, the Tree of Knowledge. Ahmed took the initiative to sell the almonds and relied on the old antiques dealer to find a buyer, the same buyer, Alexei Perchenko, who bought the bronze box. But, Ahmed sold only two of the almonds and gave the third back to Fatta for safekeeping.

"They didn't have time to enjoy their gold. Ahmed kissed one of the almonds and was contaminated by it. He lost his mind soon after. Fatta, seeing what had happened to Ahmed, decided to take Aaron's Rod back to the Ark. He followed the map on the old scroll his father had used to access the Ark originally and found the Ark of the Covenant under the Great Pyramids. He placed the rod back in the Ark and left. At home, he found the last bitter almond wrapped in a napkin in his pocket. He burned it and was infected by it, and he lost his mind as well."

"'Incredible' would be an understatement," Maximus said. "Then there are no other almonds."

"No, they're all gone," said Claire.

"The Ark of the Covenant exists, and it is buried under the pyramids, and it contains Aaron's Rod, which could sprout again," said Maximus.

"If someone were able to find it," said Claire.

"Well, you witnessed the route there," said Maximus.

"Yes, and we remember the map, but that wouldn't be enough. The map was also a key to access the Ark. One could not find the entrance or exit, or one could dig forever under the pyramids and not find the Ark of the Covenant."

"The underground tunnels must exist, and someone one day will find it," said Maximus.

"The maze under the Great Pyramids that contains the Ark of the Covenant is in another realm, another dimension. It can be accessed only with a key. Fatta had the key, which was in the form of a map, but he left it in the Ark. Unless there is another key, the Ark of the Covenant, and Aaron's Rod are out of reach."

"The Tree of Knowledge is inaccessible. That is good news," said Maximus. "Now we have to rescue Dr. Stark and find the culprits' laboratory."

The Devolution of Adam and Eve

Chapter 57. Recap

"We are at the port," announced Travis.

"In that case, I'll leave you, and good luck." Maximus signed off.

Prescott gave the pass-ID to Travis as they approached the gate. Using the voice translator, Travis presented the pass and entered the port area. The signs were in Arabic and English, and it was easy to find container area G, even without the guidance in their PAVs.

Prescott spotted container RUSU 342981 0 and they drove there.

"Prescott and Claire, wait outside until I park the car," said Travis. He drove the car inside the shipping container and discharged a small amount of phosphorus pentachloride to cover their bio-signatures. After he exited the container, Prescott and Claire closed the doors and latched it.

They walked to the east gate and left the port area without incident. As promised, two tuk-tuks were waiting nearby. The drivers had been smoking and talking while waiting for their passengers. An audio message must have been sent to them, and they drove the tuk-tuks to the curb to pick up Prescott and Claire, while Travis got inside the second one. No words were exchanged and ten minutes later, maneuvering through the traffic gridlock, they arrived at the Egyptian Yacht Club.

Inside the lobby, a red-bearded man with a captain's cap approached them. "Hello, I'm Captain Bernardo. You must be Adam, Eva, and Seth."

"Yeah, hello, I'm Seth," said Travis. "We're ready to go." Travis didn't bother to introduce his companions.

"Follow me, please," Captain Bernardo said in a Spanish accent.

They arrived at the dock where the yacht *Yolanda* was waiting. She was a thing of beauty: low and slim, sleek and aerodynamic, looking like a fast, white rocket, even when moored. It was powered by one turbojet at the aft, and the hydrofoils were raised.

Onboard, Captain Bernardo introduced his first mate, Adolfo, an Italian-looking young man. Without delay, they unmoored and navigated out of the marina. The interior of the yacht had one open cabin with ample windows on all sides. The captain sat in an elevated seat at the bow, navigating the boat. Claire and Travis sat down on the comfortable, white vinyl sofas, while Prescott was up front, looking out with much interest.

Once the boat cleared the breakwaters, the captain engaged the turbojet and the yacht accelerated, rising from the water on its hydrofoils.

"How fast will you be going?" Prescott asked Captain Bernardo.

"After we get out of Egypt's territorial waters, we'll cruise at 200 km/h," said Captain Bernardo.

"Can the hydrofoils take that kind of speed?" Prescott wondered.

"They can take up to 100 km/h. After that, we will rise out of the water and surf on the center ski only."

Travis came forward. "When do we arrive in Malta?"

"We will be near Malta in 10 hours," said Captain Bernardo. "At that point, you'll take the inflatable and navigate to Malta."

Travis and Prescott looked at each other, surprised.

"Why aren't you taking us into the harbor?" Travis asked.

"My orders are to launch you in the inflatable near Malta." Captain Bernardo shrugged.

"Thanks," said Prescott and, together with Travis, returned to see Claire chatting with Adolfo. Apparently, Adolfo had served her a cappuccino.

"I would like a cappuccino, too." Travis sat next to Claire.

"And I'll have an espresso," said Prescott.

Adolfo nodded and went down into the galley.

"Adolfo was telling me that they are from Barcelona, and that's where they're returning," said Claire. "They were chartered to take us from Alexandria to Barcelona." Claire raised her eyebrows.

"The captain said we will take an inflatable to Malta when we are near the island," said Travis.

"You mean to say that we will pilot ourselves to Malta?"

"That's the plan. We'll find out later what's the next step," said Travis.

"Maximus is being careful to prevent our discovery," said Prescott. "*Grazie*, Adolfo." Prescott thanked the first mate, taking the espresso cup from the tray.

"Anything else?" Adolfo asked.

"Thank you," said Travis, dismissing him. "We are definitely on an adventure here, and it is up to us to make it back to the US."

"That's an understatement," said Claire. "However, I agree with you. It is up to us to survive this and bring this mess to justice."

"Now you're talking like a trooper." Prescott raised his cup to her.

"We are out of Egyptian waters, and we'll now go full speed," announced the captain.

"I suggest we cloak," said Travis. "Cloaking" meant that their PAV devices would silence their voices and camouflage their mouths to prevent anyone around them from hearing or seeing that they were conversing among themselves.

"Let's sort this mess out," said Prescott, after taking the last sip from his cup. "Mossad finds out that Derek Dodd is about to sell a powerful biochemical agent on the black market, and they're afraid that radical Islamists may get it and use it against Israel. But Derek Dodd is killed, and only we can talk to him in the afterlife, where we find out to whom he sold the agent. Derek Dodd bought the agent from Alexei Perchenko, a Russian oligarch, but did not deliver it to Mohammad Abadi al Medina in Riyadh, because Dodd was ambushed and killed by two women by the side of a highway in Mexico."

"Now we know that Alexei Perchenko is the biological father of Matt Perkins," added Claire. "And there are two women killers, and another blonde woman who wore a necklace with the A&E monogram when she delivered the devolution agent to the pilots."

Prescott nodded. "The pandemic started in Africa 24 hours before the worldwide alert was issued. WHO assessed that it was a pathogen originating in Africa. We deduced that the pathogen had been dispersed from a plane, and we found the plane, which crashed in Monrovia. Pretending to help WHO with ground investigating work, we were flown to Monrovia by US Air Force and parachuted into the airport. Our intent was to talk to the dead pilots, and we did find out what happened. We discovered that the so-called pathogen is a devolution agent, which was dispersed by a plane flying along Africa's west coast before it crashed in Monrovia. We found an intact 10cc vial containing the agent, which acts as an energy field, cloning water molecules in its path, and continues the contamination up to 24 hours from the origin, or 2,000 km. The contamination ceases shortly after the energy wave passes over."

"On the other hand, WHO does not want to extract us from Africa, fearing contamination from an undetectable pathogen," said Travis. "It's worth noting that we know the cause of the pandemic and the secret of the devolution agent."

"Maximus suspects that WHO might be eavesdropping on our private conversations and that it might even be tracking our movements," continued Prescott. "We got rid of the nanobot bugs to avoid detection."

"Also, we learned that the devolution agent was made from bitter almonds from the Tree of Knowledge that sprouted from Aaron's Rod, which was retrieved from the Ark of the Covenant," said Travis.

"We do the TAP on the vial of devolution serum and find that it's made from dark-mind energy, undetectable by modern science instruments," said Prescott. "We fly to Egypt to enter the minds of Fatta and Ahmed, who are demented, and discovered what happened and who bought the bitter almonds. Luckily, Fatta placed Aaron's Rod back in the Ark, and the world is safe for now.

"We know of several suspects: Nellie Henderson, Audrey Sontor, Alexei Perchenko—who is dead—his son Matt Perkins, Matt's mother Dr. Cecilia Perkins, and Sean Cohen, all at UC Berkemore, and they are with the A&E Historical Society. We are smuggled out of Egypt, and Dr. Stark is arrested by the FBI and detained at Livermore Labs."

"Don't forget the three unknown women," said Travis.

"And we are dead or AWOL," said Claire. "Time for questions and answers."

Chapter 58. Questions and Answers

"Why are we involved in this in the first place?" Prescott asked.

"We were hired by Mossad to find out the buyer of a biochemical nerve agent," replied Claire. "Which we did."

"Why did we end up in Africa and what was our task?"

"We suspected that Africa was infected by a biochemical agent stolen from Derek Dodd and dispersed by a plane that crashed in Monrovia. Maximus offered our help to WHO, and the US Air Force delivered us to Monrovia. We worked for WHO by doing fieldwork analyzing the epidemic damage. And we worked for Mossad, and presumably the US government, to find out who was behind the pandemic."

"What did we find out?"

"We discovered that Africa was poisoned by a devolution agent, dispersed by a plane that belonged to O&C Private Jet Co., and Don O'Halloran was its CEO, who committed suicide afterward. OTTM Chemical Corporation chartered the flight, but it does not exist as a business."

"The devolution agent propagates, initially, at a speed of 500 km/h, covering 2,000 Km over 24 hours, and it is undetectable by scientific instruments," added Travis. "Also, it contaminated the pilots, and it propagates by cloning the water molecules in its path. Since it is an energy vector, the only way to survive the agent is by being protected inside a sealed Faraday cage, like Confidence was in the walk-in cooler."

"This raises another question," said Prescott. "How come we were not contaminated when we found the vial with the devolution serum?"

"In solution, the serum is inert," proposed Claire. "Maybe it's only when it is diffused that it clones other water molecules, activating the dark-mind energy?"

"Does Nellie Henderson and her associates know this? Do the villains know this fact, I wonder?" said Travis. "WHO is insistent that it is a pathogen of African origin. If they knew that the agent becomes harmless soon after the initial dispersion occurs, they would have evacuated us. Or maybe not."

"Something to keep in mind," said Prescott. "Why do they want to get rid of us?"

"When they realized what we discovered, we became a danger," said Claire. "Keeping us on the ground in the contaminated area was a short-term solution, until they could do away with us. Eventually."

"Is Dr. Warner part of the A&E?" Travis asked. "Because if he's not, we made a mistake by not divulging to him and others what we discovered."

"I agree with that." Claire tapped on a device on her wrist. "Maximus, can you hear us?"

"Yes, Claire."

"Why didn't you inform the entire WHO about the truth of the devolution agent?" Claire asked.

"The US government requested we not disclose it."

"Why?"

"For one, to prevent worldwide panic. Second, I don't think they know who made the devolution agent."

Claire, Prescott, and Travis took a moment to absorb this information.

"Then we're not sure to what degree the US government is involved?" Travis asked. "Why is it trying to kill us?"

"The US government is not involved in manufacturing the agent," answered Maximus. "However, just as Dr. Henderson is part of WHO and is one of the suspects, someone else in the government may play a dual role as well. On your second question about killing you, you're referring to the plane that was shot down over the Atlantic. The plane was getting out of the quarantine zone, and it was hailed. There was no response, and a military drone shot it down. Then again, since the suspects tracked you through the transponders in your clothes or gadgets, they knew you were onboard that plane. Through their power, WHO or Nellie Henderson made sure that the plane would not survive. Your trail went cold after the plane was shot down, with the exception of the people on the ground contaminated by the nanobots. I suspect that may be a subject of confusion among the suspects."

"Were we tracked when we went to Egypt?" Travis asked.

"No more than any other rogue plane trying to escape the infected area," said Maximus. "However, I planned your return to the US as if you were sought after."

"Henderson and Sontor with A&E are suspicious now of the identity of the two men and a woman who contacted Fatta Kazaz and Ahmed Nassief," said Prescott.

"Most likely that's the case, however, they cannot identify you based on the information provided by the Military Medical Center."

"At least that much is good news," said Claire.

"Let's continue. Why do they need more almonds?" Prescott asked.

"Maybe one almond can make only so much serum," speculated Claire. "Actually, it should be that way. It would be impossible to synthesize dark-mind energy from scratch with current scientific knowledge. New almonds might be needed for new batches of devolution serum."

"That could mean they want to make more serum to destroy humanity," said Travis.

Claire stood up and pointed outside. "What's that?"

Travis and Prescott stood up and saw a jet-hovercraft approach their yacht from the starboard side.

"That would be the US Air Force jet coming for you," said Maximus.

"What?" Claire shouted. "Did you turn us in?"

Chapter 59. The DIA

"The short answer is yes, and it was necessary," said Maximus. "Your expertise is needed in the US sooner than I can smuggle you back."

"Why didn't you tell us sooner?" Travis demanded.

"The decision was made while we were conversing," said Maximus. "I'm an AI, and I can make decisions and take actions faster than it took me to say this. You'll get an explanation soon."

"People, your names wouldn't happen to be Claire German, Prescott Alighieri, and Travis St. John, would they?" Captain Bernard asked. "A US Air Force hover-jet is inquiring."

Claire, Travis, and Prescott looked at each other with concern. Was Maximus selling them out, or was this for their own good? Either way, there was no escape.

"Never mind," said Captain Bernard. "They are ordering us to stop and be searched."

The yacht's speed decreased, and the hull settled into the water. The hover-jet came down to the window level, and they could see the pilot assessing them.

Travis walked over to the captain. "What do they want?"

"Apparently, you. I hope not me and my boat," said Captain Bernard in a heavier accent, revealing how nervous he was.

"That jet is not big enough for passengers." Travis watched as the hover-jet slowly circled the yacht.

"They just informed me that there is a transport hovercraft a few minutes behind," said Captain Bernard. "Hey, I have nothing to do with you. I was hired to transport you to Malta. OK."

"Well, hey, this is the risk you have to take when you smuggle people." Travis walked back to his teammates. "There will be a transporter coming soon."

A large US Air Force transport craft descended and hovered two meters above the yacht's aft deck, synchronizing with the yacht's movements on the water. A hatch opened and the stairway extended, sloping down to the yacht's deck. Two airmen came out and descended to the deck where Captain Bernard was waiting. They saluted and, without responding to the captain's questions, came inside the yacht. It was apparent the airmen knew the identity of CTT.

"Claire German, Prescott Alighieri, and Travis St. John, please follow us to the transporter," one of the airmen said.

Travis, Claire, and Prescott followed the first airman, with the second one following behind them. Inside the hovercraft, they were offered earphones.

They heard in their earphones, "Ms. Claire German and Messrs. Travis St. John and Prescott Alighieri, welcome onboard. My name is Colonel Karen F. Willey, and I will meet you shortly on the USAS *Alaska*."

Prescott turned to his mates in surprise. "We're being taken to an US Air Force Service Aircraft Carrier Platform? An ACP?"

The transport craft ascended quickly to 12,000 meters to a gray spot in the sky. The USAS *Alaska* was an Aircraft Carrier Platform, an ACP. It was similar in its scope and mission to the old US Navy aircraft carriers, except it was a humongous flying wing airplane, housing over one hundred fighter jets and other hovercraft. The flying wing spanned 350 meters, similar in size to a naval aircraft carrier, but it didn't have a launching deck as the naval carriers did. The planes were released from its belly and took flight immediately. This enormous carrier was powered by eight hydro-turbojets, using water from the air vapor as its fuel, and it never landed, staying airborne for years. It could fly as fast as 1,000 km/h, if needed, and was able to reach trouble spots all over the globe in mere hours. Just as the old aircraft carriers were floating airbases, so the Aircraft Carrier Platforms were airbases in the sky, accessed only by aircraft.

"I've never been on one of these," said Prescott excitedly. "The US Air Force has six of them. This must be the European/North African air platform."

The transport hovercraft caught up with the carrier and approached it from behind, aiming for bay 6 on the right wing, as indicated by a large, pulsing number 6 sign. When it was within 300 meters from the carrier's bay, the magneto-grabber latched onto the transporter and pulled it inside the bay for a safe docking. Clanking noises could be heard as the craft was latched down. Large doors opened ahead, and the transporter was pulled inside a hangar. The doors closed behind them, and an access ramp resembling a large ribbed tube attached and gripped the side of the transporter where the hatch was located.

"Please follow me," said an airman opening the hatch.

They did as instructed and, at the end of the tubular gangway, a door slid sideways, air hissing as the pressures equalized, admitting them inside the pressurized section of the carrier. The airman saluted a colonel ahead of them and stepped aside, standing at attention.

"Welcome aboard the USAS *Alaska*. I'm Colonel Karen Willey." The officer extended her hand. She was tall, with sandy hair held in a bun underneath a blue cap. She wore a dark blue jump suit, with her name and rank on the breast pocket flaps. Her uniform was different from the gray uniforms of the other airmen around. "Please take a seat." She pointed to a four-seat cart.

The vehicle was self-driven and took them through several gray corridors, which held conduits, pipes, and other raceways attached to ceilings and walls. Other vehicles speeded in the corridors, some carrying ordnance, others just personnel. Airmen were walking on sidewalks or gangways, like any other people going about their business in a city—a flying city, that is. They passed through a clear sliding door into an atrium of sorts. After they stepped out on the platform, they were taken through a maze of plusher corridors to a conference room with large, rounded corners, panoramic windows overlooking a magnificent view of blue sky and white clouds below. Judging by their direction of motion, they were at the edge somewhere along the wing.

"Please have a seat. Before we begin, can I get you any refreshments?" she asked cordially.

They shook their heads and sat down around the table, wide-eyed and mesmerized by the view outside.

"I finally get to meet one of those mysterious Trinity Teams," she said. "And by the way, you are not under arrest. You are our guests."

"Sure." Claire turned the comm on. "Maximus, can you hear us?"

"Very well. You are in good company with Col. Karen Willey."

"Why are we here, Colonel?" Travis asked bluntly.

She looked at the three of them. "We are experiencing extraordinary times, and your help is much needed."

"What section of the US military are you with?" Travis asked.

"I am a colonel in the Defense Intelligence Agency, the DIA."

Chapter 60. The Devolution of Adam and Eve

"The DIA?" Travis raised an eyebrow. "Since when is the DIA involved with health matters? Is the pandemic a military matter now?"

"It is a global and national matter," she said. "There are more agencies than DIA that are involved in this, the FBI, WHO, CDC, NIH being just a few of them. We were assigned to be the liaison with other US intelligence agencies regarding this pandemic." She pointed to the circular hologram display floating over the conference table. "Besides us, there are other concerned people watching our meeting."

Their eyes scanned the hologram, and then Maximus showed his presence in the hologram.

"Is this pandemic your doing?" Prescott asked Col. Willey.

"Of course not. We are trying to figure out who, or what organization, is behind all this. Maximus informed us of the situation, gave us the names of the suspects, and an account of your accomplishments. Arresting the suspects would be easy. But the issue remaining is the devolution agent—who possesses it, how much of it, and where the lab is."

"Then you don't believe what WHO is saying about the African origin pandemic," said Claire.

"The pathogen that infected in Africa is for the world population's consumption. We know otherwise. To our embarrassment, Mossad was the first to detect a potent biochemical nerve agent being peddled on the black market. We've been involved since we delivered you to Monrovia, under the pretext of helping WHO."

"I think there is more than what you're telling us," said Travis, narrowing his eyes.

Colonel Willey smiled thinly. "Sure. Let me bring you up to speed. Some crazed mind from the University of California at Berkemore, with connections to the DOD, thought of developing a chemical weapon that would render enemy troops mindless—not kill them but cause them amnesia. Then the oblivious troops would be taken prisoner and retrained to fight for us."

"That guy was definitely a crazed mind," said Travis. "Is he still around?"

"Yes. His name is Brian Burk, a former associate professor of bioengineering at UC Berkemore. And he ended up being the first victim of this chemical agent." said Col. Willey. "As you may know, the Lawrence Livermore National Laboratory is one of the labs where we develop new weapons. In many cases, the scientists there are also science professors at universities such as UC Berkemore."

"When did this all happen?" Claire asked.

"The amnesia agent was first proposed in 2035. Why?"

"They didn't have the bitter almonds at that time," said Claire.

"I'm not sure if it was a full-fledged devolution agent or a proto-devolution agent variety. Professor Brian Burk and his team were able to cause complete amnesia in mice, after which the mice were retrained to do new things. The experiment continued with chimps, and it had impressive

324

results. But the program was shut down and the chemicals destroyed after Brian Burk and his team started losing their minds in 2041."

"The current devolution agent does not affect animals," said Claire. "It must have been something different."

"Perhaps," said Col. Willey.

"Are these people alive today?" Prescott asked.

"Yes, in mental institutions. They couldn't be trained to become functional humans again, as had been hoped."

"A proto-devolution agent even back then, without bitter almonds," said Claire.

"However, Aaron's Rod had been in the Egyptian generals' possession since 2030," said Maximus.

"We found no evidence that Aaron's Rod sprouted before 2057," said Travis.

"But Alexei Perchenko bought the bronze box in 2031," said Prescott.

"I wonder if they were able to extract the dark-matter energy's essence from the box itself," said Claire.

"The rod was in that box for thousands of years," said Travis. "Some miasma of the dark-mind energy might have resided in the box."

"Maybe not strong enough to develop a full-fledged devolution agent," said Claire. "It acted slowly on the researchers over a period of years."

"We better quarantine the box," said Travis, standing up and then leaning over the table on his knuckles, facing the colonel. "You need to inform the Russians to quarantine that bronze box."

"What bronze box?"

"I found a picture of a box on a shelf in Alexei Perchenko's house resembling the bronze box containing Aaron's Rod." Maximus displayed its image.

"I'll make the request," said Col. Willey, and she began tapping keys on a device on her sleeve.

"You said the chemicals developed by Burk were destroyed—where, how?" Claire asked.

"The chemicals were undetectable, as you discovered in Africa," said Col. Willey. "Only the effects pointed to its existence. The department responsible for the program incinerated the lab at Livermore and sealed the area. There were no other cases of mind loss after that, and we presumed the agent ceased to exist—until the infection cases in Afghanistan, Congo, and Brazil in 2061. Nothing like that happened in China. It was a mystery how these remote areas manifested symptoms similar to those of the Livermore experiment lab some twenty years earlier. Although we were not entirely sure if the same agent was responsible, someone infected those areas with a similar agent."

"Any traces of cyanide in the 2035 experiments?" Claire asked.

"No record of any cyanide was reported in the 2035 experiment. Since no one searched for it, that's not to say it was absent," said Col. Willey. "Now we realize that the three infection cases were field trials of the devolution agent. It was not until after Mossad informed us of a biochemical agent being peddled on the black market by Derek Dodd, then your involvement, the pandemic in Africa, and finally your discoveries on the ground in

Monrovia that we could say for sure they were all related to the 2035 experiment. Maximus gave us the names of the suspects you exposed. We are monitoring them intently."

"Monitoring them?" Travis asked incredulously. "Why not arrest and interrogate them?"

"For the same reason the FBI closed the case investigating the O&C Private Jet Co. and OTTM Chemical Corp. that charted the flight to Riyadh," said Col. Willey.

"What's the reason?" Travis asked, subconsciously knowing that it couldn't be good.

"We were notified by a A&E Historical Society that there are caches of the *Devolution of Adam and Eve* agent in populated areas all over the world, ready to be activated if we investigated further or made any arrests."

The Devolution of Adam and Eve

328

Chapter 61. Dr. Stark

"And you believed them?" Travis asked.

"Look at Africa."

"The bastards are bold," said Travis. "I hope you continue investigating them."

"There's a massive investigation, by all agencies, to determine who these people are," said Col. Willey. "We stopped the FBI from investigating them directly to gain some time."

"If they carry out the threat, it would be mass murder," said Claire, clasping her hand over her mouth.

Travis smirked. "They even have a name for it, the Devolution of Adam and Eve."

"The threat should be taken seriously," said Prescott, running his fingers through his hair. "One 10cc vial would decimate the greater Los Angeles area, or New York, in less than an hour."

"Do they have enough agent to carry out their threat?" Col. Willey asked.

"They may not," said Maximus. "Mossad heard rumors that there is a buyer on the black market wanting to buy the third almond and Aaron's Rod, presumably to produce more devolution serum."

"The last almond was destroyed," said Travis. "And Aaron's Rod is out of reach."

"Are you sure?" Col. Willey asked.

"Yes, according to Fatta Kazaz's memories," said Travis.

"This is a good thing, if they don't have enough serum," said Prescott. "There are no other almonds."

"What if we presume wrong and they don't need more almonds to produce additional quantities?" Travis proposed.

"What are you thinking?" Claire asked.

"Maybe they don't want anyone else to make the devolution agent or to develop an antidote," said Travis. "I think they have all the serum they need."

"But the briefcase was the only container that was transacted . . . " Claire's words trailed off, and she shook her head. "Or maybe not—maybe they didn't sell all their inventory in that transaction."

"True," agreed Travis. "They took the case back. What if they didn't use all 100 of the 10cc vials in Africa's infection? Who's to say that all the vials in the spraying unit contained serum? Some may have been filled with plain water."

"Why? To pace Chuck List as he inserted the vials into the spraying unit?" said Claire.

"If they have all the serum they need, the threat is legit then," said Col. Willey.

"Very much so." Travis walked toward one of the windows to think, while looking at the view.

"Where is Dr. Stark?" Claire asked.

"Right here on the *Alaska*," said Col. Willey.

"Really!" said Claire, surprised. "But why here?"

"It is a safe place."

"Safe from whom?" Prescott asked.

"A&E Historical Society."

"Can we see him?" Claire asked.

"He'll join us shortly."

"Wait, we were told that he was arrested," said Travis. "Even you, Maximus, were sought after."

"That was a decoy," said Col. Willey. "We, the US government, are suspicious of everyone, you included. But WHO was sure you either had become wild or had died on the airplane that was shot down flying from Monrovia."

"Does Dr. Henderson know that she is a suspect?" Travis asked.

"Dr. Henderson is our agent," Col. Willey said with a hint of a smile.

"No sh—I mean, cool," said Travis. "You have a foot in the A&E Society."

"Unfortunately, no. We didn't even know of the A&E Society until Maximus alerted us to it."

"When was Dr. Henderson activated?" Prescott asked.

"In 2061. After the three world infections, we became suspicious that others at UC Berkemore knew the formula for the mind-loss agent. Dr. Nellie Henderson was our agent working for WHO and became a visiting professor at the University of California at Berkemore. She knows all the suspects you mentioned, and she is the one who alerted us to the danger Dr. Stark might face."

"Did I hear my name mentioned?"

"Dr. Stark!" Claire stepped toward him and embraced him. "I'm glad you're safe."

Dr. Stark's pale face turned a slight shade of pink. "Maybe I should be detained more often."

"Don't worry, I won't hug you." Travis chuckled, leaning against the window and folding his arms.

"Good to see you," Prescott said with a smile.

"Well, girl and boys, the situation is dire," said Dr. Stark. "A&E Society knows about some of the discoveries you made on the ground, but not all. Since you were far away and I was in the US, I was the obvious choice to be abducted and interrogated about what I knew. The FBI arrested me and saved me from them."

"What don't they know?" Travis asked.

"They don't know why they can't identify any trace of the agent, which they created, and what causes the propagation speed. They don't know how to properly protect themselves. They were surprised about the secondary infection aspect."

Claire, Prescott, and Travis looked at each other and nodded.

"You're saying they don't have full knowledge of what they created," said Claire.

"Besides Brian Burk and his team, other scientists working with the current devolution agent might have lost their minds," said Dr. Stark. "I have a suspicion that, after the accidents, they developed the serum using androids and remote controls."

"That's right. This serum, once allowed to dissipate, will kill its maker, even if he or she is in a protective suit," said Claire.

Chapter 62. Heartbeats

"I bet they are baffled as to why we survived for so long in Monrovia, when their scientists developing the devolution serum might have lost their minds when they were making it, even if they were better protected than we were," said Prescott.

"They've grabbed the devil by the tail and don't know how to tame it," Travis snorted.

"Do you know how to tame it?" Col. Willey asked.

"We might," said Claire.

"Good, because we have a dilemma and need all the help we can get." Col. Willey checked the device on her sleeve. "But first, the Russians acted swiftly and are transmitting to us video of what they are doing with the bronze box. They are as scared as we are about the devolution agent."

"Then you don't suspect that this was the doing of a foreign power, especially Russia," said Travis.

"We suspect everyone, especially the Russians, since Alexei Perchenko was involved in this. Here are the images from Russia." Col. Willey displayed a video hologram over the conference table of people in HAZMAT suits removing the bronze box from a shelf, placing it in a metal container, and hauling it away.

"Wait," said Travis. "Go back to where the box was visible, magnify it, and pause." The images reversed and stopped, showing a magnified, elongated bronze box. "That's not the box."

"You're right," said Prescott. "That's a replica."

"How do you know? You haven't seen the box before," said Col. Willey.

"Of course, we have," said Claire. "We saw it through the eyes of Fatta. I concur with my teammates. That is a replica."

"How can you tell?"

"This box has been cast in bronze. The original was hammered to give it shape and details."

"We can assume that A&E Society has the box now," said Col. Willey.

"We'll have to get our hands on that box, as well," said Travis.

Col. Willey nodded and made a quick note on her sleeve device. "Back to the A&E Society. With the exception of Audrey Sontor and Sean Cohen, we don't know who else is part of the Society, although it is obvious that all the other suspects are working for the Society in some manner. We didn't want to expose Dr. Henderson by having her inquire about the A&E Historical Society among her colleagues."

"Did they offer any proof of the devolution agent being planted throughout the world?" Prescott asked.

"No. Maximus told us that you could detect the agent's presence."

Travis and Prescott looked at Claire, who glanced down at one of her inner pockets.

"Only when we are close to it," said Claire, shaking her head.

"Even if we find them, then what?" Prescott asked.

"The vial has to be broken to release the agent, right?" Col. Willey asked.

"Most likely, unless it has a mini-sprayer to release the agent," said Prescott. "Are you thinking to disarm the trigger mechanism? What if they're alerted in case any of the vials are tampered with?"

Col. Willey rubbed the bridge of her nose. "We can work these details out as we face them."

"As far as releasing the agent," said Travis, "how would they trigger the release? Is someone holding a hot glove and if in danger, he would release it?"

"They told us that if any of their members' hearts stopped, the devolution agent would be released," said Col. Willey.

"Ingenious," commented Prescott.

"This sounds complicated," said Travis.

"Do you think they're bluffing?" Col. Willey asked.

"It is actually simple to set up such a triggering mechanism," said Prescott.

"Travis has a point," said Dr. Stark. "The heartbeat signal could be lost, without anyone's heartbeat stopping, and that could trigger dispersal. Not to mention that the geographical distances could complicate matters. And how many people's hearts are monitored? What happens if only one of their members dies? It's messy and unreliable."

"I'm still of the opinion that it can be done by monitoring their vital signs," said Prescott. "They must have an intelligent triggering mechanism, an AI."

Dr. Stark's eyebrows went up.

"If you are correct, then we cannot touch any of these people, whoever they are," said Col. Willey. "At least not immediately."

Mit Sandru

Chapter 63. The Colony

"Then this is the calm before the storm. What would they be doing in the meantime, hiding and saving themselves, or buying time? And for what reason?" Travis wondered.

"If they have enough serum, what would prevent them from destroying the human race right now?" Claire asked.

"Time, or better said, a lack of time, as Travis suggested," said Prescott.

"Or a lack of answers," said Claire. "Maybe they don't know where to hide if the agent is released in the quantities necessary to destroy all humanity."

"It's hard to believe that they really want to end humanity as we know it," said Col. Willey.

"That's why they call themselves the Adam & Eve Historical Society," said Travis. "Back to the good old days of Eden."

Silence settled over the meeting as their thoughts raced. Planet Earth's humans reduced to an ape-like intelligence—most of them would die due to starvation and diseases. Perhaps a million of them might survive worldwide, if they were close to a reliable source of food.

"What else is the investigation finding?" Travis asked Col. Willey.

"We're collaborating with the intelligence agencies of all major countries. Discreetly, so as not to alert A&E Society and make their fingers twitch," she said.

"Only the intelligence agencies?" Travis asked.

"We don't know if they have collaborators in the governments."

"What if our intelligence agency is behind this? Or others in other countries?" Travis pressed.

"Do you see a purpose in spooks exterminating the world's population?" Col. Willey asked.

"They're underpaid?" Travis shrugged. "Did you develop a list of possible suspects?"

"Besides Sean Cohen, Audrey Sontor, Matt Perkins, and his mother Cecilia Perkins, we compiled a list of over 100,000 suspects who are directly or indirectly connected to these four. Incredibly, most are academics. Intelligentsia."

"Is Fred Warner on that list?" Travis asked.

"Yes."

"Can you identify the environmentalists?" Travis asked.

"Why the environmentalists?" Claire wondered.

"What is destroying the environment? Overpopulation."

Claire twisted her neck as if to relieve stress.

Col. Willey pressed a few buttons on her sleeve gadget, and a list of 10,023 people scrolled on the hologram display above the table. "We also have a list of political malcontents. Seeing that Africa was infected, we suspected white supremacists as the possible culprits. Unfortunately, there are only 54 declared white supremacists or fascists among the 100,000 names. On the other hand, there are over 50,000 who are ultraleftists, anarchists, socialists, and communists."

"I'm finding it difficult to believe that socialists and communists care more about the planet than other people," said Dr. Stark.

"You forget the one-child-per-family policy of Communist China to curb their population in the twentieth century," said Travis. "Not to mention the tens of millions Stalin and Mao killed, or the killing fields in Cambodia. People are exterminated, if they oppose their cause."

"What would the cause be now?"

"If you cannot feed the people, they'll revolt, it will be hell, not a communist paradise."

"Hmm, human annihilation would pave the path for building a perfect communist society with a selected few," said Dr. Stark and sighed. "I concede."

"Besides, the conservatives are against abortions, and the capitalists want more people to exploit," said Prescott with a wry smile.

"How about the survivalists?" Claire asked.

"We have a list of those, too," said Col. Willey. "There are 69,529 confirmed survivalists in the suspect group. The four known suspects are survivalists, including Fred Warner."

"Do you monitor their families?" Prescott asked.

"Yes, but nothing unusual happened among the members of their families. There isn't any indication of their having or seeking shelter at this time."

"If we suspect a certain group of people intent on exterminating humanity for the sake of the planet, what would they do after the deed is carried out?" Prescott proposed.

340

"First, they and their loved ones would want to survive," opined Claire. "And survive well, without hardship."

"In that case, they want to maintain a community of survivors with all the skills needed to prosper in the future," said Prescott. "Doctors, engineers, high-tech experts, mechanics, specialists, agrarian workers, nurses, security, perhaps even a few musicians and artsy-fartsy elites."

"I don't see a reason to keep lawyers, politicians, insurance agents, and salesmen," quipped Travis.

Col. Willey executed a few commands and smiled. "Less than 10,000 would drop off our suspect list."

"Bureaucrats?"

"Over 20,000 of them are on the list."

"A functioning community, a colony must exist somewhere." Travis raised his eyebrows. "But where? The moon? Mars?"

Chapter 64. The Berkemore Space Biosphere

"How about on Earth? There is such a colony," said Maximus, surprising them all. "The Berkemore Space Biosphere in the Canyons State Park, near the university campus."

Maximus brought up images of the BSB. It was a proof of concept for a functional colony to be built on other planets, Mars being the future site for the first complete, self-sufficient settlement like this one. The structure was a 400-meter-diameter silo, extending 200 meters underground and capped by a transparent dome. The area under the dome was used for agriculture, while all the residences and facilities were underground. It was a settlement of 10,000 people living and working together as if it were a base on another planet. Construction began in 2057, and the colony was populated in 2061.

Travis snorted. "Why go to the moon to do this experiment, when Earth is more hospitable now and in the future?"

"They are hiding in plain sight," said Prescott. "Who initiated this project?"

"The Science Department of the University of California at Berkemore." Maximus read on, 'To assess the feasibility of colonizing Mars and other planets, a full-scale colony must be built and tested here on Earth for at least two years, with a complete community of potential colonizers capable of running, maintaining, repairing, growing food, and being self-sufficient. Note: The BSB colony does not have sufficient land under the dome to

342

provide the food needed for all 10,000 occupants, however, on another planet such as Mars, additional greenhouses will be constructed." Maximus commented, "Looking at the present colonizers' occupations, they don't have geologists, mineralogists, or mining and construction experts, just to name a few that would be needed on the new planet."

"Who paid for BSB?" Travis asked.

"The University, with secured loans."

"They have a mortgage that will never be paid off," Travis laughed. "Brilliantly evil!"

"The BSB colonists are the worker bees," said Prescott. "Why don't they have enough land to grow all their food in the biosphere? Simple. They don't need it on Earth. After devolution, the colonizers will colonize Earth, not Mars."

"This is a Noah's Ark, but for people to start a new society on Earth," said Travis. "Maximus, what's the race make-up of the colonist population?"

"The population is 50% Caucasian, 30% Asian, 10% African, and 10% others."

"This is not a white supremacist colony," said Travis. "Do they have any unskilled, uneducated, previously Idle people among them?"

"They are all skilled and educated. Most of them are in their twenties, half of them married among themselves, but have no kids, in spite of children's quarters existing in the biosphere."

"I bet all of them are perfect genetic specimens," said Travis.

"You are correct," agreed Maximus. "The prerequisites for being selected as a colonist: excellent health, college education preferred or practical skills, and between the ages of 25 and 35."

"They've been there for one year. How are they faring socially?" Claire asked.

"The original population was 10,103 people—5,050 males, 5,053 females. The current population is 9,977—4,962 males and 5,015 females. Attrition was caused by requests to leave, major illnesses, and three deaths."

"Leaving aside the deaths, this is not necessarily a true experiment," said Claire. "If they were on Mars, no one could leave. Do they say if they have any troublemakers?"

"Yes, they have a jail, with 29 men and 6 women in it."

"What does this structure remind you of?" Travis asked, folding his arms.

"A prison," said Col. Willey. "The outside walls are ten meters tall, and there aren't any doors around the perimeter."

"Or a fortress. No one can get in, either," said Travis. "Maximus, where is the entrance?"

"The official entrance is on the Berkemore University campus at the Department of Chemistry building."

"Well, well, well." Travis shook his head. "This is the perfect shelter in which to survive the human devolution."

"Maximus, please display the latest satellite pictures of the BSB," requested Prescott.

"Right now it's nighttime, but here is yesterday's satellite view."

The holo-screen filled with the round shape of the biosphere as seen from above. Several cranes were posted around it, and some kind of construction was underway.

"What's going on?"

Maximus zoomed in. "It seems they are placing a fine mesh over the dome."

"What material?"

"Metallic."

Claire and Prescott were on their feet.

"What's the matter?" Col. Willey asked.

"They are creating a Faraday cage around the dome," said Prescott. "They know how to protect themselves against the devolution agent."

"Meaning?"

"The devolution agent propagates through dark-mind energy and water molecule cloning. When a chamber, or this biosphere, is sealed and shrouded in a Faraday cage, the devolution agent cannot penetrate it. The people inside would be safe, while on the outside—"

"Doomsday," Claire finished Prescott's sentence. "That's where they're going to hide when the agent is released into the world."

"It looks as if they are at the end of their work," said Col. Willey with a worried look. She gave a quick, terse command. "I ordered a drone to survey the area now. And several thousands of fly and mosquito drones will be deployed shortly to penetrate the interior."

"If they can get in," said Prescott.

Col. Willey listened to a report in her aural comm. "According to the construction plans, there are vent shafts. That's how the mini-drones will get in."

Travis chuckled. "The dome does not have an environmental system. It is only temporary to select the right survivors until humanity is destroyed. I bet they're hooked up to the city's water and sewer system."

"Please note the water and sewer lines as an alternative access to the dome," Col. Willey spoke into her mic.

They all looked intently at the live picture of the BSB taken by the drone with a night-vision camera, but the night vision was switched off because the dome was flooded by the construction lights, as the work continued around the clock. Flashes from welding sparked around the dome's edges.

"They are practically finished," said Col. Willey. "Would it be safe to bomb it?"

"Only innocent victims would die. The real culprits would have alternative shelters," said Claire. "The BSB confirms that they are ready to destroy humanity, and the devolution agent must be ready to be released throughout the world. They were not bluffing."

"Everyone on listen-by," said Col. Willey, addressing the unseen people who were listening in on their meeting. "The only protection against the agent will be in a sealed enclosure wrapped in a metal wire mesh. Inform others, if you haven't done so already." She turned to them. "Will planes and this aircraft platform be immune?"

"No, you have windows," said Prescott, pointing at the plane's panoramic windows. "But submarines are safe."

"How long do we have?" Col. Willey asked.

"Maximus," Travis called. "Is there anything of importance upcoming at Berkemore University or the BSB?"

"As a matter of fact, yes—the one-year gala is to take place tomorrow at the Berkemore Space Biosphere. And here is a list of the invitees."

Chapter 65. The Assignment

"That's when the devolution will commence," said Travis to Col. Willey.

"General alert!" Col. Willey shouted to the unseen audience. "The place is Berkemore Space Biosphere. The when is *tomorrow*. Locate and track all the people on the enclosed list and prepare for action."

"I hope you don't plan to drop in on them," said Travis. "The big fish have still to arrive."

"No, not until we have the best plan of action," said Col. Willey. "So far we don't have an acceptable plan that prevents the devolution serum release."

"Looking at the invitee list, I see a lot of academics, some progressive political figures, a few media personalities, high-tech multibillionaires and trillionaires, celebrities, famous artists, and entertainers. *La crème de la société*," said Travis. "As expected, their significant others are invited as well. Maximus, what's the guest headcount?"

"Including their companions, 15,024."

"What's the age of the guests and the companions' education?" asked Claire.

"Average age of the guests is 39 years old. Most of the companions are educated and are Active. Just a few are Idle."

"There are more females overall," said Claire thoughtfully. "Procreation is of high importance. Maximus, are there such colonies anywhere else on Earth?"

348

Maximus took longer than usual to answer. "Negative."

"Are they all US citizens?" Claire asked.

"Only 60% of the colonists and guests. The others are foreigners."

"An international gathering," observed Prescott, as he was searching the list of names.

Dr. Stark cleared his throat. "My feelings are hurt that I wasn't invited." He pretended to be upset. "But I see Dr. Henderson wasn't invited, either. She's not part of the Society."

"We need to know who all the A&E Historical Society members are," said Travis. "If we immobilize them and keep them alive, we could find out the location of the agent and prevent this tragedy."

"Gassing the entire colony is an alternative." Col. Willey clicked a few keys on her sleeve device. "Although there may be casualties, and if the A&E members are among them, we'll run the risk of triggering a premature release."

"I don't think the members are suicidal," said Prescott. "They went to great lengths to create an oasis to survive in and to experience the future as they envision it."

"Even if we capture them all, could your people make them talk?" Claire asked Col. Willey.

"Yes, we can, but I was told that you could penetrate their memories, which is better than our interrogation techniques."

"Only if they are deeply sedated." Claire took a few moments to think. "What do you think, guys?" She asked Travis and Prescott.

"Sure, but it depends on how fast we can identify them and recover the information from their memories," said Travis.

"Also, if an AI is in charge of the system, it will be out of our control," added Prescott. "Maximus, can you investigate if there is such an AI out there?"

"I've commenced the search."

A notice appeared on the board above the table: *The suborbital jet to California is ready for departure.*

"That's our plane to take us to California," said Col. Willey. "We will need your services until we resolve this threat."

"Where are you going to land us?" Travis asked.

"At Vandenberg, and from there to wherever you may be needed."

"If our reappearance is discovered, it may alter the entire situation," said Prescott.

"What do you think they want from you?" Col. Willey asked.

"Until a few minutes ago, we thought that they didn't have a complete understanding of how to protect themselves. But they learned that much from us when we were in Africa. What they have absolutely no clue about is how the agent propagates, what the dark-mind energy is, and how it clones itself into the water molecules. Only a Trinity Team can identify dark-mind energy, which cannot be observed scientifically."

"A Trinity Team? Could they contact other Trinity Teams?" Col. Willey asked.

"None of the other Trinity Teams' names are on the guest list," responded Maximus. "And they cannot be contacted without going through me."

"But if they were to find out that you survived in Africa, how bad would they want you?" Col. Willey asked CTT.

"Oh, that's a loaded question," Travis scowled.

"I would venture to say that the Capuchin Trinity Team would be highly valuable to them," said Dr. Stark.

Travis and Prescott looked at Dr. Stark none too kindly.

"Dr. Stark has a point," said Maximus. "A direct approach by CTT at Berkemore Space Biosphere is advisable."

"Are you intending to have us knock on their door?" Claire asked. "And say what? 'Hi, remember us?'"

Claire, Travis, and Prescott exchanged apprehensive looks. They could definitely help, but they would be at the mercy of the A&E Historical Society.

"Don't you have Special Forces to enter the facility and immobilize them?" Claire asked Col. Willey.

"Of course. I'll go as far as to consider some of the colonists inside, who may have intelligence or military backgrounds and could be recruited as agents. But so far, we are not even 50% sure that we could prevent this catastrophe. I have a hunch that you could make a positive difference if you get inside the BSB."

"Have the mini-drones deployed yet?" Prescott asked.

"Yes, and we lost them by the hundreds on the first attempt," said Col. Willey. "They have anti-drone security in the air vents. The sewer passages were better, and over a thousand of them have penetrated into the dome now.

They are communicating, but they are also being hunted by their wasp-drones. We can use all the help we can get." She looked at CTT.

"The Capuchin Trinity Team is mighty resourceful," said Maximus. "They've excelled in the two short years since they've been initiated."

"They'll strip us of our weapons," said Travis.

"We will be defenseless," added Claire.

"For sure," agreed Prescott. "And they may separate and isolate us, which would make matters worse. Our power is the ability to work as a Trinity Team, although even then, we could hardly have any influence over anyone in particular. We need something else to help us on the inside."

"There are so many variables once we go there, and without intercom between us, we'll waste time and accomplish nothing." Travis saw the colonel thinking of a solution and said to her, "Comm implants will be discovered, Col. Willey. They'll run us through CCS and determine how many filled cavities we have."

"Don't you have audio-visual implants already?"

"No, that would interfere with our ability to travel to the other realms. We rely on our PAVs, but those would be confiscated when we arrived. Simply put, we will be naked and defenseless."

"We could use something new," said Dr. Stark. "A microbots network."

"What are those, Dr. Stark?" Prescott asked.

"Microbots that can form networks to help you communicate with each other, or even with us. They could disable computer-controlled electronic mechanisms and even software that you may want to infiltrate."

"Wouldn't those be detected by their CCS?" Travis asked.

"In their inert form, they are just silicon, gold, and stuff. They will cover you from head to toe and be invisible to the naked eye. When you initiate them, they'll establish networks and do what you want with them. In a cubic centimeter, there will be about one billion of them. Each one of you will receive one cc. The bots can communicate with each other to a distance of one centimeter. When you see the need to deploy them, they'll make ant trails and spider web networks to carry out your commands. Prescott, you'd be ideal to have the lead of the microbots."

"That would work," said Prescott. "We'd be able to establish some level of control and communication with you, hopefully. Can they map circuits?"

"Anything you want them to do. They have a library of commands that you'll need to learn by the time you arrive there."

"Would you take the assignment?" Col. Willey asked, with hope in her voice.

Claire, Travis, and Prescott huddled together, exchanging quick thoughts.

"One more question, Dr. Stark," said Prescott. "To use our paranormal power, we need to discard the bots from our bodies."

"That's on the menu of commands."

"And another question, Col. Willey," said Travis. "Are we immune to any criminal charges that we may incur in this mission, including ending people's life?"

"You'll be engaging enemy combatants, so you must do what's required."

Claire took out of her inner pocket the vial with devolution agent and showed it to Col. Willey.

"Is that what I think it is?" Col. Willey asked apprehensively.

Claire nodded.

"Careful with that. Could that contaminate us?"

"No, as long as it is sealed in the vial."

"Do you intend to use the devolution agent?"

"If needed. This vial may help us in case of emergency."

"What do you intend to do?" Col. Willey had a look of horror on her face. "You, could devolve as well."

"The three of us may be immune. But we're not one hundred percent sure," said Claire.

"Why don't you want to take a vial of sleep-inducing serum instead? Knock them out."

"Because the serum will be detected by the Chemical Composition Scanner."

"And that?" Col. Willey pointed to the vial.

"This is water, as far as their CCS can detect, along with our body water. Since I don't want the vial with water to be discovered and confiscated, and we must have it, one of us must carry it."

"No way I'm putting that in any of my cavities," said Travis, raising his eyebrows. "Prescott?"

Prescott shook his head in disgust.

"In that case, it will be me," said Claire.

Prescott and Travis looked at Claire in shock, sprinkled with some admiration.

Claire chuckled, seeing their faces. "It'll have to be implanted under my skin."

"It's too large, and you won't have time to heal," protested Travis.

"Not my skin—artificial skin, between my breasts. And when I need it, I can rip it open to access the vial."

"After we arrive at Vandenberg, we'll take care of that," said Col. Willey.

"Do we have immunity from the president, if we use the agent or anything else that's as deadly?" Travis asked.

"That's above my pay grade." Col. Willey looked up at the holo-screen and said, "Please forward immunity and pardon request to the president." She looked at CTT. "We'll know shortly. What else?"

"We'll need old-style sunglasses that are made of glass," said Claire.

"Not plastic?"

'The glass content in the glasses will disguise the glass vial I'll carry."

Col. Willey made a note.

"We'll need gas masks."

Col. Willey raised her eyebrows.

"We'll pretend to be infected, and as good citizens, we'd wear the masks when we knock on their door."

"In this way, they'll quarantine us together," added Travis.

A beep sounded, followed by an announcement. "The president has granted unlimited immunity and unconditional pardon to Capuchin Trinity Team."

"In that case, we'll take the assignment," said Claire.

Chapter 66. The White Room

"Excellent," said Col. Willey, visibly relieved that they would help. "We need to be on board the plane in five minutes. Dr. Stark, do you need to come with us?"

"Definitely. I'll be coordinating with CTT."

As they left to take a cart to the departing bay, Claire said to Col. Willey, "Oh, and our suits are loaded with gadgets. We'll need civilian clothes, instead."

The hovercraft flying Prescott, Claire, and Travis flew quietly and low through the hills east of Berkemore City. It was before dawn, and stealth was important. All three removed a small pillbox from their pockets and poured a fine gray powder over their pants.

"These are the microbots," Prescott told Col. Willey. "They'll spread down to our shoes and await our commands."

"I hope you don't itch easily," said Col. Willey, scratching.

"They are so fine that we don't feel anything."

"What will be your strategy?" Col. Willey asked.

"Provoke, divide, and stir the pot until they lose consciousness," answered Prescott. "Travis is good at that."

"Everyone has his talents," said Travis.

A green light signaled their imminent arrival.

Col. Willey said, "As we agreed, you have until midnight to incapacitate them. If we don't hear from you by then, we'll storm BSB or even use tactical nukes. They'll not get away with this. Good luck to you and to all of us." She shook each one's hand. "I'll be around the area with the Special Forces. I'll buy you the first round of drinks, if we survive." She smiled and saluted them.

Prescott made an uneasy face. "My stomach is in knots. No drinks for me."

"If we make it, Col. Willey, we'll get drunk together," said Travis.

The hovercraft hovered a foot over the turf of the baseball field near the university, and the CTT team jumped out quickly.

The hovercraft departed, leaving Travis, Claire, and Prescott in the middle of the field. They were dressed in dark casual attire.

"The Department of Chemistry building is over there." Prescott pointed to a monolithic eight-story building that was dark at the moment.

"And there is the Berkemore Space Biosphere," said Claire, looking at the elevated dome in the hills.

"Dr. Nellie Henderson will surely be shocked when we ask for her," said Travis. "And everyone else who knows about us."

They left the baseball field and took the University Drive to the Department of Chemistry, where they would ask for Dr. Henderson in the morning. Until then, they sat on the benches waiting for daylight and review their plans of action.

358

It was a beautiful California morning. Although it was a school day and classes wouldn't start until past eight, there were people biking and walking on the campus. At eight o'clock, they placed their gas masks over their faces and entered the building to ask for Dr. Henderson. The doorway was a CCS scanner and at that moment, the security system was alerted about them. In the hallway, they found a monitor-receptionist hologram, which came to life as they approached the reception desk.

"Good morning, how may I help you?" said the digitized machine voice, displaying the UC Berkemore Department of Chemistry logo on the holo-screen.

"We are Prescott Alighieri, Travis St. John, and Claire German, returning from Africa, and we would like to see Dr. Nellie Henderson," said Claire through her mask.

"Just a moment. Dr. Henderson is not in her office, but a message was sent to her informing her of your request. Please have a seat."

The message sent to Dr. Henderson included their picture, gas masks and all. A half-hour later, Nellie Henderson—clearly having a bad hair day— burst into the lobby, followed by a bewildered-looking Fred Warner.

"I though you people were dead!" she said, amazed to see them in the lobby. "How, why are you here?"

"Wait, they must be quarantined, Dr. Henderson," said Dr. Warner, backing away and pulling her by the arm. "Please don't take it the wrong way, but stay where you are until the HAZMAT cart arrives."

Prescott, Travis, and Claire sat down and waited for the HAZMAT bubble cart. They were asked to take a seat inside, and the cart drove itself around the building and then down a ramp to a roll-up door, which opened and admitted them. The cart drove into a large elevator, which took them down many levels. At their destination, the cart drove through gray concrete corridors, passing through many sealed gates, until they arrived at a door with a POD ID number, which was open for them.

"This is Dr. Warner," he said over the bubble's speaker. "I'm sorry for the inconvenience, but you may still be contaminated and must be inspected and, if needed, decontaminated. Please exit the HAZMAT cart and go through the open door ahead of you."

They did as told, and after they entered an antechamber of sorts, the door sealed behind them. A door opened ahead of them and they went through it into a round white room resembling a small auditorium. The door closed and sealed behind them. In the middle of the white room, at a lower level, stood a transparent dome with two oval hatches, the access doors to the dome. The dome was encircled by several rows of bleachers.

"Initiate CTT comm," Prescott ordered the microbots.

Claire, Travis, and Prescott heard a crackling sound behind their ears. Connecting micro-electronically the microbots established a link among the three of them by the use of interconnecting networks. All CTT had to do was speak from the throat with their lips barely apart, inaudible to anyone around them. The bots linked them into a perfectly coherent communication.

"Can you hear me?" Prescott linked to the others.

Claire and Travis linked back, *"Yes."*

"We will be sealed in that dome. I'll drop a batch of microbots in this room, just as I did after we left the cart," linked Prescott.

Two stairways descended to the dome's access hatches from opposite sides. The hatch in front of them swung open outwardly, as if inviting them in.

"Please enter the decontamination chamber," said Dr. Warner over the PA.

Claire, Travis, and Prescott looked at each other, understanding that once inside the dome, they were like fish in a bowl.

Claire reached discreetly inside her blouse, pulled out the test tube vial from between her breasts, and swiftly passed it to Travis.

"Place it above the frame of the hatch, Travis. Prescott, make the bots hold it in place there, until needed," linked Claire.

The plan was understood. Claire entered first, followed by Travis, who, being taller, had to hold himself by the upper portion of the opening frame as he entered, and he placed the vial above the frame. At the same time, Prescott stumbled awkwardly behind them to create a distraction, but he managed to get his equilibrium back and entered last, after making sure the vial was affixed like a cocoon above the hatch frame.

"Was the vial placed?" Claire linked once they were inside.

"Yes," linked Prescott. *"You two take charge. I'll be busy with the bots."*

Chapter 67. Quarantined

The door closed and sealed, trapping them inside the dome. There was a trace of antiseptic odor inside, but otherwise everything seemed lab normal. The dome was large enough to accommodate three stainless steel chairs, giving a sense of sterile cleanliness. The vent grills on the floor hissed quietly, and hopefully only breathable air would come in. Their hosts were considerate enough to provide three water bottles, and the caps were unbroken.

Travis noted that the dome was made of thick glass with a fine wire mesh imbedded in it. The floor was made of diamond-stamp stainless steel. *"We are in a sealed Faraday Cage."*

Prescott looked at the dome and linked, *"I think the mesh was needed to reinforce the weight of the glass, but that's good fortune for us."*

They removed their masks, sat down, and waited.

And waited.

"How long will this take?" Travis demanded into an unseen microphone, half an hour later.

"We have to perform analyses to determine if you are contaminated," said Dr. Warner through the interior speakers. "This will take time."

"We would like to speak to Dr. Henderson," said Claire.

"Dr. Henderson took her leave. She will not be involved from now on." The speaker went silent.

Prescott sat in his chair, propping his chin on his knuckles. He had his sunglasses on to hide his closed eyes as he concentrated on communicating with the microbots to establish different networks to infiltrate and control the electronic and software systems.

Another half-hour passed.

"How are you doing with the analysis, Dr. Warner?" Claire demanded.

"Working on it. Be patient."

Travis stood up and placed his hands on his hips, as if ready to start an argument, but he thought otherwise and said, "It's as if we're waiting at the doctor's office."

"That's why they call them 'patients,'" quipped Claire, who from time to time linked with Prescott to offer him assistance.

"No link to the outside yet. Door seals too tight," linked Prescott. *"Bots working for external comm via electrical wiring now. Also assessing mechanisms and controls software."*

More time passed, and Dr. Warner interrupted the silence, "You have certain items on you, which must be placed in the drop-box adjacent to door A."

"Which items are you talking about?" Travis demanded.

"Your shoes, belts, your wallet and IDs, your gas masks, and your glasses. Interesting that you don't have any electronic devices or implants. Why's that?"

"We are pure and travel light," said Travis, while taking off his shoes.

They placed all the items requested in the drop-box chute.

"If we are contaminated, then what?" Claire asked.

"We will have to decontaminate you of those nasty pathogens."

"How? You weren't able to decontaminate us in Africa."

"We need to be cautious. How did you get out of Africa?"

"We found a way," said Claire.

"That would make a fascinating story. How did you manage to pass the quarantine defense? As for you being infected—"

"Dr. Warner, this is Travis. You know and we know there weren't any pathogens in Africa. Instead, there was a devolution agent sprayed by an airplane that crashed in Monrovia."

"What devolution agent? What plane?" He asked with false curiosity.

"Spare us the drama," said Travis. "We know everything there is to know about the devolution agent and how Africa was infected."

There was no response.

"You pressed the right button," linked Claire.

Outside their dome, a haze filled the white chamber's air.

Prescott looked inquisitively at Claire, who linked, *"Decontamination."*

A minute later, the air was clear again outside.

The silence was broken for a few brief seconds when they heard several voices arguing on the speaker. Someone turned the microphone on prematurely before finishing their discussion, but they quickly turned it off again.

"Who else is with you, Dr. Warner?" Travis asked.

"Uh, my apologies. Dr. Sontor is assisting me."

Audrey Sontor, A&E member and dean of biological sciences. They weren't able to see her, but they knew what she looked like.

"Is Dr. Sontor involved with the devolution agent as well?" Travis asked.

"Who sent you here?" a new male voice asked over the speaker.

"And who are you?" Travis demanded to know.

"That's not important."

"We don't answer the questions of people we're not acquainted with." Travis made a smug face.

They heard a sigh. "Very well, I'm Dr. Xavier Gonzalez. Who sent you here?"

Xavier Gonzalez was a new name.

"Dr. Xavier Gonzalez, what's your specialty?"

"That's not important."

"Please humor us."

"Political science." Then, as if regretting his answer, he added, "Why the hell am I answering your questions?"

"Since when is political science involved with a pandemic?" Claire asked.

"Who sent you here?" Dr. Gonzalez insisted.

"What makes you think that someone sent us here?" Claire asked this time. "We came here to have a talk with

Dr. Henderson about how poorly we were treated while in Africa and about how we were never rescued. Why were we abandoned?"

"How did you get out of Africa? How come you are still alive?" a female voice asked.

"And you are?" Travis asked.

"Dr. Carla Gloss, I'm the dean of social sciences. Please answer my question."

Carla Gloss, another new name.

"Are you all UC Berkemore professors?"

Another moment of silence followed.

"Who are you people? Some Berkemore academic mafia?" Travis asked. "What do political and social sciences professors have to do with the devolution agent?"

"I suggest you let us out of here, before trouble starts," said Claire. "You will be charged with kidnapping."

"Kidnapping? We're saving California by quarantining you," said another new male voice.

"Name, please," said Travis.

"Dr. Matt Perkins."

"The sociology professor at UC Berkemore?"

"How do you know me?"

"Hey, Perkins, why did you kill your father, Alexei Perchenko?"

There was no response, and it all went quiet.

Two hours later the main door into the white chamber opened, and a group of people filed in. They recognized Fred Warner, Matt Perkins, Sean Cohen, Audrey Sontor, and Cecilia Perkins. Gonzalez was a barrel-chested Latino, and Carla Gloss was a mature black woman. The seven sat down on the bleachers, staring at them intently, like a jury.

Mit Sandru

Chapter 68. Who Sent You?

"Claire, ask him about Perchenko again," linked Travis.

"So, Matt Perkins, why did you kill your father?" Claire asked again to unsettle them.

"How dare you ask me such a question!"

"Matt, Matt," lamented Travis. "Your father brought you the bronze box with the cherubim he bought in Egypt. Or maybe he gave it to Brian Burk first, twenty-some years ago, and—"

"What the hell?" exploded the older woman.

"Ms. Perkins, what a pleasure," said Travis elegantly.

"How do you know me?" She was taken aback.

"Enough of this," said Gonzalez. "They obviously know more than we think. Who sent you here?"

"Xavier, they have information we need first." Warner pointed to CTT and asked them, "How did you three manage to survive in Africa?"

"Come to your senses, Fred," said Gonzalez, who was getting red in the face. "These three did not come back from Africa on their own without being apprehended by the quarantine forces first. Someone brought them here. We can take them to BSB and find out later all they know. We must identify who sent them. It may jeopardize our mission."

"That's for sure." A stocky man with close-cropped hair, unmistakably military and holding an unlit cigar at the corner of his mouth, entered the room. "Who sent you here, and for what reason?"

"And your name is?" Travis asked. This man was another new member they didn't know about.

"General. That will do. And who are you?"

"I'm Travis St. John. This gentleman is Prescott Alighieri, and this lady is Claire German. We are with TIO."

"Yes, when they volunteered for Africa, they said they were with the Trinity Investigation Organization," agreed Dr. Warner.

"I know who TIO is," said the general, chewing on his cigar. "Are you out of your fucking minds?" the general exploded at the group. "These people will find you even in Hell and make you pay."

"Wha, what do you mean?" Xavier Gonzalez asked timidly.

"This is a paranormal investigation team, not a scientific team. What's the name of your team?" he asked CTT.

"We are the Capuchin Trinity Team, CTT for short, with TIO," answered Prescott calmly.

"Haven't heard of your team. Are you new in TIO? Who recommended them?" the general asked the others.

"Uh, Dr. Henderson," said Fred Warner defensively.

"Minori, Heather, get Dr. Henderson," said the general into his wrist mic. He turned to CTT and said, "Who sent you?"

"Prescott has already answered your question. TIO," Travis said.

"Stop bullshitting me. TIO is a private organization. Who paid you to come all the way from Africa here to BSB?"

"The World Health Organization."

Fred Warner shook his head. "No, we didn't."

"Who paid you, CTT?"

"Let's cut to the chase," said Claire. "We know what you're up to, and you're in a world of trouble. We're here to negotiate your surrender." She stood up and crossed her arms.

They laughed, some nervously, but they all laughed.

"You're in no position to make demands," said the general, narrowing his eyes at them.

"You forget you're in the bubble," said Cecilia Perkins. "With one command, you'll be gassed. Like rats." She emphasized the last words as if anticipating what would happen.

"The way you killed Alexei Perchenko?" Travis asked.

"That's none of your business," said Cecilia Perkins.

"We're curious to know if just you or the entire A&E Historical Society were behind his demise." Claire asked.

The group outside the bubble whispered among themselves. Some were clearly surprised at being addressed as the A&E Historical Society.

Mit Sandru

Chapter 69. Ahead of Schedule

"Claire, ask them about the deal with Derek Dodd," linked Travis.

"And whose idea was it to sell Derek Dodd the devolution agent, which would later be sold on the black market?"

The group stopped their discussion and stared at CTT. Some were startled by the news. Others showed uneasiness.

"Were some of you trying to make billions on the side?" Travis pressed the issue.

"What are you talking about?" demanded Carla Gloss, dean of Social Sciences.

"You didn't know about a whole cache of devolution agent sold to Derek Dodd?"

"Hey, we regulate your air supply in there," said Matt Perkins. "Stop screwing with us."

"You didn't pay attention to what the general said. We'll come after you even in Hell," said Travis. "That's where we found Derek Dodd and learned about the devolution agent. He told us everything he knew just to save himself from Hell."

That information startled the audience even more.

"And that's where you'll go after you die," added Travis. "Hell!"

Hell existed? They hadn't planned for that, or at least not seriously.

Claire and Travis realized that they had found a rift among the society.

"Was it you, Perkins, or your father who sold the devolution agent to Derek Dodd to be resold on the black market?" Travis asked.

"You're making things up," said Matt Perkins.

"How about when the two women belonging to the A&E Society killed Derek Dodd in Mexico and took back the case with the devolution agent?"

"Is that true, Matt?" Cecilia Perkins was enraged.

The others looked either sternly or with confusion at him.

"Well, you know dad. He wanted to make some money, as usual," said Matt. "But he died in an airplane crash going back to Moscow."

"What would he have done with money in a world full of apes?" Cecilia screamed. "We will have all the money there is."

"So who killed Alexei Perchenko then?" Travis asked, faking interest.

"I repeat: He died in a airplane crash," said Matt. "An accident."

"How convenient. Just like the other people you murdered," Travis quipped. "Did you kill him to silence him after selling the cache of devolution agent to an arms dealer, which almost ended your grandiose scheme?"

Some in the A&E Society were visibly upset, while others showed concern by their shifty eyes.

"Who killed your father, Matt?" the general growled.

"I really don't know. I, like you all, thought it was an accident."

The general chewed on his cigar. "That's what you get when you team up with a bunch of amateur civilians." The general gave some of them an evil eye. Then he lit his cigar.

"No smoking in here," Cecilia Perkins said sternly.

"Or what?" The general barked back and puffed on his cigar. "Tonight it's going to be all over. Who cares about this lab?" He gesticulated toward the bubble. "Anyway, we better get info from them, and fast."

"Tonight?" Travis linked.

"They're ahead of schedule," linked Claire.

"What's going to happen tonight, General?" Travis asked.

"Nothing. None of your business," barked the general.

"Who are the two women who killed Derek Dodd in Mexico and took the devolution agent from him?" Travis asked. "Who is in possession of that agent now?"

The general hollered into his wrist mic, "Minori and Heather, forget about Henderson. Come to the lab, now!"

"I connected outside our bubble through electrical wires," linked Prescott. That was good news, as the bots would infiltrate the dome's lock controls on the outside.

The general looked at Travis. "You're a smart ass. Who sent you here?"

"Well, thank you." Travis pulled up his pants, which sagged due to his lack of a belt, seemingly pleased at what the general had called him. "Let me see if you're going to shit your pants—the DIA and the entire military force of the United States."

Travis didn't think that the people outside their bubble were going to react at all, but they did, with screams of panic. Weren't they aware of what was going to happen when the government learned of their plot? Weren't they told about the threat some of their members had made if the FBI didn't end the investigation against them? Apparently, they were not all in the loop.

"As expected." The general puffed a smoke plume. "Calm down, people. We took precautionary steps in case of that happening. Unbeknownst to all of you, in case the military tries to force its way in here, or if certain members of our society were to die, the devolution agent will be released throughout the world at that moment." He smiled, assured of having the situation under control.

Then something strange happened. They all stood up and left the white room.

Chapter 70. Lucius Levantstein

"What the hell just happened?" Travis linked.

"Do you think they're running away now that they've heard the news?" Claire linked.

"I don't like this," linked Prescott.

"Hey, where did everyone go?" Travis yelled. "Is it something I said?

No one responded.

"It's the DIA, isn't it? You play with fire but don't want to get burned, is that it?" Travis walked in place.

"What a bunch of losers," said Claire.

"Maybe they were recalled for a secret meeting," said Prescott, interrupting his work with the microbots.

"The authorities know of your threat," Travis said to stir some interest among the society. "It's better to quit while you're still alive."

But no one responded.

"I think they're trying to scare us through silence," linked Claire.

Travis nodded and sat down.

A long time passed without anyone talking to them. It must have been sometime in the afternoon already. Travis was getting concerned. If they didn't keep them engaged in a dialogue, CTT could not make any progress.

"I repeat, it's better to quit while you're still alive," said Travis.

The door to the white room swished open and three women entered. Two of them were Asian, one much older than the other, and the other was a blonde.

"There is no quitting," the older woman of Chinese descent said in a loud voice. "The United States government was informed of the consequences if we were to come into harm's way."

"And who are you?" Claire asked.

"Dr. Chen Wong, UC Berkemore chancellor. Since you said you're with the DIA, tell us what they are planning."

"We're not privy to their plans," said Claire. "We came to convince you to stop your mad plan of destroying humanity. You won't win."

"Inform us of their plan," said Chen Wong coldly.

"Are you the bad cop?" Travis asked. "Where are the others?"

Chen Wong motioned with her head. The Japanese woman and the blonde, dressed in black fatigues, approached the hatch, looking menacingly. They were not large, but a certain powerful threat emanated from their attitude.

Travis glanced at Claire and linked, *"Tell them about the third almond."*

"All right," Claire slumped her shoulders as if defeated. "You must know about the third almond. Too bad for you the US government has it."

"Who cares?" Chen Wong said.

"Maybe you will care after we tell you that with our knowledge acquired in Africa, the Center of Disease

Control and National Institutes of Health have developed an anti-devolution agent," bluffed Claire.

"What?" someone said over the speakers.

"Is that you, Dr. Warner?" Chen Wong asked.

"Yes."

"Are you all back?"

"We're all here."

"Come in here. These three are about to say something of minor importance."

A few minutes later, the society members returned to the white room.

"What did they do while they were gone?" Claire linked.

Travis had an idea. "Nice to see you all back. Did you have to leave to greet your guests at the BSB?"

They stared back.

"This is none of their business," said Chen Wong to the members with a dismissive gesture.

"How come they know so much?" the general asked.

"And if DIA knows more than they should, they haven't prevented any of our guests from arriving," said Chen Wong. "Maybe because they think the release will be tomorrow at midnight. Hmm? We're way ahead of the curve. Don't you people worry."

The members seemed to give a collective sigh of relief. This Wong chancellor was a tough cookie.

"Start telling us about the CDC-NIH anti-devolution agent. And fast, before I lose my temper," warned Chen Wong.

"Like I said, the CDC and NIH developed an antidote using the third almond with the knowledge we collected in

Africa," said Claire. "It's being distributed throughout the world as we speak by US Air Force planes. You are defenseless and ripe for plucking."

The smugness of many subsided. Some attempted to search or call on their contacts to verify what Claire had just told them. They couldn't. As long as they were inside the white chamber, no one could communicate with the outside.

"Did you hear of anything like that?" Chen Wong asked the members. "Anything from Adam or Eve?"

"Who's Adam and Eve?" Travis linked, although he knew that his mates wouldn't know.

"Sonofabitch," cursed the general. "It all makes sense now."

"Share with us your insight, General." Chen Wang was slightly annoyed.

"If the CDC developed an antidote, we have traitors among us. Someone knew the devolution agent could be neutralized, and they sought insurance by selling the agent to this Derek Dodd. Beside Alexei Perchenko, who else?" the general asked, looking furiously at the A&E members. "Minori and Heather, when did you find out about Derek Dodd?" The two women turned their heads and looked at the general.

"Heather might be the ponytail blonde who brought the vial case to the plane," linked Claire.

Travis nodded and linked, *"These two must be the enforcers and the killers in Mexico. They are armed."*

"Master Lucius told us to act immediately and retrieve the case with the devolution serum," said the Japanese

381

woman. She had short-cropped black hair and dark, penetrating eyes.

"He told us to kill Derek Dodd as well, although he seemed to be drugged when we popped him," said Heather, the blonde, without emotion.

"Unfortunately, our leaders are not here," said Cecilia Perkins.

"I've just been notified," said the general. "Lucius, Jarmal, and Lars will be joining us in a minute."

"Who are they?" linked Travis.
"Beloved leaders?" linked Claire.

"If the NIH developed an antidote," said Chen Wong to CTT, "when did they obtain the third almond?"

"Ahmed Nassief sold the last nut to a Mossad agent a week after he sold you the first two," said Claire. "The USA and Israel cooperated to develop the anti-agent after your field tests in Congo, Afghanistan, and Brazil."

"They had enough time to develop it. It's feasible," Audrey Sontor said to the others.

"I disagree," Cecilia Perkins said. "Look how long it took us to develop it after Burk synthesized it the first time, and how many brilliant scientists went berserk in the process of developing it."

"Maybe, but if it's true, we're hosed," said Sean Cohen, the professor of political science.

"Wait," said Cecilia Perkins, raising her arms as if to stop them. "The CDC-NIH developed an antidote with input from those three after they visited Africa. That's two days ago. It's impossible."

The general pointed to CTT. "When did you cooperate with the CDC, and what did you share with them?" the general asked.

Travis began to laugh. "You are still in the dark about the devolution agent. For one, you have no idea what it is and how it propagates."

The science professors blanched.

"We do, however," Claire said. "And that knowledge accelerated the production of the antidote overnight."

"That's the knowledge I want," said Warner, standing up and pointing to CTT.

"You'll get it. We'll keep them with us until they talk," said the general.

"But there is a risk in not knowing now," said Warner.

"I think these three are bluffing," said Cecilia Perkins. "If they have such knowledge, why did the DIA send them to us? Explain that. They're two-bit shysters, conning their way with the 'going beyond' BS." The corners of Cecilia's mouth went down as she used her fingers to mimic quote marks.

"Claire, tell them about the dark-mind energy," linked Travis.

"Does dark-mind energy mean anything to you?" Claire asked them.

"What's she saying?" Carla Gloss, the dean of social sciences, asked around.

"Dr. Stark mentioned something of the kind," said a worried Fred Warner.

"Maybe that's the reason you couldn't detect the agent until it was too late and your brilliant scientists went berserk," said Claire.

Most of the members of A&E Society turned pale as ghosts. They were supposed to be the experts, but here the two-bit shysters knew something they couldn't grasp.

"It's energy we cannot detect," said Cecilia Perkins bitterly. "Never understood it completely, but that explains the walk-in cooler, a Faraday cage, that kept Confidence alive. Luckily, we realized that just in time, and it will keep us safe, too."

"Any outside connection yet?" Travis linked to Prescott.

"Not yet. But the bots are in control of the bubble's electronics." Perspiration formed on Prescott's brow as he concentrated on visualizing what the bots were doing.

"Can you open the door?" Travis linked.

"Of our bubble, yes."

Travis and Claire looked at each other with renewed hope that they might be able to escape the bubble.

"I want to know something," said Matt Perkins to CTT. "Did you contact Ahmed Nassief and Fatta Kazaz?"

"Why do you want to know that?" Travis asked.

"Two men and a woman went to see Ahmed Nassief and Fatta Kazaz at Behman Hospital in Cairo," Matt Perkins said to the members. Then he asked CTT, "Were you those three?"

"Maybe." Travis rubbed his chin.

The white chamber door swished open and three new men entered.

"Yes, I, too, would like to know what your business was with those two men in Egypt," one of the three men said.

"Lucius Levantstein. The richest man in the world," Prescott linked.

"The one and only," Travis linked back.

"What's he doing here?" Claire linked.

Lucius Levantstein, the trillionaire, the genius, the wunderkind who had invented new biomaterials, cybernetic nerve systems, and AI software, and had perfected the android machine to function, talk, and do any work a human could do. Now in his forties and the wealthiest man in the world, the CEO of Eden Cybernetics was a part of, if not the leader of, the A&E Historical Society.

Chapter 71. At Midnight

"The plot cannot get any thicker," linked Claire.
"It doesn't make sense. The man who has it all wants to live the simple life of a colonist?" Prescott linked.

"I am shocked to see that you are part of this murderous gang, Mr. Levantstein," Travis said, partly tongue in cheek.

"Mr. St. John, why aren't you shocked to see the Earth sinking in human filth, and people who are multiplying like rats, surviving on manna, not working, but screwing? Come to think of it, it may be manna that caused the population explosion. Twenty billion human-parasites infest the Earth. The entire biosphere is dying off or transforming itself into hideous new forms of life. There are hardly any large wild animals left in the world. The oceans are depleted of fish. There is an island of floating garbage in the middle of the Pacific the size of Texas, visible from space. The only things that thrive today are humans, roaches, flies, and rodents. It is time for a new beginning."

"You're not God," said Travis.

"No, but I'm doing God's work here."

"Are those two gentlemen with you the Drs. Lars Ned Franke and Jarmal Patterson, Nobel Laureates in astrophysics?" Claire asked.

"Very perceptive of you, Ms. German," said Jarmal Patterson, a black man.

"Are you part of the A&E Historical Society, this lunatic murderous group?"

"Since you know already about the A&E Historical Society, yes, we are," said the third man, Lars Ned Franke, a blond-haired Caucasian.

"My God, Dr. Patterson, how could you have destroyed one billion lives in Africa? How about you, Carla Gloss? Your own black race."

Jarmal Patterson remained unfazed. "They happened to be the first victims. Caucasian, Asians, more Africans, people from all continents, from all countries, will soon devolve to allow the Earth to be reborn."

"Besides, those countries did not have nukes and could not start a premature nuclear war," added Lars Ned Franke.

Claire, Prescott, and Travis were at a loss. They had seen firsthand what happened to those exposed to the devolution agent, which meant nothing to these people, who were highly educated elites, hardly a bunch of ignorant racists.

"Who's the boss here?" Travis asked.

"That would be me," said Lucius Levantstein with a self-assured smile. "A&E Historical Society consists of twelve members. Not them." He pointed to Heather and Minori. "Now, tell me, what did you want with Ahmed Nassief and Fatta Kazaz?"

"That's none of your business," said Travis.

"You haven't dealt with Heather and Minori yet. They'll make you talk." Lucius Levantstein smirked. "Let's remain civilized, and they will not make you scream."

"Civilized? You're a murderer!" shouted Claire.

Levantstein motioned with his head toward the dome, and the two femmes fatales, showing no emotions, faced the hatch, ready to enter the bubble.

"Shouldn't we gas them first?" the general asked.

Levantstein turned to CTT. "Last chance: talk, be gassed, or lose your toenails?"

"Hold them back. I need to control the white room's door, too," Prescott linked.

"You're not going to get away with this!" Travis shouted.

Levantstein laughed. "I already have. Our plan is on schedule."

"If the DIA doesn't hear from us, they'll storm the BSB."

"That's an idle threat, Mr. St. John. Be assured that an army of android soldiers will fight back any intervention by the Special Forces. I bet you and the DIA didn't know about them." Levantstein took delight in seeing their surprised faces.

"How long do you think your android defense will hold?" Travis asked.

"All we need is a few more hours."

"This is not good," linked Prescott.

"Something is askew here," linked Claire.

"You see, just threatening the US government and the world with premature contamination in case one or all of us were killed was not an assured protection," said Levantstein. "We want to live, not die, and see Earth become a paradise again."

"It's time for us to return to BSB, Lucius," interrupted the general.

Levantstein looked around at the crowd in the room and said, "Change of plans, people. This place is safer than the BSB, in case of an attack. The latest intel I received is that they may infuse the BSB with sleeping gas early tomorrow morning. This room is sealed and armored. It has its own environmental system, and so we will not be affected. They will concentrate on the BSB. We'll stay here until it's all over."

"But the colonizers, our guests?" objected the general.

"The BSB is compartmentalized, just as any properly built planetary colony should be. In case of attack, the BSB will go into modularized lockdown mode. Some colonizers will survive, but some may not. In the worst-case scenario, they are expendable. The important guests are already here, and I took measures to send our significant others to a second lab that is just as safe as this one."

"We cannot communicate with the AI command center," said the general. "We are so well sealed that we cannot communicate with anyone outside or see what happens, unless we access the comm ports outside the inner door."

"The AIs are on automatic. If Adam fails, Eve will take over. The AIs will do what is needed. Besides, when the devolution agent is released, it will be dark outside. Nothing to see anyway. At least around here." Levantstein shrugged.

Travis, Prescott, and Claire became really worried. Something different than what they originally thought was going to happen.

"Are Adam and Eve AIs?" Travis linked.
"I think so," linked Prescott.

"You are planning to release the devolution agent sooner," said Claire, trying to keep her voice from trembling.

"Very observant of you, Ms. German. But look on the positive side." Levantstein raised his arms. "You may survive along with us. One last time: what did you want from Ahmed Nassief and Fatta Kazaz?"

"When are you planning to release the devolution agent?" Claire felt her mouth go dry.

Levantstein looked hard at them, and then asked the general, "Are they clean?"

The general nodded.

"At midnight."

Mit Sandru

Chapter 72. The Killer Androids

If that was true, the world didn't have much time.

"Prescott, what's the time?" Travis linked.

"Five past seven," linked Prescott after inquiring the time from the bots.

"We're running out of time," linked Claire. *"The Special Forces will never be able to intervene—they'll all be mindless after midnight."*

Travis eyed Lucius Levantstein. "You won't be able to devolve the entire population on Earth. Besides, the neutralizing agent the CDC-NIH developed—"

"Don't insult my intelligence," Levantstein said.

"Really? How about people and especially the authorities protected in sealed, wire mesh bubbles? Not to mention submarines and Aircraft Carrier Platforms flying over the Pacific, out of the range of the devolution agent. They will come after you and execute you for what you have done. You'll wish you were an ape."

Most of the A&E Society looked worried. Even Levantstein, displeased at the ape remark, blinked several times, indicating his concern about the ACPs over the oceans far away from the centers of dispersal. That's not how it was supposed to happen. It seems the A&E Society's equation had not considered survivors: armed survivors like the Special Forces who would hunt them down, ACPs in the sky with hypersonic planes, and submarines with cruise missiles able to destroy any place on Earth.

"The most perfectly planned endeavors carry a certain risk of being derailed," said Lucius Levantstein, gaining back his confidence. "Take you, for example—you, getting your noses in our affairs. I'm sure your investigation in Africa of the crashed airplane prompted the FAA and FBI to investigate, and they got too close to some of us. Because of that, we had to eliminate people who knew too much, like Don O'Halloran and others. To make matters worse, some of us got nervous and warned the FBI to stop their investigation, or we'd release the devolution agent. We should have stonewalled it, but it happened and the cat was let out of the bag." Levantstein threw an annoyed look at Lars Ned Franke and Jarmal Patterson.

"On the other hand, Alexei Perchenko found and bought the bronze box that held Aaron's Rod, paving the way for Brian Burk to synthesize the proto-devolution agent. General Strauss here, with DOD at the time, and Cecilia Perkins, Carla Gloss, and Chen Wong saw the initial potential of reducing the world's overpopulation using the newly discovered devolution agent. Our A&E Historical Society formed with other like-minded individuals in the 2050s.

"Alexei Perchenko did even better when he acquired the two special almonds, the bitter forbidden fruits, which resulted in the devolution agent as we know it now. With my money and some brilliant scientists who are no longer with us, unfortunately, we developed the agent for our own purpose, and after satisfactory tests, we were ready to deploy it worldwide. But Perchenko got cold feet and decided to hedge his bets, almost derailing our well-laid plans. I had to dispatch Minori and Heather to take care of the problem by eliminating Derek Dodd and Alexei Perchenko. Sorry, Matt, it had to be done."

Matt showed no emotion.

"Then doubt affected some of our members and, to assure them that the plan was sound, we did an impromptu large regional dispersal over Africa. The results were impressive, but we discovered that we used too much serum, and the agent dispersed radially from the release point. The wind had no influence. For every setback we had a contingency plan, and we persevered. You being here, or some kind of infiltrators, or Special Forces, was expected, and we prepared for those eventualities, including a brutal assault on the BSB. We have it all under control, even destroying the mini-drones that have infiltrated the BSB." He smiled ironically at them. "We have a plan for everything, as long as we don't panic and make mistakes." Levantstein looked sternly at the other members.

"How are you going to fight the survivors? They'll become guerrillas and kill you, one by one," said Travis.

"Yes, there will be pockets of survivors here and there," agreed Levantstein. "We will deal with them, as appropriate, by dispersing additional devolution agent in the troublesome spots. If needed. God knows we have enough of it. And by using our army of androids and cyber-dogs, we'll be well-protected. We have contingency plans for every situation. We are ready to begin a new life on planet Earth." He inhaled deeply, pleased at what was to come.

"But how are you going to deal with the short shelf life of the devolution agent?" Claire asked. "Make more?"

"We could have made use of the third almond, but we have enough serum on hand. And as far as the shelf life, that is and isn't an issue. The serum distributed throughout the world is good for two more days. That's why we must act tonight, without delay. But we have more serum stored in that miraculous bronze box, which keeps the serum fresh." Lucius Levantstein smiled, content with his explanation. "I've told you more than you needed to know. Now, you tell me—what did you want from Ahmed Nassief and Fatta Kazaz?"

"We're not going to tell you," said Claire.

"Minori and Heather, make them talk."

The two took an aggressive stance in front of the hatch, waiting for it to be opened.

"Heh, your two puny women against the Capuchin Trinity Team," said Travis with a smirk on his face.

"Two puny women?" Lucius Levantstein roared with laughter. "How about two killer androids?"

Chapter 73. Last Chance to Surrender

"What?" Travis stopped smirking. He never realized that those two were androids. They were so perfectly human, and androids would be impossible to defeat without weapons.

"Hey, Travis!" Heather called to him.

Travis looked at her and she released a red laser beam from one of her eyes. Travis screamed and covered his eyes. At first, he thought he was blind, but the beam was a low dose and he was able to see again, although through multicolor patches.

"Don't look into their eyes," linked Travis. *"The laser came from one of her eyes."*

"Prescott, can you keep the dome's hatch locked?" Claire linked.

"Even if I do, they'll override it," linked Prescott. *"This is ridiculous. They don't have that kind of advanced android."*

"Shit, the laser came from one of her eyes," linked Travis. *"There are no implants containing such a powerful laser."*

"All right, Levantstein. You made your point," said Claire, shielding her eyes while trying to gain some time to prepare an action plan.

"Prescott, redirect the bots to disable those two android bitches," Travis linked.

"As long as you can open the hatch when needed," linked Claire.

"Working on it, but buy me some time," linked Prescott.

"As you know, we are a paranormal investigating team, and we have the ability to go beyond the real life you experience," began Claire, shielding her eyes with one hand. Then she told them what they found out from Ahmed Nassief and Fatta Kazaz, omitting the fact that the third nut had been burned by Fatta and not sold to Mossad. She concluded with telling them how Fatta returned Aaron's Rod to the Ark of the Covenant.

"The Ark of the Covenant exists," said Lucius Levantstein, his eyes sparkling.

"Yes, but finding it may be a challenge," said Claire. "Unless you find another key-map to its location."

"You said the Ark is under the Great Pyramids," said Levantstein.

"Yes, but the maze and labyrinth leading to it open up only when a key-map, like the one the Egyptian generals possessed, is used. Without one, I doubt you'll find it."

"After the dust settles and we have the planet all to ourselves, we will bulldoze the pyramids and we will find the Ark," Levantstein said confidently.

"You say there was another bronze box in the Ark?" Audrey Sontor, the dean of biological sciences, asked.

"Yes."

"What if the other box contains Moses's staff, Lucius?" Audrey Sontor wondered. "What kind of magic would that staff possess? Since Aaron's Rod is the Tree of Knowledge, maybe Moses's staff is the Tree of Life."

"That would be something, wouldn't it?" said Chen Wong, the UC Berkemore chancellor. "We could live forever, just like the gods."

"We definitely must find it," said Carla Gloss, her eyes widening with excitement.

The rest of the A&E members seemed to be reinvigorated by such a possibility. A true paradise lay ahead, just for them and a select few.

"That will be our first priority after we carry out our plan," said Lucius Levantstein. "In the meanwhile, we'll proceed with our midnight devolution agent release worldwide." He spread out his hands and inhaled with satisfaction.

"What shall we do with them?" General Strauss pointed to CTT. "Eliminate them or keep them?"

"They have a unique talent," said Levantstein thoughtfully. "They may come in handy in the brave new world we're establishing. They could help with finding the Ark of the Covenant."

No one objected to Levantstein's decision. Many of them were nodding in approval. At least for now, CTT was safe from the killer androids outside their bubble.

"The androids and the hatch-locking mechanism are under my control," linked Prescott.

"We have less than five hours to prevent them from releasing the agent," linked Travis. *"I see no other way but to expose them to our devolution vial."*

"That would be murder," linked Claire.

"More like a disablement," linked Prescott. *"I can live with that."*

"Me, too," linked Travis.

"Unfortunately, we have no choice—disable them or allow the extinction of the human race," linked Claire. *"Disable them. Whenever you're ready, Prescott."*

"This is your last chance to surrender, or you'll suffer the consequences!" shouted Claire.

The A&E Society burst into laughter.

Claire, Prescott, and Travis held hands and said together, "Let the vial fall."

Chapter 74. The Broken Vial

The vial fell off its ledge when the bots stopped propping it. It fell down as if in slow motion, ready to crash on the floor. Minori, being closer to it, reached out to take hold of it and it landed on her palm. But the vial bounced and then fell between her fingers. She reached out again to grab it with lightning speed, but the vial had a mind of its own not wanting to be caught. Minori was determined not to let it go and when she made contact with the vial it squeezed harder and broke the vial in half. It made a pop sound as if a champagne bottle was just opened.

CTT heard the pop outside the bubble.

"What was that?" General Strauss perked up his ears, looking questioningly at the others.

"Yeah, what was that?" Levantstein ran to the hatch where the two androids stood.

"A broken vial." Minori showed Levantstein her palm with the broken vial in it.

"What the hell? Devolution agent!" Levantstein shouted in terror. "Where did this vial come from?"

"It fell from there, master Luscious." Minori pointed above the hatch. "Sorry that I broke it."

"Did you plant that?" Levantstein asked CTT with raging anger.

"Shoot those bastards!" General Strauss screamed, pointing to CTT.

Minori and Heather pulled out their guns and shot several bullets at Prescott, Claire, and Travis.

400

Tuff, tuff, tuff, tuff... was the sound of the bullets embedding themselves in the thick glass but not penetrating it.

Prescott immediately disabled the androids. Heather and Minori stood frozen, with their smoking guns pointing at the dome.

Before anyone could react, a strange phenomenon began in the white room. Dark light engulfed the entire room, except it did not penetrate into the dome where CTT were held.

"That's the dark-mind energy field emanating from the devolution serum," said Prescott, no longer needing to link with the others.

"They're toast," said Travis, running his tongue over his dry lips.

"How are you doing, guys?" Claire asked and looked around the dome. "I think we're protected by the dome."

"Thank God," said Prescott. "The dome and the embedded wire mesh prevent the energy from entering. We're good." Prescott concentrated on the bots for further action.

"I don't feel anything," said Travis. "We must be safe. But why is the dark energy still present on the outside?"

Prescott looked outside and shrugged, not knowing for sure. A certain reverberation began in the dark light. At first, it vibrated rapidly, but it slowed down to a point where the dark light sphere surrounding the dome was expanding and retracting, as if it were a visual echo. The rate of expansion and retraction kept slowing, to the point where actual spherical waves and other convoluted wavelets of dark light could be clearly seen.

"The dark-mind energy is bouncing against the white room walls," said Prescott.

"It didn't go through the walls?" Travis asked.

"Fortunately, not," said Prescott. "The room has metal lined walls, and rebar in the concrete shell prevented the energy from escaping. The energy bounces back and forth in the room until it'll dissipate."

"We're safe here until it dies down." Claire sat, watching with apprehension what was happening to the energy wave and the people outside their dome.

The A&E members stood in place, wide-eyed and unable to speak at first.

"What the hell is going on?" Jarmal Patterson shouted.

"The vial contained devolution serum, and it contaminated this room when Minori broke it," said Levantstein, shaking his head in disbelief.

Some of them began wailing, others crying. A few ran around as if seeking shelter, but there was none to be found. Xavier Gonzalez and Audrey Sontor were praying.

"How could this happen? Where did that vial come from?" Lars Ned Franke was shaking his fists in the air.

General Strauss stopped Sean Cohen, who was running around aimlessly, and slapped him to bring him back to the bleak reality.

"Lucius, do something!" demanded Cecilia Perkins.

Levantstein sat down with his head in his hands and began crying. "What have you done?" Lucius Levantstein asked looking with despair at CTT.

"No. What have you done?" Claire pointed back at him. "You are the only one who can stop this madness and save the Earth's population. You still have time."

"Ha, ha, ha!" He laughed bitterly. "Not a chance. Everything is on automatic. Not even I could reverse the process."

"Your hearts are beating and will continue to do so as you descend into oblivion. There will be no earlier release," Claire said. "Be a noble soul and stop the release of the devolution agent or tell us how to stop it."

"Not a chance. Adam and Eve are on automatic." Levantstein looked daggers at Claire. "The Earth will rise again and recover from the human parasites, even if we are not around." His voice trembled.

"Who's Adam and Eve?" Travis asked.

"My AIs. They'll take care of everything."

"Where are they located?"

"Fuck you," said Levantstein.

"Little do you know what we can do to prevent the planet's contamination," said Claire.

"Yeah. You're devolving, too, and nothing will stop the worldwide release of the agent."

"Before you sink into oblivion, you may want to know that we are protected by the bubble you locked us in," said Claire. "We are not contaminated, and we'll stop your mad plan."

Several members became hysterical.

"Calm down, people!" shouted General Strauss, taking charge like the good general he used to be. "You scientists, is this the real devolution agent?" He waved his hands in the air.

"The fuck it is," answered Warner. "How did you get in here?" He glared at CTT.

"Didn't you scan them?" Strauss barked.

Warner nodded, and then slumped his shoulders.

"It is still in this room, it is contained in this chamber," said Cecilia Perkins. "Open the doors, Matt, let the agent get out of here, and contaminate Berkemore."

"Prescott, don't let him open the white room's door," said Travis.

Prescott concentrated and ordered the microbots to counteract any attempts at opening the door.

"It's stuck!" yelled Matt, pressing frantically on the control panel on his sleeve.

"You sons of bitches!" Cecilia Perkins shouted at CTT. "It's time to give you a dose of the potion you brought with you—"

"Prescott, keep the hatch on the bubble locked," said Travis.

"Matt, open the hatch to expose them to the agent." Cecilia Perkins ran to the hatch, looking at CTT with murderous eyes.

Matt tried to do as told, but with no success. "The hatch is stuck as well."

"Prescott, get the androids ready to shoot any of them," said Travis, anticipating Cecilia's vengeful thoughts.

"Prescott, don't have them shot—have them knocked out by the androids," Claire said.

"Matt, gas those motherfuckers!" shouted Cecilia Perkins to her son.

Matt hesitated for a second, which was a fatal mistake.

Heather leaped onto Matt's back, knocking him out.

"No!" Cecilia Perkins ran to her son, who had collapsed between the bleachers.

"Put her out," Travis told Prescott.

Heather backslapped Cecilia as she tried to reach her son or his control panel. She fell back, unconscious.

"That was a good call not to shoot them," Travis told Claire.

"Let's hope their hearts are still beating," said Claire.

Per Prescott's instructions, Heather checked Matt's and Cecilia's pulses.

"They're OK," said Prescott.

General Strauss pulled his gun out and shot at Heather, but he missed and the bullet bounced off the walls. Minori gave him a blow to the back of the head. He swayed, dropped the gun, and fell down.

Heather turned him over on his back and checked his pulse.

"He's alive, too," said Prescott.

In spite of the commotion, the A&E members quieted down, becoming oblivious to their surroundings. The devolution agent started to take effect. Some began swaying their heads side to side; others, although seated, began moving their upper bodies as if following some internal rhythm. A few began groaning and growling softly, but no discernable words were uttered. Just as CTT had seen before with the other victims, the members began to space out, wandering around the room aimlessly. After several minutes, that phase passed, and a few became lethargic, withdrawn, staring into the distance, while others acted as if they were out of their minds. Carla Gloss began pounding her head against the wall. Lucius Levantstein was arguing and shaking his finger at an imaginary person, while Sean Cohen was pulling General Strauss by the legs, leaving a streak of blood on the floor from the back of his head. Chen Wong had a different idea and pulled on the general's arms. Others paid no attention to anyone else and were jumping from bench to bench, or jumping up and down, or hollering from the tops of their lungs, or howling like wolves. Fights broke out, but the members were out of shape and no one got seriously hurt.

"How long should we stay here, Prescott?" Travis asked.

"Until the agent propagation stops. Maybe 24 hours."

Mit Sandru

Chapter 75. Contact with the Outside

"The world doesn't have 24 hours," said Travis.

"I'll try to redirect the bots to make contact with the outside," said Prescott.

"By all means," agreed Travis. "What else can we do now?"

"Not much, other than observe the madness here," said Claire, shaking her head.

"Crap," said Prescott. "I can't access the outside from this room."

"Ask the androids how we can communicate with the outside," said Claire.

Prescott nodded and inquired. A moment later, he said, "There are comm ports in the vestibule between this room and the outer door."

Travis and Claire looked at each other. "Should we risk it?" Travis asked.

Claire observed the dark-mind energy outside the bubble. The bouncing waves had slowed down to the point where she could see the leading edge of each wave as it approached and departed from their bubble dome. "What do you think, Prescott?"

Prescott pulled out of his concentration. "It's been a half-hour since the agent took effect." He observed the wave pulses and timed them. "At this time, the propagation speed should be much higher. It is slowing down faster, but it's still potent."

"Everything is metal, even the outer door," said Travis.

"And the outer door should be sealed," said Claire. "But if we're wrong and this darn thing escapes into the rest of the complex and outside, we've failed."

"We should not risk it," said Prescott. "I think the agent is losing strength, either because it's enclosed and interferes with itself, or because there aren't any water molecules left to clone."

"How much longer will it take to die down, Prescott?" Travis asked.

"By the frequency I see, it is in about its seventeenth hour of propagation."

"Four more hours?"

"I'd say a lot less."

"How far could the remaining strength of the agent travel now, if it escapes?" Travis asked.

"A rough guess would be two to three km."

"I suggest we wait a little longer," said Claire.

"We don't have even two hours. Besides, we need to get out of the bubble to find out their secrets." Travis motioned with his head toward the devolving members outside.

Prescott kept exploring alternative ways to make contact with the outside, while Travis and Claire counted the frequency of the waves. A half-hour later, the dark-mind energy wave was moving as if in slow motion.

"It's definitely expiring," commented Claire. "If we open the white room's door, the additional space of the antechamber may suck energy out of the agent, I imagine."

"Sounds reasonable," agreed Prescott. "Ready?"

Claire nodded, and Prescott ordered the bots to open the white room's door. It opened as instructed, and they could see the outer door across the antechamber. The dark-mind energy wave near the door distorted as if it were being sucked into the antechamber, and it moved in. A complex pattern of waves ensued, pulsating at a higher frequency.

"It's gaining strength?" Travis became alarmed.

"The additional water molecules gave it potency," said Prescott.

"But look, it's slowing down again," said Claire.

"Are those the comm ports?" Travis pointed to a panel on the left wall of the antechamber.

"We'll find out in a second." Prescott directed the bots toward the ports and began working.

Some of the A&E members, if they were not at each other's throats, found refuge under the bleachers. General Strauss recovered from his head injury and sat on the floor, looking around in wonderment. So were Cecilia and Matt Perkins.

Prescott pumped his fist triumphantly. "Maximus, can you hear us?"

"It's about time. We were ready to accelerate our intervention." They heard him through their microbot comm.

"Listen, the devolution agent is scheduled to be released at midnight Pacific Time."

"Noted, and a warning is posted. Do you know where the serum vials are located?"

"No, or at least not yet. Two AIs, code named Adam and Eve, control the release of the devolution agent. The devolution agent from the vial we brought contaminated the A&E Society members, and they are devolving. They placed us under a dome for decontamination, and it protected us from the devolution agent outside it. The agent is contained in the room we are in, but it has residual power."

"Where are you?"

Prescott looked up to identify their location. "We're in pod Z23-A1, wherever that is."

"We've located you. You are between the Chemistry Building and the BSB, deep underground. Special Forces are on their way."

"The A&E have android soldiers and other defensive weapons protecting the compound."

"Noted."

"By the way, the leader is Lucius Levantstein, the CEO of Eden Cybernetics." Prescott gave Maximus all the names of the other members.

"Good job, people," intervened Col. Willey, who was listening in on the conversation. "How can we stop the release of the agent?"

"They did not divulge much information. We need to access their minds and extract the information. Unfortunately, if we get outside this bubble, we'll be contaminated. We have to wait until it dies down."

"How long?"

Prescott sighed and looked at the crawling energy wave. "Two hours, maybe."

"The time is 20:04 PST," said Col. Willey.

"We hear you, Col Willey, but the *goods* are contaminated, and we cannot access their minds," said Travis.

"What else do we need to do?"

"We need restraining jackets to contain the A&E members when you get here. When it is safe," said Claire, not knowing what else to suggest.

"Is it safe outside the pod you're in?"

"I think so," said Prescott. "Luckily, the pods are sealed and shrouded in metal."

"In that case, we'll proceed with penetration of the compound."

"Col. Willey," said Travis. "I'd suggest that you do not use force in trying to penetrate the compound. Force may trigger an even earlier release of the agent."

"What makes you think that?"

"They planned to release the agent a day earlier than expected," said Travis. "They thought of every scenario. Whatever you do, use caution."

"Col. Willey," called Claire. "Sealed Faraday chambers must be used for everyone's protection. We survived because of that protection. In case you haven't alerted the world on how to protect itself and in case we fail to stop the release, inform them now."

"Roger that. In the meantime, teams of investigators are searching the background and affiliates of the members that we weren't suspecting."

"Also, send as many people flying over the seas and oceans, 2,000 km or more from land and populated areas," added Claire.

"Thanks, Claire."

"Maximus and Dr. Stark," called Prescott.

"Listening," said Dr. Stark.

"We're controlling two highly advanced androids. Levantstein may have many more of them. You can hardly distinguish them from humans. I am not confident of their complete obedience to us. I only accessed the lower core, the locomotion controls. We'll need your help to access the upper core and to ensure these two androids will help us."

"Will do. Give us the link to their cyber netvironment," said Maximus.

Prescott ordered the microbots that controlled the two androids to link to Maximus, but the link ended.

"Maximus, Maximus!" called Prescott. He addressed his teammates, "The link is dead."

"Why don't you trust the androids?" Travis asked.

"Levantstein is full of surprises," Prescott answered. "Better safe than having one of them crush our skulls."

Maximus came back online. "We needed to reroute the link. It seems an AI system in the compound found out about our link. We will continue from now on multiple and interlaced links."

"Very well," said a comforted Prescott. "I'm resending the link to the androids, if you didn't get it last time."

"Are the androids awake?" Dr. Stark asked.

"Yes, and they did what we've asked of them so far," replied Prescott. "Why?"

"They are in low-core, secondary-response mode. Not trusting them was a good call. I'll let Maximus handle it from here."

The androids seemed to have been put to sleep by Maximus, as their heads dropped.

"I wish I could see what's behind that door." Travis pointed to the outer exit door.

"There are cameras in the outside passages," said Col. Willey.

"Do you have access to them?"

"We do now."

"Patch the images through to the bot network," said Prescott. "Crap!" he exclaimed, jumping out of his chair. "There are a dozen androids outside the door!"

Mit Sandru

Chapter 76. No Good Way Out

"Good thing you didn't open that door," said Travis, scratching the back of his neck.

"Maximus, can you control the outside androids?" Prescott asked.

"You are safe in there."

"Not for now, but later."

"They could be controlled through the more sophisticated androids, Heather and Minori. And now, Heather and Minori are enabled to obey you three."

Just as Maximus finished saying that, the two androids became reanimated, as if awakened from sleep. They turned their heads to assess the situation around them.

"After they address you by your names, you will have control over them," said Maximus.

"Masters Prescott, Claire, Travis—how may we help you?" Minori and Heather said in unison, looking at them.

"Now that's an improvement," said Prescott, impressed.

"Heather, how long have androids been stationed outside this pod?" Travis asked.

"Since we came in with master Lucius."

"Heather, Minori, can you see what they see?" Travis asked.

"Yes, we can."

"Are you linked to them?" Prescott asked.

"Yes, we are now."

"Maximus, Dr. Stark, it seems you have a link to the group outside."

"Working on it," said Dr. Stark.

Some in the devolved group became even more restless, and it was only a matter of time before they even might kill each other.

"Could the outside androids restrain them?" Claire asked, pointing to the A&E crowd.

"Good idea," agreed Prescott, also watching them with suspicion.

"And the outside androids are under your control," said Maximus.

"Great, if we could only open the door," Travis said. A thought came to his mind. "What would happen if we use the antechamber to get them in?"

"Part of the reduced dark-mind energy will escape from the antechamber," said Prescott.

"What if we time the closing of this room's door when the dark-energy wave is the farthest from it? Closer to us."

"That's an idea," said Prescott. "Maximus, do you understand what Travis is proposing?"

"Of course. You want to get the dozen androids into your room without letting the devolving energy escape outside. This operation will have to be coordinated externally by us."

"In that case, the wave has just bounced off the room's walls and is retreating toward our bubble."

"There is some residue in the antechamber," cautioned Claire.

"Maximus, on our command, close the room's door."

"Waiting your call."

"Close the doors," said Prescott and Claire.

After the inner door closed, the outer door opened, the androids walked into the antechamber, and then the outer door closed behind them. Finally, the white room's inner door swung open, allowing the dozen androids, although not as humanly perfect as Minori or Heather, to walk in.

"Androids, place your weapons on that bench." Travis pointed to a bench, and the androids obediently put their guns where they were told.

"Androids, restrain each one of them." Prescott pointed to the demented members. "Keep them down, holding them by their wrists."

The androids marched on and subdued one member each, holding them by their wrists as instructed. It seemed that they were trained on how to subdue humans, because as each member reacted differently under an android's restraint, that android took the necessary actions to keep each of them in place.

"That was easy," said Claire.

"Almost too easy," said Travis. "Is it normal to have them under our control so effortlessly?"

Prescott raised his shoulders. "Maximus, we need a private link."

"Yes, Prescott," said Maximus. "Are you suspicious of the androids communicating with the AIs through a back door?"

"Yes."

"We'll be monitoring any communication with the outside world and block it."

"In case we need to immobilize them when we get out, where should we shoot them?" Travis asked.

418

"Their power source is in the abdominal area," said Maximus. "Don't bother shooting them in their heads—their cyber netvironments are distributed throughout their bodies."

"So far, so good. We've got the cake, but we can't eat it yet," said Claire.

"The time is 20:37 PST," Col. Willey advised them. The midnight hour was approaching fast.

"We're still waiting for the energy wave to die out," said Claire.

"First thing we need to know is where the vials are located throughout the world," said Col. Willey.

"Our first priority," said Claire. "What's the situation on the outside, Col. Willey?"

"The Special Forces are positioned all around the campus and the BSB compound, awaiting authorization for the assault. As far as the world is concerned, there is total chaos out there. Many governments have collapsed; bureaucrats, the military, and politicians are running for shelter, and their populations are left to their own devices. Some advanced countries that are in daylight hours have deployed their military and population to find the drones on the ground."

"I hope they'll find some of them," said Claire.

"There are riots in all cities, even in the registered zones in the West. The US federal government is in transit to be sheltered or flown away to Aircraft Carrier Platforms over the Pacific. The population was informed to shelter in sealed and wire-mesh protected rooms. The United States is in a DEFCON 1 state of alert, and so are all the other

419

nuclear countries. The fear is that one or another may deploy its nuclear arsenal."

"Even if the devolution agent doesn't destroy the entire population, the nuclear aftermath could complete the job," Claire lamented.

Mit Sandru

Chapter 77. Adam and Eve AIs

Travis observed the energy wave. "The dark-mind energy is really slow, but it's also weaker. Just how much damage is left in it if we were open the outer door?"

"It's a gamble," said Claire.

"Maximus, are there other sealed doors between our pod and the outside?"

"Three more."

"What if we quarantine the dark wave in the next sealed sections?" Travis proposed.

"It's like letting the smoke get out of here," said Claire, brightening.

"That's assuming the water molecules are not infectious after the dark-mind energy passes through," said Dr. Stark.

"It's the energy converting the water molecules that's infectious. And the energy dissipates fast," said Prescott.

"We're running out of time, people," said Travis.

"Outside your pod there are three corridors with sealed doors," said Maximus. "The corridors are lined with reinforced concrete walls painted with an elastomer to seal them. The longest corridor is 50 meters. There is plenty of room for the dark-mind energy to bounce around in."

"Let's do it," said Travis.

"The energy wave is approaching the white room's closed door," said Prescott.

"Stand by," said Maximus. "The outer door is opening. The white room's inner door is not. It is blocked from opening when the pod outer door is open. I'm overriding it."

The white room's inner door finally opened, and they could see into the outside corridor. The dark-mind energy approached the opening, accelerating as if it were an escaping gas pulled out by vacuum. Even the waves bouncing off the white room's walls distorted and folded to escape from the room, searching for more water molecules in the corridor.

Clearly visible, the last waves in the room and antechamber egressed.

"Close the inner and outer doors, Maximus," said Prescott. The door closed swiftly. "And we are clean of the dark-mind energy!" Prescott shouted with glee.

"Are you sure?" Travis asked.

"Let's join hands and find out what's around us," Claire proposed, and they verified that the dark-mind energy was no longer in the white room. "We're clear," said Claire, opening her eyes.

"Time to get their secrets," said Travis, rubbing his hands.

Prescott opened the dome's hatch, and Travis was the first one to exit.

"Minori and Heather, bring master Lucius to us," said Travis.

Without objection, the two androids brought their master to them. Levantstein struggled, as if he knew that CTT would penetrate his memory, or perhaps it was just his animal instinct to resist capture. His reasoning mind was deteriorating rapidly, and CTT would have no problem penetrating his mind and memories.

Claire, Travis, and Prescott encircled Levantstein with their arms while clasping hands, and they melded their minds to interrogate Levantstein's mind. It took an instant in real time to gather all they needed to know.

"Maximus and all who are listening, we have important information obtained from Levantstein," said Claire. "The agent release is indeed scheduled for 24:00 hours Pacific Standard Time today. Vials with devolution agent are located on drones parked in inconspicuous areas all over the world. Fifty drones were deployed worldwide 24 hours ago, and they are distributed on a 1,000 km grid over the major landmasses of the world, including Oceania. The agent in each vial has a 2,000 km radius of contamination, so very few spots on Earth will remain uncontaminated.

"At 23:30 PST, the parked drones will take flight straight up, and at 24:00 PST, the power will be cut off, causing the drones to crash, breaking the vials, and releasing the devolution agent. As a backup, each drone has only one hour of battery life. Eventually all the drones will crash.

"Levantstein said that the entire project is on autopilot, which we confirmed from his memories. There are two AIs: one code-named Adam located at EDEN Cybernetics in Palo Alto, and the other AI, code-named Eve, is located in New Zealand on Levantstein's ranch. The Eden AI and its backup can stop the drones, but the AIs are not penetrable by any network. They are optically linked to the World-net—therefore, we have no chance of reprogramming them or infecting them with a virus. They

424

are rigged to self-destruct if unauthorized access is attempted. The AIs can be accessed only by the concurrent confirmation of the GeneIDs, face-voice-retina recognitions, and access codes of Levantstein, Patterson, and Franke." Claire paused.

"Sons of bitches," said not a person but Maximus.

"I'll second that," said Col. Willey. "Your report has been disseminated worldwide to all governments. Anything else?"

"We can interrogate Levantstein again, if questions arise," said Claire. "In the meantime, we'll interrogate Jarmal Patterson and Lars Ned Franke."

"Good work, people," said Dr. Stark. "Carry on."

CTT repeated the mind interrogation of the other two, but there were no new details found other than what they had already learned from Levantstein. And for good measure, they also mind interrogated all the other members, but no other vital information about drones' locations was gathered from them, either.

Time ticked on.

Chapter 78. Shut Down the Clock

"One of you androids, project the current time on a wall," Prescott ordered.

A large projection showed 20:23 PST on one wall.

"Any suggestions, anything else you need from us?" Travis asked the people listening from outside.

"We need to know the details of the BSB compound defenses," said Col. Willey.

"General Strauss has set up the defenses," said Prescott. "All the information can be accessed at the address and access codes I'm sending." Prescott operated the general's wrist control module and sent the information to Col. Willey's team.

"Thanks, that's great. How about the exact location of the AIs?"

"The AI at Palo Alto is located in a vault under the Cybernetics Center," said Prescott. "It has two access points: one shaft from the compound above. The other, which is more like a ventilation shaft, exits through the roof of the Robotic Research Lab."

"Very good. Our assault teams have just invaded the grounds of Eden Cybernetics," said Col. Willey. "How about the New Zealand ranch AI location?"

"The AI is located in an underground vault as well, under the wine cellars of the vineyards."

"Just don't break any bottles," quipped Travis.

"Can't guarantee that," Col. Willey chuckled nervously. "The New Zealand military is on its way to the ranch. Thanks."

"Are you planning to assault the BSB compound?" Travis asked.

"The command is reviewing the diagrams of the defense systems. Besides android troops stationed in the access tunnels, there are many robotic laser guns and explosive devices to be detonated on command or triggered by intruders."

"Any way to remotely disable their defense systems?" Prescott asked.

"We're looking into that as well, but the entire defense system is off the network. It is self-controlled."

"Damn it!" said Prescott.

"A new question for you," said Col. Willey. "Approximately where could the drones have landed throughout the world?"

Prescott thought for a moment. "Several drones at a time were flown by special air-transporters and ejected in a grid pattern. Each drone selected a landing spot without informing the transporter of its location. Even Levantstein wouldn't know where they are."

"Can the drones communicate?"

"No, the drones cannot transmit any information. They can only receive transmissions or commands." Prescott was visibly frustrated by the foolproof system Levantstein had devised.

"Thanks, Prescott," said Col. Willey.

In the pauses in their discussions, the devolved members, held down by the androids, could be heard growling and screaming.

"The infernal situation is," said Travis, stroking the back of his nails under his chin, "that the drones are on the ground at unknown locations, and they'll take flight at 23:30 PST time. At midnight, the power will cut off, the drones will fall to the ground, the vials will break, and the agent will disperse. To prevent the dispersal of the devolution agent, the drones must stay grounded. Since there is no other mechanism that would release the agent, that's the only option. Right, Prescott?"

"You're a genius!" Prescott got to his feet.

"I am? What, what did I say?"

"Prevent the drones from taking off."

"Well, yeah, if we could find them."

"We don't need to find them," said Prescott. "They'll take flight at 23:30 PST. That means they'll receive the official time from the GPS system."

"Are you saying that if we prevent them from receiving the GPS signal, they would stay grounded?"

"If the clock is not updated, the drones won't take off," said Prescott. "They will stay in limbo."

"I think you're correct," replied Dr. Stark. "If we can prevent the GPS system and any other networks from updating the Coordinated Universal Time, the UTC that makes all the world's computers work, we would stop the drones."

"Col. Willey," Maximus called, "the UTC and GPS must be shut down worldwide."

"Oh, my God! That will incapacitate the entire planet," said Col. Willey. "I'm informing the chain of command."

"Maximus, you'll be affected, too," said Claire.

"I'll be fine. I have my own internal clock. Somewhere."

"We have two choices," said Travis. "Shut down all of Earth's computers and revert to the Stone Age with an intelligent population, or keep the computers ticking with a dumb population."

Chapter 79. It Gets Worse

"We need another solution," said Col. Willey. "We need more solutions."

"I agree," said Travis. "What do the rest of the world's smartest thinkers suggest?"

"The ones who are not confused, hiding, or panicking are conferring," said Col. Willey. "For how long would we have to turn off the UTC and GPS system?"

"A minimum of two days, if not even longer," said Claire. "What is the concern?"

"Ignoring the hazards of shutting down the UTC, the Chinese have their own GPS system. They are not convinced that shutting down their system is necessary, and they even suspect that the US is using this as a pretext for an invasion," said a concerned Col. Willey. "The time is 20:29 PST. Too many people need to make decisions, and there is too little time."

"Could you access the Eden's AI with the information you obtained from Levantstein, Patterson, and Franke?" Maximum asked.

"We've never done it before. We need to discuss this." Prescott looked at his teammates for ideas.

"How would those three access the AI?" Travis wondered, pointing to Patterson, Franke and Levantstein. "Would they have to be together in one place, or can each one access it separately?"

"Let's ask Levantstein," said Claire.

The CTT melded their minds and extracted the information from Levantstein.

"What's the verdict?" Dr. Stark asked.

"For Levantstein, Patterson, and Franke, the accessing order is not important. But they must log in together within one minute of each other," said Prescott. "If we're successful, we might find a weakness in the AIs."

"Any risks?" Col Willey asked.

"Yes. If the AI discovers that we are intruders, it may command the drones to take off immediately," said Prescott.

"Should CTT take that risk, Col. Willey?" Maximus asked.

She took a moment to check with her bosses. "CTT is authorized to access the AI, with due caution."

"Very well," said Prescott. "With whom should we start?" he asked his teammates.

"Let's leave Levantstein for last," said Travis.

"Android, bring Jarmal Patterson to us," Prescott ordered the android holding him. "Android, hold Patterson upright. Heather, you'll be the connection to Adam, the Palo Alto AI. Face Patterson and hold him around his chest. Minori, hold Patterson's head motionless, facing Heather. Heather and Midori, be ready to perform a GeneID scan on Patterson. Heather, be ready to transmit the GeneID and the other parameters to the Palo Alto AI."

The androids complied. Claire, Travis, and Prescott surrounded Patterson and the androids, joined hands, and melded their minds, becoming "we" and infiltrating Patterson's mind.

"Access Adam at Palo Alto," we/Patterson gave the order.

Heather accessed the AI and a second later, Adam asked, "Name?"

"Jarmal Patterson," we/Patterson answered.

"Gene ID and biometrics verified," said Adam. "Code, please?"

"24X2KiNg^RB5&dZ9."

"Accessed allowed. Stand by."

CTT broke their mind meld.

"Android, bring Lars Ned Franke to us. Heather, Minori, repeat the previous procedure with Franke," said Prescott. CTT melded their minds.

We/Franke accessed Adam just as Patterson had.

Levantstein was last.

"Android, bring Lucius Levantstein to us. Heather, Minori, repeat the previous procedure with Levantstein now," said Prescott. CTT melded their minds and accessed Levantstein's mind.

We/Levantstein gave the necessary information and accessed the AI.

"Triumvirate verified," said Adam.

"Adam, connect to Eve," said we/Levantstein.

"Eve at your service. Code, please."

We had a moment of panic and searched Levantstein's mind. We/Levantstein said, "The devolution of Adam and Eve."

"How may we help you, masters?" the AIs offered.

"What is the general location of each drone?" we/Levantstein asked.

"The drops were made at the following coordinates." The AIs proceeded to give the GPS coordinates where the mother ships had ejected the drones from an altitude of 10,000 meters. The coordinates were stored in Heather's memory.

"At what time will the drones take off?"

"At the time 23:30:00 PST, current date."

"What triggers the takeoff?" we/Levantstein asked.

"UTC time synchronization at 23:30:00 PST, current date."

"What happens if the UTC synchronization goes dark?"

"Time synchronization must occur to trigger the takeoff."

"Abort mission," we/Levantstein ordered.

"As previously instructed, when the abort command is given, the drone takeoff time has been accelerated to Mountain Standard Time. The new time for takeoff, 23:30:00 MST, has been transmitted to the drones."

Chapter 80. The Drones

We frantically searched Levantstein's mind. The AI was programmed to accelerate the deployment by an hour if the cancellation of the mission, using the word "abort," were requested. There was no cancellation capability.

We broke our mind meld.

"Fuck!" screamed Prescott.

"What happened?" Maximus asked.

"We screwed up," said Prescott. "We asked the AI to abort the mission, and instead it advanced the deployment time to 23:30:00 MST."

"That's a full hour ahead," said Col. Willey, panicking. "The new take off time will be 22:30 PST now."

"We're sorry," said Claire. "We didn't know the AI was preprogrammed to accelerate the time."

"The new time table will run on MST, and the current MST time is 21:36," Col. Willey announced to the others on her conference call.

"Heather, transmit the GPS coordinates where the drones were dropped from the mother ships," ordered Prescott. "Col. Willey, for what it's worth, the drones can be found within the general coordinates Heather's transmitting. The drones probably drifted or searched for specific sheltered spots as they landed. If found, they should be prevented from taking flight."

"Thanks, Prescott. Information has been sent worldwide," said Col. Willey. "The time now is 21:37 MST. Just one hour and 23 minutes to takeoff."

"What else should we do?" Travis impatiently asked his teammates, but no one had any other ideas. He dropped his head, distraught over the lack of solutions.

"The GPS locations were useful," said Col. Willey a few moments later. "Emergency searches were launched by the militaries of most nations within the footprint of those drops."

"I hope there is enough time," said Claire. "Besides, not all areas can be searched. It is not foolproof."

"Could hovercrafts circle those areas and capture the drones when the drones are airborne?" Prescott asked. "That will give us another half-hour."

"Yes, that was the consensus as well," said Col. Willey. "Hovercrafts were instructed to immobilize any drones on the ground or in flight."

Prescott connected the microbots to Heather to listen in on any communication with Adam and Eve. The AIs patiently asked their masters every minute for new requests. Hopefully, the AIs didn't have a time limit after which another disastrous decision would be made.

"What's the AI saying?" Travis inquired.

"It's standing by," said Prescott. "I hope."

"Should Heather exit the AI?"

"No, God knows what other protocol needs to take place to exit, which we haven't discovered yet, and that may trigger another time advance."

"Who knows how many booby traps they placed within the AIs and on the drones?" Travis thought for a moment. "It seems the A&E Society was determined to carry out its mission, no matter what. Even letting the AIs make decisions without the master knowing about it."

"Or perhaps some of the society members had a hand in setting booby traps without disclosing them to the others," Claire speculated.

"I think those traps would be limited to the hardware, the drones," said Prescott.

Just as Prescott said that, Col. Willey announced, "They found the first drone in France."

"Is the drone still on the ground?" Prescott asked.

"Yes. It was located in an open field."

"Please remain alert—the drones may be booby-trapped."

"Acknowledged."

"Do they have images of the drone?"

"Yes, how can I send them to you?"

"Hold on." Prescott asked Minori, "Can you project images?"

"Yes, I can."

"Send them to Minori," said Prescott.

The images projected by Minori were converted by the android into a hologram and showed, as seen from a hovercraft, a small, quad-rotor drone resting on a field of freshly mowed hay.

Prescott asked Minori, "Do the drones look familiar to you, Minori?"

"Yes."

"Who assembled the drones with the vials?"

"Heather and I."

"Any booby traps attached to the vials?"

"That information is classified."

"Col. Willey, has anyone touched the drone yet?"

"No, but a team has landed nearby and they're approaching it."

"Stay back. They are definitely booby-trapped. Can the ground team detect any energy emanating from the drone? If they do, they should not approach it."

"What are you saying?"

"They may be equipped with motion sensors to trigger the discharge of the vials if approached on the ground," said Prescott. "I'm getting paranoid, but we discover something new every time we try to neutralize the drones."

"Understood," said Col. Willey. "But why didn't you discover that information when you searched their minds?"

"Searching their minds is like searching through thousands of virtual files," said Prescott. "We need to know what we're looking for."

"Knowing what we know now, we will search the A&E members' minds again," said Travis. "Bottom line, no one should touch the drones for now."

"Understood," said Col. Willey. "We have a new report from Russia. They found a drone 100 km east of Moscow."

The CTT repeated the mind search of every member. The mind search was instant, but getting each one prepared for the mind search took time.

"Here is the verdict," said Prescott, once they had finished. "The drones don't have motion detection, but

437

General Strauss rigged every vial with an explosive device to be triggered if the vial were to be removed. And there is no way of removing the vial without detonating it."

"That's bad news and good news," said Col. Willey. "The teams in the field can disable the drones by cutting the rotors off."

"Yes, that would work for the ones we find," agreed Prescott.

"There were two more drones found, one in China near Xi'an and the other in the Carpathian Mountains in Romania," said Col. Willey.

"Only 46 more drones to go." Travis checked the time. "It's now 22:29 MST. Only one hour and 31 minutes until the Apocalypse."

"Once the drones are airborne, there is no going back," said Prescott. "We have only one hour and one minute to prevent the drones from taking flight and ending humanity as we know it."

Mit Sandru

Chapter 81. One Minute

A rumbling was heard through the walls, and the devolved A&E members went quiet for a moment.

"Maximus, what happened?" Travis asked.

"They detonated one of the entrance gates to the compound."

"I hope the AIs don't accelerate the deployment schedule," said Prescott.

Travis scratched his head. "Last time, the AIs advanced the timing trigger to Mountain Standard Time. To accelerate the deployment, they would have to advance it to Central Standard Time, or 21:30 CST. But our time is 22:33 MST now. What would the drones do if that happens?"

"Travis, you're a genius!" said Prescott.

"I know, you said that already. Except you didn't mention that when I suggested how to get rid of the devolution voodoo from our pod."

"Don't let it go to your head, big guy," said Prescott. Both of them began chuckling. "Maximus, Col. Willey, we don't have to stop the UTC—we just have to move the time one hour ahead!" shouted Prescott.

"I'll inform everyone right away," agreed Col. Willey, her voice resonating with urgency.

"Care to explain to a genius like me what will happen?" Travis asked.

"We knew that the drones would be triggered by UTC synchronization," said Prescott. "Stopping the UTC would create havoc with all computers and satellites. But changing the time would not."

"What's the difference?"

"The UTC changes the time regularly, because the Earth slows down as it rotates around its axis. Leap seconds are added periodically without causing computers to go haywire."

"I see." Travis nodded thoughtfully, and then he thrust his chest out and folded his arms. "You're right, I am a genius."

"Col. Willey, are the people at the Naval Observatory and NIST concurring?" Prescott asked.

"Sorry, I have no answer yet."

"The clock is ticking," said Travis under his breath. "Maximus, how difficult is it to change the time?"

"It is only programing. It is not difficult. But besides the US time-keeping centers, other centers in the world have to concurrently change."

"But the GPS is controlled by UTC."

"That's correct."

"So the 800-pound gorilla is UTC."

"That's correct."

"It is 22:35 MST. Only 55 minutes to fly-on," said Travis. "How long will it take for a bureaucrat-scientist to be dragged out of bed to change the clock programming?"

"They have to go through a certain protocol: agree to do it, test it, coordinate when to do it, and do it," said Prescott.

"In the end, technology wipes out humanity," said Travis.

"Hey, people, I have good news," said Col. Willey. "The change of time was approved and scientists throughout the world are working on it."

"I hope they know they have less than one hour," said Travis. "But then, imminent oblivion makes people work harder and faster."

Claire smiled bitterly and shook her head.

"The next attempt to change the time will be at 23:25 MST," said Col. Willey. "Cross your fingers.

"And toes," added Claire, looking at her unshod feet.

"That's way too long," said Prescott. "We have only a five-minute margin of error."

"Prescott and Claire, do you feel like the proverbial fish in a blender?" said Travis, bouncing up and down on his toes to dissipate his anxiety. "I do."

"What do you want to do, then?" asked Claire.

"Why don't we probe the general's mind and see if we can shut down the BSB defense androids?"

They busied themselves with the general's mind, and to their surprise, Minori and Heather were the control centers. There were lengthy passcodes for each one of them, and once the code was given to them, they disabled the BSB defense androids and other robotic weapons.

"Col. Willey, the BSB defenses have been disabled," declared Prescott.

"Thanks," Col. Willey replied tersely. It was obvious that invading the BSB was not a high priority at the moment.

"Col. Willey," said Claire. "Just in case, the Special Forces should be seeking shelter in the BSB now. It will be safe inside."

"Thanks. Information dispatched."

Time seemed to slow down. No one in the BSB was in any danger of contamination, but the fate of the world hanged heavily on each one's mind.

"The UTC time will change in five seconds, at 23:25 MST," announced Col. Willey.

They held their collective breaths.

"The time change was aborted," said a shaken Col. Willey. "Next attempt in four minutes, at 23:29 MST."

"Only a one-minute margin of error," lamented Prescott, holding his face in his hands.

It was the longest four minutes they ever experienced. Even the devolving A&E members seemed to quiet down.

"The UTC time was changed successfully," Col. Willey announced, with relief in her voice. "The time now is 00:29:19 MST." Many shouts of relief could be heard in background.

"Less than a minute to the original deployment time," Prescott said, more to himself.

The new time turned to 00:30:00 MST. And then the seconds continued to tick away, oblivious to the fact that this could have been the end of the world.

"People, we have complete success. The drones in France, Russia, China, and Romania are remaining on the ground, past the new 00:30 MST hour. Congratulations to all of you, and thank you," said Col. Willey happily.

"Col. Willey, make sure no one touches the drones," said Claire. "They must be left undisturbed for at least 49 hours, until the devolution serum loses its potency."

"Understood and communicated."

Mit Sandru

Chapter 82. Fresh Air

Claire, Travis, and Prescott collapsed onto the benches. It was a close call. They could have exited the BSB and enter a world of ape-like creatures. A heavy load was lifted off their shoulders. They felt enlivened and euphoric.

Prescott folded his arms. "Now what?"

"We get the hell out of here," said Travis.

"Wait, is the dark energy dead outside?" Claire reminded them that the peril for them still existed.

"You're right," Travis chuckled. "It would be like drowning at the shoreline."

"We need to assess its potency," said Claire.

They walked to the pod's exit door, held hands, and attempted to sense the dark-mind energy beyond the door. It was non-existent.

"The dark energy is dead down here, Col. Willey," said Claire.

"Good. A special team is approaching your location," she replied. "You may open the pod's door." Col. Willey was heard talking in the background. "There seems to be a slight delay. The medical command is not sure if the entire room where you are and the outer corridors shouldn't stay in quarantine."

"Col. Willey, put us in touch with whomever calls the shots in the medical command," demanded Claire.

"Stand by."

"This is Dr. Henderson."

Claire's, Travis's, and Prescott's mouths opened wide.

"Dr. Henderson? How come you're involved in this?" Claire asked after she recovered from her surprise.

"I am a representative of WHO, as you know, and I've been involved with the devolution contamination since the beginning."

"OK, fine, then you should understand that there is no contamination here—"

"How do we know that?" she interrupted Claire.

"She missed the explanation about the dark-mind energy," Prescott said to Claire.

"Dr. Henderson, you are not privy to what we know about the devolution agent," said Claire. "But in short, the agent contaminates by the use of energy. It's already had its effect and contaminated the 12 members of the A&E Society. They are devolving now and are each being held immobile by an android. There is no residue of the contaminant here or anywhere. We were not affected, even though we're occupying the same room now with them. The victims are capable of transmitting a secondary infection through bites only. As long as they are kept secure, no one can get infected. I suggest you send restraining vests, mouth muzzles, or face shields down here."

Dr. Henderson and the other doctors listening in took their time to absorb what Claire had told them.

"Well?" Claire asked.

"Considering that you are the foremost expert on the devolution agent, we concur. However, Col. Willey, the team going down there should be in HAZMAT suits."

"They already are."

Without waiting for another word Prescott ordered, "Minori, open the gate."

The pod's door opened. The corridor was empty, and they took one of the carts left outside by the A&E members when they had arrived at the pod. After the last sealed door opened, they saw the soldiers in HAZMAT suits. The soldiers stepped back cautiously and then parted ways to let CTT pass through.

They exited the compound into the fresh air of the night. Life was good.

Col. Willey and the military brass, all in fatigues and gas masks, met them with visible respect, gratitude, and awe. Col. Willey saluted and then embraced each one of them.

"Before we have that drink, we need to debrief you," she said. "And also, the US Naval Observatory in DC is asking how long we need to keep the clock one hour ahead."

"Tell them that I'd prefer the clock stay one hour ahead until the serum expires. We'll need to verify the expiration in 49 hours," said Claire. "Quarantine the area where the drones may have landed. The devolution serum is still potent."

After the debriefing and a restful night, CTT and Col. Willey returned to Vandenberg, where the A&E members were being held for the time being.

"Tell me again why you need to access that bronze box Alexei Perchenko bought?" Col. Willey asked. "You want it for historical value?"

"No, we want to destroy it," said Travis.

"Why?"

"That is one bad relic," said Travis. "Would you like to repeat this nightmare?"

"Why don't you take it back to the Ark?"

"Oh, I wish I could," said Travis. "The Ark of the Covenant is beyond our reach. And it is better that way."

"The left over serum, and the bronze box need to be destroyed," said Claire.

"I'm sure whoever took custody of the box will do the right thing," Col. Willey replied. "It is the property of the US government."

"I hope they don't try to experiment with the devolution agent," said Claire, shaking her head.

"Have faith in our scientists," said Col. Willey. "Besides, as long as they don't contact you about that dark-mind energy, the box and its contents are safe."

"In God we trust," said Prescott.

"Now, how about that round of drinks I promised?" Col. Willey asked cheerily.

"Sounds like the medically prescribed thing to do," said Travis. "Call me Travis."

"Call me Karen," she said, smiling at him. "Maybe you and I can get drunk together."

"Not without us," Claire and Prescott chimed in.

The End

Author's Note:

The Ark of the Covenant is not hidden under the Great Pyramids. Please don't dig under them unless you want to find out who built the pyramids and for what purpose. And the Egyptians won't take it kindly.

The Forbidden Fruit in the Bible was the apple. But it could have been the almond, and the skin of the almonds is bitter and contains cyanide. The almonds found in the grocery stores are safe and good to eat and won't make you dumb.

The Aaron's Rod could be the Tree of Knowledge. Moses' Staff could be the Tree of Life. After all he found water with it, and water is life giving.

If you enjoyed this book and would like to help other readers with your comments please write a review on Amazon, which I appreciate very much. Amazon books link.

For more information about my books and my art please visit my website: **sandru.com**

Other Books by Sandru (Mit, DG, or Dumitru)

Paranormal, Mystery, Thriller

The Devolution of Adam and Eve (TIO Series) by Mit Sandru
A pandemic causes billions of people to lose their minds. The world's government health agencies cannot identify the pathogen and develop an antidote. It comes from another realm, and only Claire, Prescott, and Travis can solve this enigma. Will they prevent the end of humanity before it's too late?

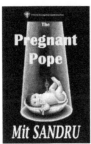

The Pregnant Pope (TIO Series), by Mit Sandru.
The 92-year-old Pope is pregnant. He hasn't undergone any medical procedures, but he carries a fetus in his abdomen. Is this a case of self-cloning, or a mutation? Is this an Immaculate Conception, or Satan's work? Find out how Claire, Travis, and Prescott solve this mystery and the bizarre outcome.

Science Fiction

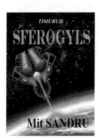

Sferogyls (Timurud Bk. 1) by Mit Sandru

The Maggotroll Empire invades the Sferogyls' planet. The Sferogyls are unarmed and have no defense against the imperial battleships. The gods resurrect Timurud and send him to help the peaceful Sferogyls fight the invaders. Will the Sferogyls win the war in space and defend their planet, or perish?

Gold Rush Mystery (Terraspantion Chronicles, Bk. 1) by Mit Sandru.

America is back on the Moon, and we intend to stay and establish a self-sustaining permanent base for tourism and mining. The work is challenging, the environment is deadly, but the astronauts Mia, Geo and Roby succeed in building the moon base, even if they landed in a mysterious crater.

Time Hole, (Terraspantion Chronicles, Bk. 2) by Mit Sandru.

Mining on the moon is a hazardous affair. Deedee and Arno, two lunar generalists, find perils beyond what they signed up for when they travel on the lunar surface at night . . . on the dark side of the Moon. Time will not be the same after they fall into the *Time Hole*.

Folding Reality, by Mit Sandru. Time Travel Adventure Mike the insurance salesman experiences perilous time travel experiences just by folding a piece of paper. He is crucified on Golgotha, almost gassed at Auschwitz, marooned in a Russian capsule going to the Moon.

Teen, Children Fantasy and Sci-Fi

Arboregal, the Lorn Tree, by D.G. Sandru.

Four youngsters, Melissa, Perry, Nathan and Michelle
materialize in a desolate world where giant, mile-high trees,
support all life. They find shelter in the Lorn Tree among the
Lorns. Soon after they discover that an evil spirit, Hellferata,
wants them dead. Fearful Lorns want to expel the youngsters
from their tree, which would be a dead sentence since monsters
roam the land at night.

Will their ingenuity, cunning, and courage help them escape, or
will Hellferata mete out her wrath before they can escape?

The Vlad V, Blue Blood Vampires Thriller & Romance

Vampire (Vlad V, Bk 1) by Mit Sandru.
Meeting a vampire isn't something that happens every night, even on the New York City subway. But never in her wildest dreams did Cat Sanders ever expect to meet the vampire Vlad V Draculesti and survive the encounter. Instead, she became his confidant. Why was she so lucky?

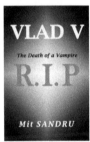

R.I.P., The Death of a Vampire (Vlad V, Bk 2) by Mit Sandru.
Vlad V Draculesti is dying because of an incident that happened decades ago. Unfortunately for Vlad V, the US intelligence agencies investigate him to find out his true identity, and centuries old life. Will Cat Sanders and vampire friends be able to help him die in peace, or will Vlad be discovered for being a vampire and die in a US Federal research laboratory?

Vampire Slayers (Vlad V, Bk 3) by Mit Sandru.
Cat Sanders is a billionaire, but not all is well. Her nemesis, Veronica Seyler, allied with a vampire-slayer drug cult, demands extortion money or she will be killed.
Cat's vampire friend, Angelique, comes to her aid. But the cult is more cunning and dangerous than even her vampire friend could handle. Would Cat and Angelique be able to come out of this alive even if Cat pays the ransom?

Vampires of Transylvania (Vlad V, Bk 4) by Mit Sandru
Cat Sanders has a simple task: spread Vlad V's ashes in Transylvania at midnight, during full moon. But in Transylvania Vlad V has centuries old enemies who take her and her friend Tudor hostage, placing them in iron cages among zombies and proto-vampires. Will they be able to escape from the blood sucking proto-vampires and flesh-eating zombies, or become zombies themselves?

The Queen of Vampires: A New Queen Arises

(Vlad V, Bk 5) by Mit Sandru

The Vampire Queen, Eleonore von Schwarzenberg, is bloodthirsty and vengeful on Cat Sanders and her friends. She plans the most painful death for them. Cat and her friends find themselves entrapped and helpless to avoid her wrath.

Will Cat and her friends be able to escape and survive the Queen of Vampires' fury?

Non-Fiction, Biography, Political

Escape from Communism, by Dumitru Sandru, a True Story and Commentary.

Life under communism is cruel and inhumane. Commit the smallest political infraction, and the secret police will arrest you. The only ray of hope is the West, but it is a crime to escape by crossing the border illegally, and anyone caught is beaten and imprisoned, sometimes even shot. This is my story of what happened and how I reached freedom.

Coloring Book

Abstract Dreams: Coloring Book 1 (Sandru's Art) by Dumitru Sandru

Reward your soul with the smooth and pleasing lines of Abstract Dreams

T-Shirts and other stuff:
Sandru's Products

Visit my e-Gallery at:
http://dumitru-sandru.artistwebsites.com/
http://www.artistrising.com/galleries/Sandru

About Dumitru "Mit" Sandru

Mit Sandru was born in the greater area of Transylvania in the last millennium; make that last century since he's not a vampire. Yet. When he was six years old, a soldier shot him at point blank range with a Kalashnikov. He survived. He outsmarted his German teacher, and survived a tornado in the middle of a wheat field. Not concurrently. When he was 18 years old, he escaped from a country resembling a concentration camp, luckily without being killed. He outran mean border patrol dogs in a foreign country, in the darkness of night, while jumping over six-foot tall stonewalls. Superman he's not. He came to the USA in search of freedom, glory, wealth, and fame. He's still searching for three of those. Lightning grazed him, and he caught a shark by the tail. Once. A monkey attacked him in Japan, but his daughter saved him. He avoided many rattlesnake bites, and built a house. No relation between the snakes and the house. Life eventually tamed him and he became a responsible citizen, with a wife, two daughters, dog and cat. And lately two grandsons. The taming part is questionable. He acquired an engineering and management degree and attempted to acquire other degrees in music, marketing, and IT. A certified student. He obtained many professional licenses, which he hardly used, but looked good on his wall. At 59-¾ years old he quit the corporate life and a six-figure salary. Rumor has it that he was given the golden handshake. He was finally free to pursue his dreams of writing, painting and music. During his professional life he painted hundreds of canvases, and composed dozens of tunes, while since his golden handshake he wrote 11 books. And that was in just the first half of his life.

Disclaimer: Everything written here is true, and the bullets were blanks.

I am Mit Sandru and I approve this unabashed bio.

Visit him at sandru.com

CPSIA information can be obtained
at www.ICGtesting.com
Printed in the USA
FSHW021940011119
63675FS